LIFE
EVERLASTING

AN ALEXIA LINDALE NOVEL
BOOK TWO

ROBERT WHITLOW

THOMAS NELSON
Since 1798

NASHVILLE   DALLAS   MEXICO CITY   RIO DE JANEIRO

Published in Nashville, Tennessee, by Thomas Nelson. Thomas Nelson is a registered trademark of Thomas Nelson, Inc.

Thomas Nelson, Inc., titles may be purchased in bulk for educational, business, fund-raising, or sales promotional use. For information, please e-mail SpecialMarkets@ThomasNelson.com.

All scripture quotations, unless otherwise indicated, are taken from the *HOLY BIBLE, NEW INTERNATIONAL VERSION.* © 1973, 1978, 1984 by International Bible Society. Used by permission of Zondervan Publishing House. All rights reserved.

Scripture quotations marked "NKJV" are taken from the New King James Version. © 1982 by Thomas Nelson, Inc. Used by permission. All right reserved.

Scripture quotations marked "KJV" are from the Holy Bible, King James Version.

Publisher's Note: This novel is a work of fiction. Names, characters, places, and incidents are either products of the author's imagination or used fictitiously. All characters are fictional, and any similarity to people living or dead is purely coincidental.

ISBN 978-1-59554-962-4 (RPK)

Library of Congress Cataloging-in-Publication Data

Whitlow, Robert, 1954–
    Life everlasting / Robert Whitlow.
      p. cm.
    ISBN 978-0-8499-4375-1 (trade paper)
    1. Santee River Valley (S.C.)—Fiction. I. Title.
PS3573.H49837L537 2004
813'.54—dc22   2004011374

Printed in the United States of America

11 12 13 14 15 RRD 5 4 3 2 1

To those who have learned that brokenness
can be the door to blessing.

• • •

Then he took the seven loaves and the fish, and when he had given
thanks, he broke them and gave them to the disciples, and they in turn
to the people. They all ate and were satisfied.

MATTHEW 15:36–37

1

The light shineth in the darkness;
and the darkness comprehended it not.

JOHN 1:5 KJV

Baxter Richardson opened his eyes.

He didn't know where he was or how he had gotten there, but the pale white ceiling pushed aside the impenetrable darkness that had threatened to engulf him. He lay still, not yet aware that he couldn't do anything else.

He heard a woman singing. With the sound came a memory. He closed his eyes. Music had rescued him from the abyss and guided him through the black mist. Without the music, he would never have found his way to the light.

He opened his mouth to speak, to ask a question of the singing voice. But all that came out was a groan. The singing voice stopped. A speaking voice replaced it.

"Mr. Richardson, I'm Sarah Locklear, one of the nurses taking care of you. Can you hear me?"

Baxter tried to open his eyes a second time, but they refused to obey.

"Mr. Richardson," the voice repeated. "You're at home in Santee in the cottage next door to your house. Your wife is there now. Do you want me to get her?"

The darkness reappeared. The young man fought to drive it back.

"Did you hear the music?"

Baxter watched in terror as the darkness grew until it met over his head like a great black bowl.

"If you can hear me, make a sound."

Baxter moaned in agony of soul. The circle of darkness was complete, and the sides began to move slowly, inexorably, downward. Once the inky gloom enveloped him, he knew he would be dead. Lower and lower it came. He gasped for breath.

"Praise God!" the voice said. "Thank you, Jesus."

The darkness moved to within inches of Baxter's face and stopped, an invisible force held at bay by an unseen power.

The singing voice returned. The stalemate continued. But as the voice grew stronger, tiny flashes of light began to streak across the dark like shooting stars, glimmers of hope in a hopeless world. Baxter listened. The melody rose to a higher place. The pinpoints of light increased. Their flickering glory didn't fade.

Baxter took a deep breath.

———

Rena Richardson rolled over in bed and opened her eyes. Her hair had fallen over her face, and when she looked sleepily toward the bedroom door, she mistook the man standing there for a few strands of blonde hair twisted together. She brushed the hair from her face. The figure remained. She jerked awake and sat up.

"Who is it?" she called out, her voice echoing in the large bedroom. She reached for the nightstand drawer.

The man stayed in the shadows without moving. Rena opened the drawer and felt the cool barrel of the pistol. She grabbed the gun.

Her voice trembled. "I have a gun!"

The man didn't move or speak. Rena pointed the pistol, but her hand shook so badly she wasn't sure she could hit the doorway, much less an intruder half hidden in the shadows.

The man still refused to budge. Rena squinted and rubbed her eyes with her left hand. Suspicion surfaced. Still holding the gun, she reached over and turned on a small lamp. The dim beam barely reached across the room to the door, but there was no mistaking the identity of her visitor.

Baxter.

Rena collapsed back onto the pillow for a moment and shut her eyes before bouncing up for another look.

"Are you still there?" she asked peevishly.

The figure continued to stare at her impassively.

"You know, if you would talk, it would make everything more realistic," she said.

Usually her husband left at the sound of her voice.

"What do you want from me? I don't have anything for you!"

The figure stayed put.

"Why don't you die and get a life?" Rena yelled.

The incongruity of her question struck her as funny. She gave a short laugh.

"That's it!" she called out. "Get a life!"

Rena threw off the covers and stood. She'd had enough. Always before, her husband had disappeared when confronted. If need be, she would put her fist through his face to prove him false. She glanced down at the floor to retrieve one of her satin slippers. When she looked up, Baxter was gone. She rushed to the hallway and turned on the light. Nothing. She went to the top of the stairs and looked down. Except for the usual nighttime creaks, the old house was deserted.

"And don't come back!" she screamed. "Do you hear me? Don't come back!"

———

Alexia Lindale sat at the desk in her makeshift office typing the last few lines of a letter to the lawyer on the other side of a divorce case. Her phone buzzed.

"Alexia, it's Rena Richardson," said the receptionist for the real-estate company where Alexia was temporarily quartered. "She says it's urgent."

Everything with Rena was urgent.

The transfer went through and Alexia picked up the receiver. "What is it?"

Rena's breathless voice held the twang of the Appalachian hills where she'd been raised. "Jeffrey came to see me this morning. He gave me the information you need to sue his father for using the power of attorney to transfer property out of Baxter's name."

"What kind of information?"

"Names of companies, how much Baxter owned before the accident, and the amount that he owns now."

Alexia picked up a folder from the stack of Richardson files on the corner of her desk. Inside was a copy of a durable power of attorney Baxter had signed at age eighteen giving his father, Ezra, absolute control over his personal and business affairs.

"Give them to me."

Rena listed the names of the companies and percentages of ownership. Alexia didn't recognize any of the entities. In a small town like Santee, the identity of every viable local business enterprise should be common knowledge.

"They're probably shell companies or subsidiaries of Richardson and Company set up for particular projects," Alexia said.

"I don't know what you're talking about."

The lawyer ran her fingers through her dark hair. "I'm thinking out loud. I'll need you to fax Jeffrey's list to me. Did Jeffrey tell you why he is willing to sabotage his father?"

"He wants to help me and thinks it's wrong what Ezra's doing to me and Baxter."

Alexia had heard this before, yet remained unconvinced of Jeffrey's altruism.

Her client continued, "And he still doesn't know that you know he's giving me information. He wrote down the names of several Richardson employees and said I should mention them if anyone asks how you found out what Ezra is doing."

"I'm not going to do that," Alexia retorted. "And I won't let you do it either. If you're questioned under oath about your sources, you'll have to tell the truth. Jeffrey can't hide behind you."

"You don't understand," Rena said. "It's not like that. He wants to help me."

Alexia drew a small target in the margin of her legal pad and put Rena's initials in the bull's-eye.

"Why would Jeffrey turn on his father and risk so much to help a woman who married his brother only six months ago? How can you trust him?"

Rena's voice revealed a hint of panic. "Don't argue with me. Just check out the information. I can't make Jeffrey . . ." she stopped.

"Mad?" Alexia offered. "What is going on, Rena?"

The phone was silent for a moment.

"It's not that," Rena answered in a calmer tone. "It's best for me to cooperate with him. We can help each other. He doesn't think it will be necessary to go very far with a lawsuit before his father will back down. Then it won't be necessary to tell who gave us the information."

"I can't count on that," Alexia said. "And it's foolish to think that filing a lawsuit against someone as powerful as your father-in-law is going to scare him into doing the right thing. Using the power of attorney to transfer property from Baxter's name is technically legal, and it will take a court order to stop him. A judge won't do that without convincing evidence that Ezra is wielding the power of attorney as a weapon to defraud you."

"He backed down about the money he took from our checking account and returned it," Rena countered.

"True," Alexia admitted. "But that was only a few thousand dollars. How much do you think Baxter's share of these companies is worth? Did Jeffrey give you any idea?"

"No, but he said he could get whatever you need. He just doesn't want to do anything that will ruin the businesses."

"How would making Ezra restore the status quo hurt the businesses?"

"That's just what he told me."

"It's not good enough."

"Why are you giving me such a hard time? You're supposed to be helping me, not making everything more stressful than it already is."

"Okay," Alexia said. "Fax over the information, and I'll think about what to do."

"Will other people at your office see it? I'm sure Jeffrey doesn't want anyone else to know what he's doing."

Alexia sighed. "If you promise to send it in the next five minutes, I'll stand by the fax machine and snatch it up before anyone else can read it."

"And when will you file suit?" Rena asked. "I want to do it as soon as possible."

"I'll call you."

Alexia hung up the phone and walked down the hallway to the small room that contained the fax and copy machines. In less than a minute, the fax machine began to spit out a single sheet of paper. Alexia held it lightly in her fingers as it inched out of the machine. She glanced down at the list of companies. During the six years she worked at Leggitt & Freeman, Alexia knew that Ezra Richardson had hired Ralph Leggitt to set up multiple companies and perform legal work in scores of business deals. Though Alexia had avoided business law to focus on domestic litigation, she wasn't a total stranger to corporate structures. In divorce cases she often had to uncover information that businessmen concealed from their wives, and ferreting out key pieces of financial data was one of Alexia's strengths. Many ex-husbands still bore the fiscal scars of the beatings she'd given them when they tried to hide assets.

The lawyer took Jeffrey's list back to her office and put it in her briefcase. It was late afternoon, and a new investigation would have to wait. As she snapped her briefcase shut and entered the hallway, she almost collided with Rachel Downey, the startlingly blonde real-estate broker who owned the building. Rachel, a short, jolly woman with a penchant for multiple rings, was always ready for a chat.

"Glad I caught you," Rachel said. "I drove by the house on King Street this afternoon. I'm even more convinced that it's going to make a great office for you. When is your contractor going to start the renovation?"

"Soon. We were together this afternoon, but we didn't talk business."

Rachel raised her eyebrows. "Gwen Jones told me you were spending a lot of time with your contractor. Isn't he also some kind of minister?"

Alexia smiled. "Yes, he's the music minister at the Sandy Flats Church. What else did Gwen say?"

Rachel stepped closer. "That she was going to leave Leggitt & Freeman as soon as your office is up and running. She's already picked out a secretarial desk and credenza."

"Well, keep that quiet. If one of the partners finds out, they'll fire her before I'm ready to start paying her."

Rachel lowered her voice. "Your plans are safe with me."

Alexia was less sure.

Rachel continued. "Tell me more about your music-loving contractor."

Alexia stepped back. "There's not much to tell. He's a minister who plays the piano."

"And from what I've heard, he's quite a bit older than you are."

"He was in the seventh grade when I was born."

Alexia watched as Rachel quickly did the math in her head.

"With a daughter almost as old as you are," the Realtor added.

"She's in her early twenties, Rachel. I'm pushing past thirty-one."

Rachel sniffed. "A virtual old maid. I was already on my second husband by your age."

Alexia laughed. "So, what's wrong with me trying to catch up? Don't you think it's about time I got married? I need at least a couple of husband scalps under my belt before I turn forty." Alexia patted Rachel on the arm. "And that's all the personal information you're prying out of me. The reason Ted and I were together today had to do with Baxter Richardson."

Rachel raised her pencil-thin eyebrows. "I didn't think the Richardson clan went to church."

"Sandy Flats is not their church. Ted asked me to go with him because I represent Rena and could get him in to see Baxter." Alexia paused, not knowing how to explain to Rachel that Ted Morgan saw music as a form of prayer for a sick person. She wasn't sure about it herself.

"Is it true that Rena put Baxter in the cottage next door to their house?" Rachel asked.

"Yes. They've turned it into a long-term care facility."

"How is he doing?"

"No closer to waking up than the first time I saw him in ICU in Greenville. He's in a coma and paralyzed from the neck down. He's breathing on his own, but that's about it. His mental status is a mystery."

Rachel shook her head. "He's the best of the lot. I've brokered some deals with his father, but I had to watch him like a hawk, and Jeffrey is just as bad or worse. He tried to cheat me out of a commission but backpedaled in a hurry when I caught him."

Rachel's tongue could be smooth as soft butter when describing a house for sale, but she wouldn't hesitate to use it as a dagger if attacked or swindled. Jeffrey was wise to back down.

"If anybody else tries to take advantage of you, call me," Alexia said. "I'll write them a nasty letter."

Rachel fluffed up her hair. "That's okay. You did great work getting me out of my last huge marital mistake. I'll save you for the big problems."

"Then get a prenuptial agreement and don't fall for a guy just because he buys you rings."

Rachel held up her hands and wiggled her bejeweled fingers. "Don't worry, I've run out of room."

"Good."

Rachel pointed to the lawyer's bare left hand and exclaimed as if making a grand discovery, "Look, Alexia, you've got plenty of space!"

2

Music heard so deeply that it is not heard at all,
but you are the music while the music lasts.

T. S. ELIOT

Ted Morgan sat alone on the front pew in the quiet sanctuary of the
Sandy Flats Church. The two-hundred-year-old building had occupied the same plot of ground for so long that it had become as much a
part of the Low Country landscape as the ancient live oak trees that bor-
dered it. The late afternoon shadows cast darkness over the church's
stained-glass windows, which depicted miracles from the life of Jesus.
The exhilaration Ted felt earlier in the day while playing a portable keyboard in Baxter Richardson's room had subsided and been replaced by a
simple, practical question.

Was he doing any good?

He ran his fingers through his curly brown hair and closed his eyes.
Just as he worked with wood to build something that would last generations, he wanted to use his musical talent to create something enduring
in God's kingdom. Results in wood he could see; any sign of healing in
Baxter had so far eluded him.

The greatest surprise of the afternoon had been the participation of a
total stranger—Sarah Locklear, the private-duty nurse who supported
with her voice what Ted played on the keyboard. Ted and Sarah's seam-
less improvisational worship would have made veteran jazz performers
jealous. Nevertheless, upon reflection, Ted was disappointed. He wanted
results, not a sensory high. The music minister didn't play so that he
could feel good; he played as a way to bring heaven to earth. While he
savored the emotional by-products that flowed to him through musical
expression, his fingers touched the keyboard for other reasons.

Ted glanced down at the polished wooden floor of the church. Hadn't Jesus spit to make mud that healed the eyes of a blind man? Didn't Peter's shadow cast the power of God on those it touched? The music minister hadn't been called to spit, but to play. He believed that the gospel included healing through worship. Thus, while the session at the cottage had been glorious, it had not produced any change in Baxter Richardson's condition and could not, in Ted's mind, be labeled a success.

Frustrated, he stood and looked up at the lightly stained beams that met in sharp points overhead like the skeleton of an ancient ship. Years before, he'd defeated the artistic seduction that ensnares some musicians in narcissism. His current enemies had simpler names, like doubt and unbelief.

"What else should I do? What else can I do?" he asked.

No answer came from the rafters.

He approached his piano, a seven-foot Steinway made in Hamburg at the apex of early twentieth-century European piano craftsmanship. In the gathering dusk, the black instrument waited patiently for him to bring it to life, but he hesitated. He ran his fingers over the cool surface of the lid and then lightly stroked a few keys without producing sound. Without inspiration, he didn't want to run through a few scales or technical exercises. He left the sanctuary and started to walk across the crushed-shell parking lot to the old parsonage where he lived. It was almost supper time.

But suddenly, the inner nudge he learned not to ignore stopped him.

Recognition of the prompting brought a wry smile to the minister's face and made his forehead wrinkle. He returned to the sanctuary, sat quietly on the piano bench, and waited. It didn't take long. He touched the keys. For now, he knew what to do. God had created him to play, and that was what he would do until more faith or insight came.

———

Alexia left Rachel Downey and walked across the parking lot at the rear of the building. Mornings were chilly in late November along the South Carolina coast, but the temperature was usually comfortable by the late afternoon. Petite yet muscular from many years as a long-distance swimmer, Alexia draped the jacket that she'd worn earlier in the day across her arm. With summer's humidity gone, she was surrounded by a crispness enhanced by the salty air from the ocean several miles to the east.

Santee wasn't the easiest place for a female attorney to find her way, but Alexia loved where she lived and had the pioneering spirit of her mother, who had defected from a Soviet youth soccer team during a tour of the United States in the 1970s. Alexia had moved to Santee after graduating from law school in Florida and worked as an associate at Leggitt & Freeman, where she earned a measure of respect through hard work and an undeniable ability to handle herself in the courtroom. A few months before she would have achieved partnership status, however, she ran into trouble when her representation of several divorce clients created conflicts of interest with the general business clients of the firm. The dispute between Rena Richardson and her father-in-law, Ezra, one of Leggitt & Freeman's biggest clients, was the final blow. When Alexia refused to disclose confidential information about Rena to Ralph Leggitt, he told her to clean out her desk and leave.

After briefly debating whether to slink out of town, Alexia decided to stay and open her own law office. Most of her clients followed her from the old firm, and a ten-thousand-dollar retainer from Rena gave her an instant cash reserve. Soon, the house on King Street would become Alexia's new headquarters. It was only a couple of blocks from the courthouse, and she anticipated turning it into a place that reflected her own tastes.

All in all, now that the shock and disappointment of her termination had worn off, Alexia was glad for the transition. She had no doubt that in a few years she would look back on her dismissal and consider it a blessing in disguise.

She drove along Highway 17, the coastal road that ran like a hemline along the Atlantic Ocean, and thought about the time she and Ted had spent with Baxter Richardson. Ted Morgan could perform classical works of piano with a skill that rivaled her collection of recordings, and Alexia had been equally amazed at his ability to improvise. But when the music minister played a portable, electric keyboard as an instrument of prayer and healing, something unique occurred. The manifestation of God's presence invaded the room. The air took on a weight, a heaviness, as if a thick robe of glory had been thrown over the small living room.

And when the private-duty nurse with long black hair and deep, dark eyes began to sing, Alexia bowed her head in awe. She'd never seen a miracle, but the fact that Baxter remained unchanged when the music stopped was almost more surprising to her than if he had awakened and asked for a glass of water. Of the trio present, only Alexia knew that if Baxter returned from the shadowlands, he would have to face the consequences of his attempt to take his wife's life.

Alexia turned her silver BMW onto Pelican Point Drive. Her dog, cat, and house on the marsh awaited her.

———

Detective Byron Devereaux lightly rubbed his fingers back and forth across his thin, dark mustache. Various items from the Claude Dixon murder investigation littered his desk. He adjusted his round glasses.

A picture of Rena Richardson's red convertible, the car stopped by Deputy Dixon for traveling twenty-five miles per hour more than the speed limit, held his attention for a moment. Then his eyes drifted to a written transcript of the deputy's garbled radio transmission to the Charleston County sheriff's office. The transcript stated that the driver was "male," but in listening to the actual recording at slow speed, Devereaux couldn't rule out the possibility that the deputy said "female."

In the center of the desk was a picture of Claude Dixon's body at the scene. There were no visible marks or bruises on the overweight officer, and no evidence of a struggle. At first, Devereaux surmised the driver was a juvenile who took the sporty car for a joy ride and then panicked when stopped by a police officer. But that theory didn't explain how the patrolman was killed. Perhaps the driver was an expert in martial arts who could deliver a quick, deadly blow; however, the autopsy showed no evidence of injury to Dixon's face or solar plexus. The cause of death was "cervical fracture"—a broken neck. A bruise on the back of the deputy's head and the position of his body left little doubt that he died when his head struck the asphalt pavement. But what caused the deputy to fall? A careful inspection of the ground around the body revealed no footprints except those made by Dixon's size-twelve boots.

Dixon's service revolver, handcuffs, wallet, car keys—everything except his notebook—were present and accounted for. Devereaux suspected that the murderer had taken the notebook because Dixon had recorded incriminating information.

Again, the detective reviewed the notes of his conversation with Rena Richardson and her lawyer. Richardson reported the convertible missing about an hour before it was found in a Charleston parking lot. She'd not allowed anyone to borrow the vehicle and hadn't seen anyone suspicious in the wealthy Santee neighborhood where she lived.

Someone knocked on his door.

"Come in!" he called out.

The door opened, and a rookie detective with sandy hair entered the room.

Devereaux glanced up. "What is it, Bridges?"

Rick Bridges handed Devereaux a stack of fingerprint images.

"These are from the Richardson vehicle. The steering wheel and gearshift lever had been wiped clean before the car was abandoned, but there were prints everywhere else, inside and out. We sent the best specimens to the FBI. Two matches."

Devereaux looked at the prints.

"One is a very good right thumb," Bridges continued, indicating the print. "The other is a partial ring finger, also the right. Both were taken from the passenger-side door handle."

"Are they from the same individual?" Devereaux asked.

"That's what the report says."

"Who is it?"

Bridges handed Devereaux a brief written report sent with the prints.

"Henry L. Quinton. Thirty-four, Caucasian. He's originally from Newark. He's wanted for questioning in the murder of a police officer in Providence."

Devereaux looked up from the report in surprise. "How old is the Rhode Island case?"

"Five years."

"Did you talk to anyone about it?"

Bridges nodded. "Yes. They're sending me what they can, a mug shot and psych profile from an arrest about eight years ago. Rhode Island thinks Quinton had links to an organized crime syndicate in New York. Still might. The officer killed was under investigation by internal affairs in Providence. It may have been a preemptive hit."

Devereaux sat back in his chair. "So much for the idea that this was a joy ride."

Bridges nodded. "And someone with a New Jersey accent would stick out like a 1930s gangster in Santee. When we get the mug shot, we'll canvass every convenience and liquor store in the area. If the guy opened his mouth, someone will remember him."

"Maybe," Devereaux said. "A lot of people from up north are moving into the fancy golf course communities."

"If he's still stealing cars and killing police officers, I doubt he spends his free time on the golf course."

Rick Bridges's optimism was as green as he was. Devereaux put the lid on his own skeptical observations.

"Do you want to get more involved in this case?" he asked.

"Yes."

"Okay. You're in charge of running down Quinton. I'll let them know upstairs."

3

Pelican Point Drive accessed a large tract of land tied up in bankruptcy court since its developer went under. Alexia had acquired an odd-shaped lot on the north end of the parcel from the bankruptcy trustee, who wanted to square up the tract before seeking a buyer. To date, he was still looking.

She drove a half-mile to the edge of the coastal marsh and prepared to turn left on an unmarked, one-lane road covered with broken seashells. The isolated location of her home did not frighten Alexia. In fact, in the spring and fall she occasionally slept on her screened porch in a wide Pawleys Island hammock.

Not expecting any traffic, she was startled when a gray van appeared. Occasionally the curious would drive into the area, but the van was traveling too fast for someone taking a leisurely drive along the marsh. The vehicle veered toward her so suddenly that she had to swerve to avoid being struck.

"Watch it!" she yelled. The tires on the right side of her car went off the crumbling asphalt into the sand. The van came within inches of her, and she caught sight of the driver, who wore a cap pulled down over his face. She glanced in the rearview mirror but couldn't identify the vehicle's out-of-state plates.

Rattled, Alexia put the car in reverse and backed up. The left rear tire slipped off the pavement into the sand. Not realizing what had happened and still upset, she jerked the car into drive and stepped on the gas pedal. A few seconds of spraying sand later, she was stuck.

Alexia had lived on the coast long enough to know that fighting the sand was as futile as punching a tar baby. Hitting the steering wheel in frustration, she got out and inspected the damage. The right rear wheel was sunk halfway to the axle. The left rear wheel was within an inch of a piece of asphalt that would have given her enough traction to move forward. She could walk home but didn't like the idea of abandoning her car for the night. Anyway, she would have to get it out eventually.

Retrieving her purse, she flipped open her cell phone and called her roadside-assistance service. The lady who answered took down her information, put her on hold, and then told her it would be at least an hour before someone could arrive to help her.

"I'm not far from my house," Alexia said. "I can walk home, and the driver can come there first."

"I'm sorry, but your plan only provides towing service from the location of the disabled vehicle to your residence."

"It's less than a quarter mile from the car. If it's going to be an hour before someone gets here, I'd rather wait at home than here at the car."

"Just a minute," the woman said.

Alexia took off one of her shoes and dumped out a spoonful of sand. She loved the coast, but not when it invaded her nice shoes.

"Thank you for holding," the woman said. "I checked with my supervisor, and the rules require you to stay with the car until the driver arrives."

"That's ridiculous!" Alexia blurted out.

"It's a security measure. We can't be responsible for any damage or theft before the wrecker arrives."

"But he'll be picking me up before towing the car," Alexia protested.

The woman adopted the tone of a mother addressing a stubborn child. "Ms. Lindale, we're a towing company, not a taxi service, and we can't assume liability for matters not covered by your plan."

Alexia silently blamed the unknown attorneys who had sued roadside-assistance companies and scared them into curtailing services. She spent a few frustrating seconds trying to come up with an alternative but couldn't think of one.

"Okay," she said. "I'll be here."

"Thank you for this opportunity to serve you," the woman replied. "Your service number for this call is 23892. Please reference this number if you need to call back."

Alexia closed the phone. As soon as her membership came up for renewal, she'd try another company.

The sun dropped toward the horizon. Shadows from a stand of scrubby trees began to lengthen and stretch across Pelican Point Drive. Alexia leaned against the hood of her car and looked across the marsh. A few hundred yards away lay a narrow barrier island too fragile for commercial development. Alexia had claimed it as her private refuge. She owned a small, battered aluminum boat with a tiny motor, and as often as possible, she would take the boat to the island and swim on the ocean side while her black Labrador, Boris, happily paddled alongside her. There would be no time for a swim this evening.

She leaned over, picked up a broken clam shell, and tossed it into the inky waters of the marsh. The muddy bottom was crawling with blue crabs. A couple of times a year Alexia would set out a trap near her house and invite her secretary, Gwen Jones, over for a crab boil. Gwen, in her early fifties, had lived all her life in the Santee area and ate crabs Cajun style, leaving nothing but the shell. Alexia was more traditional and extracted the morsels of sweet white meat from the claws and legs before dipping them in melted butter.

Alexia checked her watch and saw it had been almost an hour. She wandered slowly up the road toward Highway 17. Beyond a bend on the other side of the trees, the road was straight, and it was possible to see almost all the way to the junction. Alexia walked through darkening shadows into the small grove and rounded the bend. She looked to the west in hope of seeing the wrecker. Instead, she saw the gray van, parked under the trees at the beginning of Pelican Point Drive. Alexia eased back into the shadows.

Alexia knew the spot as a place where people would swing off Highway 17 and have a picnic. But it was not the time of day or season of the year for a picnic. She couldn't see any lights or signs of movement. She glanced up at the sky. Darkness would overtake it completely in a few minutes.

Alexia was caught between anger and apprehension. She was mad at the driver but concerned that he hadn't immediately left the area. Why would he risk the possibility that Alexia might call the police and report him as a reckless driver?

Alexia had no neighbors. Her house didn't have an expensive security system. She didn't own a gun. She had a canister of pepper spray in the glove compartment of her car, but she'd not taken it out since the last time she traveled to Atlanta.

The lights of the van came on. Alexia turned and fled back down the road as fast as her shoes would let her go. She plotted her strategy as she ran. She would lock her car and take a path through the brushy undergrowth that led to the other side of her house. If the van appeared, she could call the police.

She reached her car, locked it, and scurried down the path. Lights from a vehicle cut through the gloom and came through the small wooded area. Alexia crouched and took out her cell phone. Her hand shaking, she was punching in 911 when the vehicle came into view.

It was the tow truck.

Alexia looked down at the ground and exhaled in relief. She came out of the shadows as the driver climbed from the cab and inspected the status of her BMW. The wrecker's diesel engine rattled as Alexia crossed the road.

"I'm glad you're here," she said.

The driver jumped at the sound of her voice.

"Where did you come from?" the young man asked. "I thought you were going to be with the car."

"Oh, I just went for a little walk. Did you see a gray van as you turned onto Pelican Point Drive?"

"Uh, I didn't notice anyone."

Alexia glanced back up the road. "Okay."

"Do you have your membership card?" the driver asked.

In a matter of minutes, the car was back on terra firma. Alexia got in and waited for the wrecker driver to turn toward the highway. Instead of driving home, she followed him. She didn't want to take the young man's word about the absence of the gray van. When they reached the picnic area, it was empty. But her sense of safety was gone. Her refuge by the marsh had been violated.

A full moon was coming up as Alexia climbed the steps and unlocked the front door of her house. Built close to the marsh, the house was perched atop six concrete pillars. Two times since the house had been built, storm surges swept beneath the structure, but Alexia wasn't home for either event. During hurricane season, she kept a close eye on the weather and stayed with Gwen in town if the ocean turned ugly.

Alexia could hear Boris barking on the other side of the door. She pushed it open and was met by a deep growl. An instant later, Boris, barking fiercely, bolted past her, skidded down the front steps, and started running up the road toward Pelican Point Drive.

"Boris!" Alexia yelled.

The dog slowed at the sound of her voice.

"Come!" Alexia commanded.

Boris was an unruly, boisterous juvenile, but he stopped running and continued barking as he stood in the middle of the road. Her heart pounding, Alexia peered into the darkness illuminated only by the light of the moon. Nothing. Boris turned around and trotted back up the steps and into the house. Alexia closed the door behind him and quickly flipped the dead bolt. Misha, her silver Persian cat, rubbed against her leg in greeting. Alexia leaned against the door frame until her heart returned to a normal rhythm. She leaned over and scratched the cat's neck.

"You don't seem worried," she said.

Alexia carefully inspected the house, but everything was as she'd left it that morning, except for an expensive shoe Boris had gnawed. Alexia picked it up and shook it in front of the dog's face. One of the narrow leather straps was dangling where it had been ripped loose.

"Bad dog," she said. Boris wagged his tail. Alexia dropped her hand to her side and continued. "But, like most criminals, without immediate punishment, you don't have a clue about accepting responsibility for your crime."

Reassured that everything was in order, Alexia calmed down. She walked through the living room and dropped the remains of the shoe into the trash compactor in the kitchen. The kitchen, on the south side of the house, contained a breakfast nook with large windows that overlooked the marsh. Nestled in the nook was a small, glass-topped table and two chairs.

Alexia fixed a sandwich and a bowl of soup, and then sat in one of the chairs to eat. Misha hopped into the other chair and kept her company. Boris lay at Alexia's feet in case a morsel fell to the floor. She dropped a piece of smoked turkey as a treat.

Alexia didn't do a lot of entertaining, but the large, open living room was a comfortable place for a crowd to mingle. Because the house wasn't a vacation home, she didn't fill it with common wicker beach-house furniture. Her tastes ran more to steel, glass, and leather. On the other side of the living room, a screened porch jutted out from the north side of the house. It was bare except for a large Pawleys Island hammock and a small table. The main floor also contained two small bedrooms and a broad deck that stretched across the rear of the house.

The second level was smaller than the first and dedicated solely as Alexia's bedroom. The spacious area had a sitting room where Alexia had set up her computer, and she'd positioned her bed so that the sun rising over the barrier island could greet her with a glorious good morning.

She went upstairs, put on her pajamas, and turned on her computer. She slipped a CD of a pianist performing Debussy's *Claire de Lune* into her music system. In the quiet of the night, her bedroom filled with the composer's musings about French evenings when the diaphanous veil between the imagination of man and the beauty of nature lifted for a glimpse of an enchanted land.

Alexia sat down in front of her computer screen. After she deleted a long string of uninvited e-mails, she read a brief note from her mother about the weather in Florida. She was about to turn off her computer when she decided to do a preliminary search of the Richardson companies. Going downstairs, she retrieved the list from her briefcase and then accessed the records for the South Carolina Secretary of State, Corporations Division. She typed in the name of the first company. It came up unknown. She tried a minor variation and didn't score a hit. One by one, she went down the list. None of the businesses had been incorporated in South Carolina or even registered to do business in the state. Puzzled, Alexia pushed back her chair and stared at the screen.

Obtaining governmental approval to do business in South Carolina was a simple process. Companies meant jobs; jobs meant greater tax revenue.

Government bureaucrats made it easy for companies to transact business in the state, and a corporation that didn't register with the Secretary of State ran needless risks. Alexia couldn't imagine Ralph Leggitt failing to process Ezra Richardson's business activities through the proper channels.

She tapped her fingers on the wooden surface of her computer stand and then typed in the keywords for the Delaware Secretary of State. For generations, Delaware had cultivated a reputation as a place where businesses could be birthed cheaply, confidentially, and without the regulatory entanglements of New York and other northeastern states. As a result, more companies listed tiny Delaware as their place of incorporation than any other state.

Alexia typed in the first name on the list, Jasmine Corporation, and received immediate confirmation. The registered agent served as the Delaware contact for companies wanting to keep the names of the people in control hidden from public scrutiny. Four of the ten companies on Jeffrey's list had been incorporated in Delaware. Each one listed the same registered agent as the legal contact. The other six companies remained a mystery.

She printed out the information she'd found and considered her next step. In recent years, Nevada had emerged as a competitor to Delaware in preserving the secrecy in corporate records. She searched for information on the remaining six companies through the Nevada Secretary of State and scored four hits, the last a company named MetBack, Inc. She printed out these results as well. As the last sheet came out of the printer, the pianist performing Debussy struck the final poignant notes. Alexia hadn't thought about the shadow over her paradise for the past hour.

———

Rena didn't have to wonder if someone was watching her every move. She had a videotape to prove it. Jeffrey had handed the tape to her with a sick smirk and suggested she might want to view it alone while she ate. The first time she watched the surveillance video on the small television in the kitchen, she lost all desire for food and didn't eat for a day and a half. When the screen went blank, she swore she'd never watch it again. It had been impossible, however, not to revisit the images.

Close to midnight, moody and depressed, she took the tape upstairs to her bedroom and slipped it into the VCR. Each time it started to play, her secret hope rose: maybe this time the plot would be different.

It began with a shot of the front of her house and the red convertible in the driveway. The date and time stamp counted minutes at the bottom of the picture. As she watched, the front door of the house opened, and she saw herself coming outside. She got in the red convertible, turned the car around, and drove down the driveway. The grainy picture followed her through two stop signs and a traffic light that turned red as she sped through it. When a truck pulled in between her car and the vehicle following her, the video ended.

That day, she had taken her joy ride down the coast toward Charleston, and the stupid, fat policeman stopped her for speeding. He slipped and broke his neck all by his brilliant self, but who would believe *that* truth? So she made up the car-theft story. She really had no choice. The occurrence of a second serious accident so close in time to Baxter's fall would have raised awkward questions. Unfortunately, the tape undermined her fictitious alibi, and Jeffrey gleefully held it over her head to ensure her cooperation.

Watching the tape again made Rena so mad that she didn't know whether to cry or to scream. She paced across the bedroom several times. Glancing up, she saw her reflection in a decorative, gold-framed mirror on the wall. The contorted image made her even more furious. She went to a window and threw open the curtains. Raising the window, she leaned out into the darkness and looked across the broad lawn toward the street. Rena saw no cars. She didn't know if her handlers took the night off or not. She glared, trying to bore a hole into the future. In a few moments, she sighed in despair. At the end of sight was only more of the unknown.

She glanced toward the cottage. Ultimately, this was not her fault. Her husband did a long-distance free fall onto unforgiving rocks and survived. The obese policeman keeled over backward and died instantly. It wasn't fair.

Rena slammed the window closed. No, it wasn't fair.

4

Baxter Richardson opened his eyes a second time.

The white ceiling was now a dim gray. His thoughts were a jumbled mess, impossible to decipher and categorize into coherent concepts. Words without context ran through his mind. He opened his mouth to speak, but all that came out was gibberish. A female voice spoke, not the singing voice that had helped vanquish the darkness.

"Mr. Richardson. Can you hear me?"

The words entered his ears, but he couldn't process them. He tried to respond, but it was hopeless. He moaned.

"Are you hurting?"

All he could muster was the sound of a single letter.

"Buh," he said.

The voice called out. "Make a note of the time in his chart. We need to call his doctor first thing in the morning. I don't think this is random. He's waking up."

———

The sun, rising from beneath the ocean waves, changed from a massive orange ball to a circle of yellow fire. Alexia was putting on the last touches of makeup when the phone rang.

"You've got to come over here," Rena said frantically. "The night-duty nurse stopped by the house a few minutes ago and told me Baxter may be coming out of the coma."

Alexia forgot about her eye shadow. "What did she say?"

"That he's trying to open his eyes and make sounds."

"Any words?"

"No."

"Is he still paralyzed?"

"I think so. I was so shocked I didn't ask."

"Have you been over to the cottage?"

"Not yet. I'm afraid to go. The last time I looked into Baxter's eyes he was trying to kill me. What would I say to him? Should I ask him why he tried to push me off the cliff? Warn him about his father? Tell him that he's paralyzed? Threaten to talk to the police?"

Alexia waited for her to stop and catch her breath.

"I'm not sure what you should say to him," Alexia finally interjected. "If he doesn't know what's happened, it wouldn't make any sense to confront him. I think you should keep everything simple until we know more about his mental status. Wait and see what happens."

"Wait and see!" Rena exploded. "That's all I've heard since the first meeting with the doctors in Greenville! I'm the one who's paralyzed here! I can't go anywhere or do anything because I don't know what's going to happen. What did I do to deserve this?"

"You haven't done anything wrong," Alexia reassured her. "We just have to take everything one step at a time. Did the nurse contact one of the doctors?"

"Yes."

"Which one?"

"Dr. Leoni, the neurologist from Charleston."

Alexia had not yet met Dr. Simon Leoni, the neurologist recommended by the neurosurgeon who originally treated Baxter.

Alexia rested the phone against her shoulder and applied the final touch of faint eye shadow. "There's no use in my coming over now, but I'd like to be there when the doctor arrives. If Baxter regains consciousness and can think for himself, it will make our lawsuit against his father moot."

"What do you mean?"

"Unnecessary. If Baxter is mentally competent he would have to pursue his own claim. You wouldn't have legal standing to complain."

"But I'm his wife!"

"I'll explain in more detail later. First, let's find out what the doctor thinks about Baxter's condition. I'll be at my office in an hour and can come over when Dr. Leoni arrives."

Rena was silent for a few seconds. "I'm scared," she said in a subdued voice. "I'm sorry I got upset, but I don't have anyone else to talk to."

Alexia gave her short dark hair a few more quick brushes. She had come alongside Rena as her legal champion, but there was a limit to the role she could play as counselor. She had waited for this opening.

"Rena, you may need a professional to help you cope with what this is doing to you. A lot of my clients talk to a psychologist or psychiatrist."

"I'm scared, not crazy."

"You're not crazy, but extreme stress can affect you more than you might realize. A lot of people need a counselor or therapist to help them work through traumatic situations. When the crisis is over, they go on with their lives."

"I don't know," Rena spoke slowly. "It's hard for me to trust anyone, and I don't know any psychologists or psychiatrists."

Alexia responded in her most soothing tone of voice. "I'll give you some names to consider. In the meantime, focus on getting through this day one moment at a time."

"Okay, thanks."

After she clicked off the phone, Alexia quickly finished getting ready. She stepped onto the deck and called Boris home from his morning jaunt. In the clear air of a new day, the unsettling events of the previous night faded. Boris ran up the steps onto the deck with happy eyes.

"Anything bad in our world?" Alexia asked him.

Boris wagged his tail.

"Good."

Alexia opened the door and followed the dog inside. He walked over to his water dish and began lapping noisily. Alexia removed the cover from the doggie door so the Labrador could come and go during the day.

"And there aren't any shoes under my bed today," Alexia continued. "If you get bored, gnaw on the big piece of rawhide I bought you last week. I saw it in the corner of the living room."

On her way to the front door, Alexia paused to stroke Misha's back. "Watch the dog and let me know if he gets into mischief."

Alexia drove past the spot where she'd been stuck the previous evening. The tide had flowed in and erased tire marks from the sand. The road was empty, the picnic area deserted. She decided to call Ted Morgan and tell him about Baxter.

The music minister didn't know the truth about the events leading up to Baxter's injuries because the information was protected by the attorney-client privilege. So when Ted asked Alexia to help him gain access to play his keyboard and pray for Baxter, she hesitated. Baxter's condition seemed just punishment for his conduct. But in the end, Alexia agreed to help. Rena didn't care, and the treating neurosurgeon wrote a note authorizing "music therapy."

She turned onto Highway 17 and punched in Ted's number. The phone rang several times before a sleepy voice answered.

"Hello," he said.

"Did I wake you?" Alexia said as she glanced at the clock in her car. "I thought you got up a lot earlier than this."

"Normally I do, but I was up late last night."

"What were you doing?"

"I couldn't sleep and went over to the sanctuary. I played the piano for a while and then prayed for Baxter."

"Well, I'd say you got through."

"Why?" Ted's voice grew stronger. "What's happened?"

"Rena just called and told me Baxter's waking up. He opened his eyes and tried to talk."

"Is he moving his arms or legs?"

"I don't think so."

"Didn't Rena give you any details?"

"Not really. She was in shock herself. I asked her to let me know when the doctor comes to check him."

"Did he recognize her?"

"She hasn't seen him yet. The nurse told her what happened, and Rena called me."

"That's odd. Why didn't she rush over to the cottage?"

Alexia hesitated. "I'll find out more today and let you know."

"Okay, but I won't be satisfied if all he did was flutter his eyelids."

"I understand. Get some sleep."

"Not now. I'm wide awake."

Alexia snapped the phone shut. In a few minutes she entered the downtown area of Santee. The center of town was about eight miles from her home on the marsh and retained the slow-paced atmosphere that predated the area's commercial development.

Land use along the South Carolina coast was divided into narrow strips. Along the sandy beach, condominiums for tourists mingled with the vacation homes of those wealthy enough to afford oceanfront real estate. Just beyond the coastal area, commercial developments selling beach chairs, sunscreen, and body boards had sprung up. Next came restaurants featuring seafood buffets laden with enough calories and cholesterol to clog a water main, and trendy clothing boutiques that charged high prices for skimpy women's garments. Golfing communities provided a third level of expensive residential development for year-round residents who had moved south to escape colder weather.

The town of Santee was home to a small number of people who had resided in the area for generations. Natives avoided houses with high property-tax values, wore hats to ward off the sun, and considered loud-mouthed tourists as pesky as mosquitoes. Alexia had represented several local residents and earned a measure of acceptance into their tight-knit circle.

Most of the buildings along the town's two main streets had been built thirty or forty years ago, but local government officials were proud of the attractive new sandstone courthouse and their success in luring several out-of-town banks to open branch offices.

Alexia entered Rachel's building through the back door, the shortest path to her temporary office. The lawyer had recently purchased a very nice cherry computer table and telephone stand in anticipation of her move to the King Street house, and the new items looked out of place in the rectangular room with cheap, paneled walls. A single window gave a limited view of the parking lot.

Alexia walked down a long hallway to the front of the office to check for phone messages. As she stood by the receptionist's desk and flipped through the pink slips of paper, one name caught her attention. Startled, she gave it a second look. She handed the note back to the receptionist.

"Are you sure this call is for me?"

The young receptionist glanced down. "Oh, yes. He called a few minutes ago. I was too busy to fill in your name. Sorry about that. That's the direct number for his personal assistant. He wanted you to call as soon as you arrived."

Alexia returned to her office and put the note from Jeffrey Richardson on her desk.

5

Detective Giles Porter sat in a squeaky chair behind an old wooden desk. He shared a large, open room with the other detective who worked for the Mitchell County Sheriff's Department. In a corner, hunched over a radio transmitter, crouched the dispatcher, who monitored and directed the activities of the county's seven full-time deputies. Porter ran his hand over the top of his bald head. Underneath his fingers he felt the familiar crease of the reddish scar left by the shotgun blast that thirty years before blew out the windshield of his patrol car. At that time, the sheriff's department only had two patrol cars. But those cars were special.

To be effective, law-enforcement officers needed vehicles that could compete with those driven by the moonshiners, who transported homemade liquor from the mountains of northwestern South Carolina to the dry counties of the Piedmont. Giles Porter, just discharged from the army and working as an inexperienced deputy, had spent many nights parked under the trees along rural roads. Rolling down the window of his patrol car, he would watch the stars overhead and listen for the deep-throated rumble of a Ford coupe whose backseat was filled with gallon plastic jugs of white lightning.

The sons and nephews of the men Porter chased down winding roads on moonless nights now raced legally under bright lights at dirt tracks and short asphalt ovals from Walhalla to Gaffney. The final surrender of prohibition ended the need for hidden mountain distilleries; however, some modern stock-car racing fans romanticized the criminals of the past who hauled illegal whiskey. Not Porter. He'd seen men who lost their sight after drinking a bad batch distilled through a rusty radiator, and on two occasions he called a hearse to pick up the bodies of those who consumed contaminated white liquor that bit with poisonous venom.

Porter shuffled papers across his desk and picked up an information bulletin about the death of Claude Dixon, a long-time deputy with the Charleston County Sheriff's Department. He stared at the small picture, trying to decide if he'd ever met Dixon. Porter's memory was legendary. The detective carried multiple phone numbers in his head and had an uncanny knack for recalling obscure details at crucial times. Few felonies in Mitchell County remained unsolved, and over the years Porter had received several generous job offers from larger police departments. But his heart remained in the mountains where he'd risked his life and raised his children. Preserving law and order in Mitchell County was his enduring passion.

It took a moment, but he remembered sharing a table with Dixon at a training event in Columbia. He read the brief summary of the circumstances surrounding Dixon's death. The officer died during a traffic stop, when he was knocked to the ground and broke his neck. The car he stopped, an expensive red convertible, was stolen from the Richardson residence in Santee. Porter leaned forward in his chair, causing it to give a loud screech. In the third drawer of a gray filing cabinet behind his desk was a folder with the name "Baxter Richardson" across the top. Porter's encounter with the Richardson family occurred while Baxter was in the hospital in Greenville, but he knew the wealthy family resided in Santee.

"Paul!" he called out to the dispatcher. "Is your computer turned on?"

"Yes sir," replied the young officer.

"Find out the full name of the owner of a red convertible stolen in Santee two weeks ago. It was recovered in Charleston County as part of a homicide investigation."

"Do you know the VIN?"

"No, but the last name is Richardson."

"That will take a minute."

Porter waited patiently as the young man's fingers flew over the keys. Paul Fletchall didn't have the physical stature to break up a brawl;

however, he knew how to usher the sheriff's department into the age of modern technology, and as a lifelong resident of Mitchell County, he knew every street and road better than any other dispatcher in the department.

Giles Porter's thoughts had returned on a regular basis to Baxter and Rena Richardson ever since he learned that the young man had survived his quick trip to the bottom of Double Barrel Falls. From the first day he met Rena, Porter had been certain the attractive young woman wasn't telling him the whole truth about the events surrounding her husband's accident. His subsequent investigation substantiated his suspicions. In the evidence room next to the cleaning closet was a walking stick Porter had brought back from Double Barrel Falls. Other evidence remained in a secure location in a medical lab at Greenville Memorial Hospital. No one knew about the results of the tests except Porter and the forensic pathologist who performed them. The detective was itching to ask the local solicitor to seek an indictment against Rena from the grand jury, but his professional patience kept him in check. He hoped other evidence would surface, making it impossible for Rena to bat her eyelashes at the men on the jury and wiggle free.

"Got it," Paul called out. "Baxter Calhoun Richardson. Hey, isn't he the guy who fell from the cliff and ended up in a coma?"

"Yes. It seems he's had a string of bad luck."

Porter picked up the phone and dialed the number for the Charleston County Sheriff's Department. After a few transfers, Detective Byron Devereaux answered the phone. Porter introduced himself.

"We have a mutual interest in Baxter Richardson," he began.

"Baxter Richardson?"

"He's the owner of the red convertible stopped by Deputy Dixon. Richardson spent several weeks on life support in Greenville Memorial Hospital following injuries suffered in a fall here in Mitchell County. You may have talked to Rena, his wife."

There was a brief pause. "You have my attention."

———

Alexia returned her other calls before picking up the message from Jeffrey Richardson. Baxter's older brother had given Rena the money to hire

Alexia after his father gutted Rena's bank account, but Alexia remained wary. Rena seemed afraid of her brother-in-law, and while the lawyer wasn't naive about Rena's tendency toward paranoia, sometimes paranoid people had reason to be suspicious.

She considered phoning Rena but decided it would only upset her client. Until Alexia knew why Jeffrey was contacting her, there was nothing to discuss. She flipped over a clean sheet on her legal pad and touched the numbers on her phone. A pleasant female voice answered.

"Good morning, Jeffrey Richardson's office."

"Mr. Richardson, please. It's Alexia Lindale returning his call."

The woman put her on hold. While she waited, Alexia listened to a recording of music suitable for a dentist's office. Every so often there was a faint beep that made her wonder if the phone was hooked to a recorder. Finally, a male voice with a soft, coastal accent came on the line.

"Ms. Lindale?"

"Yes."

"Thanks for calling. I know you're busy, so I'll get to the point. My father is using the power of attorney Baxter signed when he turned eighteen to secretly transfer my brother's interest in several companies."

Because Rena had told Alexia that Jeffrey wanted his identity as a source to remain confidential, she was surprised by Jeffrey's frankness.

"I'm aware of the possibility," Alexia replied deliberately. "From the first day I learned about the power of attorney, I knew your father might attempt to transfer assets."

"Of course you did. I've heard you're a smart lawyer with a knack for seeing through corporate smoke screens."

Alexia remained noncommittal. "I'm simply doing my best to represent your sister-in-law."

"And I appreciate it. If Baxter could talk, he'd thank you too. Rena needs someone like you so she won't make any mistakes."

"What kind of mistakes?"

Alexia heard Jeffrey clear his throat. "Rena is a great girl, but I'm sure you've seen that she can be a little bit flighty. Occasionally, she says things she later regrets. She needs someone steady to guide her and keep her out of trouble."

"Why are you calling to talk about this? I thought you wanted to remain behind the scenes."

"Not really. You need to be able to talk to me directly if you have any questions. It will be a lot more efficient that way."

"That will be up to Rena, but I'll mention it to her."

"Good. Do you have a list of the companies involved in the transfers?"

"Yes, but I wasn't sure they were all directly implicated."

"They're not, but we can sort that out later."

"Okay," Alexia answered. Then she waited until the silence felt uncomfortable. "Is there anything else you wanted to tell me?"

"Actually, I wanted to invite you to dinner Saturday night."

Alexia was startled. Gwen had told her Jeffrey Richardson approached women like a big-game hunter tracked exotic prey.

"No, thank you," she responded curtly.

Jeffrey laughed, which annoyed Alexia. "Oh, it's not a date. It's a charitable fund-raiser for a nonprofit organization that operates homes for abused children. I've agreed to sponsor a table and need to fill it. You could bring a friend. The entertainment will be a classical pianist. Victor Plavich from San Francisco. I've been told he's very good."

Alexia sat up straighter in her chair. "Won't your father be there? That could be awkward. I mean, I haven't filed suit yet, but I cross-examined him during the hearing in Greenville to terminate Baxter's life support, and with what might be coming up—"

"Don't worry," Jeffrey interrupted. "I wouldn't do that to either one of you. He bought a table, too, but he'll be out of town on a business trip to the Caribbean."

Alexia's resistance melted. "Okay. I have a good friend who loves piano music. Could I invite him?"

"Sure. What's his name? I'll pencil him in on my sheet."

"Ted Morgan."

"Call back and confirm with my assistant as soon as possible. I don't want to be dining alone."

"I'll let her know by the end of the day tomorrow."

Alexia put the phone back in its cradle and wondered what she should wear. It might be a formal affair. She had several dresses for fancy occasions, and she mentally tried on each one, imagining herself walking into the banquet hall with Ted. She thought of the rustic music minister in a tuxedo, and the scene made her smile.

———

Rena looked out a window toward the cottage. She resented the money shelled out by Ezra for Baxter's nursing care. The amount spent every week for skilled medical care would have fed and clothed Rena and her brothers for a year when they were growing up. What a colossal waste.

Several days had passed since Rena last stepped across the driveway to the cottage. There wasn't any reason to drop in for a visit to watch her husband breathe while an RN or aide scurried around acting busy. Rena's few happy memories of the cottage had been obliterated by its transformation into a fancy hospital room to preserve the life of the man whose survival threatened her own.

She decided to go to the spa and had put on expensive workout clothes. Hard physical activity gave her a temporary respite from the constant pressure that surrounded her. She was in excellent physical condition and could run an hour on a treadmill. She'd occasionally tried to persuade Baxter to join her for workouts, but he was more interested in relaxing.

"Go ahead," he'd tell her, and then return to his wine or golf magazine.

Rena walked out the side door and toward the four-car garage connected to the main house by a short covered walkway. Instead of entering the garage, she paused and then continued walking. She had to see for herself whether Baxter had improved enough to become a clear danger.

Dark shutters and a red door accented the white wooden cottage. The landscaping service had planted beds of cheerful pansies on either side of the brick walkway. Winter along the coast was merely a season for a different crop of flowers. Carefully shaped shrubs grew beneath the front windows. It was a perfect dollhouse.

She pushed open the door. Baxter lay on his back, his eyes closed. She could detect no visible change. The open blinds let in the morning light. An aide Rena didn't recognize was placing a tray on the adjustable table beside Baxter's bed. The young woman looked up in surprise when Rena entered the room.

"Uh, may I help you?"

"I'm his wife," Rena said.

A nurse stuck her head around the corner from the kitchen.

"Good morning, Mrs. Richardson," she said.

"Have you heard from the neurologist?" Rena asked.

"No, but I saw the notes from the night-duty personnel. It looks hopeful."

Rena grunted. "Leave me alone with him for a few minutes."

The nurse withdrew to the kitchen. The aide joined her. Rena stepped close to the edge of the bed and looked down at her husband.

Baxter's right leg, broken in the fall, was in an air cast. Because of the injury to his spinal cord, he couldn't move the leg, making it unnecessary to do anything to stabilize it. A white sheet and lightweight blanket covered all but his head and neck. The cuts and bruises he'd suffered at the waterfall had healed without leaving serious scars. Someone had trimmed his sandy brown hair and shaved his face. To a casual observer, he could have passed for a young man recovering from an appendectomy.

After Baxter fell from the cliff and while he lay unconscious in the ICU of the Greenville hospital, Rena had maintained a consistent propaganda campaign designed to reprogram his recollection of the incident at the cliff. She had no idea whether her lies had taken root, but at least they helped pass the tedious time spent at his bedside. She pulled up a wooden chair and sat down so that her mouth was close to his ear. She wanted to scream at the top of her lungs for him to die and leave her alone.

"Hello, darling," she said and then watched closely for any reaction.

Seeing nothing, she continued, "It's me. You're in the cottage where we lived after our honeymoon. You've had a terrible accident, but you're going to be okay. I've been here with you the whole time. You may have had some bad dreams, but you slipped and fell—"

Baxter suddenly groaned so loudly that Rena jumped in her seat. His eyelids fluttered, and for the first time since he pleaded for help as he slipped over the cliff, her husband opened his eyes in her presence. He didn't turn his head but stared straight up at the ceiling.

Rena's mouth dropped open, and she watched in disbelief. A knot cramped her stomach, and she leaned over in pain.

"Oh no!" she said.

The nurse peered around the corner.

"Are you alright?"

Still gaping, Rena pointed at Baxter's face.

The nurse spoke. "He's opened his eyes a couple of times since I came on duty."

The pain in Rena's stomach eased slightly. She spoke in a hoarse whisper.

"Does he understand anything?"

The nurse stepped into the room and approached the bed so that she would be in Baxter's line of sight. Moving her hand from side to side in front of his face, she watched his reaction.

"He doesn't follow the motion of my hand. The doctor will have to examine him, but I don't know what he can see or understand." The nurse leaned over. "Mr. Richardson, if you understand that someone is talking to you, blink your eyes one time."

Rena watched Baxter's eyelashes from the side. There was no movement. The knot in her stomach relaxed, and she took a deep breath.

"See?" the nurse said. "Each time I've asked him to blink his eyes I couldn't establish a distinction between involuntary and voluntary activity."

Baxter blinked.

"So you don't even know if he can see?" Rena asked.

The nurse shook her head. "I don't want to speculate. The doctor will be able to give you a better idea about his status."

Rena reached out and tentatively touched Baxter's cheek. His eyes fluttered and seemed to roll back in his head. Rena withdrew her hand.

"Did you see that?" she asked.

"It's not unusual."

Rena suspected the nurse knew more than she was saying, but didn't press her for information. She wasn't sure she wanted to know the truth. She pushed back the chair and stood up.

"Have you talked to the doctor since you came on duty?" she asked.

"No. The night nurse called Dr. Leoni's answering service, but we haven't heard from him. As soon as we know his schedule, we'll notify you."

Rena straightened. "I'll be out for a while, but you have my cell number. Could I have one more minute alone with him?"

The nurse returned to the kitchen. Rena leaned over so close to Baxter's right ear that her lips almost touched it.

"Sweetheart, it's Rena. Remember that I love you very, very much. You can't trust everyone, but you know that I'd never do anything to hurt you."

Baxter's head jerked slightly so that his ear brushed against Rena's lips. The physical contact overloaded her circuits. Rena fled from the room.

6

Eat to live, and not live to eat.
POOR RICHARD'S ALMANAC

Shortly before noon, Alexia called Leggitt & Freeman and asked to speak to Gwen Jones. The receptionist put Alexia on hold. Anyone waiting to speak to a lawyer or staff member at Leggitt & Freeman listened to a random series of beeps and tones. Alexia once suggested Rachmaninoff might be a sophisticated alternative, but Ralph Leggitt dismissed her idea as snobby.

In a minute, her former secretary answered in a harried voice.

"Hold, please."

Before Alexia could protest, she returned to the never-never land of beeps. She was about to hang up and try later when Gwen's voice returned.

"Gwen Jones. How may I help you?"

"You can tell the office manager to get rid of the infuriating sounds that play when a person is on hold. Are you too busy to talk?"

"I'm swamped. Leonard has been trying to make up for goofing off the past two weeks, and the new lawyer wants all his correspondence to go through three drafts. How many times can you change a cover letter for a client receiving a draft copy of a simple will?"

"Can you sneak away for lunch?" Alexia asked.

"Isn't there a federal law that gives me an hour for lunch?"

"No, but you'll not be able to type one hundred words a minute if you don't keep up your strength."

"I can squeeze in an hour. Are you willing to feed my soul as well as my stomach?"

Alexia knew what that meant. "Yes, but we'd better leave now if we want to get a table."

"I'm already turning off my computer."

Gwen loved soul food, and when she and Alexia went to lunch, she often insisted they go to Cousin Bert's. Having lived all her life in South Carolina, Gwen recalled with bliss old-fashioned Southern dinners at her grand-mother's house, and Cousin Bert's capably fed her childhood memories.

Owned by an African-American family, Cousin Bert's was located behind Main Street in a low concrete-block building painted white. For many years it had been one of the special places where blacks and whites came together to sit down in mutual respect for perfectly seasoned col-lard greens, expertly fried chicken, and sweet tea garnished with a thick slice of lemon. Few tourists stumbled upon the hidden culinary glory, and local residents didn't reveal the secret to strangers. An old Pepsi sign on a rusty iron pole beside the front door announced the name of the eating establishment.

Alexia arrived before Gwen and parked carefully in Bert's small gravel lot so that she would be able to exit unhindered. By 12:30 PM cars would pack themselves in so tightly that it might be hard to find a path back to the street. She opened her car door, careful not to nick Judge Garland's new white Lincoln. A van with the name of a local plumbing company stenciled on the side rested at an angle on the other side of the judge's sedan.

Inside, the tide of lunchtime patrons was beginning to rise. Waitresses carrying plates heaped with food scurried from the kitchen into the brightly lit dining area filled with simple tables and plain chairs. Alexia saw Judge Garland sitting in a back corner with two men she didn't know. He didn't look up when she entered.

Alexia selected a table for two against the wall next to a narrow win-dow and sat so she could watch the door for Gwen. Pictures of Bert and members of his extended family decorated the walls, along with photos of other members of the community. A picture of a white brick mason hung beside a photo of a distinguished-looking black man in a dark suit, white shirt, and dark tie. Alexia didn't know the rationale behind the eclectic collection but suspected each picture was the beginning or end of a story. An older, dark-skinned waitress came up to her. Alexia recognized her face.

"Just you today?" she asked.

"No, Gwen Jones is coming."

The waitress nodded and scribbled on her pad.

"I'll bring out two teas—sweet for Gwen and unsweet with extra lemon for you."

Alexia glanced over at Judge Garland. This time he saw her, smiled, and nodded in greeting. Alexia was relieved. She'd not been sure how the judge would view her since she'd left Leggitt & Freeman. She'd worked hard to earn his respect, but his long-standing personal relationships with other attorneys and judges could trump her competency. Since she was no longer associated with an established firm, Alexia worried she might be viewed by the local bar as a maverick.

Gwen entered just as the tea and two small cornbread cakes arrived at the table. In the few days since Alexia had last seen her, Gwen had changed her hair color from a reddish-blonde to brown with auburn tips. Gwen loved brightly colored clothes and kept a perpetual tan. She hurried over and sat down.

"Sorry, I'm late," she said. "Leonard gave me a document that had to be changed before a closing scheduled this afternoon."

"Had you made a mistake?"

Gwen picked up a steamy cornbread cake and broke it in two. "No, he miscalculated and dropped the last zero for the proceeds to the seller. It would have been ugly."

"Ouch."

Gwen put a generous swath of whipped butter on the cornbread and took her first bite. She closed her eyes.

"That's the ultimate," she said.

Alexia also liked the cornbread. Bert's rendition was sweeter than typical cornpone.

"He's going to make a mistake someday and cost the firm a bunch of money," Alexia said.

Gwen sipped her tea. "When he does and gets booted out, promise me you won't take him under your wing."

Alexia laughed. "I won't be on his radar screen. Leonard will forget my name in six months."

"Yeah, I don't think he knew me when I showed up on Monday with my new hair."

"It's nice."

Gwen fluffed it gently. "It's close to my natural color."

"Liar. Your hair has forgotten its original color."

They ordered lunch. Gwen selected dark-meat fried chicken with mashed potatoes and green beans. At Cousin Bert's, the green beans were cooked with tiny pieces of bacon and brown sugar for an hour before the lunchtime crowd arrived. Alexia preferred green beans steamed for two minutes and covered with toasted almonds. She chose the soup of the day, which was always a seafood gumbo seasoned with a generous touch of cayenne pepper.

"That gumbo is more than I can handle," Gwen said after the waitress left. "It's potent enough to raise the dead. If I ate a bowl for lunch, I'd be miserable all afternoon."

"Maybe a bowl is just what Baxter Richardson needs to bring him all the way back to consciousness."

"What do you mean?" Gwen asked in surprise.

Alexia told her about Rena's call.

"He opened his eyes," Gwen repeated. "What do the doctors say?"

"Nothing yet. The local neurologist may come by this afternoon. If he does, Rena is going to call me so I can be there to listen."

Gwen shook her head. "I guess Rena feels terrible about trying to cut off Baxter's life support."

"It's hard to know what she thinks," Alexia said. "That seems to depend on how she feels at any given moment. She still faces the possibility that Baxter will be a total invalid with significant brain damage. Even if he wakes up, he'll be a quadriplegic. On top of it all, she's got that wild card of a father-in-law. He's the ultimate control freak."

Gwen nodded. "It might have been better if Baxter had slipped quietly away."

The waitress brought their food. The mashed potatoes were flecked with tiny pieces of brown peel that conclusively established their link with potatoes harvested from the ground rather than poured from a box. Alexia took a sip of soup. It made the edge of her tongue sizzle.

"Ted Morgan and I went to see Baxter yesterday," she said after they'd eaten in silence for a few moments. "He wanted to pray for him, and Rena agreed to let me take him in."

Gwen nodded. "Rachel told me."

Alexia stopped her spoon between her bowl and her mouth. "What else did Rachel tell you?"

"I hope everything."

"You've never had me under such an intense microscope. Did you talk this much about Jason and me when we were engaged?"

"Not with Rachel. Jason was always a long way off, and I only met him once. I kept my thoughts to myself."

"Really? Let's hear them."

"You asked me at the time. Don't you remember my response?"

It had been more than a year since Jason Favreau last visited Santee on his way to a job in southern France. Alexia was scheduled to join him a short time afterward for a week in Marseilles to finalize wedding plans. The day before she left, he called and broke off the engagement. Barely a month passed before he married a French girl.

"No."

"That's because you weren't paying attention. I grunted twice, which meant I was as concerned for you as a mother bear is for her cubs when a hunter comes tromping through the woods."

"Why didn't you speak up?"

"Would it have done any good? You thought Jason was a perfect match. Your head was filled with a lifetime of exotic trips to places I've never heard of."

"Ouch."

Gwen leaned forward and patted her hand. "I didn't want to hurt you, Alexia. That's why I didn't say anything."

"And I'm glad to know how you really felt. Promise not to keep your thoughts to yourself in the future."

"But I can be wrong."

"Sure. However, I respect your opinion," Alexia paused. "What about Ted Morgan? What do you think about the difference in our ages?"

"His age is a plus in my book. Most men don't know how to walk through a door before they're thirty-five. Ted is in his midforties, right?"

"Yes, forty-four."

"Then you have a clearer picture of who he really is than if he were wandering around in a typical male postcollege identity crisis."

"Well, I'm comfortable with the age difference. It's not something I think about when I'm with him, and he's more tuned in to how I feel than anyone I've met. We're not too serious, but there's potential."

Gwen slowly chewed a piece of chicken before continuing. "I've never met him, and there's no substitute for looking a man in the eye, so I'll reserve final judgment. But I have to know, are you attracted to the man or the music?"

Alexia's quick answer died on her lips. She ate a spoonful of soup before responding.

"I love the music, and he has a unique gift," she admitted. "But it's more complicated than that. There's also the influence he's had on what I believe. He's been my spiritual guide. Until I met him, Christianity was on the fringe of my world. Now it's become much more important, and Ted is at the center of what's happening to me in that area of my life."

"All of which means you need to take your foot off the romance pedal. He may be a great piano player and a good counselor, but it's hard for me to see you happy with a minister. You're too ambitious to sign up for that kind of lifestyle."

Alexia shrugged. "I don't know."

"It looks to me like the pendulum may have swung the other way. With Jason, you would have been hopping all over the world, never knowing where you'd be from month to month. Ted Morgan might not even have time to take you to Charleston for a weekend."

Alexia sipped her tea. "You're right. I've been too narrow with him. I need to understand the bigger picture of his life."

"And where a woman like you would fit into it."

The two women split dessert, a massive piece of coconut cream pie that towered at least four inches above the plate.

"How could one person eat all this?" Alexia asked.

Gwen carefully carved out another sliver and sighed with content. "One heavenly bite at a time."

Alexia left the last crumbs for Gwen and grabbed both checks when the waitress set them down.

"We always pay our own way," Gwen protested.

"I invited you," Alexia replied.

Gwen withdrew her hand. "Okay, but I need to talk to you about more than Ted Morgan."

"What is it?"

Gwen's face became serious. "I think my neck is on the chopping block at Leggitt & Freeman. You know I can hack into Ned's computer?"

Alexia nodded.

"I was reading Ned's interoffice e-mail, and I'm on the agenda for the partner's meeting tomorrow."

"That could mean a lot of things."

"Name a good one."

Alexia thought for a moment. "I can't. But why would they want to fire you? Leonard would commit monthly malpractice if you weren't there to clean up his messes."

"It may be a youth movement. I know they're interviewing clerical people in their early twenties. They can pay them thousands less than I'm making—"

"And lose more than that in productivity."

Gwen shrugged. "Go figure. I know it will be a while before your new office is ready, but if it happens, do I still have a place to land with you?"

"Of course. I'm not sure Rachel has an extra office, but we could set you up at home."

"Rachel has an office. She's willing to clean out the storage room across the hall from you."

Alexia smiled. "You talked about more than Ted Morgan and me last night."

Gwen held her thumb and forefinger close together. "Just a little bit. She can give me some work and pay part of my salary for a while if it puts a strain on you to do it all."

Alexia motioned to the empty plate. "We'll find a way to keep you in coconut cream pie."

Gwen once again touched her hair. "And color. I'd be afraid to find out what's really lurking inside my scalp."

———

Detective Rick Bridges passed the city limits sign for Santee. On the seat beside him, a manila folder held a criminal arrest photograph of Henry L. Quinton. Nothing about Quinton's appearance signaled anything sinister. Even though he wasn't smiling for the camera, his clean-shaven face and carefully combed dark hair made him look more like a twenty-something corporate business trainee than a professional hit man.

Bridges stopped at three convenience stores with no success before turning into the parking lot for a liquor store on the south side of town. He took the photograph inside and put it on the counter in front of a middle-aged man, who deposited a cigarette into an ashtray beside the cash register. The detective placed his badge beside the picture and introduced himself. Several customers milled about. Two immediately left at the sight of the badge.

"Have you ever seen this man?" Bridges asked the clerk. "He would have a New Jersey accent."

The man held the picture close to his eyes and squinted.

"Can't say that I have, but that doesn't mean anything."

"Why not?"

"I've only been working here a week. Before that I was living in Georgia."

"Is anyone else here?" the detective asked.

"Yeah, the manager is in back paying bills."

"I'd like to check with him."

The clerk led Bridges past a long rack of cheap wines and opened a thin wooden door. "The office is the second door down the hall on the left. I need to stay here with the customers."

The detective rapped twice on the closed door. A gruff female voice answered. "What is it?"

"Detective Bridges with the Charleston County Sheriff's Department.

Please open the door so I can show you a picture of a man I'm trying to locate."

Bridges heard someone sneeze, the sound of a drawer being closed, and a chair or other piece of furniture being knocked over. The door opened, revealing a large, overweight woman wearing blue jeans and a bulky sweater. She was rubbing her right shin and holding a tissue to her nose.

"Ran into the chair," she said, not moving away from the door.

"Sorry to bother you. I just have a quick question."

"Yeah, let me see."

The detective handed her the photograph and looked past her into the office.

"He's not from around here," he said, surveying the room. "Probably New York or New Jersey. The picture was taken about eight years ago, so he'd be around thirty-four by now."

The woman stuffed the tissue in her pocket. "A lot of people with faces like that come in here. I can't remember anyone in particular."

She handed the photograph back to the detective. When she did, he saw a white, powdery smudge on the side of her right index finger. She saw his glance and quickly stuck the dirty finger in her mouth.

"Taking a powder for a headache?" Bridges asked.

"Uh, yeah."

Bridges stared at her face for a second longer than necessary. The woman's nostrils were red and inflamed. Without permission, a search warrant, or illegal drugs in plain view, he couldn't take another step. But he could send a message.

"I'd rather not come back later," he said. "Are you sure you don't know who this might be?"

The woman glanced over her shoulder at the desk. "You might want to ask at the Beachcomber Club on Highway 17. People from up north like to go there at night."

"Who should I talk to?"

"Uh, Harry is the main bartender. He's been there a long time."

7

Alexia was about to call Ted and invite him to the benefit concert when the receptionist buzzed her. Rena again.

"Dr. Leoni is going to be here in thirty minutes," Rena said over the phone.

"Did you talk to him?"

"No, it was his nurse. He's making a special trip from Charleston. Do you think I should call Ezra and let him know? I don't want to talk to him, but—"

"He's out of town," Alexia interrupted.

"How do you know?"

Alexia bit her lip. "Jeffrey mentioned it."

"You talked to Jeffrey?" Rena asked, her voice getting louder. "Why?"

Alexia kept her tone matter-of-fact. "He phoned me. Don't worry. It was a positive conversation. He's willing to give us more specific information about the companies on the list and thought it would be better to contact me directly. He knew you were passing along information from him anyway. It will be easier for me to ask him what I need to know than relay everything through you. Normally, things would be handled this way with an insider cooperating in a case."

"You can't trust him."

"Oh, I'll double-check everything he says, but it will help me ask other people the right questions about the businesses."

"But he doesn't want you to do that."

"Then why is he giving us information?"

Rena didn't answer. Alexia waited. "Are you still there?"

"I don't want to talk about Jeffrey anymore."

Alexia picked up her pen and tapped it on the top of her desk. "We'll have to talk about him if you want me to file a lawsuit against Ezra based on information Jeffrey has provided. If that information isn't true, we shouldn't waste your money and my time trying to do something about it. All we'll accomplish in filing a lawsuit is making Ezra madder at you than he already is."

"But you told me if Baxter wakes up we can't do anything anyway."

"Yes, but that's not what we're talking about now."

Rena's silence lingered for a few seconds.

"I need to sort through everything else before making up my mind. I've got to change clothes."

Rena hung up before Alexia could respond. She slowly returned the receiver to its cradle and tried to assess Rena's reaction. Alexia had no doubt that Jeffrey intimidated Rena, but she didn't have a clue why her client feared him.

Then it hit her.

As a divorce lawyer, she should have suspected the possibility of an affair between Jeffrey and Rena. If true, an affair would cast new light on the entire sequence of events from Baxter's fall to the present. As she worked backward in time, each link in the chain joined its neighbor in logical progression.

Somehow, Baxter learns of the relationship between Rena and his brother. He confronts Rena at the falls and in a rage tries to push her over the edge. Instead, he plummets to the rocks. She thinks he's dead, and when interviewed by Detective Giles Porter, decides it's easier to say Baxter slipped and fell than reveal they had a struggle.

But Baxter survives. And Rena has a dilemma.

She meets Alexia and tells her part of the truth, i.e., there was a fight at the falls and Baxter tried to push her over the edge. Probably at Jeffrey's suggestion, Rena then asks Alexia to file a request with the court in Greenville to terminate Baxter's life support. Prior to going to court, Rena tells Alexia that Jeffrey is willing to support the petition to terminate life support because he believes it would provide a merciful and quick end to Baxter's life. Ultimately, Jeffrey keeps his allegiances secret and doesn't attend the hearing, but his money makes it possible. When Ezra uses the power of attorney to pillage Rena's bank account, Jeffrey comes to her aid and gives her the ten thousand dollars needed to retain Alexia. His intimate relationship with Rena explains everything—why he would bankroll her efforts to end Baxter's life and why his loyalties would lie with her rather than his own father.

In his latest move, Jeffrey seeks to restore Baxter's financial stake in the Richardson businesses, not to help his brother and sister-in-law, but because he wants to gain greater control himself. Working behind the scenes through Rena, he can avoid tipping off Ezra and keep his personal motivations secret. The stakes are probably higher than Rena suspects. He controls her like a puppy on a leash.

Alexia's stomach felt slightly queasy. For the first time, she considered the possibility that Baxter Richardson didn't deserve what had happened to him. Her mind racing, she looked at the clock. It was time to go. She tried to force herself to calm down.

———

Located in an older part of town, Baxter and Rena's house was even more of a showcase than when built by Ezra's father almost eighty years before. When Baxter married Rena, he renovated the ancestral home and thoroughly modernized it. They'd been living in it less than four months when the accident occurred.

Alexia drove up the long, curving driveway and parked near the guest cottage to the left of the house. Rena came out a side door of the main house. As Alexia watched her walk down the steps, she wondered briefly how closely her new theory followed the truth. Then she tried to banish the images whirling through her mind and concentrate on what was happening in real time. Rena looked frazzled.

"Is the doctor here?" Alexia asked.

"Yes, that's his car," Rena said, pointing to a new Lexus. "The nurse just called and told me he's ready to meet with me."

Alexia followed Rena into the cottage. Baxter was lying on his back with his eyes closed. On the far side of his bed stood a nurse Alexia didn't recognize and a short, slightly balding man with intelligent brown eyes. He introduced himself to Alexia and greeted Rena.

"I've had an opportunity to examine your husband, and there is no question that he shows signs of regaining consciousness."

Alexia glanced at Rena and saw her swallow. The doctor continued.

"Without an MRI scan we can't be sure, but I suspect the swelling in his brain has diminished. He suffered an axonal, or localized, head injury instead of one involving diffuse trauma, so his chances of recovering a greater level of cognitive functioning are increased. It's also fortunate that he didn't have an appreciable period of hypoxia, or loss of oxygen to the brain, prior to arriving at the hospital. On the other hand, the fact that he has been comatose for several weeks makes prognosis for specific sensory abilities more difficult to predict."

Alexia wished doctors would use understandable English.

"Can he hear?" she asked simply.

The doctor leaned closer to the bed and spoke in a slow, distinct voice.

"Baxter, if you can hear me, open your eyes."

Everyone stared at Baxter's closed eyelids. Nothing happened for several seconds. Then, Baxter Richardson slowly opened his eyes.

Out of the corner of her own eye, Alexia saw Rena step back. Baxter looked straight up at the ceiling. Alexia couldn't tell if he was focusing on anything, but she saw him blink and then keep his eyes open. As she continued to watch, the doctor placed his right index finger on Baxter's chin.

"If you can feel my finger on your chin, close your eyes."

Baxter's eyelids slid downward. Alexia watched and believed.

"This is all very basic," the doctor observed.

Basic maybe, but definitely significant. Alexia couldn't wait to tell Ted. A skeptic might chalk the improvement up to coincidence, but she'd been in the room just yesterday when the minister played and the nurse sang, and she had felt the air thick with the presence of God.

"Can he move his head, or blink once for yes and twice for no, or send any signal that he understands something more complex?"

The doctor removed his finger from Baxter's chin. "Before you arrived

I tried more difficult commands, but he wasn't able to respond. However, all in all, I'm pleased."

"No words?" Alexia continued.

The doctor shook his head. "And don't be discouraged if the first words he speaks are nonsense. Until he regains the ability to organize sounds into words and words into sentences, his vocabulary might spill out randomly."

"Like baby talk."

"Similar, only he would likely say actual words, perhaps complex ones."

Alexia glanced over her shoulder at Rena, who was staring at a spot on the floor somewhere on the other side of the bed.

"Do you have any questions for the doctor?" Alexia asked her. "I'm not trying to monopolize his time."

Rena looked up and asked in a soft voice, "What about his memory? I don't want him to remember the bad things that have happened to him."

"Most likely he won't," the doctor responded, "at least initially. People waking from a coma usually begin by opening their eyes and obeying simple commands such as squeezing a hand. Because of the injury to your husband's spinal cord, we have to rely on blinking. Then, as I said, there will be some form of verbal communication that often begins as nonsense. Be patient. Communication often improves as time passes. Memory is more difficult to predict. Post-traumatic amnesia, or PTA, is common in cases of severe head trauma. Generally, the longer the coma, the longer it takes to recover. Both recent and remote memory are affected. This means he will not remember what is happening to him at this stage of his recovery, and any statements he makes about what took place prior to his injury won't be retained in his long-term memory."

"Wait," Rena said, her voice stronger. "He may remember something from the past and then forget it again?"

"Or remember an event incorrectly. The possibilities are limitless. But whatever happens during this transition period will almost certainly not stay with him. We don't know the type and extent of permanent impairment to the areas of the brain injured, or the capability of other areas to compensate for what he's lost. He may also experience changes in more intangible aspects, such as his personality."

Alexia had read about head-injury patients who became aggressive and hard to manage. If he exhibited irrational rage, Baxter, bound in a prison of paralysis, would at least pose no physical threat.

The doctor continued. "Recovery may be rapid for a period of time, slow down, speed up, or stop completely. Actually, it's really premature to talk about memory, communication, and personality, but I want to give you a big picture of what might take place in the coming weeks and months. All I know with confidence is that he's doing much better than the last time I examined him. As for the rest, we'll have to wait and see."

Alexia quickly glanced at Rena to see if she was going to react to the hated phrase. She didn't.

"Should I keep talking to him?" Rena asked.

"Yes, it's even more important now than before. The stimulation will be good for him, and the sound of a familiar voice will help orient him to his surroundings."

"What if he acts upset?"

"Take a break and try later. There's no need to push him too hard at this point."

Rena stepped forward and touched Baxter on the cheek.

"I love you, honey. I'm glad you're getting better."

Baxter didn't move.

The two women walked outside together and past the beds of multi-colored pansies. Dr. Leoni stayed behind to talk to the nurse. He was writing in Baxter's chart as they left.

Beside Alexia's car, Rena asked, "What do you think?"

"It's amazing that he's waking up. When we came yesterday, I saw nothing to suggest he was coming out of the coma."

"No, I mean about the lawsuit against Ezra. I shouldn't have gotten upset with you for talking to Jeffrey. You're right. It will be easier to put everything together if the two of you don't have to go through me."

"All right," Alexia said slowly, "but his information is going to be the cornerstone of any case we build against your father-in-law. If he's un-reliable it will make my job harder instead of easier."

Rena looked past Alexia's shoulder toward the street. "You can't trust Jeffrey," she said simply. "He only cares about himself."

Following Rena was like tacking a sailboat into a shifting headwind.

"Then what do you want to do?" Alexia asked. "Having to verify everything Jeffrey tells me will be an awkward way to proceed."

Rena turned her gaze to Alexia, who saw a deep sadness in the young woman's eyes.

"This has all been so horrible that I've thought about leaving town in the middle of the night. It's not worth fighting over a bunch of stuff I don't understand. Let Ezra and Jeffrey have everything. There's nothing to keep me from getting in my car and running away, except that I don't have anyplace to go. My mother is dead, my brothers are broke, and my stepfather"—Rena paused—"doesn't know where I am. If Baxter had died, at least I would have received part of my inheritance and could move away to start over. Now, if he wakes up there's no telling what type of condition he'll be in, and after what happened at the waterfall, I can't stay married to him."

This time Alexia followed Rena easily. The sorrow in the young woman's eyes could be the by-product of two failed relationships: Baxter had not been able to keep her love; Jeffrey had proven fickle and manipulative.

"Divorce?" she asked.

Rena nodded. "I have to figure out a way go on with my life, even if it means divorcing Baxter, changing my name, and moving far, far away. A property settlement will provide enough for me to go somewhere else for a while."

Alexia measured her words. "Divorce is an option. But a big property settlement is unlikely because Baxter's future medical-care costs will be very high."

Rena bit her lower lip. "But he has insurance, and his father has enough money to pay for everything. I'm entitled to my fair share."

"That's not the way the court would look at it. Insurance coverage can change. The company might go out of business or cancel the policy, and even though Baxter is his son, Ezra has no legal obligation to help. The court would set aside a lot of money to pay for lifetime medical care."

"How much?"

"Medical-cost experts calculate those types of things, but it would certainly be millions of dollars."

"So he's better off dead than alive," Rena said bitterly.

Alexia didn't respond.

Rena continued. "I should have done this as soon as the accident happened. The thought of having to live with Baxter for the rest of my life is crazy. Even people who don't know the truth wouldn't blame me for getting out, not that I care what anyone thinks. I mean, he tried to kill me!"

Alexia couldn't argue with the facts behind Rena's feelings, but she kept her tone on a professional level.

"Although it isn't required by law, you definitely have grounds for divorce. It wouldn't be necessary to tell what happened at the waterfall. Getting a divorce is easy. The problem is the property settlement. Baxter was rich before he married you, and it will be hard to show how you made him richer in such a short period of time."

"Maybe it would be worth it to divorce him even if I didn't get a lot of money. How soon could you draw up the papers?"

"You need to think about the financial implications first. Don't make a spur-of-the moment decision."

Rena's eyes flared as she pointed toward her house.

"What do you think I've been doing while I've been locked up in that house?" she asked. "I can't keep living like this!"

"Once the petition is served, it will set a lot of things in motion."

The fire in Rena's eyes died as quickly as it had sprung up.

"You're right. I don't want to make a mistake."

Surprised by yet another sudden shift, Alexia thought it best to continue the conversation later.

"We'll talk," she said simply.

Alexia got in her car. Looking in the rearview mirror, she could see Rena, her shoulders sagging as she plodded toward the exquisite old house that had become her fancy prison.

8

Unless you change and become like little children,
you will never enter the kingdom of heaven.

MATTHEW 18:3

Alexia returned to the office and tried to phone Ted, but he didn't answer at the parsonage. She plowed back into her business, returning phone calls and typing letters. She was a competent typist but paused between two long letters and wished for Gwen's speedier fingers.

Leaving the office, Alexia drove out of town and turned down the road to the Sandy Flats Church. Ted's truck was parked in front of his house, but Alexia didn't ring the doorbell. She went directly to the sanctuary. Late afternoon was practice time, and she would steal whatever chance she could to listen to Ted Morgan play the piano.

Twenty years ago, her mother's old recordings of Artur Schnabel playing Beethoven's thirty-two piano sonatas sparked Alexia's love of classical piano music. The piano was the greatest instrument on earth, and Alexia could identify by name and composer most well-known piano compositions and many obscure ones.

The finely crushed shells crunched under Alexia's feet as she walked across the parking lot to a brick walkway that ran in front of the sanctuary. Five broad steps took Alexia up to a pair of dark-stained wooden doors held in place by strips of hammered iron. The latch was unlocked, and Alexia quietly entered the narthex. The sound of music greeted her, and she stopped to listen.

It was Weber's Sonata in A Flat, a fashionable piece from the early Romantic era that often found its way into the repertoires of pianists competing in the Van Cliburn and Tchaikovsky competitions for young pianists. Two wide entries led into the sanctuary. Alexia slipped through the one on the left and walked softly halfway down the aisle to a spot where the acoustics were optimal. Engrossed in the music, Ted didn't seem to notice her. She sat in a pew and closed her eyes. Gwen was at least half right—Alexia was definitely attracted to the music.

When he finished, Ted stretched. He was wearing jeans and a light-green shirt with long sleeves. His hair appeared slightly damp, as if he'd recently taken a shower.

"Good afternoon!" Alexia said. "I liked the Weber."

Ted turned on the bench and smiled. "He's bold at times, like a wind surfer bucking across the chop."

"Do you wind surf?"

"No, but I watched them off the Outer Banks last year when I was on vacation at Buxton."

Alexia walked down the aisle to the front of the church. Sitting down on the front pew, she curled her legs up beneath her.

"Do you want a report on Baxter Richardson?" she asked. "The neurologist from Charleston came by today."

"Of course I do."

Ted listened intently but didn't react as Alexia relayed the events.

"Did the doctor know I've been playing for Baxter?" he asked.

"He didn't mention it. He was all business and didn't get too excited about what's happened, but I was amazed. When Baxter opened his eyes, it was like someone coming back from the dead."

Ted pointed to a stained-glass window that depicted Lazarus stepping out of a cavelike tomb with grave clothes still draped about his face. Jesus stood with his back to the viewer, his arms stretched out toward his friend.

"Do you really think there is a connection between the time we spent with him and the improvement in his condition?" Ted asked. "Don't you think Baxter could have gotten better anyway? I'm sure the doctors would say that the swelling in his brain finally subsided, and he woke up."

Alexia gave Ted a puzzled look. "Are you kidding?"

"No. I'm glad he's improving, but I want something dramatic to happen. Something that can't be explained by anything except God's power."

"Why can't God's power be gradual? I don't claim to understand what was going on while you played and the nurse sang, but I could feel something in the air. Today, it was easy for me to believe that God was involved."

"Good for you."

"Don't patronize me."

Ted held up his hand. "Sorry. If an analytical lawyer can believe, then so should I. God has the right to do what he wants to do the way he wants to do it. I'm just letting you know how I feel."

Alexia nodded and relaxed a little. A man with feelings was good. Add that to his score.

Ted continued. "My hope is that people besides Baxter will be affected by what happens."

"Like Rena?"

"And others. Was she there?"

"Yes. Baxter's father is out of town, and I don't know if his brother knows the latest news. He and Rena have an odd—" Alexia stopped in midsentence and changed direction. "Would you be willing to help Rena?"

"How?"

"She's been through a lot and needs someone to talk to about it. I can't mention specifics without her permission, but she is depressed and reluctant to see a psychologist or psychiatrist."

"I'm a music minister, not a professional counselor."

Alexia leaned forward. "But you've helped me so much. And I didn't even know how much I needed it!"

Ted chuckled. "You were easy. All I did was encourage you to walk in the path cleared by your grandmother's prayers. The only type of counsel I can give is spiritual. Is that what Rena wants?"

"I don't know if she's thought about it in those terms."

"Well, I don't mind you finding out if she's interested in what I have to offer. But I don't do any one-on-one counseling with women."

"I could be here."

"That would help."

Alexia nodded. "I'll talk to her and let you know."

"Okay." Ted turned back to the piano and plunked out a few random notes. "Will I be able to play again for Baxter?"

"Do you want to?"

"Yes."

"That shouldn't be a problem. I'll call Dr. Berman's office and let him know that Baxter is responding well to music therapy. If something dramatic does happen, maybe you'll be featured in a medical journal someday."

"Maybe gradual is better. I'm not looking for fame."

Ted hit a few quick notes. Alexia recognized it as the opening measures of Scriabin's Sonata in F Major.

"That's Scriabin," Alexia said. "I have a recording of that piece performed by Horowitz at Carnegie Hall."

Ted nodded. "Speaking of famous performers, have you heard of Victor Plavich?"

Ted wrinkled his brow. "The pianist from San Francisco?"

"Yes."

"We both studied under Aube Tzerko in California."

"Do you know him?"

"No, he's several years younger than I."

"Plavich is giving a charity concert in Charleston on Saturday night, and I've been invited. We'd be the guests of Jeffrey Richardson. He's sponsoring a table."

"Baxter's brother?"

"Yes. I talked to him yesterday about business matters, and he invited me to come and bring a friend. You're the only friend I have who would appreciate the evening."

Ted abandoned the cheerful piece and hit the lower octaves with the dismal opening notes of Chopin's Sonata in C Minor. "I'm not sure I could handle it if you think Plavich is better than I am. I'd rather not go than have you tell me on the spot."

Alexia laughed, though she wondered if Ted was kidding. The look on his face was hidden behind his furrowed brow and glasses.

"I'm used to fragile male egos cloaked in jealousy," she said. "I knew several of them at Leggitt & Freeman. They were called the senior partners."

Keeping his head bowed, Ted asked, "How did you treat them?"

"With outward respect and inward disdain. They were as bad as little boys on the playground. But really, are you envious of Victor Plavich?"

"Not if I talk it out. It helps to bring it in the open. I've chosen a different path and can't let someone else's success upset me."

"Let's talk about it."

Ted looked up and smiled. "We just did. I'm okay."

Alexia laughed again. "Your psychiatrist would go bankrupt."

"If he shrunk my head, I'm not sure he'd find much more in there than a hammer and some bent nails. Can I wear my painting overalls to the concert?"

"I'll have to find out. Do you own a tuxedo?"

Ted nodded. "Sometimes I put it on when I come over to the church late at night and pretend that I'm on a European concert tour. It's ancient and a little bit too small, but I can wear it if I don't eat too much for dinner."

Alexia stood up. "I'll call you with the details about Saturday night."

"Okay, and please contact the nursing service and find out when Sarah Locklear is going to be on duty with Baxter. I think she's supposed to help."

"I can do more than that. Rena could call the nursing service and request that she come on a regular basis."

"That would be great. Two are better than one."

Alexia's eyes narrowed, and she turned her face away so he wouldn't notice. "You mean three?"

"I was just talking about the musicians."

———

Detective Rick Bridges kissed his pregnant wife, Amy, good-bye and left Charleston in an unmarked car as the sun set behind a grove of pine trees. There was no point in arriving at the Beachcomber Club too early. The sky darkened as he drove north on Highway 17. The investigative file on the seat beside him had grown since his first trip in search of Henry L. Quinton. He'd learned from a homicide detective in Rhode Island that Quinton sometimes used the name Hank Quincy and had a wife named Gayle, who lived in Baltimore. A couple times a year, a detective would contact Gayle Quinton and ask if she'd had any contact with her husband. Whether from loyalty or fear, she always said no, but she lived in a large house on Chesapeake Bay and drove an expensive car that didn't fit her part-time job as a bookkeeper for a landscaping business. So far, the sporadic instances when officers staked out the house hadn't yielded any clues about Quinton's whereabouts.

A more puzzling piece of the file was the memo prepared by Byron Devereaux after his conversation with Giles Porter in Mitchell County. After reading it the first time, Bridges left his desk and knocked on the opaque glass door to his boss's office.

"Come in," responded the slender, bookish detective.

"What's this supposed to mean?" Bridges asked, laying the memo on Detective Devereaux's desk.

Devereaux shrugged. "He talked; I listened. At first, I thought there might be something to it, but in the end I couldn't see a strong connection. He believes Rena Richardson didn't tell him the truth about her husband's accident, and therefore didn't tell me the truth when I interviewed her about her car."

"Has she been indicted?"

"No, but Porter has circumstantial evidence, skin scrapings from a hiking stick. I'm sure a jury in Mitchell County can be educated about DNA tests, but I doubt twelve people would find her guilty on that evidence alone."

"Unless her husband wakes up from the coma and talks."

Devereaux nodded. "Yeah, that would be ideal, but for now it's like a murder case. The person who can tell us what really happened isn't able to give a statement."

"Should I interview her again?" Bridges asked.

Devereaux picked up a thick paper clip and slowly bent it between two fingers.

"Not until you have something new to ask her about this case. The hard evidence points to Quinton. He's the one with the proven criminal record."

———

When Bridges arrived in the Santee area, it was still too early to go to the club, and he detoured into the downtown area. He flipped open the file and found the address for the Richardson house. Stopping at a convenience store, he asked for directions from an older sales clerk who not only told him where to turn but also gave a detailed description of the residence.

The neighborhood where Rena Richardson lived lacked the illuminating streetlights of downtown. He took a wrong turn, doubled back in the darkness, and found the correct street. Only a few of the mailboxes bore house numbers. Apparently, mail delivery in Santee wasn't dependent on specific address information. A get-well card addressed to Baxter Richardson, Santee, SC, would find its way to the correct destination without any trouble.

Bridges peered through the darkness at older dwellings concealed on spacious lots behind large oak trees, clumps of dune grass, and lush bushes. He saw the Richardson home and slowed to a stop at the end of the driveway. The house was in a class by itself, primarily because of the unusually broad expanse of lawn that served as a buffer from the street. A gas lamp flickered in the curve of the driveway. In the dim light, Bridges could make out several cars parked beside a small guest house.

There was no sign of the red convertible stopped by Deputy Dixon, but a four-car garage stood between the main house and guest quarters. He inched slowly forward along the street, stopped again, and noticed the bright lights of a vehicle behind him that had stopped. He moved forward and pulled to the side of the road so the car could pass him or turn into the driveway. Instead, it flashed its bright lights. Bridges smiled. The headlights were shaped like those of a common model of police interceptor. He guessed he'd encountered local police patrolling the prosperous neighborhood.

Bridges put his car in park and opened the door. Getting out, he took out his police identification and held it up with one hand, shielding his eyes from the high beams with the other. As he stepped forward, the vehicle turned sharply and accelerated toward him. Bridges fell back against his car as the other swept past him. It struck his right leg and then slammed into his open door with a sharp screech of metal. The driver turned off his lights and skidded around a corner. The detective saw that the car was a blue sedan but in the shock of the moment didn't get a clear look at the license plate. He wasn't even sure whether it was a South Carolina vehicle. He tried to run forward, but his leg almost gave way.

He limped as fast as he could to the corner, but his assailant had disappeared into the darkness.

Returning to his car, he sat down and gingerly pulled up the right leg of his pants. Blood trickled from his raw knee and shin. He touched it and glanced angrily down the street. Whoever was driving the car didn't want to meet a police officer. Bridges, on the other hand, very much wanted to meet him.

9

A shout that tore hell's concave,
and beyond frighted the reign of chaos and old night.
PARADISE LOST

In the morning, Alexia called the nursing service and asked about Sarah Locklear's schedule.

"I'll check the computer," the girl on the phone responded. After a few seconds, she said, "Yes, she will be working tomorrow night from eleven to seven."

"Third shift?"

"Yes, the night shift. She asked to be put on a regular schedule, and the only slots available are at night."

After she hung up, Alexia phoned Ted with the news.

"What do you want to do?" she asked.

"I'd like to go back."

"Do you want me to be there?"

Ted hesitated. "That's up to you. You may have to be up early in the morning to go to work."

Alexia answered with a slight edge in her voice. "It's not that. I've stayed up late plenty of times when preparing for a trial. I just don't want to be a third wheel. You and Sarah Locklear have something to contribute. I'll just be sitting there."

"Wait a minute. That's not the way it works. Yesterday, you encouraged me to believe. Today, it's my turn. God doesn't measure significance the same way we do. All that's important to him is obedience motivated by love. Your comment yesterday at the church set me straight. Whether it's my playing, Sarah Locklear's singing, or your praying that causes a breakthrough, we all share in the end result."

Alexia relaxed. "Okay."

"What time do you want to be there?"

"About midnight. That will give Sarah time to complete the shift change. Should I try to contact her in advance?"

"Do you have her phone number?"

"No, only the agency."

"Don't go to any trouble. Based on how quickly she caught on the other night, there shouldn't be a problem."

Alexia thought about Gwen all morning. On partnership meeting day, the six equity partners at Leggitt & Freeman met for a catered lunch served at a fancy table in Ralph Leggitt's massive office. As an associate, Alexia had been invited to attend several times to give brief reports. She'd concluded that the meetings were a cross between a fraternity bull session and an old-fashioned gentlemen's club. The partners even passed around a silver-inlaid cigar box at the conclusion of the meal. Today, Gwen's immediate future would be decided between bites of crab cakes with wild rice and a dessert tray guaranteed to add a half an inch to Leonard Mitchell's waistline.

At 1:30 Alexia began watching the clock and listening for the beep of the phone that signaled a call. Whenever Leggitt & Freeman fired an employee, he or she left immediately. The firm administrator, a retired military officer who rarely smiled, stood beside the terminated employee's desk to ensure a swift and harmless departure. Alexia had thought the gesture melodramatic until Gwen told her of the time a young paralegal downloaded a virus that knocked out the central server as a parting gift.

Alexia's phone beeped. She punched the line.

"It's Gwen Jones. Do you want to take the call?"

"Yes."

The several seconds it took to transfer the call seemed longer than usual. When the light came on, Alexia picked up the receiver.

"What happened?" she asked.

"I'll give you a clue: I'm calling from my cell phone in the car."

"I can't believe it! You've been there longer than anyone except Sue Geller."

"Nine years, seven months, twenty-seven days."

"Who gave you the ax?"

"Leonard broke the news, which surprised me since I wasn't sure he had it in him to do any dirty work in person. In fact, he seemed upset. Maybe he's got to train someone else to decipher his handwriting now." She barked a laugh. "But I think he may have voted to keep me. It was a tender moment, to the extent that's possible with Leonard. I told him not to worry about it."

"Did he give you a reason?"

"He said I was too old."

"That's an invitation to a discrimination lawsuit!" Alexia exclaimed. "I know a lawyer in Orangeburg who will chew them up and spit them out—"

"Alexia," Gwen interrupted, "I was kidding. He told me they were reallocating personnel and don't have a spot for me. Strictly business."

"Right. How do you feel?"

"Not as bad as you did when Ralph Leggitt canned you."

When she was fired, Alexia left the senior partner's office, stormed past Gwen's desk, and slammed the door to her office so hard it knocked pictures off the wall.

"Do you want to go home or come see your new spot? It still has boxes of paper and office supplies in it, but you can get an idea of the layout."

"Not today. I think home and a bubble bath are in order, and it will be nice to watch *Oprah* without having to record it. I think today's show is about women who found true love and riches after age fifty-five."

Alexia smiled. "Okay, but you can start work tomorrow morning if you want to. I haven't talked to Rachel, but I'm sure we can work out the details by the time the coffee is ready."

"Would it be alright if I take the rest of the week off and come in on Monday? I need a few days to unwind, and then I'll show up ready to be my usual vivacious self."

"Of course. That will give us time to get everything set up."

The following evening, Alexia kept looking at the clock. Normally, she relaxed when she arrived home from work, but the anticipation of going back into town to see Baxter had her as fidgety as if she was waiting to cross-examine a hostile witness. She wanted to believe Ted Morgan's reassurance about her involvement in praying for Baxter, but his perspective didn't stand up to her analytical scrutiny. Alexia was active, not passive. She wanted to be doing something, to experience the surge of adrenaline that accompanied intense activity. She paced through the house.

Boris, lying on his cedar bed in the corner of the living room, lifted his head each time she came into view. Misha, curled up on the small rug in the middle of the living-room floor, didn't move except for an occasional twitch of her silver tail. When Alexia opened the door and went onto the deck, Boris pattered outside to keep her company. It was several hours until midnight.

Heavy afternoon rains had rendered the night cool and damp; however, with the expanse of the ocean nearby, the coast was unimpressed with rain unless wrapped in the fury of a hurricane. Alexia could feel the remaining moisture in the air on her cheeks. Overhead, the stars hid behind invisible dark clouds that promised to release more showers before morning. She put her hands on the wet railing of the deck and wondered what to do. She didn't want to listen to music, read a book, or watch TV. She stood in the darkness and probed herself for an answer. None came. She sighed and uttered a prayer that was no more than a question mark. She followed up with a few halfhearted petitions that God might help them during their time with Baxter.

Alexia wanted to pray, to prepare, but didn't know how except in words that traveled no farther than the top of her head. She'd encountered God in Ted's backyard, and felt a divine presence when the music minister played the piano and Sarah sang, but how to bring the same reality to her life on a regular basis eluded her. She felt drained.

Boris leaned heavily against her leg. She reached down and scratched behind his right ear. The dog closed his eyes in contentment.

"It doesn't take much for you, does it?" she asked.

Boris didn't budge. To move would jeopardize bliss. Alexia smiled.

"Okay, I'll try not to make it too complicated." She patted Boris's head and looked out over the marsh. "Lord, I'm leaning against you. Please touch me."

She waited.

No lighting bolts illuminated the sky. No tidal wave of glory swept over her. But a quiet peace crept over the edge of her consciousness—an inner confidence that, at least temporarily, removed uncertainty. She took a deep breath and stood still. It wasn't much, but it was enough. She reached over and scratched Boris's ear.

The quiet peace stayed with her while driving to the Richardson house. The main house slept. Rena was either away or in bed. Ted's truck was parked in front of the cottage beside two other vehicles, one of which Alexia assumed belonged to Sarah Locklear.

When Alexia entered, Ted was sitting in a chair beside Baxter's bed with the keyboard across his lap, adjusting the settings. Sarah was standing at the foot of the bed with an open Bible on her hand. Sarah was in her midforties. She was taller than Alexia and had the clear complexion and fathomless dark eyes of her Native American ancestors. Ted glanced up when Alexia entered.

"We're just getting started."

Alexia looked down at Baxter, clad in light-blue pajamas. His eyes were closed and his arms rested outside the sheet. His sandy brown hair looked dark next to his pallid skin.

"How is he?" she asked Sarah.

"No real change since he initially stirred," Sarah replied. "I reviewed all the notes as soon as I arrived, and everything is routine. The neurologist is coming again tomorrow."

"Have the nurses tried to communicate with him or ask him questions?"

"Yes, it's part of the protocol. We talk to him throughout the shift and include direct attempts to elicit a response. The results haven't been consistent. He's opened his eyes some but hasn't been able to blink in response to yes-or-no-type questions."

"Sarah and I have been talking," Ted said. "We've decided to thank the Lord for what he's already done before moving into something new. We're not under a time restraint, so we don't have to hurry."

"Where is your aide?" Alexia asked.

"She's in the kitchen. She knows we're going to be playing and singing, and I've given her enough paperwork to keep her busy for a while."

Alexia walked around the bed and sat in a chair against the far wall of the tiny living room. Ted nodded toward Sarah. Standing with an open Bible still in her hand, she began to sing in a soft, low voice.

"At midnight I will rise to give thanks unto thee."

Several times she repeated the words. The third time, Ted joined in with the keyboard, and Alexia felt a prickly sensation on the back of her neck. The words came alive when married to the notes. Alexia closed her eyes. The atmosphere in the room became intense but not stressful. The peace she'd felt after praying on her deck remained. Thankfulness soon joined it and became the unspoken song of her soul. She opened her eyes and looked at Baxter. No change. The nurse transitioned into another passage.

"Blessed be the name of the Lord from this time forth and for evermore. From the rising of the sun unto the going down of the same, the Lord's name is to be praised."

From midnight to dawning, the Lord was worthy to be blessed and praised. Each moment was a cup to be filled. Alexia listened and learned. Acknowledgment of the Lord's worthiness to receive praise from his people was legitimate in itself.

The music from the keyboard grew stronger, and Sarah fell silent. Ted transitioned into another key and moved forward in strident chords. In a few moments, Sarah joined him.

"The Lord is my rock, and my fortress, and my deliverer; my God, my strength, in whom I will trust."

After declaring the entire verse, Ted and Sarah returned to each phrase, repeating the words again and again until satisfied that it was time to go on. For Alexia, the experience was like turning in a circle on top of a mountain. Each viewpoint offered a slightly different panorama. She continued to watch Baxter for signs of a response. Nothing seemed to penetrate.

———

All day long, random thoughts had been running across the surface of Baxter Richardson's mind like water poured out on the floor. They refused to take form and shape, and he couldn't command them to array in regimental lines so he could review them and issue appropriate orders. Earlier in his life he had faced a similar challenge—when he first learned to talk.

Now, as then, the mysterious connection between the sounds and the concepts that create language remained as obscure as the theory of relativity.

The darkness compounded his confusion. Without the defense of a will that could filter stimuli entering his mind, Baxter floated at random. He continued to fill his lungs with oxygen, but his soul gasped for air. Voices from the abyss harassed him with covert threats that bred despair. Walls of blackness pressed in around him and covered him like the lid of a casket. His survival instinct fought the darkness but without enduring hope.

It was probably fortunate that he didn't realize the seriousness of his injuries. The prospect of life held captive within a body that couldn't move and a mind that wouldn't work was bleak beyond words. Death would be a friend, not an enemy. If he'd had the ability to comprehend his true condition and respond to it, Baxter would likely have taken his own life.

The female voice that whispered love into his ear didn't bridge the gap of recognition. Distant memories, not recent ones, were closer to the surface of his understanding. He needed to lay a foundation upon which he could stand and view the timeline of his life. Unfortunately, in the swollen and damaged tissues of his brain, the building blocks lay scattered about with no one to collect and organize them.

Into the chaos came the music.

It wasn't the beauty of the notes but their orderliness that touched him. The sounds entered his soul like tiny rays of light, each one dispatched on an individual mission. Wherever the light touched, restoration emerged.

God is good, and everything he does is perfect. The musicians were earthen vessels, but the treasure within them had no blemishes. As they played, the treasure was released to bless Baxter with divine grace. Confusion inched backward. Brain cells began to send signals to the correct destination. The healing process took another step forward. The music stopped.

Baxter opened his eyes.

———

Alexia stood and stepped quickly to the bed. At the sound of her approach, Baxter turned his head slightly and looked at her face. They'd never met, so she didn't expect recognition, but the question in his gaze was encouraging.

"I'm Alexia Lindale," she said. "If you liked the music, blink your eyes."

Baxter immediately blinked.

Alexia had never seen a more remarkable yes. She turned toward Sarah, who had moved to the other side of the bed. Ted put his keyboard on the floor and stood up. Sarah reached over and stroked Baxter's cheek.

"You're in the cottage next to your house in Santee," the nurse said. "If you understand me, blink again."

Baxter blinked.

"Yes! He understands!" Alexia exclaimed.

A thousand questions bubbled to the surface, but she'd never cross-examined a witness who could only answer by blinking.

Sarah spoke, "Try to speak. Make the sound of a *b*."

Baxter weakly put his lips together and then closed his eyes. Sarah didn't move.

"If you want to talk more, open your eyes," the nurse said.

The three waited. Baxter's breathing became regular with the rhythm of sleep. His eyes remained closed.

"That's it for now," Sarah said.

She laid her hand on Baxter's head and began to pray. She started simply but with earnest conviction. As she continued, her voice grew louder and more authoritative.

She finished by saying, "In the strong name of Jesus of Nazareth, the one and only Son of God. Amen!"

10

The lines are fallen unto me in pleasant places;
yea, I have a goodly heritage.

PSALM 16:6 KJV

For several days, Rena had been waking before dawn and spending the last hour of the night in restless frustration. But this morning, she didn't stir until the sunlight peeked around the edges of the thick curtains that covered the windows of her bedroom. She stretched for several seconds in enjoyment of the comfort of her bed before anxiety, her constant companion, rolled over and greeted her. She shut her eyes and burrowed into the covers, but it was no use. Reality had returned.

She got out of bed and pulled the curtain a few inches from a window, then looked across the front yard. The clumps of dune grass at the end of the driveway swayed in the wind. There was no sign of the spies Jeffrey had dispatched to guard her, nor the blue car that frequented the street. She suspected Jeffrey's men worked in shifts, just like the nurses who took care of Baxter.

She went downstairs to the kitchen. Rena didn't have any pets. Shortly after her honeymoon, Rena bought an expensive macaw that lived for two weeks in an elaborate cage in one corner of the kitchen. One day he nipped Rena's finger while she fed him a piece of fruit. The bird returned to the pet store in Charleston.

Rena fixed a cup of coffee, turned on the TV, and sat morosely at the kitchen table. The minutes that passed may as well have been days.

The phone rang and jarred her back to the present. She glanced at the caller ID. Jeffrey. She didn't want to answer, but the uncertainty of not knowing why he called would be worse than finding out bad news.

"Hello," she said in a flat tone of voice.

"What's going on with Baxter? Any changes?"

"The doctor says he's at a plateau and may be there for a while."

"Or forever?"

Not for the first time, Rena wondered about Jeffrey's true feelings toward Baxter.

"Maybe."

"Did you hear the commotion in front of your house last night?"

"No, what happened?"

"A police detective from Charleston tried to talk to your bodyguards and lost the door of his car when they drove past."

"Why did they do that?"

"He forgot to close it when he got out."

Rena shook the fog out of her head. Jeffrey seemed almost happy about the incident. "What do you mean?" she asked.

"The detective probably wanted to ask you more questions about the deputy who died, and the bodyguards surprised him before he could contact you."

"I already met with a detective," Rena responded sharply. "Why would he want to talk to me again? You haven't told them anything, have you?"

"Of course not."

"How do you know he was from Charleston?"

"I have friends at the police department."

Rena bit her lip. "If you're just calling to harass me, I don't have anything else to say."

"Calm down. I just wanted to make sure you were okay. If the police question you again, just make sure you tell them the same thing that you did the first time."

"I'm not stupid, Jeffrey. I won't talk to anyone unless Alexia Lindale is with me."

"Good. She'll take care of you if you let her."

"Yeah, that's what I'm paying her to do."

Jeffrey continued. "In fact, I'm going to be spending time with Ms. Lindale tonight at a benefit concert in Charleston. I'm looking forward to it."

Rena flushed. Alexia had not said anything about going on a date to Charleston.

"She's hardly your type," Rena managed.

"It's too soon to tell, but I think it will help if I get to know her better. I'm always careful when I mix business and pleasure. Anything personal will be a bonus. Do you have any inside information about her social life?"

At first, Rena couldn't remember anything about Alexia's taste in men but then recalled that the lawyer had brought a music minister to the cottage to see Baxter. She smiled slightly.

"She likes preachers. She's very religious."

She heard Jeffrey grunt. "Then she'll be a challenge. I'll let you know what happens."

Rena brooded while she finished her coffee. As she drained the last drops, she decided what to do. She always made her best decisions in the morning. She picked up the phone and dialed Alexia's home number.

The wind brushed Alexia's cheeks as she crossed the marsh in her boat. On weekdays, she would occasionally go for a swim in the late afternoon, but on the weekends, without the pressures of work, she could reverse her schedule.

Every dawn was a glorious good morning to Boris, and he skidded across the deck when Alexia let him out for his morning run. Misha followed at her own pace and silently padded down the steps to the sandy soil. Alexia put on a black wet suit. When Boris returned and saw what she was wearing, he ran straight through the house to the front door and began barking. Alexia kept her old aluminum boat underneath the house, and the dog knew that next Alexia would go down the front steps and unlock the rusty chain that secured the boat.

She slipped into a pair of old deck shoes. Her house was so close to the marsh that it didn't make sense to hitch the boat to her car and tow it a few feet to the edge of the water. Except for the initial effort to get the trailer moving, the feat depended on balance rather than strength, and Alexia had perfected the process. Boris posed her greatest danger, running excitedly around her feet.

"Anchors aweigh!" Alexia shouted as she dug in her heels.

The small trailer tires made a slight indention in the sandy soil. Fortunately, the soil contained enough clay to keep the trailer from sinking to its frame. With Alexia walking backward, the trailer moved steadily across the hundred feet between the house and the edge of the marsh. As she approached, Alexia deftly turned the trailer around and raised the tongue so the boat slipped smoothly into the water. She grabbed a rope tied to the bow to keep the boat from slipping away into the narrow canal. Before she could give him a command, Boris bounded into the boat. His feet scratched the aluminum bottom as he ran from one end to the other.

Alexia joined him, but lost a shoe in the thick black mud that lined the edge of the marsh.

"Man overboard!" she called, as she jumped out of the boat into the knee-deep water and retrieved her shoe.

Alexia used the boat to travel short distances through the marsh. When she first bought it she used oars, but quickly decided to buy a small trolling motor. The engine started on the second pull, and she turned the boat around and pointed the bow toward the barrier island.

With no direct route across the marsh, she followed a zigzag path along narrow openings through the swaying reeds. From the shore, the twists and turns weren't obvious, but to Alexia the marsh was like a familiar patch of woods, and she didn't take any wrong turns leading to grassy dead ends. Boris stood at attention in the bow, carefully watching the water for mullet. Alexia suspected the dog believed the small fish responded to the sound of his bark, and he would occasionally yelp a command. Twice before, when a large school of fish broke the surface like silver popcorn, Boris leaped over the side in excitement, and Alexia had to pull him back into the boat by his collar. Today, however, he was content to be the figurehead of the ship and guardian of its mistress.

As they neared the island, the marsh grass gave way to a narrow stretch of open water maintained by a current that swept around the north end of the island. A stiff breeze ruffled the water more than usual. The boat bounced and Boris almost lost his footing. Alexia steered the boat directly onto the sand. As soon as it scraped the bottom, Boris jumped out and bounded over the dunes. Alexia climbed out, pulled the boat onto shore, and tied it off to a straggly bush, which had chosen a difficult spot on earth to fight for survival.

Carrying a beach bag containing her towel, swimming goggles, and a bottle of fresh water, Alexia trudged to the top of the dune. She stopped at the crest and savored the unhindered view of the Atlantic. The sun was playing hide-and-seek with a band of clouds blown across its path. Directly in front of Alexia, six pelicans looking for breakfast glided inches above the whitecaps. The north end of the island lay to her left, and to her right the beach stretched for almost a mile to its southern end. Below her, Boris splashed into the surf with his tongue hanging out.

In warmer weather, Alexia would occasionally see visitors who came to the island in boats for a picnic or to sunbathe in a secluded spot, but after mid-November, she usually had the island to herself. She walked down a steep dune into the edge of the surf. After several weeks of cooler nights, the water temperature had dropped, and without the wet suit, she wouldn't have wanted to go for a swim. Boris ran up to her, shook himself, and followed her as she waded through the deepening water. Donning goggles, she dove through a chest-high wave. The cold water on her face and head made her gasp, but she knew she would soon adjust. She swam slowly beyond the breakers and turned south.

Alexia ignored her mind's message that she wasn't making any progress in the rough water and brought herself into rhythm with the rolling waves. Although she wouldn't have considered trying to cross the English Channel, Alexia was a strong swimmer. Boris, always positioning himself between Alexia and the beach, paddled alongside her.

As she swam, Alexia began to think. Not about when to breathe and how hard to kick—those activities were second nature to her. Her mind soared, free to consider anything. In the past, she'd planned the cross-examination of witnesses, daydreamed about meeting a man with whom she'd want to spend the rest of her life, and outlined the itinerary for her next vacation. Today, her thoughts stayed close at hand, and she meditated on the world surrounding her. Love of nature was nothing new to her, but since her experience with God in Ted Morgan's backyard, the sky appeared more vibrant, the marsh more varied, the ocean more awe-inspiring. She tasted the salt water on her lips. It was bitter, yet contained the exact combination of chemicals needed to sustain an almost infinite variety of life. She glanced sideways at Boris's head as he steadily paddled along beside her. He, too, was an amazing creature—a mixture of personality and instinct that when packaged together made him her friend.

Because time was not a factor, Alexia swam farther than usual before turning back toward shore. Her legs were slightly wobbly as her feet touched the bottom and she stood up. At that moment, a wave hit her in the back and caused her to pitch forward into the water. Boris was immediately beside her. She came up sputtering. In a few more steps she was in the shallow surf and then onto the hard sand. She sat down just beyond the reach of the tiny lines of foam that marked the edge of the ocean and took off her goggles. Boris padded over to her and licked her cheek.

"Did you enjoy your swim?" she asked him. "You have a natural wet suit."

Often, Boris would shake himself dry and then run down the beach, but today he stayed close to her. He sat down beside her, and she scratched behind his right ear. Boris closed his eyes and panted.

When the incoming tide reached her feet, Alexia stood and began to hike toward the north end of the island. The wind had died down as the sun climbed higher in the sky, and the air temperature rose to a pleasant level. As she walked along the edge of the surf, she looked for shells. Few intact specimens made it to shore; waves pounded them into small pieces before allowing them passage. But today was different. Half buried in the sand lay a medium-sized, pinkish conch. Alexia had turned over hundreds of similar conchs only to find them broken and marred. She nudged the shell with her big toe, but it didn't move. She pushed harder, and it rolled over. It was in one piece. Leaning over, she picked it up and washed it off in the shallow water. Even the small spikes along the leading edge were in good shape. She carried it in triumph to her beach bag. Later, it would take its place as the centerpiece for the clear glass table in her kitchen.

Alexia's hair had dried in the stiff breeze by the time she crossed the marsh. She hooked a rope to the front of the boat and cranked the winch to pull it onto the trailer. She dropped the tongue of the trailer beneath the house and stepped with Boris into the small, outdoor shower stall. Both she and Boris had dirty feet, caused by a combination of sand and mud. The dog didn't mind the spray so long as he could shake off the excess moisture within close proximity of Alexia. Alexia finished cleaning herself and her dog, then sat on the steps and wiped her feet with a towel.

She went into the kitchen to drink a glass of water and saw the message light blinking on her phone. She dialed in the access code.

"Alexia, this is Rena. I need to talk to you before your date with Jeffrey. I'm also leaving you a message on your cell phone. Call me at home."

Alexia considered taking a warm shower before calling but decided to correct Rena's misunderstanding as soon as possible. Her client's tendency to ruminate could be toxic. Alexia finished the glass of water and punched in Rena's phone number. As soon as her client answered, Alexia launched into corrective mode and told her that she'd invited Ted Morgan to accompany her to the benefit concert.

"That's not the reason I called," Rena said. "It's about Baxter. I've definitely decided to file for divorce."

"I thought we were going to talk—"

"And I don't want you giving Jeffrey any information about me."

"I wouldn't do that anyway. My plan was to get information from him."

"Well, I wanted you to know before you had any other contact with him. Will I have to pay you more money?"

"Uh, yes. The balance of your retainer will barely cover the beginning stages."

"I'm sure I can get it from Jeffrey."

"Are you sure? How will he react to you filing for divorce?"

"He'll be fine after I explain. Just don't say anything to him tonight. Jeffrey is a snake. I've got to go. Bye."

Her head spinning with possible reasons for the conflicting signals her client was sending about Jeffrey Richardson, Alexia slowly returned the phone to its cradle.

11

A talent is formed in stillness,
a character in the world's torrent.

GOETHE

Alexia listened to Rachmaninoff while she dressed for the evening. Her long silver gown fell gracefully from her shoulders and highlighted her short black hair and green eyes. Around her neck she placed an emerald necklace and added matching earrings she'd purchased with the first large bonus she'd received while at Leggitt & Freeman. Strappy black shoes and a black shawl completed the ensemble.

"What do you think, Misha?" she asked the cat, who lay curled up on the bed watching her. "If I make a big fee, should I buy you an emerald collar?"

The sun was inching below the tree line as Alexia descended the steps to the living room. She gave Boris a quick pat as she left.

Ted's work truck wasn't a suitable carriage for a formal affair, so Alexia drove her car to pick him up. She arrived at the old parsonage a few minutes late. With a mixture of anticipation and curiosity, she knocked on the door. Ted opened it. The change in the music minister's appearance was dramatic. Except for his Sunday choir robe, Alexia had never seen him in anything but casual attire. Tonight, his hair was carefully brushed in place, his black tie knotted neatly at his throat.

"You look ready to perform," Alexia said. "When you said you had a tuxedo, I forgot to ask if it was decorated with red sequins."

"I've never played Las Vegas, and black is probably better for Charleston." He looked at Alexia and smiled. "You, on the other hand, are beautiful enough to go anywhere."

Ted took her hand and touched it to his lips. Alexia smiled quizzically.

"Who needs to go to Charleston?" Ted asked. "Let's go over to the church for a private concert. We can barter. I'll play a song for a kiss—the longer the composition, the longer the payment."

Alexia stepped away. Either her dress or Ted's mood was making him more amorous than usual.

"That's not tonight's program," she said. "I don't want you to have to work. This is your chance to listen to someone else."

Ted frowned. "I'd rather work."

"Then you drive."

They left the parking lot and retraced Alexia's route. They passed the intersection of the coastal highway and Pelican Point Drive. The sign for her road leaned slightly to one side.

"That's where you turn to go to my house," she said. "Follow that road to the marsh and turn left. I live in the only house on the road."

"Tell me about it."

Alexia described her refuge by the marsh and life with her pets.

"Boris and Misha," Ted said. "That's the Russian influence."

"Yeah, they're my best friends, and I talk to them all the time. Living alone has made me a little bit eccentric."

Ted laughed. "I've been solitary a lot longer than you have. Do you think I'm eccentric?"

"Do you talk to your piano?"

Ted nodded. "Yes, and I talk to my fingers if they're not doing what I want them to do on the keys." He held up the middle and ring fingers on his right hand. "Except for these two. I don't scold them."

"Why not?"

"I'm just grateful I can use them at all. I had an injury over twenty years ago when I was preparing for the Tchaikovsky competition."

Alexia was impressed. The International Tchaikovsky Competition for young pianists was the Olympics of the piano world.

"You went to Moscow?"

"I wanted to. I'd moved from Atlanta to Hollywood so I could study under Aube Tzerko. Are you familiar with him?"

"Yes," Alexia replied.

"At first, Tzerko didn't want to take me as a student, but I did some carpentry work on his sunroom, and he agreed to give me a chance."

Ted set the car on cruise control as they entered a long, deserted stretch of highway.

"I took lessons too," Alexia said.

"Tell me about your teacher."

"She had perfectly coiffed gray hair and a huge diamond ring that probably slowed down her finger speed on her left hand. At the beginning of a lesson she wound up a metronome and put it on top of the piano. When it started ticking, I began playing. Every swing of the arm gave me a mental beating. Fortunately, a lesson only lasted thirty minutes."

Ted laughed. "Tzerko had an internal sense of meter more musical than a metronome. He set up two Steinways in his studio. He would sit at one and the student at the other. Our sessions lasted two hours. He was unbelievably demanding—very intimidating. He believed if a student could survive the emotional onslaught of the lessons, the pressure of the competition would be bearable."

"I had law-school professors like that," Alexia said. "They sometimes made me stand up and attempt to answer ridiculously difficult questions for an entire class period. It was rough, but it prepared me for what I face in court now."

"Tzerko never allowed his students any break from the spotlight."

"Were you working too?"

"Yeah, I did small remodeling jobs, but I always reserved time to practice several hours a day."

"Did you meet Roxanne in California?"

Alexia knew nothing about Ted's first wife except that the marriage didn't last very long, and they had a daughter who was now in her early twenties.

"Yes, on a job. I did some work for her parents while she was home on Christmas break. We dated for several months while she finished at UCLA, and we married in mid-June."

Ted stared ahead with a faraway look in his eyes. Curious, Alexia wanted to conduct a quick marital-history cross-examination. Instead, she settled on an easy question.

"Did she enjoy piano music?"

"Perhaps more than she liked me." Ted turned toward Alexia with a serious expression. "Do you want to know about Roxanne or my preparation for the Tchaikovsky competition?"

Alexia retreated. She wanted him to enjoy this night.

"The competition," she responded in what she hoped was a cheerful voice.

Ted passed a slow-moving truck before continuing. "Every pianist going to Moscow has to memorize and master about three hours of difficult piano music and be ready to play whichever piece the judges request. My lessons with Tzerko were open to other piano students, so occasionally people would come to the studio and listen."

"Like me at the sanctuary."

A slight smile returned to Ted's face. "Yes, only they were more likely to be critical than complementary. One day, Tzerko got caught up in the piece we were rehearsing and didn't stop when my two hours ended. The next student arrived and sat in the gallery with the spectators. We kept going another two hours. Another student arrived. We continued. Five hours later, he finally let me leave."

"Weren't you exhausted?"

"Yes, but also invigorated. To Tzerko, music was everything, and at the time, I shared his passion."

"Do you remember what you were studying?"

"One of the *Transcendental Études* by Franz Liszt. It's glorious, but structured."

Alexia thought for a moment. "The improvisational music you play is simply glorious."

Ted smiled. "That touches me at a deeper level. It helps me communicate with God."

Alexia nodded. She'd felt the presence of a power from beyond this world when Ted touched the keys.

"Does anyone else do what you are doing?" she asked.

"I don't know of anyone, but if the Holy Spirit is leading me, I'm confident he's inspiring other musicians as well. I want to talk to Sarah Locklear about it. She caught on so quickly the other afternoon that I suspect she's thought about these things."

Alexia felt a pang of jealousy about the nurse, but she brushed it off.

"Why didn't you go to Moscow?"

The minister took his right hand from the steering wheel and wiggled his middle and ring fingers. "I damaged the tendons and nerves in these fingers and couldn't extend them properly. It became so severe that it hurt to play the simplest pieces, but I kept practicing anyway. I saw some of the top doctors in Southern California. They recommended surgery as the only way to save my career, so I agreed to an operation. But the surgery made my hand worse. I had to give up my dreams of going to Moscow or becoming a concert pianist."

"That's terrible."

"I was devastated. The problem even limited my carpentry and painting work, and my income dwindled. Roxanne couldn't take the pressure and moved back in with her parents. In a few weeks, I received divorce papers. Angelica was only a year old."

"I wasn't trying to bring up—"

Ted shrugged. "It's part of the piano story. That was my long, dark night of the soul. But I found hope. I became a Christian through the influence of a friend who worked with me on a construction crew. The next weekend he took me to a home fellowship that met in his apartment complex. They prayed for my hand, and God healed it. The folks in the meeting didn't know about my career as a pianist; they thought I needed a healthy hand so I could drive nails. Every note I play to God's glory goes into the heavenly bank account of the people in that group."

"What about your lessons? Couldn't you still prepare for the competition?"

"By that point, I couldn't have gotten ready in time, and in four more years I would have been too old. The competition is only open to people under twenty-eight. So I went home to Georgia, finished my degree at a community college in Atlanta, and went to seminary at Emory."

Alexia glanced out the window at the dark silhouettes of the low trees that lined the highway.

"Are you still upset about what happened to your hand? Even though it's okay now, it ruined your career and wrecked . . ." she paused.

"My marriage?"

"Yes."

"It wasn't that simple. I doubt my marriage would have survived anyway. I was so self-centered that it would have taken a saint to live with me, and Roxanne was not a saint."

"What about your career?"

"The injury to my fingers destroyed my ambition. It needed to happen. People in California music circles were beginning to say complimentary things about me, and I couldn't handle the praise. I had unhealthy fantasies about my future that went beyond my own hopes and dreams. I began to envy—maybe even hate—other pianists."

"Knowing you now, it's hard to believe you felt that way."

Ted glanced at her. "It's true. Most people with a talent can easily fall into this trap. Some don't see it; others don't care. I'm glad you think I'm different, but I'm not the same person who walked into Tzerko's studio for my first lesson, and I wouldn't relive that season of my life for anything in the world."

"Okay," she said. "But it's still a shame that we're not driving to Charleston to hear *you* play the benefit concert."

———

It was dark by the time they passed the small side road where a patrolman had discovered Officer Claude Dixon's body. Byron Devereaux's thorough examination of the area had yielded no hard clues, and subsequent rains washed away the tire tracks left by Rena's convertible. The site of the officer's death bore no more sign of what had happened than an unmarked grave.

Within a few minutes, Alexia and Ted approached the outskirts of Charleston. The banquet and concert were being held at the Francis Marion Hotel on the corner of King and Calhoun Streets. Opened in 1924, the recently refurbished hotel now exceeded its original splendor.

The often stifling humidity of summer had fled to regions closer to the equator, replaced by cooler—tonight almost crisp—air. A big crowd had gathered for the benefit event, and Alexia and Ted had to wait several minutes for a valet to take Alexia's car. As they walked up the sidewalk, Alexia tried to spot Jeffrey.

"Did he tell you where to meet him?" Ted asked.

"No, his administrative assistant told me there would be a guest list for his table inside."

"Anyone else you know going to join us?"

"I'm not sure. I didn't think to ask."

They stepped onto the thick carpet inside the building and joined a line of people waiting for table assignments. When they reached the front, Alexia gave her name to a tall young man, who scanned down a sheet of paper.

"Here it is," he replied. "Table fourteen. Second row from the front on the left."

Alexia slipped her arm into Ted's as they entered the banquet hall. The best china and silverware glistened on the round tables, and the servers scurried about in formal attire. Bottles of wine stood ready in the center of each table. Alexia and Ted zigzagged to the front of the room. Table fourteen was on the same side of the room as the eight-foot Steinway that sat waiting for Victor Plavich.

Alexia saw Ken Pinchot, her former mentor and one of the senior partners at Leggitt & Freeman. Their interaction had recently turned adversarial when the older trial lawyer helped Ezra Richardson prevent Rena from terminating Baxter's life support. Alexia inwardly kicked herself for not anticipating that one of her former bosses would attend. The links between the Richardson family and Leggitt & Freeman ran deep and wide.

Pinchot, immaculately dressed in a professionally tailored tuxedo, had clear, perceptive blue eyes that quickly evaluated Alexia and her escort. He extended his hand with a wry smile.

"Good evening, Alexia," he said. "I checked my weapons at the door. How about you?"

Alexia nodded. "Yes, Ken. It's good to see you."

She introduced Ted and greeted Nanette Pinchot, Ken's third wife, a blonde in her early forties who endeavored to be as perfect as her husband.

Nanette wore a classic black dress and a stunning pearl necklace. Gwen Jones knew Ken's second wife and told Alexia that if Nanette didn't measure up, Pinchot would trade her in for a newer model without a backward glance.

They sat down. The noise level in the room increased as the crowd gathered. There were four empty places at the table.

"Who else is joining our table?" Alexia asked Pinchot.

Pinchot shrugged. "Maybe Jeffrey and three girlfriends. I didn't talk to him about the guest list."

Alexia realized her own inclusion in the group had probably been a surprise to Pinchot. She took a sip of water and didn't volunteer an explanation. With Ken present, Jeffrey and Alexia would not have the opportunity to strategize against Ezra.

Jeffrey arrived with his guests. Instead of three women, Jeffrey was accompanied by two men that Alexia recognized as officers of the largest bank in Santee, and a third man she didn't know. Jeffrey introduced the bankers and the stranger, a stocky man in his forties with dark eyes and a swarthy complexion.

"This is Nicholas Valese," Jeffrey said. "He's visiting from New York."

When Valese learned Alexia was a lawyer, he smiled and spoke with a clipped accent that sounded harsh when contrasted with the others' Southern lilts. "A female attorney handles a lot of my business. She's better than any man in a fight."

Pinchot responded, "That's what we used to say about Alexia when she was with our firm. There are scores of men walking around Santee with a lot less money in their pockets because she gave it to their ex-wives."

"Oh, a divorce lawyer," Valese said with a wink. "That's how my lawyer got her start. She's told me about what she's done to guys who try to hide stuff from their wives—"

Before Valese could bore Alexia with secondhand war stories, a waiter arrived and announced the banquet entrees. Alexia selected the salmon and Ted chose a glazed pork chop.

Valese wanted to order à la carte.

"Bring me a steak," he insisted, his voice rising. "Don't talk to me about a cardboard salmon or rubber chicken!"

The waiter stuttered a reply, and Valese's face grew red. He swore in a coarse whisper that could be heard around the table. Jeffrey intervened.

"Just a minute, Nicholas. I'll talk to the man in charge of the food."

Jeffrey left the table. Alexia leaned over and whispered in Ted's ear. "I'm sorry about our dinner companions. I imagined we'd be left to ourselves."

Ted kept his voice low. "Do you see the bulge under our angry companion's jacket?"

Alexia quickly glanced at Valese. His large coat looked smooth to her.

"No," she replied. "Do you think he'd bring a gun in here?"

"Not really, but he seems to fit the part."

Alexia kicked Ted under the table.

Small talk swirled around the table while they waited for the first course. Jeffrey was sitting across from Alexia. He didn't engage her directly in conversation, but several times she caught him watching her. When their eyes met, he smiled. Based on Rena's comments and Rachel Downey's negative opinion, Alexia had expected Jeffrey to be more sinister. In reality, he was very pleasant. Alexia could see why he had no trouble attracting female companions. Wealth and good looks create a potent attraction to women who fail to look beneath the surface.

Alexia glanced sideways at Ted, who was listening politely to the two bankers. She picked up snippets of conversation about new types of financing available to churches and hoped the entertainment would be more invigorating than present company.

12

Unlike most mass-produced banquet fare, the food was delicious. Cooked perfectly, the salmon arrived attractively garnished with a crisp array of vegetables. Valese received a thick steak that seemed to mollify him. Toward the end of the meal, waiters appeared pushing carts of desserts. Alexia, debating between a strawberry cheesecake and blueberry torte, saw a small, balding man hurry over to Jeffrey and tap him on the shoulder.

"Mr. Chandler," Jeffrey said when he glanced behind him. "Let me introduce you."

Chandler was the executive director of the organization receiving the proceeds from the event. Alexia could see beads of perspiration on the top of his head, and he was obviously distracted as he shook hands with the men at the table. He turned back to Jeffrey and spoke in a frantic voice that Alexia could hear across the table.

"Mr. Richardson, as one of the primary sponsors of the evening you should be alerted to a problem. Mr. Plavich has been having severe abdominal pains. He tried to rest, but the pain became so severe that a short time ago his wife took him to the emergency room. They say he has acute appendicitis. He's obviously not going to be able to perform tonight."

"That's good news to me," Valese grunted.

Chandler ignored the comment and continued talking to Jeffrey. "Do you think it would be out of order if we still made an appeal for the capital-fund campaign? My board members are split on the issue. The table sponsors have covered the cost of the evening, but we need the extra money to go forward with our building project."

Alexia leaned over to Ted.

"You could do it." she whispered.

Ted shook his head. "I couldn't take on a building project in Charleston. Even if I worked on a crew, by the time I drove—"

"No," Alexia interrupted. "You could play the piano."

Ted's eyebrows went up. "Uh, no, that's not possible. I don't have any music with me."

"Don't be silly." She touched his arm lightly. "You have a repertoire at your fingertips. You'd be the hero of the evening."

"Or the embarrassment."

Ken Pinchot was leaning forward, listening. "You play the piano?"

"Ted is an accomplished pianist," she said in a bold voice that caused the rest of the table to turn toward her. "He could substitute for Victor Plavich."

"What?" Chandler asked.

Jeffrey seemed embarrassed. "We appreciate the offer, but fourteen verses of 'Just As I Am' is not what this crowd came to hear."

Alexia flushed. "He's professionally trained. I've heard him play, and he's superb. When he was younger he prepared for the Tchaikovsky competition and studied under a famous piano teacher in California."

"The Tchaikovsky competition?" Chandler asked with surprise.

"That was more than twenty years ago," Ted answered. "I'd like to help, but I've not prepared a program."

"Give it a try," Pinchot interjected. "It's a worthy cause."

"Do you still maintain a classic repertoire?" Chandler asked.

Ted nodded.

Chandler glanced down at his watch. "If I can find a private room, would you be willing to let me hear you play?"

"I don't know—"

"Be a good sport," Jeffrey said. Alexia found his grin mocking. "It's the Christian thing to do, right?"

Ted looked at Jeffrey and started to speak but stopped. Taking off his glasses, he rubbed his eyes and then placed his napkin slowly beside his plate.

"Where is the private room?" he asked.

"Yes!" Alexia said in a voice so loud that she immediately clamped her hand over her mouth.

Chandler looked over his shoulder. "Come with me, and we'll ask one of the staff."

After they left, Alexia was so excited she ignored the dessert tray as it trundled off to the next table. She turned toward Ken Pinchot.

"I've heard him play several well-known pieces that would work fine," she said.

"Where did you meet him?" the older lawyer asked. "I didn't think you went to church."

"I interviewed him as a potential witness in a divorce case. When I arrived, he was in the sanctuary playing. I couldn't believe my ears. He's as good as the performers on some of the CDs I own."

"It's one thing to practice a closing argument in front of a mirror," Pinchot replied. "It's another to carry it off in front of twelve people in a jury box."

"He can do it," Alexia answered. "I know it."

———

In a few minutes, Mr. Chandler and Ted reentered the banquet hall. Chandler returned to the head table. Ted came over and sat down. Everyone looked at him.

"Well?" Alexia asked.

"I'm going to do it," Ted replied with a wan smile.

"Splendid!" Pinchot said. "This will be an event worth remembering."

Ted looked at Jeffrey. "He gave me permission to substitute 'Jesus Loves Me' in B Minor for 'Just As I Am'."

Jeffrey's eyes narrowed.

Alexia leaned over to Ted. "What are you going to play?"

"Different stuff," he replied.

"Tchaikovsky?"

"No. Three periods: baroque, classical, romantic."

Before Alexia could ask another question, Chandler took his place behind a podium and the room quieted. He began by identifying a number of dignitaries, then introduced the board members and asked Jeffrey and another man who apparently paid more than their *pro rata* share of the evening's expenses to stand. Chandler then cleared his throat.

"Many months ago, we scheduled a performance by nationally acclaimed pianist Victor Plavich, who was to be the highlight of this event. Unfortunately, Mr. Plavich became ill this evening and has been admitted to the hospital. I received a call a few minutes ago that he will be fine but unable to perform for us tonight."

A low murmur rippled across the crowd. Alexia reached underneath the tablecloth and squeezed Ted's hand. It was cold and clammy.

Chandler looked at their table. "However, one of our guests has graciously agreed to substitute for Mr. Plavich. Mr. Ted Morgan from Santee studied classical piano in California and was scheduled to participate in the Tchaikovsky competition for young pianists before an injury shortened his competitive career. In the true volunteer spirit that typifies those who support our work, he will give a brief concert. Please welcome Mr. Ted Morgan."

Modest applause filled the room as Ted stood up and walked to the piano. Alexia wanted to cheer. She quickly glanced around. The most common expression on the faces of those at nearby tables was curious doubt.

Ted sat on the bench and bowed his head, obviously praying. Jeffrey Richardson looked up at the ceiling and rolled his eyes. Alexia's excitement was suddenly replaced by a wave of anxiety. She'd pushed Ted forward even though he'd told her that performing classical music in public was not part of God's plan for his life. She bit her lip. If this didn't work, she'd owe everyone in the room an apology—especially Ted. She said her own silent prayer. Ted put his fingers on the keys and began to play.

Alexia quickly recognized Bach's *Chromatic Fantasy and Fugue*, a Baroque composition. Ted stumbled several times in the opening measures and glanced apologetically toward the audience. Alexia inwardly groaned. Under the table, her hands grasped her napkin and twisted it in a death grip. Ted lowered his head and pressed forward. He made another serious miscue that caused Alexia to wince. Even a listener unfamiliar with the piece could tell something was amiss.

Alexia felt Jeffrey's gaze turn toward her but avoided looking in his direction. She didn't take her eyes from Ted. She knew that within him lay the ability to do this. He paused and stared for a second over the top of the piano toward a spot on the wall behind the head table. His focus returned to the keyboard. He lowered his head.

And the music exploded.

The composer would have been proud. An intense, latent drama that must have been within Bach's heart filled the piece. Originally written for harpsichord, the Steinway liberated the music from the emotional straightjacket imposed by the tinny, one-dimensional sound of the harpsichord. Ted skillfully wove the work's three primary voices into a tapestry of unexpected and inviting harmonies, yet maintained the integrity of each as a musical depiction of the Godhead—Father, Son, and Holy Spirit. The ultimate goal of Bach's gift was worship, and when performed by someone who shared the composer's faith, the music communicated not only the beauty of sound, but the fragrance of a soul that loves God.

Alexia began to weep. She sat motionless and erect as the first tears flowed down her cheeks and fell onto her dress. She glanced down and discreetly touched the corner of her napkin to her eyes.

Ted finished the piece with a pause so brief that there was no time for applause. Alexia glanced at the faces around her table. Ken Pinchot was hard to impress, but she caught the hint of tentative approval. Nicholas Valese didn't try to suppress a yawn. Jeffrey was inscrutable.

Ted moved immediately into Beethoven's *Moonlight Sonata*. He played the familiar piece with only a few minor mistakes and then launched into Chopin's *Grand Polonaise Brillante*. Alexia was stunned. The composition lasted more than twenty minutes and contained some of the most challenging music in the piano repertoire. For Ted to play it from memory without having prepared was very risky. The extremely rapid, yet tranquil, grace notes that surrounded the melody of the opening movement, deceptively labeled *tranquillo* by Chopin, required a high degree of technical proficiency. Alexia held her breath. Pinchot's expression registered obvious surprise. Even a person unfamiliar with classical piano music could appreciate the challenge of such speedy finger movement across the keys.

As she watched Ted's face, Alexia realized that he'd entered into the realm of the music and left the room. He was as relaxed as if he was alone in the sanctuary of the Sandy Flats Church, and yet as focused as he must have been while playing for five hours with Aube Tzerko in California.

Ted moved into the second movement, the allegro molto. Legendary for stretching the capability of the piano beyond what others dared imagine, Chopin treated the keyboard as if it were a full orchestra. The allegro molto contained sounds so varied and intense that they caused Alexia's chest to ache. It required every ounce of the pianist's endurance and strength, because it ended with one of the most brilliant displays of virtuosity and grandeur known in the entire piano repertoire. Knowing what lay ahead, Alexia's nervousness returned. It would be tragic if, after performing so brilliantly, Ted faltered at the end.

Instead, his determination and drive didn't let up until he had summoned the last notes with power and authority. He stopped, and his hands dropped to his side.

Alexia knew her eyes were shining, but not with tears. Pride in Ted filled her heart. Enthusiastic applause erupted. Chandler stood immediately, clapping vigorously. Alexia joined him. Most of the room followed. Everyone at Alexia's table stood—whether from genuine appreciation or social duty, she could not tell.

Chandler hurried across the room to Ted and pumped his arm. He then leaned over and spoke into his ear. Ted nodded. The host returned to the podium as the crowd settled down. He mopped his face with a napkin, and Alexia realized he'd been more nervous than she about Ted's ability.

"Ladies and gentlemen, what a remarkable performance we've heard this evening," Chandler said. He looked toward Ted before continuing, "Especially the Chopin. Forgive me for not announcing beforehand what Mr. Morgan intended to play, but in my haste, I forgot to ask him. However, he has agreed to a brief encore."

Standing beside the piano, Ted announced in a loud voice, "My final number will be Robert Schumann's *Kinderscenen,* or *Scenes from Childhood in F Major.* I think it contains one of the finest melodies in the world."

He returned to the piano bench and began to play. As Alexia listened to the composition unfold and swirl across the room, she had to agree. What a beautiful sound. Ted finished to polite applause and returned to his seat. When he sat down next to her, Alexia could see the beads of perspiration on his forehead. She gave him her glass of water.

"That was magnificent," she whispered.

"Well done," Pinchot added.

Jeffrey nodded in Ted's direction and gave him a thumbs-up.

"I've been working on the Chopin for weeks," Ted said in a low voice to Alexia. "I wondered why I was spending so much time reviewing it. It was the feature number of the last concert I gave in California."

Chandler returned to the podium and a picture of a proposed building was projected onto a large screen behind him. The fund-raiser commenced, but Alexia didn't want to leave the concert.

"What were you feeling while you were playing?" she asked.

Ted took a long drink of water. "I was thirsty."

Alexia pursed her lips. "Okay, Mr. Nonresponsive. What else?"

Ted took another drink, set the glass down, and pointed to the ceiling with his finger. "I felt his pleasure. I wasn't sure that I would, but it was the only way I could have done it."

"I saw you hesitate toward the beginning of the *Chromatic Fantasy and Fugue*. After that it was incredible."

Ted nodded. "That's when it happened. We'll talk later."

The evening progressed, and Alexia signed a card for a donation beyond what she would have contributed if Ted hadn't performed. In her case at least, the entertainment had the desired effect.

When the event ended, several people immediately came over to Ted and began talking to him. Alexia stepped over to Jeffrey.

"Thank you for the invitation," she said.

Jeffrey smiled. "I should thank you for inviting your piano prodigy. He saved us from an embarrassing evening. What's the name of the church where he works? I forget."

"The old Sandy Flats Church on McBee Road."

"Let him know I'll send him a check for his work this evening. After paying Victor Plavich, there's nothing in the nonprofit's budget to do anything, but I'll take care of it myself."

Alexia glanced at Ted. He was still occupied with the crowd swirling around him.

"Uh, okay."

"And I'd like him to perform for a party I'm hosting in Santee. We have a big event just before Christmas. People come in from all over the country. He could play some classical music and then take requests."

"He doesn't do that sort of thing," Alexia responded without thinking.

Jeffrey raised his eyebrows. "I'll pay him a lot more than he makes pushing the buttons on an organ."

Alexia bristled. "Actually, you'll have to ask him. I'm not his agent."

Jeffrey shrugged and pointed to the growing crowd around Ted. "Maybe you should be."

———

Several minutes later, Ted saw Alexia out of the corner of his eye. She stood relaxed and beautiful, talking to a handsome young man. Ted pulled away from three older women who were all talking to him at once and joined her.

"It's time for Elvis to leave the building," he whispered in her ear.

Alexia willingly disengaged from her conversation. Ted took her hand and started walking, but before they reached the front door, two people asked Ted to play at weddings and three others begged him to give their children lessons. Finally, they stepped into the fresh air outside.

"Tough being a star?" Alexia asked.

Ted didn't answer, and they walked in silence to the car.

"You drive," Ted said. "I'm beat."

As she pulled out of the parking deck, Alexia said, "I'm sorry for calling you a star. I know you don't want to draw attention to yourself."

Ted yawned. "It's okay, but I want to return to who I am. The farther we get away from the hotel, the better I'll be."

"Are you sorry that you played?" Alexia asked in surprise.

Ted closed his eyes for a moment before responding. "No, but I'm not interested in trying to launch a career. This evening was fine, even though dealing with the people afterward was a strain."

They passed a row of older homes illuminated by flickering street lights. The wrought-iron work cast long shadows on the wall of the houses.

"Does that mean you won't play for Jeffrey Richardson's Christmas bash?" Alexia asked. "It's a huge party with lots of rich folks at one of the country clubs his family developed. He suggested that you play a few classical numbers and then take requests."

"Are you serious?"

"Yep, and you'll make a lot more money than you will painting my new office. If you hire me as your agent, I'll get a piece of the pie too."

Ted laughed. "Okay, be my agent and decline. In return, I'll furnish a free can of paint and buy you a piece of pie. What kind do you like?"

"Peach cobbler with ice cream at Cousin Bert's. They only serve it on Thursdays."

Ted reclined the seat and stretched out his legs. "It's a deal."

13

Here is the charming evening, the criminal's friend;
it comes like an accomplice, with stealthy tread.
CHARLES BAUDELAIRE

Rick Bridges switched the handset to his other ear and spoke to Byron Devereaux's wife.

"I'm sorry his father is in the hospital," Bridges said. "Tell Byron I'll see him on Monday."

Bridges hung up. This turn of events dealt a setback to his plans to locate Henry L. Quinton, a.k.a. Hank Quincy. It would be a week before another Saturday-night gathering at the Beachcomber Club.

"Who's driving tonight? You or Byron?" Amy called from the kitchen.

The detective made a quick decision. "I am." He would take the opportunity to do some fact-finding and wait until he wasn't solo to make an arrest.

Forty-five minutes later, Bridges pulled into the parking lot for the Beachcomber Club. The sandy lot in front of the bar was filled to capacity, and the detective squeezed into a spot next to a pickup truck with one orange door and one green door.

The Santee police had yet to receive any credible information about the hit-and-run driver who struck his leg and smashed the door of his car. The detective's right leg remained stiff and had kept him off the racquetball court this week, though the orthopedist who examined the leg assured him full recovery.

Every Carolina cowboy wore his best footwear Saturday nights. There weren't any real cowboys along the coast, but boots were a popular honky-tonk fashion statement. Bridges had polished his until they shone. Faded jeans, cleaner than most of the patrons', a lightweight jacket, and a western-style straw hat that concealed his military haircut completed the ensemble.

Strapped underneath the detective's left shoulder rested a smaller version of his standard service revolver. As a detective, Bridges could carry a wide variety of weapons. A set of stainless-steel handcuffs that he didn't intend to use jingled in his jacket pocket. If the bar required patrons to pass through a metal detector, Rick Bridges would set off more alarms than a knife collector returning from a convention.

The Beachcomber Club was painted a bright pink with green trim around the door and window frames. Boards painted the same pink as the building permanently sealed the windows. Above the front door, a neon sign with a flashing cocktail glass announced the name of the club. Bridges walked across the parking lot and reached the door at the same time as a large, overweight man escorting two women. Under the light, Bridges could see that one of the women sported a jagged scar across her nose. Both women paused and looked at the detective. The woman with the scar smiled and revealed several prominent gaps in her grin. A bouncer, sitting on a stool by the door, spoke to the man and gave Bridges a quick inspection without comment.

Inside, a pale, gray haze of smoke hung in the air. Small round tables scattered about the room offered a few vacant seats. On one wall hung an enormous blue marlin. On another, several smaller fish swam in single file toward a row of video poker machines. A light sprinkling of sand covered the floor, giving credence to the Beachcomber name and serving as a line of first defense against sloshing beer. Opposite the poker machines was a small, empty stage. Instead of live music, a jukebox blared a country tune.

Bridges walked over to the bar. A chunky, middle-aged barmaid with long blonde hair wiped off a spot in front of him.

"What do you want, sweetheart?" she asked.

Bridges ordered a beer. When she brought it, he asked, "Is Harry here?"

"No, the ice machine broke, and he had to go buy some bags of ice. He should be back in a few minutes."

"Then maybe you could help me. I'm looking for Hank Quincy. Do you know him?"

The woman's eyes narrowed. "Are you a cop?"

Bridges laughed and tilted his hat up. "Do I look like a cop?"

The woman shrugged. "I don't want any trouble. Hank can be moody. If you've got a problem with him, you take it outside."

Bridges smiled. "If there's a problem, it won't start with me."

He saw the woman scan the room. Her eyes stopped in a corner near the deserted stage. Bridges followed her gaze. Four men slouched around a table with two half-empty pitchers of beer in the middle. Two had dark hair, a third had brown, and a fourth was balding.

"He's in the corner with his buddies."

"Which one is he?"

"The one with dark hair."

"There are two guys with dark hair."

"Hank doesn't have three rings in his right ear. He's got too much class."

Bridges was too far away to distinguish ear decorations.

A man standing at the other end of the bar called out, "Do I have to pour my own beer?"

The woman sneered. "No, but I want to see your money on the counter before I pull the tap."

When the barmaid left, Bridges took a drink and looked down at the wet ring left on the bar from the mug's condensation. He could get a close look at the suspect and compare his appearance with the file photo. He might also get additional information. Police-department protocol discouraged solitary action with a potentially dangerous suspect, and attempting to make contact might cross the line, but Bridges rationalized it as an investigative mission.

He picked up his beer and started weaving his way across the room. As he approached the corner, he could see that the man sitting across the table had three silver earrings in the upper cartilage of his right ear. That left the dark-haired man with his back to Bridges as the most likely candidate for Hank Quincy. The detective turned sideways to pass between two tables. A woman suddenly stood up and knocked his arm, causing his beer to tip and soak the right side of her dress. It was the woman with the scar carved across her nose. Her male companion jumped to his feet.

"Watch it!" he said.

The woman dabbed the wet spot with a paper napkin. "I'm gonna smell like beer the rest of the night!"

The room grew quiet and all eyes turned in the direction of the table.

"Excuse me," Bridges said softly, tipping his hat. "It was an accident. Could I buy you a drink?"

The woman's countenance softened. Her male companion's glare increased.

"No, move along!" he ordered.

Bridges complied as the woman directed her ire toward the man.

"Why'd you go do that?" she demanded. "I was gonna get a free drink out of it!"

Bridges didn't hear the man's response as he reached the table in the corner. The man with the earrings glanced up at him.

"Don't come over here spilling your beer, cowboy," the man said.

The balding man chuckled. Bridges looked down at the other dark-haired man. From his profile he looked somewhat like Quinton, but not similar enough for a positive identification.

The detective spoke slowly, making his natural drawl even more pronounced. "That wasn't intentional. I was wondering if y'all could help me?"

"What is it?" the balding man asked.

Bridges looked down at the dark-haired man. "Do you have a car for sale?"

The man looked up coldly out of the corner of his eye.

Before he answered, one of his companions replied, "He don't have a car; he drives a beat-up old van."

The dark-haired man turned in his seat. When he did, Bridges knew it was Quinton—older, of course, but with the same narrowly set brown eyes and neat appearance that seemed inappropriate for a mug shot and now out of place at the Beachcomber Bar.

"I don't have a car for sale," Quinton said in a distinct, nasal accent. "Who told you that I did?"

Bridges stepped back. He'd verified his identification, and it was time to move on.

"Sorry I bothered you."

He quickly retreated to the bar and sat on a high stool. He glanced over his shoulder and saw that Quinton had turned sideways to watch him. Bridges took a sip of beer and made a decision. While Quinton was potentially implicated in Deputy Dixon's death, he was definitely wanted for questioning in the Rhode Island murder. Bridges had located him, and the opportunity to apprehend him couldn't be squandered. He left the rest of the beer in the mug on the counter and slipped outside to his car. He called the Santee Police Department and asked for two patrol cars. The dispatcher told him it would be ten minutes before the officers would arrive.

While he waited, Bridges got out and walked up and down the haphazard rows of cars to see if Quinton had driven his van. A license-plate check might reveal additional information. The single light in the parking area didn't illuminate the back corner of the lot, where several vehicles stood. One of them was a gray van that fit the "beat-up" description. Bridges took out a small notepad and squatted to record the license-plate number. The last two characters were covered in mud. He reached forward and wiped the plate with his fingers.

His face smashed into the back of the van. Someone grabbed his shirt, jerked back his head, and slammed it into the bumper. Dazed and with blood pouring from his nose, Bridges tried to stand but was thrown to the ground. Someone put a foot on his neck. Two more hands grabbed the detective's arms and pinned them behind his back. He was lying with his face partly buried in the sandy soil.

"Get his wallet," a voice said.

In a few seconds, another voice said, "It's too dark. I can't read it. He was writing something on a pad."

"Open the door of the van, so we can see," the first voice said. "Keep him on the ground."

"You should keep out of other people's business, cowboy," the person with the foot on his neck said, pressing down harder.

Bridges gagged. The door of the van opened, and the dome light came on.

"He was writing down the license plate number. Richard Bridges. Lives in Charleston."

Someone leaned close to the detective's ear. "Why did you want the license-plate number?"

Bridges moaned.

"Check him," said the voice near his ear.

A hand reached around his side and felt the lump under his left arm. "He's carrying a gun!"

"Get it!" the nearby voice commanded.

The hands holding his arms tightened their grip as he was rolled onto his side. Dirt, sweat, and mud stung his eyes. He gasped for air. His gun was pulled from its holster. Another hand felt inside his jacket.

One of the men swore. "Handcuffs! He must be a cop!"

"What are we going to do?"

There was a moment of silence. Bridges tried to spit some of the filth from his mouth.

"Cuff him and put him in the back. We'll take care of him somewhere else."

Someone clamped the handcuffs on him. He was half-kicked, half-shoved into the back of the van, where he landed on some tools. His head stung as it struck something metal. A dirty shirt quickly enveloped his head and covered his face. He heard the front two doors of the van open and close. The engine started. The driver backed up and turned around. As he started to move forward, the man in the front passenger seat cried out.

"Cop cars! He must have called them!"

"It doesn't matter," the man behind the wheel responded. "I'll ease past them."

The van moved forward. The vehicle turned to the left. Lights flashed. Sirens wailed.

"He's blocked me!" the driver yelled.

Pandemonium hit the inside of the van. Bridges heard the front and back doors fly open. He could hear the shouts of the police as they chased the men through the darkness. He tried to sit up but felt dizzy and slumped back onto the floor. The shirt around his face was soaked in blood, making it harder and harder to breathe. He heard a single gunshot, and his heart sank. He desperately hoped it wasn't his gun being used against a fellow officer. His stomach lurched.

He lay still. Slowly, his head began to clear enough so that he could sit up. Restrained by the handcuffs behind his back, Bridges couldn't reach up to dislodge the shirt. He scooted to the back of the van and attempted to stand up. He could still hear the sounds of the chase, and the blue lights of the patrol cars flashed through the cloth of the shirt. Suddenly, a bright light shone directly at him.

"Don't move!" a deep male voice commanded. "Put your hands over your head and stand up slowly."

The detective shook his head. "I'm Bridges," he managed in a muffled voice. "Help me."

He tried to stand but collapsed into unconsciousness.

———

Returning from Charleston, Alexia and Ted passed the Beachcomber Club. The blue lights of several police cars flashed in the parking lot, and the siren of an ambulance wailed as it pulled out. Alexia slowed down as the ambulance sped away.

"That's a rough place," Alexia commented. "I won't try to book you there. I doubt they'd appreciate Debussy."

Ted had dozed off until the commotion swirling around the club roused him. He yawned and looked out the window.

"I wonder what happened."

"Probably a fight."

When they reached the church, Alexia parked in front of the parsonage.

"You were great tonight," Alexia said. "But I respect your desire to maintain a low profile. The next time we go to a charity concert I promise not to volunteer you."

Ted smiled. "The evening certainly turned out different than if you'd let me lure you to the sanctuary."

"Oh, and I'll resign as your agent if you think that will help."

"Not necessary. Are you going to come to church in the morning?"

Alexia nodded. "Yes."

"Good. I'll see you then. Maybe we can go to lunch."

Ted opened the car door. Alexia put her hand on his arm. At her touch he leaned over, and they briefly kissed.

"I had a wonderful evening," Alexia said. "Are you going to practice any more tonight?"

Ted laughed. "Do I need to?"

Alexia kissed him again, a little more strongly.

"No. You've had enough Chopin for one evening. You need something else to think about as you go to sleep."

14

Rick Bridges struggled toward consciousness like a swimmer seeking the surface. He almost reached air and light before darkness dragged him down again.

He next found himself on a table underneath bright lights. His vision was blurry, but he could make out a nurse standing beside his bed adjusting an IV bag.

"What happened?" he asked in a slurred voice.

The nurse looked down at him. "Don't try to move. I'll get the doctor."

He closed his eyes and groaned. As he became more aware, he moved the fingers on his left hand. He lifted his hand a few inches from the bed, but it was connected to the IV. He commanded his right hand to touch his nose, which was swollen and sore. His hand slowly came up from his side but missed his nose and poked his left eye. A female voice spoke.

"That's good, Detective Bridges. I'm Dr. Garinger. Move your left fingers."

Bridges complied and then cooperated with a series of commands. He wiggled his toes and answered some simple questions. The doctor shone a light in his eyes.

"You're neurologically intact," she said. "You have a concussion and a broken nose, but your neck seems fine."

Bridges began to tap the memory of where he had been and what had happened.

"Quinton," he said.

"What?" the doctor asked.

"Quinton? Did they catch him?"

"I'm not sure whom the police arrested. All I know is that you were struck in the head and face and knocked unconscious. You arrived at the Santee hospital in an ambulance about an hour ago."

"An hour?"

"Yes. We ran a CT scan of your head and neck. It showed evidence of the concussion and broken nose but nothing that shouldn't improve in a few days. You have no damage to your spinal cord."

"What about my wife?" Bridges asked in alarm. "Does she know where I am?"

"She's on her way. I already told her about the results of the CT scan."

Bridges sank back into the bed and closed his eyes. When he opened them again, Byron Devereaux stood beside his bed. His supervisor's thin bespectacled face was filled with concern.

"Welcome back," Devereaux said. "You had a close call. How do you feel?"

Bridges felt better but credited the drugs dripping into his left hand. Underneath the numbness lurked pain.

"I'll make it. How's your father?"

"He's going to be okay. I was on my way up here when I received the call."

"Did they catch Quinton?"

Devereaux nodded. "Yes. Two of the men got away. They found Quinton hiding underneath a car."

"I heard a gunshot. Was anyone hurt?"

"Only you. I don't know about the gunshot. Quinton is on his way to Charleston in the back of a patrol car."

Bridges winced. "How does my face look?"

Devereaux tilted his head to the side. "Like you kissed a windshield at fifty miles an hour, but the doctor says you'll be fine. Were you trying to make an arrest on your own? That's not very smart."

"No, just trying to get Quinton's plate number." Bridges gave Devereaux a brief account. "I don't know why the Santee deputies stopped the van. I hadn't mentioned it when I called the dispatcher."

"The driver was in too much of a hurry. He just seemed suspicious."

Bridges closed his eyes. "That was close. If the guys from the bar had taken me someplace . . ."

Devereaux sighed and looked at the floor. "I'm going to ask the solicitor to keep Quinton here instead of shipping him up to Rhode Island. He's killed one of our deputies and came close to killing you. I'd rather see him on death row in South Carolina than anywhere else I can imagine."

———

Alexia was scooping out a bite of grapefruit for breakfast when the phone rang. She looked at the caller ID. Weekend calls from Rena never brought good news, but Alexia wouldn't dodge a problem on Sunday if it stood any chance of growing bigger by Monday. Rena probably wanted a detailed account of the evening with Jeffrey. Alexia answered.

"Did you watch the news this morning?" Rena asked excitedly.

After dropping off Ted, Alexia had crawled into bed. The only sounds of her morning had been Boris barking as he ran through the marsh grass and a few chirping birds perched near her deck.

"No, what is it?"

"They caught the man who stole my convertible," Rena said. "He was at a bar on the coastal highway."

Alexia remembered the flashing lights. "Was it the Beachcomber Club on Highway 17?"

"Yeah, that's it. He attacked a policeman from Charleston. The TV reporter just interviewed the detective who talked to us after the car was stolen. He said that they're going to hold the man on multiple charges."

Alexia could imagine the list: auto theft, murder of the policeman who stopped him for speeding in Rena's car, assault against the officer who tried to arrest him, and anything else the solicitor's office could tack on.

"What's the man's name?" she asked.

"I wrote it down. Uh, here it is. Henry L. Quinton. He's from New Jersey and was driving a gray van with New York license plates."

The blood drained from Alexia's face.

"Which channel carried the story?" she asked.

Rena told her. "Will I have to testify at his trial? It was horrible at the hearing about Baxter's life support. I almost passed out."

Alexia picked up the remote control for the small TV she had in the kitchen and turned on the power. "Oh, it will be routine," she said after a brief pause. "Don't worry about it. You'll have to identify your car and confirm that it was stolen, but you don't know who took it so you won't get an antagonistic cross-examination. No criminal-defense lawyer wants to create extra sympathy for a victim."

"I'll still be nervous."

"We'll rehearse if you want to. I'm just glad they caught someone. I want to watch the news myself. We'll talk on Monday."

She clicked off the phone and turned in her chair to view the newscast. The rest of her grapefruit remained uneaten in a bowl on the table. The arrest of Henry L. Quinton led the broadcast. She stared intently at the mug shot; however, she'd not gotten a clear view of the driver of the van on the dusky evening she encountered him. When a photo of the vehicle briefly flashed on the screen, Alexia compressed her lips tighter. It was either the same gray van that invaded her territory or its twin. When the news anchor switched to a story about erosion on a barrier island, Alexia turned off the TV.

Why would someone like Quinton be in the vicinity of her house? Almost no one trespassed on her tiny corner of the marshlands. And why did Quinton try to run her off the road? Alexia posed a threat only to recalcitrant husbands who wanted to rip off their wives. She'd never represented Mrs. Henry L. Quinton, and she could deduce no other possible connection between herself and a thief and killer. Her thoughts turned to Rena. Why would Quinton steal Rena's car? Of all the fancy cars in the golfing developments that surrounded Santee, why hers? Alexia's mind continued to spin, but her questions only led to other questions.

She arrived at the Sandy Flats Church in a somber mood. Walking across the parking lot, she saw Mrs. Marylou Hobart. Ted had taken on Mrs. Hobart and her rambling, ramshackle house as an ongoing rehabilitation project. The older woman, dressed in a faded brown outfit that had probably been new when Alexia attended elementary school, waved happily.

"Alicia!" Mrs. Hobart exclaimed as they drew closer together. "It's good to see you."

The partially deaf woman hadn't mastered the name Alexia, and Alexia was content to answer to anything close.

She leaned forward and shouted, "Good morning, Mrs. Hobart!"

"No need to holler, my dear," Mrs. Hobart chided. "This is a good day. My euthanasia tubes are more open than usual."

The dark cloud over Alexia lifted, and she smiled at the woman's mala-propism. "I'm glad you're still with us. Maybe you can enjoy Ted's playing. Last night, he performed at a benefit concert."

Mrs. Hobart nodded. "I always benefit from being around him. He's very handy around the house. He can fix most anything. I never thought I'd be able to get the toilet in my upstairs bathroom to stop running, but he put a rubber thing in it, and it's been as still as a summer pond ever since."

Alexia helped Mrs. Hobart up the steps to the sanctuary. That the extraordinarily talented music minister was willing to hug the older woman's toilet was proof of the practical effect of his faith. The two women sat on the right side of the church about halfway toward the front. Alexia knew from experience it was the best spot, acoustically speaking, in the two-hundred-year-old sanctuary.

The room was three-fourths filled. The men wore suits and ties, and the women were clothed in nice dresses with a smattering of hats. Christian roots ran deep among longtime residents of the Santee area, and a church that traced its founding to the early settlers in the Lowcountry didn't easily adopt casual, beachfront religion. Only the teenagers showed signs of breaking with tradition. Whether the young people would return to the formality of prior generations would not be answered until they reached adulthood.

Ted and the senior minister, John Heathcliff, entered the sanctuary. Both men wore robes. Ted sat at the piano and played an excerpt from a Bach fugue as the prelude. Music was the heart language Alexia best understood, but other parts of the service also touched her spirit. When the congregation stood for the responsive reading, her soul echoed the antiphonal agreement with the words of David from the Psalms. On this Sunday, three-thousand-year-old poetry came alive in a small church in South Carolina.

The sermon, a message about giving, was hard to follow, and Alexia wasn't sure what Reverend Heathcliff wanted her to believe. If he'd been arguing a case in which Alexia served as a juror, she'd have sent word to the judge that she needed more information.

After the minister pronounced the benediction, Alexia lingered while Ted played the postlude. She didn't recognize the music and suspected he wrote it. The other people on the pew moved into the aisles and toward the back of the sanctuary. Mrs. Hobart tapped her on the arm.

"Didn't the preacher say amen?" she asked.

Alexia nodded. "Yes ma'am."

"That means it's time to go."

Alexia pointed toward the piano. "I'm listening to Ted."

Mrs. Hobart nodded, and the two women stood together in silence until the music minister's hands lifted from the keys.

Mrs. Hobart sighed. "It was the same way with my husband, Harry. I could listen to him play for hours."

"Did he play the piano?" Alexia asked in surprise.

"Oh, no, but he could make a fiddle talk. You'll think I'm crazy, but he could play songs, and I could see what he was a-playing. He could make flowers pop out of the ground and rain fall from the clouds."

"That's beautiful."

"It sure was. There ain't nothing like a man that makes music," the old woman paused, then added with a twinkle in her eye, "especially one that can fix a stubborn toilet."

Ted the toilet fixer came up the aisle. He unzipped his dark robe, slipped it from his shoulders, and draped it over his arm. Underneath he wore a white shirt, yellow tie, and gray slacks.

"Two of my favorite people!" he called out.

Mrs. Hobart grinned. "You did good today. I could hear you a lot better than the preacher."

"We have a pew equipped with speakers connected to ear pieces," Ted said, pointing to one of the front rows.

The older woman shook her head. "I don't like those things. They make it sound like I'm listening to everything through a seashell. It roars bad."

They walked to the back of the sanctuary. The congregation had moved to the parking lot. Parents with babies and toddlers were collecting their offspring from the nursery. Those without children were already on their way to the local restaurants.

"Can you join me for lunch?" Ted asked Alexia.

Mrs. Hobart thought the question was directed to her. "Not today," she responded. "Ann Briscoe is taking me out to eat and then driving me home. She picked me up this morning."

Mrs. Hobart's voluntary chauffeur saw her and motioned toward the car.

"It's good seeing you," Alexia said. "Have a nice afternoon."

"I'm sure you will," Mrs. Hobart responded. "Ted is a good cook. He brought me a piece of coconut pie that was almost as good as I used to make."

They watched Mrs. Hobart navigate across the fine gravel and crushed seashells that covered the parking lot.

"She tells me you're a miracle worker when it comes to toilets," Alexia said.

Ted nodded. "Yeah, that toilet was draining the water table for the whole eastern seaboard."

"I'll add that to your list of talents."

They walked down the steps together.

"Let's eat at my place," Ted said. "After all the rich food last night, I'd like something light. I bought some fresh shrimp yesterday. We can boil them and eat them plain or make a shrimp salad."

"With coconut pie for dessert?"

Ted chuckled. "I didn't make the pie. A lady in the church gave it to me, and I shared it with Mrs. Hobart. She was confused about where it came from, and it wasn't worth the trouble trying to straighten it out."

Alexia noticed several heads turn and watch them cross the parking lot. After Ted first took Alexia to lunch with Mrs. Hobart, news of the music minister's interest in the young lawyer had rippled through the congregation.

"Have you ever been to a drive-in movie?" she asked as Ted pushed open the door.

"Once or twice when I was a kid. Why?"

"I feel like I'm on the screen, and the show is about to begin."

Ted looked past Alexia at the cars sitting in the church parking lot.

"I see what you mean," he said.

Alexia stayed put on the front stoop. "Is it okay? I don't want to cause you any problems."

Ted stepped into the house. "Don't worry. The church secretary asked me about you last week, and I told her. She circulated the news, and it has probably reached the outer limits of the Sandy Flats Church universe by now."

"What did you tell her?"

"The truth."

"Which is?"

"That you like classical piano music. She's seen your car outside the sanctuary when I've been playing in the afternoon. I told her that you are a very interesting and unique person, and I wanted to get to know you better."

"That's bland. Did it satisfy her curiosity?"

"Probably not. But it's all I gave her. Anything else floating through the drive-in movie crowd is as true as a rumor from Hollywood."

Alexia followed Ted through the living room to the kitchen at the back of the house. The old wooden floors creaked under their feet. They passed the picture on the mantel of Ted's daughter, Angelica, at the time of her graduation from Juilliard. In the kitchen, Ted opened the refrigerator and took out a plastic bag filled with shrimp, their heads intact. He poured the shrimp into a plastic bowl and took out a knife and cutting board.

"Cook them with the heads on," Alexia said. "It will give them more flavor."

Ted stopped with the knife in midair. "Do you eat them with the heads on too?"

Alexia sat down at the small table against the wall of the kitchen and propped her feet up on the opposite chair. "Yeah, most lawyers eat shrimp with the heads on. First they bite off the heads and then take their time nibbling away at the body. It's one of the first things I learned in law school."

Ted returned the knife to the drawer. "No argument from me."

"Where's the pot you use to boil them?"

Ted retrieved it from underneath the counter. Alexia joined him at the sink as she filled the large pot with water. Their arms touched. Alexia looked up at him. The insecurity caused by Sarah Locklear faded as she spent more time with the minister.

"Thanks for inviting me."

Ted wrinkled his forehead and smiled.

"I needed to be with someone today," Alexia continued. "I didn't want to go back to my house and spend the day alone."

Ted took the pot from her and put it on the stovetop.

"Why not?"

Alexia sat back down.

"Do you remember the police cars outside the bar last night?" she asked.

"Yes."

Alexia told Ted about Quinton's arrest and the phone call from Rena. When she mentioned her recent encounter with the gray van, Ted's expression grew more serious.

"I've lived alone ever since I moved to Santee," Alexia said with a sigh. "And I've been in my house on the marsh for four years. This is the first time I've felt afraid, and I can't shake it."

Ted dumped the shrimp into the boiling water. "It might not be the same guy. Can you find out more about him?"

"I need to ask questions because of Rena's situation, but I'd also like to investigate a few things myself. The detective might talk to me if I tell him my story. It's just unsettling to think someone like that was near my house."

The shrimp instantly turned pink. Ted looked at his watch.

"Ready in two minutes," he said. "Yeah, you need to find out what was in Quinton's head before the Charleston County prosecutor tries to bite it off."

15

To every action there is always opposed an equal reaction.
SIR ISAAC NEWTON

After talking to Alexia, Rena tried to contact Jeffrey. She was nervous about his reaction to the arrest of one of his spies. He didn't answer his cell phone, and she didn't leave a message that might accidentally be retrieved by someone else.

Rena went to her computer in the corner of the kitchen. Turning it on, she continued her Internet research into the nature and duration of comas. Her anxiety about Baxter's return from the netherworld had abated somewhat when he showed no ability for complex communication. Medical information she located on-line reassured her that partial amnesia, particularly as to events immediately preceding an injury, commonly occurred in cases of severe head injury. Even if a person's ability to speak returned, conversation was often disjointed and confused.

Baxter's vulnerability would give Rena time to plan. Something subtle would be ideal; something that could not be connected to her would be essential. The most promising scenario would be death by a means naturally associated with prolonged inactivity. How to promote deterioration via infection or systemic failure presented a challenge. She typed in another key word and clicked the search button.

An hour later she turned off the computer and left the house to buy a cup of coffee and a pastry. Walking past the garage, she decided to detour toward the cottage. The young nurse's aide on duty was giving Baxter a sponge bath. Her husband's chest and arms had atrophied significantly during the weeks he'd been immobile. He was lying with his eyes closed as the older nurse gently rubbed his arm with a damp cloth. Rena stared at him for a moment.

"Has he shown any other signs of waking up?" she asked.

"His eyes have opened a few times but didn't focus on anything. I asked him a few questions but didn't get a response. He wouldn't blink."

Rena continued to stare down at him. She lightly touched Baxter's hair. It was soft and slightly damp.

"The nurse is making you look nice," she said. "Your father is coming back into town this afternoon and will come by to see you."

Baxter remained motionless. Rena was satisfied. Though he stubbornly clung to life, he couldn't be far from the limit to what he could endure. She turned and left.

"You have a pretty wife," the aide said as she patted Baxter's arm dry with a soft towel. "After I'm finished, I'll turn you onto your side, so you won't get any nasty bed sores. One of the nurses brought some pretty plants that you can enjoy. They are red, green, orange—"

As the aide rattled on, Baxter opened his eyes. His mouth was dry. He licked his lips.

"Father," he croaked. "Talk."

The aide jumped and let out a shriek. She dropped the towel. The nurse in the kitchen came rushing into the room.

"What happened?" she asked.

The aide pointed toward Baxter whose eyes were now closed.

"He spoke."

"What did he say?"

"He asked for his father and wants to talk to him."

The nurse leaned over closer to Baxter's head. "Mr. Richardson, if you want to see your father, open your eyes."

Nothing happened.

The aide stood on the other side of the bed. "Ask him again."

The nurse touched Baxter's cheek. "Mr. Richardson, if you want to talk to your father, open your eyes."

Baxter slowly raised his eyelids.

"Do you want to talk to your father?" the nurse asked again.

"Huh," he managed before his pupils rolled back in his head.

The aide looked at the nurse. "What do you think?" she asked.

The nurse picked up Baxter's arm and slipped on the hospital gown. "I think he's coming back. I hope his father gets here before our shift is over. I want to see what happens."

———

A few hours later, Rena called Jeffrey again. This time he answered.

"Is anyone listening?" Rena asked.

"I assume you mean other than me. No, we're the only ones on the line."

"Did you see the news on TV?"

"Yes."

Rena waited for Jeffrey to continue, but he didn't say anything.

"Do you know anything about the man they arrested for stealing my car?" she asked.

"Only what you know. That's he's not guilty. He didn't steal your car, and he didn't kill the policeman."

Rena bit her lip. When she spoke, she couldn't suppress a slight tremor in her voice.

"I didn't do anything to the policeman. That video you sent to blackmail me doesn't prove anything. I was driving the convertible earlier in the day and then parked it in front of the house with the keys in it. Quinton must have stolen it while I was in the house."

Jeffrey spoke slowly. "The clock running at the bottom of the screen doesn't lie, Rena, but who said anything about blackmail? Nobody has a copy of the tape but you and me."

"Quinton doesn't have a copy?"

"Forget about him. He'll be convicted and that will be the end of it. You need to focus on the important things."

"Uh, I'm cooperating. I know Alexia is doing research on the companies you gave me, but I don't know when she's going to file suit. Did you talk to her last night?"

"No, there wasn't an opportunity, but I'll contact her if I need to."

"So, there's nothing I have to worry about?"

"Not from me."

"What about Quinton's lawyer? What if he tells his lawyer about the tape?"

"Quinton wasn't working the day you took your ride to Charleston, and I doubt he knows a tape exists. The man who shot the film was checking out some new equipment. It was totally random. Pretty, lucky, eh?"

Rena didn't appreciate the barb. It was infuriating to think that chance had placed her in such a dangerous situation.

"Then why were his fingerprints on my car? Did Baxter know him?"

"No. Quinton dropped off the money I gave you when my father gutted your bank account."

Rena paused. "Oh, when he opened the car door he left fingerprints."

Jeffrey gave a short laugh. "Yeah, which was stupid on his part."

"Won't he try to drag others down with him? Maybe even you?"

"No, I've never met him. I talk to the people who give him orders."

"What if he mentions my name and talks about the money? What should I do?"

Jeffrey hesitated, and Rena realized she'd mentioned something her brother-in-law hadn't thought about.

"Look, Rena, people like him know not to talk to the police, but if he mentions you, he makes himself look guilty. The last thing he wants is a connection with you because your car is directly linked to the deputy who was killed."

"He wasn't killed; he slipped and fell!"

There was a momentary silence on the other end of the line. When he spoke, Jeffrey said,

"Will you repeat that for the tape?"

"What!" Rena exploded. "You said—"

Jeffrey laughed.

"I'm kidding," he said. "Don't be so edgy. I'm sure you haven't done anything wrong in years. Keep your cool, and everything will work out. If the police contact you, make sure your lawyer is there when they interview you. She's sharp, and I'm sure knows how to take care of nosy detectives. She's good-looking, too, but you're right, she's not my type—a bit too uptight."

"So you're not worried?"

"I've not done anything wrong, and you should be okay too if you keep your mouth shut and do what your lawyer and I tell you to do. We've talked enough about this. How's Baxter?"

Rena was unconvinced but didn't know what else to ask him.

"No different. Everyone got excited when he opened his eyes the other day, but I don't think he recognizes me. It's depressing."

"My father left the office a few minutes ago on his way to see Baxter. If you run into him, don't talk to him about the car, Quinton, or anything else. In fact, avoid him. There's nothing you can say to him that will help us."

"That won't be a problem."

Rena hung up the phone. While drinking a glass of water, she looked out the kitchen window toward the cottage and saw Ezra Richardson's black Mercedes come up the driveway. She stepped away from the window but stayed close enough to watch. Ezra parked in front of the cottage and got out. Dressed in a dark suit, he looked like an older, slightly overweight version of Jeffrey. They shared dark, penetrating eyes, as well as a well-shaped nose and strong jaw. Both faces were compatible with an unyielding personality.

While in the Caribbean, Ezra received word that his younger son was beginning to emerge from the coma. He'd considered flying home immediately, but a brief conversation with Dr. Leoni convinced him to complete his business. The extra time proved troubling yet valuable. All was not as it should be in the Richardson empire.

At the cottage, he pushed open the door and found Baxter, his eyes closed, lying in the same position Ezra had last seen him. The nurse on duty stuck her head around the corner from the kitchen.

"Mr. Richardson," she said excitedly. "We were hoping you'd come. Your son spoke for the first time a few hours ago. He said 'father' and 'talk.'"

Ezra stepped quickly to the side of the bed.

"Baxter!" he said in a loud voice. "I'm here!"

"There's no need to yell," the nurse said. "If he wants to respond, he will—"

Baxter opened his eyes and looked up at his father. Ezra could see the light of recognition come on in his eyes.

"He knows you," the nurse whispered.

Baxter shifted his gaze to the nurse.

"Go," he said in a voice that slightly cracked.

Ezra shooed her away with his hand. "You heard him. He wants to talk privately."

The nurse started to protest, but the look on Ezra's face didn't invite debate.

"Yes sir," she said meekly. "I'll be in the kitchen if you need me."

———

Thirty minutes later, Rena heard the doorbell chime. When she came down the stairs and leaned over the banister to look out the sidelight, she saw Ezra and froze. She wanted to flee, but the older man saw her and beckoned urgently. Trapped, Rena descended slowly and opened the large door. Ezra stepped inside without being invited.

"I just finished talking to Baxter," he began abruptly. "As soon as I spoke his name, he opened his eyes. We were able to talk for several minutes."

Rena put her hand out to steady herself against the wall. "Uh, I didn't know he was talking," she managed. "What did he say?"

"He knows his name and who I am. He recognized the cottage but still thought his mother was alive and that Jeffrey was away at college." Ezra paused. "When I mentioned your name he shook his head."

"You mean he doesn't know who I am?"

"I don't know. Maybe when he sees you and hears your voice, he'll remember you."

Rena's heart was pounding in her ears. "Uh, did he remember the accident?"

"I don't know. I didn't say anything about it except to tell him that he'd been hurt. I told him about the coma but not the paralysis. I'm not sure he understood any of it. He tired quickly and fell asleep. I waited to see if he woke up, but he didn't."

Rena took a deep breath. "That's good. I'll give him plenty of time to rest before I go over. Is the nurse going to contact Dr. Leoni?"

"Yes, he's scheduled to come by tomorrow afternoon. I left instructions for the morning shift to let me know the specific time so I can be there."

Rena stepped away from the wall. Her heart had calmed down. Ezra rubbed his chin.

"Rena," her father-in-law said slowly, "Now that Baxter is beginning to recover, I hope we can put aside our differences. I disagreed with you about terminating Baxter's life support, and my opinion has proven right. But I think we should open the lines of communication between us. I've been taking care of Baxter's business interests and realize that I need to let you know what's going on and get your input as his wife."

Ezra's overture baffled Rena. It was so contrary to their previous relationship and completely at odds with Jeffrey's portrayal of his father selfishly manipulating Baxter's business affairs. She stared at him for several seconds.

"What have you been doing for Baxter?" she managed.

"Maintaining the status quo, except when a sale or transfer was the best thing to do for his long-term needs. And yours."

Rena wasn't ready to instantly forgive and forget. "Why did you take the money out of my checking account after Baxter was hurt?"

"It was an unnecessary measure, and I'm sorry."

"And everything else Baxter owned at the time of the accident is still in his name?"

"Yes, though I've transferred some investments. We're always looking at new ventures, acquisitions, and developments. Baxter's net worth has actually increased a little in the past few months. I know you don't have a lot of experience in business, so if you like I can pass along information directly to your lawyer. Ralph Leggitt tells me she has a good grasp of business and can advise you."

"That might be a good idea. Do you and Jeffrey make the decisions?"

"Jeffrey isn't involved in everything, but much of what we do is linked. Baxter wasn't as interested in the business as Jeffrey."

Rena knew Ezra's statement about Baxter was true. Her husband always preferred a wine magazine to a corporate balance sheet.

"But does Jeffrey know what you've done with Baxter's stuff?"

As soon as she asked the question, Rena regretted it. Ezra raised his eyebrows.

"Have you been talking to Jeffrey about it?"

"A little bit," she admitted, her face turning red, "but I don't know very much. Please don't mention it to him. I don't want either one of you mad at me."

Rena squeezed her eyes shut and summoned a weak tear. She opened them slowly, uncertain whether she could face Ezra's wrath. He greeted her with compassion.

"Don't worry. I'll keep this conversation to myself, and I suggest you do the same. In fact, keep the lines of communication open with Jeffrey and let me know what he thinks."

Rena nodded. Ezra took out a business card and wrote a phone number on the back.

"This is one of my private lines. Call me anytime."

Her mind reeling, Rena slowly closed the door behind her father-in-law. When she turned around, she clapped her hand over her mouth to stifle a scream.

It was Baxter.

He was wearing one of his favorite golf shirts and khaki pants. He looked at her, shrugged with a slight smile, and disappeared.

16

Hear not my steps, which way they walk,
for fear the very stones prate of my whereabout.
MACBETH, ACT 2, SCENE 1

When Alexia arrived at the office Monday morning, Gwen's vehicle was already in the parking lot. Alexia parked beside her with a sense of relief. Since leaving Leggitt & Freeman, Alexia had been like a car that wasn't firing on all cylinders, and the secretary's support would make everything run more smoothly. She went inside, deposited a large bouquet of fresh-cut flowers in a stylish vase on Gwen's desk, and walked up front, where she found Gwen introducing herself to other members of Rachel's staff. Alexia laughed.

"I didn't realize I was getting a different Gwen Jones from the one who ate lunch with me at Cousin Bert's," she said. "You're changing hair color faster than most women do shoes."

Gwen turned and smoothed her hair, now short and deep brunette.

"This really is my natural color, and I'm going to stick with it. I took my beautician a picture of myself as a little girl and told her to match it. This is also what I looked like when I married my second husband. He was the best of the lot. What do you think?"

Alexia nodded. "It looks good. Mature and intelligent."

Gwen frowned, "I was hoping for sexy."

"Someone else will have to be the judge of that."

"I think you look great," said a cute young receptionist. "I bet you're older than my mom, but you look a lot younger."

"Don't tell me your mother's age," Gwen responded quickly. "I'd rather savor the compliment as it stands."

Alexia turned toward her office.

Gwen followed her after giving a parting wave to the other women. "I've got to go to work," she said over her shoulder. "Alexia is a real slave-driver, but I'll be back later when she goes to court and tell you the first chapter of my life story."

Rachel Downey had hired two men to clean out the storage room across from Alexia's office and turn it into a cozy secretarial space. Gwen walked in and saw the bouquet on the desk beside the computer screen. She touched the soft petals.

"Thanks, Alexia, they're beautiful."

"I'll try to keep the place bright until we move to our new office with multiple windows. Will you get claustrophobic in here?"

"How many windows did I have at Leggitt & Freeman?"

"None."

"I only felt claustrophobic when Leonard surrounded my desk with files."

"I haven't even dictated anything yet, but I'm closing on the King Street house this afternoon, so there may be some last-minute stuff to do."

"I'm here if you need me. Don't be in a rush. I'll be happy setting up." Gwen pulled open the bottom drawer of her desk. It was empty. "Plenty of room in the candy pantry. I'll make a run during lunch."

"When Rachel arrives, find out if there is anything she needs you to do."

"Sure, or I'll see if I can help any of the girls up front."

Seeing Gwen at her desk, Alexia felt a sudden surge of emotion. She'd not allowed herself to think about the day her friend would join her, and now that it was a reality, the threat of tears caught her off guard. Alexia cleared her throat and turned away.

"I have some calls to make," she said.

Still looking down, Gwen didn't notice.

Alexia went into her office and closed the door. After clearing her head, she located Byron Devereaux's phone number in Rena's file and called the detective. She reached his voice mail and left a message requesting a call back without furnishing any details. She dictated letters in several files and interrogatories in a divorce case involving a chef at a local restaurant. Her intercom buzzed.

"Who is it?" she asked the young receptionist.

"Sean Pruitt, a lawyer in Charleston."

The name didn't sound familiar to Alexia. It wasn't unusual for her to litigate with Charleston attorneys, and she knew most of the ones who specialized in divorce cases. She left the phone on speaker and pushed the talk button.

"Alexia Lindale."

"Sean Pruitt in Charleston. Are you the lawyer representing Mrs. Rena Richardson?"

The lawyer's accent was as deeply steeped in Charleston as a tea bag in boiling spring water. He also sounded young, and the billowing intonation seemed almost contrived.

"Yes," Alexia answered with a slight smile. "What can I do for you?"

"I've been appointed by Judge Moreau to represent Henry L. Quinton, and I'd like to talk to your client about the theft of her car."

"What are the charges against Quinton?"

"Felony-murder. There's a chance the solicitor may seek the death penalty, seeing the murder involves a police officer."

Pruitt sounded casual about the responsibility of defending a man's life.

"There's not much my client can tell you," Alexia said. "The car was in her driveway with the keys in it. She noticed that it was missing in the early afternoon and called the police. The car was recovered in a parking lot in north Charleston within a couple of hours."

"I don't doubt that's an accurate summary, but would it be possible for her to tell me about it in her own words?"

Alexia tapped her pen on the top of her desk.

"Do you handle a lot of criminal cases?" she asked.

"Only when the judge makes me," Pruitt answered.

"What do you do the rest of the time?"

"I'm building a robust personal-injury practice."

Alexia wasn't impressed. Personal-injury lawyers included the best and worst of the legal profession, and the number of tadpoles swimming at the edge of the pond greatly exceeded the few who became big frogs sitting on a water lily. If Pruitt was any good, she'd have heard about him. He was probably a hack trying to pretend he was the descendant of an Old South barrister.

"In the criminal cases you've handled, can you name a time in which it was in the victim's favor to agree to a pretrial interview with the defendant's lawyer?"

"Almost every case."

"You're kidding."

"No. After I talk to the victim and tell my client the nature of the testimony that will come to light in court, I persuade most of them to enter a plea agreement with the State. The victim doesn't have to come to court to testify, and I consider that a plus."

"And if your client doesn't enter into a plea agreement?"

"Uh, that hasn't happened very often."

Alexia sat up straighter. "You mean the defendants in every criminal case you've handled have entered into a plea agreement?"

"If that's what I've recommended. I've only had to try a few of them."

Alexia wanted to ask about the outcome of the trials, but etiquette held her tongue. She was shocked that Judge Moreau had assigned a green lawyer to a potential capital murder case. Why invite a posttrial habeas corpus petition before the trial even started?

Pruitt continued, "Of course, if the State seeks the death penalty, another lawyer will be appointed to help me, but for now, Quinton is my baby."

Alexia hesitated and then saw an opportunity.

"I'll talk to my client about it. If we agree to an interview, I'd like to talk to Quinton."

"I have no problem with that," Pruitt answered without hesitation. "If you cooperate with me, then I'll work with you. Here's my number. Call me as soon as you talk to Mrs. Richardson."

Alexia wrote down Sean's number and hung up the phone, mystified. Sean Pruitt was either incompetent or unreasonably self-confident.

After lunch, Alexia finalized the purchase of the King Street property. The owners lived in New Jersey and closed by giving a power of attorney to Rachel Downey. The Realtor signed the deed transferring the property to Alexia with a flourish after they'd waded through a small mountain of disclosure forms, waivers, and documents required for the loan. They walked out of the bank together. Rachel slipped the check for her commission in her purse.

"I talked to Gwen," Rachel said. "It will be fun having both of you around, but I'll miss you when your renovation is finished. You have such a glamorous life."

Alexia gave Rachel a puzzled look. "What's glamorous about it? I represent my clients and go home."

"Oh, I heard about your minister friend's impromptu performance Saturday night," Rachel responded with a knowing wink. "He saved the day, and you were there leaning on his arm in a silver dress and an emerald necklace."

Alexia laughed. "How did you find out?"

"Gwen Jones is not my only spy. It takes several people to keep tabs on you."

"Your spy is accurate except for the part about me leaning on his arm."

"That's not what I heard. You whisked him out of there before someone else tried to take him home for a pet. The more I hear about Reverend Morgan, the more impressed I am that you saw his potential."

"Well, I hope he's as good with a hammer and paintbrush as he is with a piano," Alexia added. "It's time to get busy with the renovations."

"I'm sure he's a Monet. If you need any ideas with colors and fabrics, let me know. I'd love to see that old house sparkle."

———

Late that afternoon, Alexia cleared a block of time to call Rena Richardson. With her office door open, she could hear the welcome sound of Gwen pecking away on the computer keyboard. Alexia was reaching for the phone when the receptionist buzzed her.

"Rena Richardson is here to see you," she said.

Although some of Alexia's clients had a bad habit of showing up without an appointment, Rena hadn't been one of them. Alexia walked to the waiting area. Rena was sitting on the edge of a chair with an anxious look on her face. When Alexia entered the room, she jumped up.

"I need to talk to you," she said. "It's important."

Alexia opened the door to the smaller of the two conference rooms adjacent to the waiting area. Inside, the two women sat down at a round cherry table with four chairs. A decorative vase sat in the middle of the table.

"What is it?" Alexia asked.

"Baxter is talking."

"That's an improvement."

"No, it's not," Rena replied. "He's talking nonsense. Dangerous nonsense."

"What do you mean?"

Rena spoke rapidly. "It started yesterday. He talked to Ezra first. I wasn't there and don't know exactly what he said, but Ezra told me it was just stuff about the family, nothing about the accident. Then he told me that Baxter didn't remember me. That hurt, but considering his injury I guess I shouldn't take it personally. Anyway, I waited an hour or so and went over to see him myself. When I stood by his bed and called his name, he opened his eyes and stared at me. It was obvious that he didn't recognize me. It was spooky. I stayed for a while and talked to the nurse on duty. The nurse went to the kitchen with his tray of food, and I stepped closer to the bed to say good-bye."

Rena glanced at the closed door of the conference room and lowered her voice. "When I leaned over the bed, he opened his eyes and glared at me with the most hateful expression you can imagine. It was exactly the way he looked at me when he attacked me at the cliff. He made a horrible sound in his throat. Alexia, the rage bottled up inside him is still there, waiting to get out. It was so scary that I ran out."

"I thought you said he was talking nonsense," she said.

"I'm not finished. I didn't stop running until I got back home and slammed the front door behind me. I leaned against the wall with my heart pounding out of my chest. I didn't want to ever go back to the cottage again. And then the nurse called. She said Baxter was asking for me. I didn't know what to do. I tried to call you, but you weren't here."

"I was at the bank."

Rena continued, "I mean, he's paralyzed and can't hurt me, but I'm going to have nightmares about the way he looked at me. The nurse's aide kept calling, so I went back. I didn't want the nurse to hear anything, so I told her to leave us alone. Baxter's eyes were closed, but when I came closer and told him I was there, he opened them and looked up at me."

"With the same look?"

"No, he was calmer, but that's when he began talking nonsense."

"What kind of nonsense?"

"He asked me 'why, why, why' over and over in a scratchy voice, but I knew what he was saying. And then he said, 'why did you do it, why did you do it' about five or six times. That's when I got scared. The nurse didn't hear him, but if Ezra finds out and calls that detective with the horrible scar—"

"Giles Porter."

"Yeah. I know Baxter is confused, and what he says shouldn't give anyone a reason to accuse me of anything." Rena's face flushed red. "But I don't know what might happen! It's not fair! I'm the victim! Something has gone wrong in Baxter's mind, but you know that detective would believe him instead of me!"

In Alexia's mind, the most incriminating implication of Baxter's questions pointed to the possible affair between Rena and Jeffrey. While morally wrong, adultery wasn't a criminal offense that would interest the Mitchell County detective.

"Don't jump to conclusions, Rena. Those words could mean a lot of things. Why are you so afraid?"

Rena gaped at Alexia. "Are you kidding? You don't see what he's trying to do?"

Alexia shook her head. "Tell me. Honestly, I don't get it."

Rena stared at Alexia for a few seconds. She reached forward and touched the side of the vase. Her hand trembled for a few seconds then stilled.

"Okay. Maybe you're right. I lost control and assumed something crazy. It's just that I've been worried out of my mind that Baxter would accuse me of pushing him off the cliff as a way to avoid responsibility for attacking me. I thought that's what he was trying to do. He's rich and has the support of his family. I'm a poor girl from the mountains with no one to speak up for me."

"Except for me."

Rena looked at Alexia again.

Alexia spoke in a level tone of voice. "You should have told Porter the truth when he first interviewed you, but that's in the past. There isn't any reason for you to be afraid of a criminal prosecution. Baxter sounds like he's still incoherent. If he says something and people ask you questions about it, we'll deal with it then."

"I feel so insecure."

"That's understandable."

"And I hate it when people hassle me. It was horrible when Porter kept interrogating me. He asked the same questions over and over. He was trying to trick me."

"If he ever talks to you again, I'll be there." Alexia leaned back in her chair. "Try to calm down."

Rena ran her fingers through her hair. "I know too much worry can drive a person crazy."

"Together, we'll face whatever comes up."

Rena managed a weak smile. Alexia leaned forward.

"Speaking of interviews," Alexia said. "The lawyer appointed to represent Henry Quinton called me this morning. He wants to talk to you about the theft of the car."

"Tell him no."

"That's what I started to do, but I need to tell you something that might change your mind."

Alexia told her about the incident with the gray van.

"You think he was stalking you?" Rena asked skeptically.

"I don't know, but I'd like to find out. Quinton's lawyer agreed to let me talk to his client if I let him talk to you. This lawyer is inexperienced and wants to convince Quinton to plead guilty. If that happens, you won't have to testify in court. You don't know anything except that the car was stolen, so I don't think there is any harm in answering a few questions. It would be similar to the interview with Detective Devereaux. And of course, I would be there with you."

"No," Rena said.

Surprised, Alexia asked, "Why not?"

Rena shrugged. "I don't want to do it."

Rena was Alexia's ticket to Quinton. She started to argue, but stopped. She couldn't pressure Rena to do something designed primarily for Alexia's purposes.

"Okay, but if you change your mind, let me know."

Rena stood up. "I won't. And I want to file for divorce right away. The sooner the better."

———

After Rena left, Alexia tried to reach Sean Pruitt, but he wasn't available. She tried Ted in hopes of making arrangements to begin the renovations, but she had to leave a message in his voice mail. Shortly before Alexia left to go home, the receptionist buzzed her.

"Rena Richardson is on the phone."

Alexia punched the button for her speaker phone.

"I've changed my mind," Rena said abruptly.

"About what?"

"About talking to Quinton's lawyer. Go ahead and set it up."

"Why?"

"I've thought about it some more since leaving your office. There are some questions I want you to ask Quinton."

"What kind of questions?"

"I'll write them down and give them to you later."

"Okay, but I can't guarantee that his lawyer will let me ask them or that Quinton will answer."

"I know."

Alexia didn't want to call Sean Pruitt twice—once to agree and then to back out.

"Are you sure you won't change your mind again?" she asked.

"No. Set it up."

17

The hidden soul of harmony.
JOHN MILTON

Ted's cell phone beeped as he drove through a dead zone northwest of Santee for his meeting with Sarah Locklear. He'd check the message later. Ted had contacted the nurse through her agency and suggested they get together for supper. Sarah accepted immediately. On the seat of Ted's truck, a scrap of paper bore the name and address of the restaurant she had suggested for their meeting.

Farther inland, the houses became smaller, the driveways unpaved, and the cars older. Sandy soil costing barely a hundred or a thousand dollars per acre replaced the exorbitantly priced oceanfront property. As the distance to the shore increased, the wealth and extravagance dissipated like a wave retreating from the beach.

A billboard on the right-hand side of the road announced his arrival at the Southside Restaurant. He applied the brakes and turned into the diner's parking lot in a cloud of dust. A fresh coat of lime-green paint brightened the exterior of the wooden building. He saw Sarah's car near the front door and parked nearby. Ted ran a comb through his hair before he got out of his truck.

Inside, the nurse, dressed casually in jeans and a yellow shirt, her dark hair in a French braid, sat alone at a table. She waved when he entered, and he joined her, pulling out a cane-back chair. A large chalkboard attached to the wall above an open pass-through to the kitchen announced the day's specials. Sarah sipped an iced tea. As soon as Ted sat down, a small, older woman with her gray hair in a tight bun came up to the table.

"Is everybody here now?" she asked.

Sarah nodded.

"What do you want to eat?" the waitress asked.

"Uh, is there a menu?" Ted responded.

"First-timer, eh?" the woman said. A plastic name badge identified her as Nancy. "I'll let Sarah tell you how it works. How do you want your tea?"

"Sweet," Ted replied. "With extra lemon."

When the waitress departed, Ted asked, "No chance to mull over a menu?"

Sarah pointed to the blackboard. "Get one of the specials. They have other choices, but the best food is always on the chalkboard, and the cook doesn't like special orders."

Ted scanned the three meat entrees and a variety of vegetables.

"Any recommendations?"

"It's the best chicken-fried steak this side of Dallas, and the sautéed squash is perfect. All the vegetables are good except the mashed potatoes. They're runny."

"Have you been to Dallas?"

"Yes. I worked at Baylor University Medical Center on the ortho-pedic floor for five years."

Nancy was lurking in the corner of Ted's peripheral vision, and when he looked away from the chalkboard, she returned to his elbow. Sarah gave her order, adding okra with tomatoes to the squash and chicken-fried steak.

"Same for me," Ted added, "except I'd like cornbread instead of a roll."

The waitress left, and Ted leaned forward.

"Is your house nearby?"

"A couple of miles. I live with my aunt. She had a stroke two years ago, and I moved here to help take care of her."

"No family of your own?"

"Three brothers, four sisters, and more nieces and nephews than I can keep up with, but no children of my own. How about you?"

"I've been divorced for years and have a daughter in her twenties. She's a musician in New York."

"Pianist?"

"No, she plays the viola."

Ted squeezed the juice from two lemon slices into his tea.

"Thanks for coming," he said. "I've been thinking a lot about Baxter Richardson and have so many questions that I'm not sure where to start."

Sarah's tone turned professional. "Well, he had a fracture at C4-5 of the cervical spine that caused damage to his spinal cord and resulted in the paralysis—"

"No," Ted interrupted. "Not the medical part. I want to know about you and your singing."

Sarah looked surprised. She took a sip of tea. "Oh, it's not too complicated. I've been singing since I was a little girl."

"Where did you grow up?"

"I'm a Lumbee from Robeson County, North Carolina."

"Lumbee?"

Sarah touched her brown arm. "We're the largest Native American group in North Carolina. The Cherokees live in the western mountains; we live in the southeastern part of the state not far from the coast. Some folks believe we're descended from the survivors of the Lost Colony who intermarried with the Cheraw, but it's impossible to prove. Many family names in the area sound English: Locklear, Oxendine, Revels, Carter, Briggs . . ."

"Any Morgans?"

Sarah smiled. "Not that I remember."

"And the singing?"

"My father was a hog farmer and part-time preacher. Our family often sang in church. When I was a little girl they let me support the lead, but as soon as my voice matured, I started singing alto. I can't remember a time when there wasn't a song in my heart. It's not always been a happy tune, but it's wrapped up in who I am. I still sing in the choir when I'm not working and in ensembles if I'm asked to participate."

Ted nodded. "I can relate. How long have you been a nurse?"

"About twenty-five years. I was always playing nurse when one of my brothers or sisters was ill. If they were all healthy, I'd find a pet or animal to take care of. Everyone told me I should be a nurse, and when I went to college at UNC Pembroke, that's the direction I took."

"Do you sing for your patients?"

"Occasionally I'll hum or sing softly. It seems to calm people who are agitated. But what we did the other night in Santee was a new experience for me."

The waitress brought the food. The chicken-fried steak covered a third of the plate and was topped with a broad band of white gravy speckled with black pepper.

"I'm glad I had a light lunch." Ted said.

Ted cut into the meat. It was crispy on the outside and just the right thickness on the inside. He took a bite. The meat was juicy, the gravy slightly salty.

"Mmm. This is good."

Sarah pointed her fork at the chalkboard. "There's a reason they call it a special."

They ate in silence for a few moments.

Sarah cut off a piece of meat. "What about you? Have you played your keyboard for a lot of sick people?"

"No, this is my first serious attempt. Honestly, I'd hoped the results would be more dramatic."

"He's waking up."

Ted shrugged. "That could be explained by natural improvement."

"Possibly, but the presence of the Lord was in the room when you played, and the next day Baxter opened his eyes. One of the nurses called me today and told me he is beginning to talk. That's pretty amazing improvement, considering the severity of his injuries."

Ted ate a bite of squash. "Alexia Lindale told me the same thing. For the past year, I've been thinking that God can use worship in more ways than we realize."

"What do you mean?"

Ted put down his fork and held out his calloused hands with the palms up. "I believe the universe is in the hands of the Lord as Creator. If that's true, then there is a divine connection between sounds, words, pictures, music, and all other forms of creativity that are submitted to his authority. Our job is to find practical ways in which God can use our creative gifts to advance his kingdom on earth. I pray with words, but I also pray with my music. I play music to worship, but I also want to play to heal. I want to go into the uncharted realms of worship." He suddenly stopped. "Do you think that's nuts?"

"If I did would it change your mind?"

"No."

"Then keep talking. I'm interested."

"Late at night, I'll go alone into the sanctuary, open my Bible, sit down at the piano, and play melodies that I believe are musical expressions of the truth on the page. At other times, I'll play a few notes and let them linger in the air like incense. When they're gone, I'll play a few more. On and on it goes while my spirit breathes air from another realm."

Sarah's dark eyes narrowed, and she looked past Ted's shoulder.

"I understand." She nodded thoughtfully. "I've been to those places, although I didn't try to analyze it like you're doing."

"I'm not trying to analyze—"

"Don't get defensive," Sarah interrupted with a slight smile. "Understanding what God is doing doesn't threaten freedom of the spirit. It just helps us cooperate with him."

"Sorry, you know what I'm talking about. Few people have a clue, and I'm hesitant to say anything to anybody."

"Musicians are supposed to think outside the box."

"Maybe a musician in New York, but not a music minister in South Carolina. My box is small, and my senior pastor thinks I should stay in it. He doesn't have any idea what I'm doing with Baxter Richardson."

"That's not a problem."

"Why not?"

Sarah lifted her chin. "If God does a miracle in Baxter's life, the Richardson family will come to the church and give so much money that everyone on the staff will get a big raise with enough left over to hire assistants to do all the real work."

Ted laughed. "That's a plan John Heathcliff would support, especially if it included unlimited green fees at his favorite golf courses."

The waitress returned to the table. "Any dessert?" she asked.

Sarah asked for a box to take home the remains of her meal. Ted looked at the chalkboard. No desserts were listed.

"What kind of desserts?" he asked.

Nancy looked at Sarah and rolled her eyes. "Peanut-butter pie or chocolate cake."

"Unless you hate peanut butter, get the pie," Sarah said. "It's a cream pie crowned with meringue, and a thin layer of peanut butter is mixed into the crust."

"Done, with two forks."

Sarah held up her hand. "Ministers are supposed to help us flee temptation. My body doesn't metabolize pie as efficiently as it used to."

"You can sing away the calories."

While they waited for the pie, Ted asked, "What do you think we should do next with Baxter?"

"Let's continue doing the same things, while being open to a new direction. Do you know whether he is a Christian?"

"No."

"Have you ever played the Gospel?"

"Not without words."

Sarah's eyes glowed. "Oh, I'll provide the words. I've never seen a dramatic physical healing as the result of music, but I've witnessed people with no hope of survival receive life everlasting in response to a song."

It was dark when Ted left the restaurant. The peanut-butter pie exceeded expectations, and he was more convinced than ever that Sarah Locklear was a remarkable woman. Never had he met anyone with spiritual DNA so similar to his.

———

The following morning, Alexia left a message for Sean Pruitt. Within thirty minutes he called her back.

"You can interview Rena Richardson," Alexia told him. "I'd like to talk to Quinton on the same day."

"How about this afternoon at my office in Charleston? After I talk to Mrs. Richardson, we can go to the jail and meet with my client."

Surprised, Alexia glanced down at her calendar. It was clear after 2:00 PM. Rena had said she wanted to meet as soon as possible.

"Uh, I'll call Rena and find out if that works for her."

"My client isn't going anywhere," Pruitt replied in his aristocratic voice. "His schedule isn't an issue."

"Does he know I want to talk to him?"

"Not yet. I'll spend some time with him before you ask him any questions."

"What if he won't talk to me? I don't want to waste a trip."

"Oh, I'll encourage him to tell you anything that doesn't prejudice our defense. It shouldn't be a problem."

It was risky, but Alexia wanted access to Quinton, and Rena had ordered her to set up a meeting.

"Okay. Where is your office?"

Alexia wrote down the address and directions to an area heavily inhabited by lawyers, near the old courthouse.

"I'll see you around three," she said. "If you don't hear from me in the next hour, it means we'll be there."

"I'll look forward to it."

When she hung up, Alexia called Rena and told her about the immediate opportunity.

"That will work for me," Rena said briskly.

"Do you want to ride together?" Alexia asked. "That way you can let me know the questions you want me to ask Quinton, and we can review what you're going to tell his lawyer."

"Sure."

Alexia gave her a time to be at the office.

———

Shortly before lunch, Ted returned Alexia's call.

"Sorry I haven't been available," he said.

"No problem, I've been busy. I closed on the King Street house yesterday, and I'm ready to get started on the renovation. Could you meet me for a few minutes after lunch? I have to leave for Charleston around two."

"Sure. Where?"

"On King Street."

Ted's truck was in the driveway when Alexia arrived. The small house was a plain-looking 1950s bungalow, but Alexia's imagination could see potential for a chic law office. Ted was inspecting the seam where the chimney connected to the house. Alexia joined him.

"Is it okay?" she asked.

"Yes, I checked it before you made your offer. Have you decided on a new color for the exterior? This gray has got to go."

"Pink."

Ted nodded without smiling. "That narrows it some, but there are still a lot of shades of pink: pale, rose, neon. You'll need to view some paint chips and get specific."

"Pale pink for the siding with hot pink for the shutters. From now on pink will strike fear in the heart of every deadbeat ex-husband within twenty miles of Santee."

"And give you a nickname—Santee Barbie."

"That won't work," Alexia replied. "You're the artist. What color do you recommend?"

Ted looked over the stretch of wall between the front door and the end of the house. It was the longest section of wooden surface, broken only by a single window. He motioned with his hand.

"This long section would be perfect for a mural of you cross-examining a witness. I could work the window into the picture as part of the courtroom. It would be unique."

Alexia nodded. "And I'd be called 'the billboard lawyer.'"

"No, that's already taken by those two guys who handle personal injury and worker's compensation cases with the big signs on Palmetto Street and Highway 17. Yours would be better. Their suits don't look right and the heads are too big for their bodies."

"But that's the way they really look."

"Well, your mural wouldn't need retouching to be beautiful."

Alexia smiled. "Thanks, but I'm not tempted. Seriously, what do you think about cream with sandstone-colored shutters?"

Ted walked over to his truck and returned with a card of paint colors. He pointed to one that he'd circled.

"What about this for the base? I already picked it out."

Alexia took the card from him and held the rich creamy color against the house.

"This is why I hired you," she said approvingly. "Let's move inside."

As they walked through the house, Alexia talked and Ted took notes.

"Rachel Downey offered to help me with the design," Alexia said. "Have you ever worked with her?"

"No, I'd never met her before the day I did the inspection."

"She's very interested in you. She knew all about what happened in Charleston the other night."

"How did she find out?"

"I'm not sure. There must have been other people from Santee at the benefit."

Alexia glanced down at her watch. "I've got to go in a few minutes. I'm going back to Charleston myself. The lawyer representing the man who stole Rena's car has agreed to let me interview him."

"Isn't that unusual?"

"Yes, but so is the attorney. I've never met him, but I can tell from our phone calls that he's a bit off-the-wall."

"Which means?"

"Usually, 'incompetent,' but I'll know for sure after today."

They walked out of the house together. When they reached the front stoop, Ted's cell phone rang, and he answered it.

"What night are you working?" he asked then paused. "Good. I'll be there. See you then."

He put his phone back into the front pocket of his shirt.

"Who was that?" Alexia asked.

"Sarah Locklear. We met for supper last night. She'll be working with Baxter on the third shift Wednesday. We're going to meet around midnight."

Alexia fell a step behind Ted as they approached his truck. He looked over his shoulder at her as he opened the door.

"Will you be able to make it?" he asked.

"Uh, other than sleeping, I don't have any other pressing plans at midnight on Wednesday."

"Good."

Ted waved as he backed his truck out of the driveway. Alexia didn't notice. She was mulling over Ted's mention of his restaurant rendezvous with Sarah Locklear. As she drove to her office for her meeting with Rena Richardson, she looked at but did not see the familiar sights of Santee passing her by.

18

The true way to be deceived is to think
oneself more clever than others.
LA ROCHEFOUCAULD

Alexia mulled over the reason for Ted's contact with Sarah Locklear. She had no doubt where it would lead. The nurse was strikingly beautiful, musically gifted, spiritually mature, and closer in age to the minister than Alexia was. If all the relevant data about Ted and Sarah was fed into a computer dating service, their names would flash onto the screen next to a five-star rating for relational success. Alexia felt like a ninth-grade schoolgirl watching a senior quarterback walk away with the captain of the cheerleading squad. She bit her lip in anger and hurt as she pulled into Rachel Downey's parking lot. Rena's car was already there. Alexia pushed her feelings aside. She had to focus on the task at hand.

When Alexia opened the door, she saw Rena sitting on the edge of a chair in the reception area. She'd twisted the tissue in her hand into a thin white rope.

"I need to get the file from my office," Alexia said. "I'll be ready to go in a minute."

"Wait!" Rena called out, picking up a videotape from the table beside her chair. "You have to watch this tape before we leave."

Alexia stopped and came over to her. "What is it?"

Rena handed the tape to her. There were no markings on the outside.

Rena spoke in an intense whisper. "It has to do with the questions I want you to ask Quinton."

Alexia glanced down at her watch. "We need to leave in a few minutes so we won't be late. What's on it?"

"It's not long, but you have to see it before we go. I should have shown it to you before now, but I was afraid."

Alexia had encountered Rena's fears before. Some were reasonable, others harder to understand.

Alexia turned toward the receptionist.

"Does Rachel have a TV with a VCR here?"

The receptionist pointed toward one of the conference rooms. "There is one in a cabinet in the corner."

The tape in her hand, Alexia went into the room with Rena close behind. She leaned over, opened the cabinet doors, and turned on the TV.

"Are you going to give me a preview?" she asked.

"Just watch it," Rena replied as she sat down. "You'll see."

Alexia slid the tape into the machine and pressed the play button. A few seconds of gray snow was followed by a panorama shot of Rena's house. The front door opened and the camera zoomed in on Rena as she walked down the steps and got in her red convertible. She backed into the turnaround area near the cottage and drove down the driveway. The pictures followed her through two stop signs before losing her at a stoplight that changed to red as Rena zipped through it. The gray snow returned.

"So what?" Alexia asked. "You ran the stoplight on Vincent Street. Who shot the home movie?"

"Did you see the date and time on the bottom of the tape?"

Alexia had noticed the numbers but not connected them to a specific event.

"Yes."

Rena looked directly at Alexia. "The date on the tape is the day my car was stolen and driven to Charleston. The time is less than an hour before the police officer was killed."

Alexia's mental wheels whirled. "You told Detective Devereaux that you hadn't driven the car since early that morning."

"And that's the truth," Rena responded slowly and emphatically. "Someone has taken the video and inserted a date and time to make it look like I drove to Charleston instead of the thief."

"How did you get this?" Alexia asked sharply.

Rena sighed. "Jeffrey gave it to me. It's his way of blackmailing me into doing what he wants me to do with his father. Can you keep it for me without telling anyone?"

"Of course. It's as confidential as anything you tell me."

Rena relaxed slightly. "Good. I'm tired of looking at it."

Twenty questions immediately fought to the surface of Alexia's mind and clamored for answers. She hesitated and then selected an easy one.

"Do you know where Jeffrey got the tape?"

"I'm not sure, but I think Quinton was the one watching the house."

"That's what I thought," Alexia said under her breath.

"You thought he was watching me?" Rena asked with surprise.

Alexia shook her head. "No. Remember, I told you that I suspected he was watching me."

Alexia looked again at her watch. Even if they left immediately they would be late for the meeting with Pruitt.

"Let's talk in the car," she said. "This is going to be different than I suspected. I may not let Quinton's lawyer talk to you, especially if he has a copy of this tape."

"Jeffrey told me that Quinton doesn't know about it."

"But if Quinton shot the film—"

"I don't know that for sure," Rena interrupted. She put her head in her hands. "I don't know what to think except that I'm going to go crazy."

Alexia put her briefcase in the backseat of her car. In addition to the investigative file for the theft of Rena's car and her list of questions to ask Quinton, the briefcase now contained the videotape. She pulled around to the front of the building. Rena stood outside waiting for her. As soon as Rena got in the passenger seat, Alexia began her cross-examination.

"Why would Jeffrey blackmail you so that you would sue his father? You have plenty of reasons not to trust Ezra, not to mention the legal right to find out what he's done with Baxter's assets."

"Jeffrey is paranoid. He came up with this scheme to scare me so that he could make me do anything he wants."

Alexia was blunt. "What else does he want you to do?"

"I'm not sure. When we first talked in Greenville, Jeffrey acted nice and told me he would protect me. After he gave me a bunch of money when Ezra emptied my checking account, I felt better, but now I'm scared of him."

"Has he physically threatened you?"

"Not yet, but I can feel the same thing in him that I saw in Baxter's eyes at the waterfall."

Alexia suspended the interrogation before asking her next question. When she did, she spoke in a matter-of-fact tone.

"Have you and Jeffrey ever had a romantic relationship?" she asked.

Rena turned in her seat. Alexia glanced over and saw that her client's eyes were blazing.

"How dare you!" Rena screamed. "Why would you accuse me—"

"I'm sorry," Alexia interjected quickly. "Calm down. I should have asked if Jeffrey tried to hit on you. I didn't mean to insult you."

Rena faced forward like a pouting child, and Alexia could see out of the corner of her eye that she was still fuming. After a few seconds, Rena spoke in a softer but still angry voice.

"Why would you ask me that?"

Alexia couldn't see a way to keep going without causing Rena to sizzle.

"It was a stupid thing to say," she said. "Forget it. Help me understand why Jeffrey wants to pressure you."

"Don't ever say anything like that again."

Alexia turned onto the main coastal highway. Rena clammed up. They passed the deserted Beachcomber Club and drove for a couple of miles in silence.

"Because I know what he's doing," Rena said.

"Huh?"

"That's why Jeffrey is blackmailing me. I know things about his business that he doesn't want to come out in the open."

"What kind of things?"

"He's involved in something illegal."

Alexia waited.

In a moment, Rena continued, "Jeffrey is in a fight with his father for control and wants me to help him get the upper hand. That's why he wants us to sue the companies on the list he gave me. He thinks a lawsuit will cause Ezra to back off and let Jeffrey do what he wants to do."

Alexia immediately thought about her former bosses at Leggitt & Freeman and wondered what they might know about the inner workings of Richardson and Company. Ralph Leggitt and his partners loved money, but Alexia couldn't imagine them risking prison to make a few extra bucks.

"Did Jeffrey tell you anything about the companies that you haven't mentioned?"

"No. He provides information in tiny drips, and I didn't want to know very much."

"Baxter never told you?"

Rena looked out the window for a few seconds before answering.

"That's another thing I need to tell you. I found out that Baxter's family was doing something illegal and confronted him about it while we were hiking. I begged him to get out. I told him we could move somewhere else and start over. I've been poor before and would have been willing to live in a mobile home and work at a convenience store to escape the situation here. He became furious, asked me if I was going to tell the police. I told him that I loved him and wouldn't do anything to hurt him, but he went berserk. That's the reason for the fight. When I thought he died on the rocks, I came up with the story that he slipped because it was easier than telling the truth."

"Why didn't you tell me this before?"

"Whoever is working with the Richardsons wouldn't think twice about hurting me if I mess up their plans. I was trying to take care of everything on my own and not get you involved."

"Is there anything else you're not telling me?"

Rena shrugged. "I don't think so. I know you need the whole truth to help me. I'm sorry I didn't say anything before. It's a relief to get this out in the open."

They drove past a succession of manicured entrances to resort communities. Alexia was skeptical of Rena's story.

"And in case something happens to me," Rena said.

"What?"

"You need to know the truth in case something happens to me. I've been thinking about leaving town, forgetting about my rights to any money, and letting Ezra or Jeffrey take control of everything. If Baxter had died, I could have done it. Now, I have to figure out a way go on with my life. That's why I want to file for divorce, change my name, and move far away."

"Even if a court sets most of the money aside for Baxter's future medical needs?"

Rena turned slightly in her seat. "No matter what happens with the money, I have to get out. Would you stay in this situation if you were me?"

Alexia didn't answer. She wasn't sure Rena's tale contained a consistent strand of truth. Accusing the Richardson family of involvement in organized crime was far-fetched. Alexia's theory that Baxter and Rena fought over an affair, while less exotic, remained more plausible. Jeffrey would use the tape to keep Rena quiet in case he wanted to end their relationship without an untidy mess.

"What do you want to do about the videotape?" Alexia asked. "If Quinton's lawyer gets his hands on it, he will try to convince the solicitor to dismiss the charges against his client and indict you."

"You have to protect me. That's why I showed it to you. You saw what happened when that awful detective harassed me at the hospital."

Alexia hated it when clients wanted guarantees in advance. "We can have it analyzed to find out if the date was added later."

"Of course it was added later," Rena said.

"Then testing will prove it. In the meantime, let's see what Quinton will tell us. His fingerprints were on the car for a reason, but if neither you nor Quinton drove it to Charleston on the day the officer was killed, we need to find out who did and why."

They reached the outskirts of Charleston. Touches of urban sprawl had crept up the coast as the city spilled beyond the peninsula bounded by the Ashley and Cooper Rivers. The newer areas were no different from any other suburban region: strip centers, restaurant chains, and movie theaters. After penetrating the outer ring of modernity, Alexia and Rena moved down the peninsula into the older part of town, where the speed limit dropped to thirty-five miles per hour and the pace of life slowed by more than a century.

The Charleston County Courthouse, at the corner of Broad and

Meeting Streets, was the site of the provincial capitol while King George ruled the Lowcountry. Several years later, the citizens of Charleston gathered in the street below a second-story balcony and listened to a herald read the Declaration of Independence. The building yielded its place of prominence only after it burned at the time of the Constitutional Ratification Convention of 1788. Rebuilt in 1792, it settled comfortably into its more mundane role as the legal hub of the region.

Sean Pruitt's office was on Beaufain Street, a couple of blocks from the courthouse. Alexia parked on the street in front of a peach-colored structure with short white columns. The three-story building housed several law offices. At the top of the signage was a notation reading, "Sean P. Pruitt III, Attorney at Law."

"Here's our man," Alexia said. "Let me do the talking first. If I let him question you, keep your answers short and simple, just like you did when the detective interviewed you. The real questions will be for Quinton when I go to the jail."

"Okay."

They walked up a brick sidewalk and climbed five steps to the large front door, which was painted white with a shiny brass kick plate and a large lion's-head knocker. Alexia pushed it open and stepped into what had once been the foyer of a large home but now served as a common reception area. A young woman seated behind a fancy wooden desk and wearing a headset greeted them.

"We're here to see Sean Pruitt," Alexia said. "I'm Alexia Lindale."

"He'll meet with you in the conference room across the hall," the woman said, pointing to a pair of sliding pocket doors. "Please go in and have a seat."

Alexia pushed back the doors. The antique furniture and a hand-woven rug gave the room a museum feel. Rena sat down in a side chair and began to fidget. Alexia inspected the paintings on the wall. The most impressive was a nineteenth-century oil portrait of a man wearing a gray suit with stiff collar. She heard footsteps. Turning around, she faced a dark-haired young man about six feet tall with piercing blue eyes. He wore a white shirt, red tie, and gray slacks. He extended his hand toward Rena, who hurriedly stood up.

"Ms. Lindale?" he asked in the deep Southern voice Alexia had heard on the telephone.

"No, I'm Rena Richardson," she said.

Pruitt bowed slightly to Rena and shifted his gaze to Alexia. The clear, intelligent look in his eyes belied her first impression. Alexia stepped forward and firmly shook his hand.

"Thank you for coming," he said.

"Nice room," Alexia replied. "I was admiring the portrait. Who is it?"

"My great-grandfather, Harrison Pruitt. He built this house in 1880. His father lost everything in the War, but Harrison bounced back by importing cheap goods from the North during Reconstruction. Sort of a Southern carpetbagger."

Alexia raised her eyebrows. "And you're proud of that?"

"Just honest," Pruitt said with a shrug, "a scarce trait among families who have lived in Charleston as long as mine. Everybody pretends their ancestors had the integrity of Lee, the oratorical skills of Calhoun, and the military genius of Jackson. Any coffee or tea for you ladies?"

Alexia opted for tea. Rena declined.

While Pruitt was out of the room, Rena whispered, "He's kind of weird."

"Yeah," Alexia replied.

Pruitt returned with Alexia's tea, which he poured himself from a small silver teapot. He picked up a sugar cube with a set of tiny silver tongs and gave Alexia a questioning look. Alexia didn't know sugar cubes still existed in the modern universe. When she nodded, he plopped the cube into the steaming cup.

"Does your family own the house?" she asked.

"I do," Pruitt replied. "I live on the third floor and have an office on this floor. I rent space to the other lawyers. It's a convenient way to handle overhead."

Alexia took the cup and sipped gingerly.

Pruitt continued. "My mother is the antique collector. She sold her house in town and lives at Hilton Head. A lot of the stuff in here came from her side of the family."

Alexia set her cup on a matching white saucer and moved to business.

"What do you want to ask Ms. Richardson?"

"Oh, not too much." He looked at her. "I'd like a basic chronology of the events of the day. As you can imagine, I'm still at the preliminary stages of my investigation and don't have enough information to convince my client to plead guilty."

Alexia was perplexed, but it wasn't her job to convince Pruitt that his client deserved a competent defense. She looked at Rena and nodded.

"Go ahead," she said to Pruitt.

The lawyer slipped a small, handheld tape recorder from his pocket and put it on the table in front of Rena. Alexia held up her hand.

"No recordings. Take notes if you like."

Pruitt didn't argue. He turned over a new page on a legal pad and began asking Rena a series of questions very similar to the ones posed by Detective Devereaux. Rena performed well. Pruitt wrote Rena's name at the top of the page but didn't take any notes. As she listened, Alexia decided he either had a remarkable memory or was too lazy to remove the cap from his pen. Pruitt soon reached the part in the story where the police contacted Rena and told her that her car had been found.

"Just a few more questions," he said, "but first, a replenishment for your lawyer." He reached for her teacup.

"No, I'm fine," Alexia replied.

Pruitt set his blank legal pad on the table and stared past Rena at the portrait of his great-grandfather.

"Very well," he said. "Tell me about the videotape that shows you driving the red convertible less than an hour before Deputy Dixon's death."

All the color drained from Rena's face.

"Don't answer that," Alexia snapped. She turned to Pruitt. "You sandbagged me."

Pruitt remained calm. "I'm not sure what you mean, but I think it's highly relevant that I find out about this alleged tape. The solicitor's office doesn't know about it, and I don't have a copy, but my client insists a videotape exists that shows your client exiting her house, getting in the red convertible, driving down the street, and running a red light before giving the camera crew the slip. Across the bottom of the tape is the date and time it was filmed. Unless the car was hijacked on the way out of town, Mrs. Richardson is the only person who could have driven it to Charleston within the time period during which the crime occurred."

Stalling for time to decide what she should do, Alexia asked, "What else is Quinton telling you?"

"That he traveled to Savannah on the day in issue and has a witness to prove it. I don't know how or why Deputy Dixon died, but it wasn't my client's fault. Quinton was out of town all day, and, with or without the tape, I don't think the charges against him will stick. However, a zealous advocate wants to marshal all forces and mount a vigorous defense. Unless you give me a reason not to subpoena the tape from your client, that's exactly what I intend to do. Once it's in the solicitor's hands, the matter is out of my control. To me, it looks like someone could be interested in getting your client into a lot of trouble."

"Maybe so," Alexia replied, "but it's not something we can discuss at this time." She handed her card to Pruitt. "Ms. Richardson doesn't have anything else to say. If you decide to serve a subpoena, let me know."

Pruitt remained seated. "I take it you don't want to talk to Quinton?"

Alexia glanced at Rena, whose eyes were glazed over. She looked like she was about to faint. "Let's go," Alexia said.

"Wait!" Rena cried out. "This is all wrong!"

Alexia saw a dam about to break and didn't know what was behind it. She spoke in a sharp voice. "No, Rena! Not here, not now."

Rena stared straight ahead and spoke rapidly. "The policeman stopped me for speeding and told me to get out of the car. When I opened the car door, he tripped and fell backward. I had no idea he was dead. I was scared to death and drove off. It was an accident. That's it."

Alexia was furious but not with Pruitt. Rena had supposedly delivered a heartfelt revelation of the whole truth less than an hour before. That story was now thrown out the window. Her client's world of truth was pockmarked with sinkholes.

Pruitt rubbed his chin. "That would be a Class F felony for filing a false police report alleging the commission of a crime. You could go to jail for up to five years."

Rena looked up at him with desperate eyes. "I can't go to jail. I'd rather kill myself than be locked up. But I didn't do anything wrong."

Pruitt lowered his hand. "Or the solicitor might choose involuntary manslaughter due to criminal negligence, which also carries a five-year maximum sentence."

Rena covered her ears. "Stop! I don't want to hear any of this!"

Alexia didn't intervene. At this point damage control was impossible.

Pruitt continued in a matter-of-fact tone of voice, "Of course, the solicitor can charge you, but proving the case is another matter. Without the videotape or a confession, I doubt you'll ever be indicted. To me, your story about what happened with Deputy Dixon is plausible."

Alexia finally trusted herself to speak. "Why didn't you tell me this when you showed me the videotape at my office?" she asked sharply.

"I was afraid." Rena said through tears. Turning toward Pruitt, she pleaded, "You're a lawyer and what I tell you is confidential. You won't turn me in, will you?"

"I'm not your attorney, so I have no restriction of confidentiality."

"But you won't tell anyone because you believe me," Rena pleaded. "I mean, if you'd been in my place you might have done the same thing—"

"Don't go there," Pruitt interrupted in a surprisingly stern voice. "This is not about me, and I won't commit to anything until I find out what is going to happen to the charges against Quinton. If the murder and theft charges are dropped, then the tape is irrelevant. If not, there's nothing I can do to help you."

Rena sobbed. Alexia felt her face flush. Pruitt looked toward her and continued in a calm voice.

"You've kept your side of the bargain. Do you want to interview Quinton?"

Alexia bit her lip. Her wounded pride wanted to leave, but there might yet be something to salvage from Quinton. She glanced at Rena. Watching her client cry wouldn't accomplish anything positive.

"Yes," she said.

"Very well. Let's go to the jail."

"I want to stay here," Rena said through her sniffles.

"That's fine, so long as no one else needs the conference room," Pruitt replied. "I'll check the schedule."

Pruitt left the room, and Alexia fought the urge to berate Rena for lying to her and then blurting out her story in front of the other lawyer. However, there wasn't time to properly chastise her client, and Alexia waited in stoic, tight-lipped silence. Rena's emotions subsided, but she remained sitting with her head bowed and her shoulders slumped over. Alexia took a deep breath.

"Don't talk to anyone while I'm gone," she said curtly.

Rena didn't look up at her. "It was an accident, and I was scared. I drove the car to Charleston, abandoned it in a parking lot, and caught a taxi back to Santee."

Alexia stared at the top of Rena's blonde head and wished she could cut it open and sort the truth from the lies. The veracity of everything Rena had told her in the past was open to debate. Baxter. Jeffrey.

"We'll talk later," Alexia said.

19

'Tis strange—but true; for truth is always strange;
stranger than fiction.

LORD BYRON

P ruitt turned the dead bolt and held the door open for Alexia. She
stepped onto a landing above a very nice courtyard that featured a
fountain surrounded by carefully manicured bushes and an array of late
fall flowers. When they reached the fountain, Pruitt stopped and faced
her. The sound of water from the mouths of three marble birds perched
on top of the fountain tinkled in the background.

"Do you really think I had an obligation to tell you that a tape exon-
erating my client existed?" he asked.

"No," Alexia admitted. "And I can't—"

"Tell me what your client has told you," Pruitt completed Alexia's
thought. "But it's obvious she's been spinning tales, and now you don't
know what to believe."

Alexia didn't respond.

"Would you like my opinion?" Pruitt asked.

Alexia raised her eyebrows. "Maybe."

Pruitt put his hands in his pockets. "I believe her mea culpa is the
truth. Your client is not the type of person who would kill a police officer over a speeding ticket. The autopsy showed no evidence of assault,
the deputy was grossly overweight, and the drop-off to the shoulder of
the road was sufficient to cause someone to lose balance and fall."

"Okay, that's one man's opinion. But why would someone be filming
my client's activities in the first place?"

Pruitt picked a leaf from the water at the edge of the fountain. "I'll
let you ask Quinton that question, and he'll be free to answer."

Alexia shrugged. "I doubt your client will be as spontaneous as mine."

"I can assure you that I have not sandbagged your interview. You'll have a fair chance to find out everything you can."

"That's all I can ask."

Pruitt dropped the leaf on the brick walkway. "My car is in a garage behind the garden."

Pruitt led the way past a wrought-iron chair, covered with a cushion, nestled between two large potted plants.

"That's where I like to sit in the evenings and read until it gets dark," he said.

Alexia didn't respond. Pruitt's recreational habits were of no interest to her. They walked underneath an arbor and came to the back door of a small wooden garage. Inside was an unusual silver sports car with the silhouette of a horse on the back. Pruitt pressed a button that caused the opposite wall to flip up, revealing a back alley.

Alexia eyed the car. "What is that?"

"My car. I have to drive something to the grocery store."

Pruitt followed Alexia to the passenger side and opened the door for her. She sat mere inches above the ground. Pruitt slid behind the wheel and started the engine. It came to life with a muted roar. He pulled straight out of the garage into the alley.

"It's a Ferrari," he said. "I bought it used."

Alexia was not a college sorority girl impressed by a red Corvette, but riding in the Italian sports car was a different experience. It was impossible not to notice the heads that turned in their direction as they pulled onto the street.

"How do you handle the curiosity?" Alexia asked. "Everyone stares at you."

"By pretending that I'm someone famous."

"Who are you today?"

Pruitt downshifted smoothly, and the car slowed to stop at an intersection. "I'll let you choose."

Alexia glanced at the lawyer's silhouette. He was a handsome man but didn't remind her of anyone.

"Uh, how about Evgeny Kissin?"

Pruitt burst out laughing.

"Do you know who he is?" Alexia asked.

Pruitt turned a corner. Three young men standing on the sidewalk stopped talking and watched the car drive past.

"He's a Russian pianist with hair like a lion's mane, but I don't think those guys on the sidewalk would consider him famous."

"He is to me."

"I recently bought Kissin's new recording" Pruitt said. "It's an all-Brahms CD."

Alexia remembered reading a review of the performance on the Internet. She'd ordered it, but it hadn't arrived.

"How is it?" she asked.

"Excellent. He knows how to communicate emotion."

They passed the Francis Marion Hotel.

"Did you attend the benefit concert at the Francis Marion the other night?" Alexia asked.

"No, I was invited but couldn't make it. Were you there?"

"Yes."

Pruitt downshifted again. "I read in the paper about the substitute pianist from Santee. Do you know him?"

Alexia nodded. "Yes, uh, he's a friend. He did a great job."

Pruitt accelerated through two stoplights before the third one caught him.

"Quinton's alibi seems tight," Pruitt said while they waited for the light to turn green. "But I didn't know the truth until I saw your client's response to the mention of the videotape. That settled it for me, even before she told what really happened. Your client reminds me of a young woman I represented last year who was charged with manslaughter in the death of her husband. She changed her story so many times that I wondered if they shouldn't have charged her with murder. When the truth finally came out, she had a legitimate defense."

"What was it?"

"Her husband had been cheating on her with her best friend and punching my client in his spare time. One night he took the abuse to a new level and threatened her with a gun. He tripped and fell, and the gun went off, sending a bullet into the ceiling. She tried to grab the gun out of his hand. They fought, and it discharged again. The bullet went straight up through her husband's mouth and out the top of his head."

Alexia winced.

"At first, my client told the police it was a suicide, but when her prints showed up on the weapon, she changed her story and claimed she'd cleaned the gun for him earlier in the day. When tests showed gunpowder on her clothes, she hired me."

"Did she tell you the truth?"

"Not at first. She denied any problems in her marriage and concocted a conspiracy theory that the assistant solicitor, a fraternity brother of her late husband, had decided to frame her. It was nuts. The more I learned about the dynamics of her marriage, the more I suspected the killing was either in self-defense or an accident. One day, I walked through my accident theory with her. She broke down and cried. It was similar to what just happened with your client."

Pruitt turned a corner into the parking lot for the Charleston Correctional Center.

"Did you have to try the case?" Alexia asked.

"Yes, it was one of the few criminal cases in which my client didn't enter a plea. Each one of her conflicting confessions was read into evidence by the detective who interrogated her. On paper, she looked like a pathological liar, and I think it surprised the prosecutor when I called her to the witness stand to tell what really happened. The solicitor couldn't wait to begin his cross-examination. He tried to tear her apart with her prior inconsistent statements, but the more he harangued her, the more it looked like she had finally decided to tell the truth. The jury acquitted her after deliberating three or four hours. Jurors can usually smell the truth."

Alexia had also found jurors to be good judges of common-sense facts. Lawyers, caught in the niceties of legal maneuvering, often trusted in their own ability to thread the legal needle with a thin strand of evidence that jurors rarely accepted as strong enough to support a verdict.

The modern Charleston County Correctional Center dwarfed the ten cells and detoxification tank on the outskirts of Santee. The guard on duty at the initial checkpoint examined their identification and pressed an electrical switch that allowed Pruitt to push open a heavy, solid steel door. Alexia stepped into the hallway and waited for Pruitt to lead the way. They went through another steel door and arrived at a desk where a female officer radioed a guard in the cell block and informed him of Pruitt's request to see Quinton. She told them to wait in interview room number two. They passed through yet another steel door into a short hallway lined with interview rooms. Interview room two was a window-less space containing a small table and three plain metal chairs.

"Will you be here while I talk to him?" Alexia asked. "I'd like the same chance that you had to find out the truth."

Pruitt smiled slightly. "Mrs. Richardson didn't appear to be restricted by your presence, but I promise not to needlessly interfere."

The door opened and Quinton, wearing leg-irons, handcuffs, and an orange jumpsuit, was ushered in by a burly correctional officer.

"With a woman present, I'm going to leave on the restraints," the officer said.

"It's alright. She's an attorney," Pruitt responded.

The officer inspected Alexia. "Is she also representing him?"

"No."

"Then the restraints stay on."

The door banged shut. Quinton sat and put his manacled hands on the table in front of him.

"They don't give accused cop-killers much slack in here," he said in a nasal New Jersey accent.

Alexia glanced down at the prisoner's hands. She noted his neatly trimmed fingernails, clean-shaven face, and tidy hair. He certainly didn't have the look of a deranged murderer.

"Before Ms. Lindale asks you any questions," Pruitt began. "Let me tell you what her client, Mrs. Richardson, just told me."

Alexia listened again to Rena's admission of fault. It brought back a taste of the frustration she'd felt at Pruitt's office. When his lawyer finished, Quinton turned to Alexia.

"Do you have copy of this tape? It's not right for me to be locked up for something I didn't do."

Pruitt responded before Alexia spoke. "I'll subpoena the tape if we need it. My first step is to present your alibi evidence to the solicitor's office. If that works, we won't need the tape. However, even if the theft and murder charges are dropped, you'll still be facing assault charges because of the incident involving the detective at the Beachcomber Club."

Quinton responded with a shrug. "One of the other guys knocked him on the head. He was snooping around my van. It looked like he was trying to steal it."

"Are those charges pending in Charleston County?" Alexia asked.

Pruitt nodded. "Yes, we waived jurisdiction and venue in Santee so everything could be handled here." He spoke to Quinton. "I told Ms. Lindale that she could ask you some questions."

Quinton looked at Alexia with a slight smirk. "Go ahead. I don't have any plans for Saturday night."

Alexia ignored the innuendo. "Would you recognize Rena Richardson if she walked into this room?" she asked.

"Yeah. All the guys hired to watch her had her picture. Cute blonde in her midtwenties, a little bit taller than you. We were her guardian angels."

"Who hired you?"

"I'm not going to tell you, but we were there at the request of Jeffrey Richardson."

"He hired you?"

"That's not what I said."

"Who told you what to do?"

Quinton's eyes narrowed. "You don't want to know."

"Why not?"

"Because if he thinks you're interested in him, he might become interested in you. You don't want that kind of attention."

Alexia kept her voice level. "Then why mention Jeffrey Richardson?"

"He's a money guy but nothing else. Besides, if you didn't already know about his involvement, you wouldn't be sitting here."

Quinton spoke with the confidence of a man who had everything figured out. Alexia decided to test him.

"What else do I know?" Alexia asked.

"Oh, I'm no psychic, but I'm sure Jeffrey Richardson is trying to scare your client with the videotape. I'm not sure what he wants to do and don't really care, but that tape is my ticket out of here. I didn't steal that car or kill the deputy."

"Why were your fingerprints on the door of Rena Richardson's convertible?"

"Check the police report. They were on the passenger door. I delivered a package to her one night and left it in the seat of the car."

"What was in the package?"

Quinton shrugged. "Drugs, diamonds, money, I don't know. It wasn't addressed to me. If I'd worn gloves I wouldn't be sitting here. It was a stupid mistake."

"Who told you to deliver a package?"

"A person who had the right to tell me what to do."

"Why were you watching Rena?"

"I told you. It was my job."

"Did you shoot the video?"

"No, it was my day off, and I went to Savannah."

"How did you find out about it?"

"One of the other fellows mentioned it to me after the deputy turned up dead, and Mrs. Rich claimed her car had been stolen."

"It's Richardson."

"We called her Rich. It seemed to fit."

"Were you watching anyone else?"

"Not when I was protecting her."

"It sounds like you were spying on her. Did she ask for protection?"

"I've never met her, but my instructions were to make sure that nobody bothered her."

"Why did she need protection?"

"There are people who might try to hurt her. We were supposed to keep that from happening."

"Who would want to hurt her?"

Quinton looked directly into Alexia's eyes. "Counselor, there are bad people in this world. Some of them are in the cell block where I'm locked up; a lot more are out on the street. As long as I was on the job, your client was safer than if a police cruiser slowed down in front of her house every five minutes."

"Can you tell me the names of any of these bad people?"

"I could, but I won't."

"Why not?"

"For the same reason you don't need to know the name of my boss."

Alexia remembered the man who accompanied Jeffrey to the benefit concert. "Is Nicholas Valese your boss?"

"No, and we're not going to play any guessing games."

Without a judge to force answers, Alexia retreated and regrouped.

"Have you seen me before?" she asked.

"You look familiar, but I can't place you. Santee is a small town. We could have been in the same store or passed by on the street. Where do you buy your liquor?"

Alexia bought an occasional bottle of wine in Charleston but couldn't remember the last time she went into a liquor store in Santee. She refused to let Quinton take over direction of the questions.

"Do you know where I live?" she asked.

"No."

"Do you own a gray van?"

"It's mostly gray. It used to be totally gray, but it's lost a lot of paint."

"Recently, someone driving an older-model, gray van near my house ran me off the road into the sand. Was that you?"

Quinton shook his head. "No. Where do you live?"

Alexia ignored the question. "Do people borrow your van?"

"Sure, all the time. I'm a generous guy."

"Can you describe any of the people who have borrowed your van in the past couple of weeks?"

Quinton raised both his hands to scratch the side of his nose. "I'm not too good at that type of thing." Before Alexia could ask another question, he added, "And I'm not going to tell you any names either."

"Are they still in the area?"

"I'm not really sure. I've been out of touch with everyone lately."

"Was anyone watching me?"

Quinton grinned, but it didn't make him look friendly. "I'm sure a lot of people are watching you. My lawyer hasn't taken his eyes off you the whole time we've been talking."

Pruitt spoke up. "Ms. Lindale, I asked Mr. Quinton to cooperate to the extent he wants to do so and so long as I don't think it's detrimental to my representation. From your questions, I assume you believe a coworker of my client may have been in the area near your house."

"'Coworker' is an interesting way to describe someone who tried to run me off the road. I'm not claiming anyone violated the law, but it made me wonder if an accomplice was in the neighborhood, and why."

Pruitt looked at Quinton and then spoke to Alexia. "Step outside for a minute and let me talk to my client."

Alexia opened the heavy, metal door and stood in the hallway. Unlike Rena, Henry L. Quinton didn't seem interested in disgorging any helpful information. Alexia wasn't particularly surprised; however, the fact that Rena had bared her soul to Sean Pruitt made Alexia's inability to pry anything from Quinton more frustrating.

Except for the heavy, metal doors, the hallway could have been a hospital ward. An inmate operating a large buffing machine and wearing a white jumpsuit with the words "Correctional Center Trustee" stenciled in large black letters across his chest approached her. Alexia stepped to the other side of the hall as the man sprayed the floor with a pink substance from a bottle attached to the machine. As he passed by, the floor glistened. The door opened and Pruitt motioned to her. She reentered the room.

"Have a seat," Pruitt said.

Alexia glanced at Quinton, but he was looking down at the table. She resumed her place.

Pruitt spoke. "Ms. Lindale, you've probably been the subject of surveillance because of your representation of Rena Richardson. Lawyers often play a big role in what people do, and it's not unusual for their activities to be monitored. In fact, there is a strong possibility that we were followed from my office to the jail. Mr. Quinton's life would be at risk if his superiors suspect that he is discussing anything other than the charges against him with either one of us."

His words confirmed what had been at the edge of Alexia's imagination. But even hearing it didn't make it real.

"So what does this mean?" she asked. "I'm not doing anything out of the ordinary for Rena."

"It depends on what she wants you to do," Pruitt said.

Alexia quickly reviewed the current status of her representation of Rena. The only thing on her desk was the preliminary research into the companies identified by Jeffrey.

Pruitt continued. "I suggest you be careful. Information that might not seem significant to you could be very important to someone else."

Alexia looked at Quinton, who stared back at her impassively.

"Okay," Alexia said. "Is that all you're going to say?"

"I didn't say anything," Quinton replied. "That was my lawyer talking. As far as I'm concerned, we didn't discuss anything except how you can help get me out of here."

Quinton got up from the chair. The leg irons scraped against the floor.

Pruitt held open the door and spoke to his client. "I'll let you know as soon as possible about the solicitor's response to our alibi evidence."

They exited the building, and Alexia glanced around the parking lot. Pruitt saw her.

"We won't know who is watching us," he said calmly. "Everyone stares when a Ferrari goes by."

20

He who watches over Israel will neither slumber nor sleep.

PSALM 121:4

Pruitt didn't say anything on the ride back to his office. Alexia glanced over at him but didn't try to intrude. When they turned onto the side street leading to the garage, Pruitt looked in the rearview mirror.

"Did you notice the black Suburban that's been behind us since we left the jail?"

Alexia looked over her shoulder in time to see the dark vehicle slow down and then continue past the alley.

"He's going around to the front of the building," Pruitt said. "He'll pick you up when you and your client leave the office."

"Are you sure?"

"No, but I'm paranoid enough to be suspicious."

Alexia barely noticed the quaint garden during her second trip past the fountain. At the bottom of the steps leading up to the rear entrance, Pruitt stopped and leaned against the black iron railing.

"Of course, I'll send you a copy of any subpoena for the tape."

Alexia hesitated. "Unless you hear otherwise from me."

"Thinking about bailing out on your client?"

Alexia shrugged.

"No one would fault you," Pruitt said. "She's lied to you and is possibly facing criminal charges. You're primarily a divorce lawyer, aren't you?"

"Yes."

"I looked you up in Martindale-Hubbell, but the listing still had you at Leggitt & Freeman."

Pruitt had been exponentially more thorough than Alexia in his preparation for their meeting.

"I recently went solo," she said.

"You'll enjoy it. It's great being your own boss."

Alexia walked up the steps. "That's encouraging," she replied without enthusiasm. "I need to get Rena and go."

Pruitt opened the door. "I'll let you know about the charges against Quinton. I'm not so sure the assault charge involving the detective is going to evaporate, but that doesn't concern you."

"Right," Alexia said over her shoulder as she passed by him into the house.

Rena was sitting in the conference room reading a home-decorating magazine. Alexia's mouth dropped open. She wasn't sure what she expected Rena to be doing, but fantasizing about a new décor for her sunroom wasn't one of the possibilities.

"How did it go?" Rena asked in a normal tone of voice.

"Mostly generalities," Alexia answered. "I'll fill you in on the drive to Santee."

The receptionist stuck her head into the room and spoke to Pruitt.

"Dick Bowley is on the phone."

"I'll be right there," he replied and then turned toward Alexia. "Sorry, I have to take the call."

Alexia waved her hand. "Sure. We'll find our own way out."

As they descended the front steps, Rena asked, "Are you still mad at me?"

It was a juvenile question. Rena was only a few years younger than Alexia but at least a decade behind in maturity.

"Your lies could be a huge problem," Alexia replied simply.

"I know, but it felt good to get the truth out. While you were gone, I decided everything is going to work out. I didn't do anything wrong except lie to the police about what happened."

"Which is a felony."

"But you won't turn me in, and I don't think Sean will do anything to hurt me."

"Sean?"

"He's too young to be called Mr. Pruitt."

They reached Alexia's car. She glanced up and down the street. No sign of the black Suburban. They got in, and Alexia started the engine before she replied.

"Young Sean Pruitt isn't required to keep anything confidential," she said.

"I know, but there wasn't any meanness in his eyes."

Alexia pulled out into traffic. "That's a quick judgment."

"Oh, I'm sure. It was the same with you at the hospital in Greenville. I knew immediately that I could trust you."

Alexia clammed up. Rena had overused her ability to pull on Alexia's sympathetic heartstrings. They entered a newer part of the city. Rena broke the silence.

"What did Quinton tell you about spying on me?"

"He didn't deny it. He even claimed he was a guardian angel."

"Those are the same words Jeffrey used."

"You've been under twenty-four-hour surveillance, but except for identifying Jeffrey as the one paying the bill, he wouldn't tell me who he was working for."

Rena nodded. "Yeah, it fits exactly with what he told me in Greenville."

"Perhaps you should tell me what you're talking about."

"It's all tied in with what I mentioned earlier today. Baxter's family is involved in illegal activity, and I'm caught in the middle of a struggle between Jeffrey and his father."

Even after talking with Quinton, Alexia was unwilling to give credence to Rena's story.

"Other than keeping the videotape secret, what's in this for you?" she asked.

"Jeffrey promised me a lot of money. If Baxter dies, I'll inherit his part of the companies."

"Which was the reason why you wanted me to file the petition to terminate Baxter's life support?"

"No," Rena replied in a hurt tone of voice. "I did that because Baxter would have wanted me to do it."

Alexia started to argue but stopped. The issue was dead and Baxter alive.

Rena continued. "Jeffrey wanted me to be his new partner, but I don't want to be involved in any way with him," Rena paused and then spoke with emphasis, "either business or personal. But when his father tried to take over everything, I didn't have a choice. Jeffrey came to the hospital, caught me at a vulnerable moment, and persuaded me toward his side of things. Now I feel trapped."

"Me too," Alexia muttered under her breath.

"What do you mean?"

Alexia looked out the window of the car before answering. They slowed to a stop as a shiny car turned into the beautifully manicured entrance of an expensive new housing development. Every plant was in its place, and a light mist from the sprinkler system created a moist cloud over a bank of brightly colored winter flowers.

"Rena, you hired me to help you sort through the legal paperwork affecting your relationship with Baxter and his family. I did that and more. I protected you from the detective in Greenville and filed the petition to terminate Baxter's life support. I sat with you while you lied to Detective Devereaux, and I came with you to the meeting today and interviewed a man who is probably a professional criminal."

"You've been a lot of help. I don't know what I'd have done without you."

Alexia maintained her momentum. "But I'm not a criminal-defense lawyer. You may be charged with one or more crimes. If that happens, I'm not going to represent you."

Rena sat with her lips tightly compressed. Sensing an impending explosion, Alexia continued, determined to go ahead with what she wanted to say.

"And if you think Jeffrey, Baxter, and his father are doing something illegal, you should hire a lawyer who can talk to the police. If everything you're telling me is true, this situation has gotten out of hand. You may have to leave Santee and go someplace safe."

Alexia stopped and waited for Rena to react. She glanced sideways and saw Rena staring out the opposite window.

"It's odd," Rena said slowly. "When I finally have the courage to tell you the truth, you don't have the guts to help me."

Alexia refused to be manipulated by guilt. "That's right. I'm not willing to risk it. We don't have anything pending in court, so I will withdraw and refund the balance of your retainer. You'll need to hire someone with criminal law experience as soon as possible."

"Who should I hire?"

"I don't know."

"What about filing suit against Ezra for stealing from Baxter?"

"I won't do it."

Rena took a tissue from her purse and began twisting it. "What about divorcing Baxter and leaving Santee? Would you handle my divorce if I decide to walk away from everything?"

Alexia hesitated. She couldn't claim inexperience in divorce cases.

"I'll let you know."

With nothing further to discuss, it was a tense ride from Charleston to Santee. Alexia sighed in relief when she pulled into the parking lot for Rachel's building and Rena got out of the car.

"When will you let me know if you're going to handle the divorce?" Rena asked.

"By five o'clock tomorrow afternoon. Does anyone but you have access to your answering machine?"

"No."

"Then if you're not home when I call, I'll leave a message."

Alexia watched Rena walk to her vehicle. The emotional link between them had grown strong. Shared secrets and common battles against powerful foes had forged a bond. But Alexia didn't have to wait until the following day to decide what she wanted to do.

She went inside the office. It was deserted. On her desk was a neat stack of letters and pleadings. Alexia flipped through the documents and signed them with gratitude for Gwen's invaluable help. First thing in the morning, Alexia would ask her to copy Rena Richardson's files so she could give a set to her client along with a letter withdrawing from further legal representation.

———

At home, Alexia kicked off her shoes and plopped down in her favorite chair in the living room. Misha hopped into her lap and curled up in a contented ball. Boris happily gnawed a rawhide bone at her feet. The living room's large picture window faced the marsh, which turned dark purple for a few minutes before pulling a black blanket over its head for the night. Alexia watched the passing of day to night, the ebb and flow of the tide, without turning on any lights. The relentless rhythm and power in nature had a calming effect on Alexia and put the events of the day in perspective, shrinking them to photographs she could hold in her hand. She sat quietly. The darkness descended; the marsh went to sleep. The anxiety of the day flowed from Alexia's soul, leaving her tired but without the tyranny of fear.

———

Ted Morgan had learned to treat sleep as a privilege, not a right. Most nights he went to bed around 11:00 PM and woke up seven hours later; however, the small alarm clock on his nightstand was not the final arbiter of his schedule. God neither slumbers nor sleeps, and at times he calls his servants to do the same.

The nudge came at 1:00 AM. Ted woke up, glanced at the clock, turned over, and found a comfortable spot on his pillow. But when he closed his eyes, sleep didn't return. He lay still to make sure he wasn't experiencing a brief moment of wakefulness. Consciousness reigned. Rolling onto his back, he opened his eyes and stared up at the dark ceiling. He was awake; his mind sharp. Without arguing, he swung his feet over the edge of the bed and went into the kitchen to drink a few sips of water.

Ted's nighttime vigils varied. Sometimes he walked the floor of his house and prayed in response to images that came to mind. Faces appeared, and petitions for people or places welled up in his spirit. At other times, he would open his Bible and read in a loud voice a verse that seemed to lift from the page. His proclamation of truth might not carry beyond the walls of the old parsonage, but he longed for the power of anointed words unrestricted by the limits of natural speech. Occasionally he received an answer to his prayers, but more often, he did not receive feedback. One of his greatest struggles centered upon an unanswered question: Why had his best efforts at obedience yielded so little in tangible results? Alexia Lindale and Sarah Locklear might be confident about his ministry to Baxter Richardson, but Ted rode a roller coaster of faith that both soared to heaven and plummeted to earth. To him, viewing the reward of prayer as reserved for another time and another place seemed an inadequate cop-out. Nevertheless, he persevered.

"What's up, Lord?" he asked.

It wasn't an eloquent prayer, but it was sufficient for the moment. In the middle of the night while wearing his pajamas, Ted didn't depend on formality to get God's attention. A clear answer didn't come, but he sensed the nudge toward the sanctuary. Leaving the red-trimmed choir robe hanging in the closet by the front door, he put on a blue bathrobe made of tattered terry cloth to ward off the chill and an old pair of dock shoes that served as house slippers.

He picked up the large sanctuary key from the table in the foyer and grabbed a flashlight from the closet. When he stepped outside, a stiff breeze whipped his robe. The narrow beam of the nearly new moon helped him locate the keyhole for the large wooden door. The lock turned smoothly.

Ted didn't turn on the interior lights but relied on the flashlight to guide him down the aisle to the piano. The wooden floors creaked under his feet, and the walls groaned as if trying to wake in response to the late-night intruder. He found the piano bench and turned off the flashlight. Ted liked playing in the dark. That way, light emanated from the music.

Finding the right notes was as easy as buttoning a shirt. He placed his hands on the keys and began to play softly in the middle of the keyboard. Peace came. He closed his eyes, knowing he was in God's will but not yet clear on the specific mission. Within a few minutes, the purpose for his time rose distinctly to the surface of his mind. The notes painted an inner por-trait of a face that was becoming increasingly familiar to him. The eyes, the cheeks, the lips, the nose, the dark hair—all came into focus. He looked into the eyes and saw reflected a request, not directed toward him, but to the One who held all answers in his hands. Ted bore down harder on the keys and moved rapidly from the lower notes to the higher ones. Release didn't come easily. Undeterred by the lateness of the hour, he continued. Whatever the need, he was determined to play his part in seeing it fulfilled.

In the life of Sarah Locklear.

21

A very ancient and fish-like smell.

THE TEMPEST, ACT 2, SCENE 2

Alexia awoke to a bright morning. A storm in the night had cleared the air. She released Boris for his run, and he scampered off to explore the new smells unearthed by the large raindrops that had pounded the sandy soil. Misha walked gingerly across the wet deck to the steps, pausing now and then to shake a paw free of water.

Alexia drank a cup of coffee and ate some yogurt with strawberries in the kitchen nook. The windows welcomed the marsh into the house. Several egrets stood motionless in the shallow water at low tide, and a large flock of seagulls glided overhead. Occasionally, a few dived into the opaque water for a bountiful breakfast.

She arrived at the office before Gwen and placed the papers she'd signed the night before on the secretary's desk. Sitting down to update her list of things to do, she put at the top of her sheet, *Gwen to copy all of Rena Richardson's files*. Number two: *Call Rena before five o'clock*. Alexia had reached number twelve, which involved research on a new case she'd taken in the previous week, when Gwen stuck her head in the door and greeted her.

"Same hair color?" Alexia asked.

"I'm not fickle. How was your trip to Charleston? I waited a few minutes after five but couldn't hang around any longer."

Alexia snapped shut her pen. "Come in and close the door."

Gwen sat down with an expectant expression, and Alexia summarized the events of the previous afternoon. Now that Gwen worked for her, she could share the details of her representation of Rena. The secretary asked a few questions but grew quiet when Alexia mentioned the videotape and Rena's allegations about Richardson and Company.

"This is like something from a movie."

"Rena claims it's real. If it is, I don't want to have anything to do with it."

Gwen put her hands together under her chin. "You're going to fire her?"

Alexia nodded. "Yes, and that brings me to your first assignment for the day. I need you to copy all her files so she can pick them up and take them to another lawyer."

Gwen didn't move. "What will that solve?"

Alexia gave her a puzzled look. "It will get me out of this mess. Rena's problems have been taking up too much of my time and dragging me into legal quagmires."

Gwen shrugged. "Do you know who you sound like?"

"No, who?"

"Ken Pinchot. He only liked to litigate on his terms and sloughed off any cases he thought he might lose or didn't want to handle. Remember? You were on the receiving end of some of those junk files. The only cases in his cabinets were the ones that would bring in a ton of easy money or make him look good."

"Yes, and I'm glad those days are over. But this is different. I'm not trying to dump something on an associate. Rena has the money to hire the best available legal talent. And I'm not a criminal attorney; it's been three or four years since I handled a misdemeanor. She needs both a corporate lawyer and a litigator to fight her father-in-law or Jeffrey over the business issues."

"What about her domestic problems?"

"Yeah, we talked about that." Alexia started to tell Gwen what had happened between Rena and Baxter at the waterfall but hesitated.

Gwen spoke first. "I mean, it's pitiful to divorce a guy who is paralyzed and coming out of a coma."

"Oh, she has legitimate reasons to end the marriage, but I don't want to be involved in it. I have too much else to focus on."

Gwen stood and picked up the Richardson files stacked on the corner of Alexia's desk. "Okay, I'd better get started, but I hope I don't have to pull a bunch of staples. My dentures can't handle it."

"You don't wear dentures."

"We both should if we're going to lose our bite."

Alexia smiled. "It's not that bad. I'll dictate the disengagement letter."

Gwen took the files from Alexia, who felt an immediate sense of relief. Tomorrow, Rena Richardson wouldn't occupy the top two spots on her to-do list.

―――

Giles Porter had not traveled to the coast for several years. His wife preferred the gurgling sound of a mountain creek to the roar of the ocean surf, so for recreation the Porter clan enjoyed frequent Saturday picnics in the hills of Mitchell County. The detective knew no happier sound than the excited squeal of a barefoot five-year-old grandchild standing in the cold, shallow water of a fast-moving stream.

The edges of the scar on top of his scalp were especially susceptible to sunburn, and from April to October, Porter always wore a battered hat when he stepped outside. October was past, but he'd thrown the hat onto the seat of his car. The sun along the coast presented a danger long after it went into winter hibernation in the mountains, and Porter didn't want to take any chances. He was a thinker, not a gambler.

The detective's stomach rumbled. He stopped at a local drive-in that sold hamburgers and hot dogs. He ordered a corn dog, which he dipped in a small pool of mustard laced with ketchup that he'd squeezed onto a paper plate. Sitting at an outside table under an aluminum awning, he ate the corn dog in four bites. It was much better than the ones at the Mitchell County Fair, and he ordered another one. When he finished it, he deposited his trash in a trash can at the corner of the building and returned to his car, unaware that a streak of the mustard-and-ketchup mixture stretched from the corner of his mouth partway up his right cheek.

Porter had memorized the address for Baxter and Rena's house. He unfolded a map of the Santee area and found the correct street on the northwest outskirts of town. He drove through the downtown area and then southwest. At the Richardson house, he slowed at the end of the driveway and inspected the fine home, nicer than just about any dwelling in Mitchell County. An older man walking a golden retriever came around the corner. Porter stopped the car and rolled down his window. The man approached the car.

"Good afternoon," the detective said. "Do you live in the neighborhood?"

The man stopped and replied in a voice that sounded more like Cape Cod than Cape Fear. "Yes, a couple of blocks that way."

"Nice dog."

The retriever sniffed the air and wagged his tail.

"That's Buddy."

Porter reached out the window and patted the dog's head. "Hello, Buddy." The detective pointed toward the Richardson home. "Do you know who lives there?"

The man's eyes followed the direction of Porter's finger. "Oh, that's the Richardson place. It's one of the oldest houses in town, but a young couple lives there now. It's a sad story. The husband was in a serious accident a few months ago, and now they're taking care of him in the cottage beside the house."

Porter could see part of the small white building from his vantage point at the end of the driveway.

"What's wrong with him?"

"In a coma and paralyzed from the neck down. He was a nice guy. Whenever I saw him, we would talk about wine. For someone so young, he knew a lot about the fruit of the grape. Most of the locals think bottled beer is a fine beverage, but he had a lot of class."

"Has he gotten better?"

The man shrugged. "My wife heard a rumor that he said a few words the other day when his father came by for a visit, but I don't know myself."

"You haven't visited him?"

"No. I stopped by when they first brought him home, but the nurse on duty told me they were restricting visitors to people on a list."

"I guess that's for the best."

"Yeah, it would be a shame if he picked up a bug from a visitor. My brother-in-law was in a coma after he had a stroke. He caught a cold and died of pneumonia."

Porter glanced down at Buddy. The dog stood motionless beside his master.

"That's a well-behaved dog."

The man smiled with obvious pride. "He used to walk around the ring when we lived in Connecticut."

"I bet he has a wall of ribbons."

"He did well, but now all he has to do is keep me company."

Porter nodded. "I bet he does that better than anyone else. Nice talking to you. Have a good walk."

"Thanks."

Porter watched the man proceed briskly down the street. He drove past the Richardson house and returned to the downtown area. Finding the courthouse, he parked on the street near the front entrance. He went inside and found the office of the clerk of court. A young woman was behind the counter.

"I need to find out whether a guardian has been appointed for an adult," he said.

"Who is it?" the woman asked.

"Baxter Richardson."

The woman's eyes widened. "We don't do that in this office, but I can find out for you."

Porter smiled. "That would be great."

The woman walked over to a simple wooden desk and picked up the telephone. She punched in some numbers and talked for several minutes before hanging up.

"There's no record of a filing. Do you know him?"

"I've been around him a little. How about you?"

"Oh, I grew up here, and everybody knows the Richardson family. My older sister went to school with his brother, Jeffrey, and Baxter and I were in the same class in elementary school."

"What was Baxter like as a kid?"

"Kind of quiet. Jeffrey was a big talker, always getting in trouble for smarting off to the teachers, but Baxter was a good kid. Everybody liked him."

"How about Baxter's wife?"

"She's from somewhere else. I think they met in college. I recognize her when I see her around town, but I've never talked to her."

Porter tapped the counter with his fingers. "Thanks for your help."

"Uh, just a minute," the young woman said with a sheepish grin on her face. "Did you know you have some food on your face?"

"Where is it?"

The girl pointed to her own right cheek. Porter reached up and felt the dried mustard-ketchup concoction.

"That must be left over from the corn dogs I ate for lunch," he said. "I stopped at the drive-in on the north side."

"Yeah, they have the best corn dogs, a lot better than the ones at the fair."

"That's what I thought too."

Porter pulled a clean handkerchief from his pocket, wet the corner with the tip of his tongue and then rubbed his cheek.

"Did I get it all?" he asked.

The young woman nodded. "Yes. You know, Baxter liked to eat there. He could go to any restaurant in town, but I've seen his SUV parked in front of the drive-in many times. They also have delicious soft-serve ice cream."

"I didn't try that," the detective paused. "Have you eaten lunch today?"

"No sir," the young woman said with a short laugh. "I guess I have food on the brain. I'll be on my lunch break in a few minutes."

"Will you get a corn dog?"

"No, I have some carrots and celery in the refrigerator in the break room. I'm trying to lose weight for my wedding. I'm getting married in two weeks."

"Congratulations."

Porter left the courthouse and returned to the drive-in. The same woman was behind the counter. She eyed him with curiosity when he approached.

"I enjoyed the corn dogs," he said.

"Most folks do. We mix the batter and dip them ourselves."

"Is that what Baxter Richardson would buy before his accident?"

"Do you know Baxter?"

"Not well, but I know he liked to come here."

The woman shook her head sadly. "It's awful what happened to him. He was one of our best customers. He liked corn dogs, but his favorite food was our fish sticks, an order of onion rings, and an ice cream topped with chocolate syrup. We make the fish sticks ourselves."

"What did Baxter put on his fish sticks?"

"Ketchup with a few pieces of raw onion. I made it up for him special."

Porter nodded. "Give me the Baxter special without the onion rings."

"Ice cream too?"

"Yep."

Back in his car, Porter placed the paper tray containing the fish sticks and ketchup mixture on the seat beside him and ate the ice cream as he retraced his route through Santee. The smell of the fried fish filled the car. He passed the courthouse and continued to the Richardson house. When he reached the driveway, he turned in and drove toward the house. The SUV Rena and Baxter had driven to the trailhead for Double Barrel Falls was parked in a detached four-car garage. Porter remembered the license-plate number. He parked in front of the cottage and sat in the car for a couple of minutes until he finished the ice cream. The young woman at the clerk's office was right. The soft-serve was good. Picking up the fish-stick tray, he approached the door of the cottage and knocked. A middle-aged woman with a badge identifying her as a registered nurse opened the door. She looked suspiciously at the detective and the food in his hand.

"May I help you?" she asked.

Porter produced his badge with his free hand and identified himself with a smile. "I was involved in the efforts to rescue Mr. Richardson after his fall and kept up with his status at the hospital in Greenville." The detective took a step forward. "How is he doing?"

The nurse retreated, whether before the badge or the pungent smell of the fish, he couldn't tell.

"Uh, better. I guess you can see him for a few minutes, but keep it brief. And you can't eat in here."

"Of course not."

Baxter was lying on his side facing the open door. His eyes were closed.

There was a chair beside the bed, and Porter moved it close to Baxter's head and sat down.

"Hello, Baxter," he said.

The young man didn't move.

"It's not quite as nice a day as the first time I saw you at the hospital in Mitchell County," Porter continued. "All the leaves are gone from the trees in the mountains."

The nurse, who was standing at the foot of the bed, stepped toward the kitchen. "I need to prepare his afternoon meds," she said. "When I come back, you'll need to leave."

Porter nodded. As soon as the nurse was out of the room, he held the fish sticks and ketchup-onion mix up to Baxter's nose.

"I brought you some fish sticks with ketchup fixed just the way you like it."

Baxter opened his eyes and blinked. Porter leaned closer.

"My name is Giles Porter. I'm a police detective from Mitchell County."

Baxter licked his lips. "Po, pop," he said.

Porter looked into the young man's eyes. Their bleariness signaled an absence of comprehension.

"I'm a policeman," Porter continued. "Do you know what that means?"

Baxter shifted his head slightly and closed his eyes for several seconds. Porter stayed close to the bed. Baxter reopened his eyes. This time they were in focus.

"Yes," he said in a weak voice. "Do Rena?"

Porter leaned even closer. "Yes, I know Rena."

"Ba, bad."

"Did she do something bad? If so, say yes."

Baxter blinked his eyes and said, "Yes."

"What did she do?"

Porter held his breath. Baxter opened and closed his mouth several times. No words came out. Porter spoke again.

"Did she push you over the edge of the cliff at the waterfall? If that's what happened, all you have to do is say yes."

"Here's your medications," the nurse announced as she burst in from the kitchen.

Porter kept his eyes glued to Baxter's mouth. "Yes or no?" he asked.

"Yes," Baxter managed in a weak voice.

Porter sat up in the chair. He wanted to cry out in triumph but kept cool.

"No," Baxter continued.

Porter immediately leaned over closer to Baxter's head.

"Which is it?" he asked quickly. "Yes or no. It's very important."

"It's very important that the patient have his medications," the nurse interrupted. "Please, it's time for you to leave."

Porter held up his hand. "We haven't finished talking."

The nurse glanced down and saw that Baxter's eyes were open. She set the medicines on the hospital tray.

"I'm sorry, Detective Porter, but we have to give priority to medical protocol. I'm sure Mr. Richardson has enjoyed your visit."

Porter didn't move. "This isn't entirely a social visit. I'm conducting a criminal investigation."

The nurse raised her eyebrows. "Why didn't you tell me?"

"Because you're neither a witness nor a suspect. I realize Mr. Richardson needs to conserve his strength, but I need to talk to him. I'm almost finished."

The nurse took a step back. "Do I need to leave?"

"If you don't mind."

"Okay. I'll be in the kitchen."

As soon as the nurse was gone, Porter spoke. "Baxter?"

The young man's eyes were closed. They didn't open. Porter held the fish and ketchup close to Baxter's nose.

"Baxter, please open your eyes so we can talk."

Whatever ability the familiar food had to rouse Baxter had waned. His eyes remained closed. Porter reached over and touched Baxter's cheek.

"Wake up."

He waited. The eyes remained closed. Baxter released a long sigh. Porter leaned back in the chair.

"Nurse!" he called out. "You can come back."

Immediately, the nurse stuck her head out of the kitchen.

"How long will he sleep?" Porter asked. "We weren't finished."

"It's impossible to know. It could be hours or minutes."

Porter stood up. "I'll be back later. When does your shift end?"

"At three o'clock."

The detective turned to leave.

"Detective Porter?" the nurse asked.

Fish sticks in hand, Porter turned around. "Yes?"

"Is Mr. Richardson a suspect or a witness to a crime?"

22

When you come to a fork in the road, take it.
YOGI BERRA

Alexia intently reviewed a set of proposed interrogatories. The precise wording of the written questions was important. She wanted to force the opposing party's attorney to either provide answers damaging to his case or file groundless objections that would justify a motion to compel. Whatever the response, Alexia would continue to narrow the avenue of escape for the man seeking to dodge future financial responsibility for his wife and two children.

On her desk rested a complete set of the documents Gwen copied from the Rena Richardson files. Beside the stack was a standard disengagement letter. It was easy for Alexia to withdraw from representation without any lawsuits pending. No judge needed to authorize her retreat. As soon as she finished correcting the interrogatories and dictating a demand letter in another case, Alexia intended to call Rena and deliver the news.

The phone buzzed. All Alexia's calls were now being routed through Gwen, and she'd told the secretary that she didn't want to be disturbed except for an emergency.

"What is it?" she asked with a slight edge in her voice.

"It's Rena Richardson."

"I'm going to call her in less than an hour."

"She wants to talk to you now."

Alexia tapped her pen against the top sheet of the interrogatories. She could back out as easily now as in another sixty minutes.

"Okay, I'll take it."

She picked up the receiver.

"Rena, I'm glad you called," she began.

"He's here!" Rena screamed into the phone. "You've got to come!"

"Who?" Alexia asked in alarm.

"The detective with the horrible scar on his head!"

When Alexia crossed swords with Giles Porter at the hospital in Greenville, she expressly told him not to have any contact with Rena. Unless initiated by her client, communication between the two violated Rena's constitutional right to have an attorney present when questioned by the police.

"Put him on the phone," Alexia said grimly.

"He's at the cottage with Baxter."

"Where are you?"

"At the house."

"Then stay inside and don't talk to him."

"But he's talking to Baxter! You've got to tell him to leave!"

Alexia hesitated. Rena had the right to order Giles Porter to leave her property unless he was there pursuant to a valid arrest or search warrant. But sending Rena over to the cottage to deliver an ultimatum wouldn't work. Alexia would have to maintain the status quo as Rena's advocate for one more skirmish.

"I'll be there in less than five minutes."

Alexia hung up the phone and grabbed her purse. As she hurried out the door, Gwen called out.

"Attorney Alexia Lindale to the rescue! I knew you wouldn't abandon a woman in distress!"

Alexia didn't answer. She glanced at her watch as she backed out of her parking space. Less than three minutes passed before she sped up the Richardson's driveway. When she got out of her car, she could see Rena peeking out one of the windows on the front side of the house. Alexia motioned for her to come outside. Rena hurried down the steps, glancing furtively toward the cottage.

"I need you with me when I tell him to leave. This is your house, not mine."

"What if he tries to arrest me?"

Alexia hadn't considered that possibility. "Uh, just let me do the talking."

"I don't want to see him."

"If you want him to leave now, you have no choice."

Alexia turned to avoid further argument and led the way to the cottage. Rena trailed a step behind. Alexia reached the door and opened it without knocking.

The detective sat in a chair near Baxter's head. His body blocked Alexia's view of Baxter's face, but Porter was leaning over with his head tilted as if listening to what the paralyzed man said. Alexia stepped forward. Rena stayed behind her at the threshold.

"Detective Porter, you need to leave! Now!" Alexia commanded.

Porter cut his eyes toward Alexia, but he didn't move. A nurse came in from the kitchen and stopped in her tracks.

"Mr. Richardson hasn't asked me to leave," he responded in an even tone. "And we're having a nice talk. He's doing much better than the last time I saw him."

"You are on private property, and unless you have a warrant, you have no right to be here."

Porter turned toward Baxter.

"Baxter, do I have your permission to talk to you?"

Alexia moved to the side so she could see Baxter's face. The young man's eyes were open, but he didn't look in her direction. His mouth moved, but no words came out. The sight of the helpless man being interrogated by the detective infuriated Alexia.

"Look! He's in no shape to talk to you! Go now!"

The detective remained impassive. "No guardian has been appointed for him, so I can assume that Baxter is mentally competent. If he is willing to talk with me, then you have no legal standing to order me to leave. Am I correct in assuming that this property is titled in both Baxter and Rena Richardson's names? If so, he has just as much right to let me stay as your client has to ask me to leave."

Alexia glanced back at Rena, who shrank away from the door. Alexia came closer to the bed.

"Baxter," she said. "Please, look at me."

The young man's eyes shifted slowly in her direction, but Alexia couldn't tell if there was comprehension in his gaze.

"I'm Rena's lawyer," Alexia began. "You don't have to talk to this man if you don't want to."

Baxter blinked his eyes but said nothing. Alexia felt ridiculous. It was like cross-examining a mannequin.

"Do you want to talk to him?"

Baxter's expression shifted from bland to puzzled.

"Who?" he managed.

It was the first word Alexia had heard Baxter Richardson speak. Her eyes grew wide at the realization that the young man might really return from the living dead.

"The detective," she said in a softer tone. "Do you want him to stay or go?"

Baxter closed his eyes. In a moment his breathing became even.

"He's asleep," Porter said. "It happened earlier when I was here, so I left to give him a break."

"You were here earlier?" Alexia asked sharply. "Who gave you permission to come in?"

Porter didn't answer, but the nurse standing near the kitchen answered in a voice that trembled slightly. "I did. He showed me his badge and told me that he had helped Mr. Richardson after the accident. I thought it would be okay for him to see him."

Rena made an anguished noise behind Alexia, who ignored her and turned toward the nurse.

"From now on, stick to the list. Detective Porter does not have permission to interrogate Mr. Richardson."

"Do you represent him?" Porter interjected. "You never informed me that Mr. Richardson was your client."

"He's not. But his wife is the co-owner of this property, and as her attorney I'm telling you to leave. If Baxter wants to contact you, that's his business. But don't come back on any fishing expeditions."

Porter rubbed the top of his head and gently massaged the area around his scar. Alexia found it impossible not to watch the gesture.

"I brought the fish earlier in the day."

"What?" Alexia asked.

Porter continued. "I'll take any and all steps I consider necessary in my investigation of this matter." The detective looked past Alexia toward Rena. "Today has been very enlightening."

Rena didn't answer. Alexia moved sideways and blocked the detective's line of sight. She heard footsteps and turned in time to see Rena running back toward the house. Alexia spoke.

"Are you finished with your juvenile games, or do I have to call our local police to escort you from the property?"

Porter stood up and faced Alexia. His dark eyes were glinting.

"Let me tell you something, Ms. Lindale. You can ask me to leave, but you're not going to keep me from doing my job. I'll be back and finish what I've started. You can count on it."

The detective brushed past her. Alexia watched him from the doorway to make sure he wasn't going to the house to arrest Rena, but he got in his car and left. Alexia took a deep breath and realized that her heart was pounding. The nurse had joined her at the door.

"Uh, I'm sorry," the nurse began. "I didn't mean to cause problems."

"I'll ask Rena not to report what happened to the agency," Alexia replied. "I can imagine what he told you. He's a clever manipulator."

"His concern seemed genuine. After he'd been here for a while he said something about a criminal investigation but didn't tell me any details."

"Did you hear what he asked Baxter?"

"No, I was preparing the medication tray the first time he came, and when he came back he asked to be alone with Mr. Richardson for a few minutes. Since he's a detective, I thought it would be okay."

"How long was he here?"

"Five or ten minutes the first time, and then he left for an hour." The nurse looked at her watch. "He was here longer this time. Maybe twenty minutes."

"And you don't know anything that was discussed?"

The nurse shook her head. "No, but I doubt it was much. Mr. Richardson hasn't communicated with anyone beyond simple yes and no responses."

"In a legal proceeding, a few words can have a big impact," Alexia replied soberly.

Alexia returned to the main house and knocked on the door. Rena peered at her through one of the sidelights and then opened the door.

"Is he gone?"

"Yes, for now."

Rena was wringing her hands. "This is another reason why I've got to divorce Baxter and leave Santee."

Her response provided an opening for Alexia to deliver her decision to withdraw from further representation. Things were happening on so many fronts that the sooner Rena made the transition to a new legal team, the better. Alexia looked at Rena's face and searched for the perfect words.

"Rena," she began then stopped. "Can you come back with me to my office? I'd rather talk there."

"Yeah, I need to get away from here."

———

Alexia glanced in the rearview mirror at Rena's vehicle. In the amplified stress of the moment, she'd not had the heart to cut Rena loose. She hoped the short drive and change of scene from the house to Alexia's office would allow her to communicate in a calm, professional manner. She parked behind the building. Rena pulled in beside her.

"We'll go through the rear door," Alexia said as they got out of their cars.

Alexia led the way into her office and closed the door. The documents Gwen copied sat conspicuously on the front right corner of Alexia's desk. She assumed a professional posture by leaning forward with her arms resting lightly on the desk.

"Rena, I told you yesterday that I'm not a criminal-defense attorney."

"I thought you did fine just now," Rena interjected. "There's no way I could have ordered the detective around the way you did."

"Which doesn't mean anything if criminal charges are filed against you either in Charleston or Mitchell County. Porter is after you, and if the Charleston solicitor gets a copy of the video, you may face charges related to Deputy Dixon's death. You need someone advising you now, not after an indictment, and I'm not the person to do it. Also, the impact the criminal investigations may have on your domestic situation with

Baxter is something a new lawyer should review. I've done all I can do for you."

Her argument that Rena needed a whole new set of lawyers due to the interrelationship of potential criminal charges and a divorce proceeding lacked logic, but she made it anyway. Rena's eyes showed a mixture of hurt and fear.

"But you're the only one who knows everything," she said in a pleading voice. "I can't imagine starting all over with someone I don't trust. Would you give me a chance—"

Rena was stopped by a knock at the door.

"Come in!" Alexia called in irritation.

The door opened, and Gwen tentatively poked her head around the corner.

"Sorry, I knew you were in a conference, but while you were gone, a lawyer named Sean Pruitt called twice. He asked me to let you know as soon as you returned. He said he has some news that affects Ms. Richardson."

Alexia stared across her desk at Gwen without focusing. Possible reasons for the call scrolled through her mind. Gwen held out a slip of paper.

"Here's his number."

Rena put her head in her hands. "No! This can't be happening!" she wailed.

The sound of Rena's voice summoned Alexia back to the immediate situation.

Sitting up straight, she said to Gwen, "There's no use putting it off."

Gwen glanced sideways at Rena and retreated from the room. Alexia started to punch in the numbers, then stopped. She looked at Rena, who had taken her head from her hands to watch. Alexia held out the slip of paper.

"Rena, here's the number. Take it home and call Pruitt from there. I'm withdrawing from representation, and you're going to have to take care of this on your own."

Rena didn't scream. Instead, two large tears suddenly appeared and rolled down her cheeks. She reached out with a trembling hand and took the slip of paper.

"Uh, what am I supposed to say?"

"Just ask why he called me."

"Could you at least find out what's going on? Then I promise to leave."

Alexia paused. Abandoning a woman in distress had never been her modus operandi. "Okay," she said with resignation.

Taking back the slip of paper, she dialed. As the call went through, she activated her speakerphone so Rena could hear both sides of the conversation.

"Good afternoon. Attorney Sean Pruitt's office," a pleasant female voice answered.

"Alexia Lindale returning his call."

"Just a minute, please."

The receptionist placed them on hold. As they waited, the sounds of Schubert's *Wanderer-Fantasie* came through the tiny speaker. Alexia wondered what Henry Quinton thought about listening to Schubert while on hold from the Charleston County jail. The pianist transitioned from the adagio to presto sections.

"What's wrong?" Rena asked anxiously. "Do you think he's not there, and the receptionist forgot—"

Sean Pruitt's distinctive voice cut off Rena's question.

"Ms. Lindale. Thanks for returning my call."

"We're on a speakerphone," Alexia responded. "Rena Richardson is in my office listening to the conversation."

The Charleston lawyer immediately adopted the more formal tone he used at the time of his initial contact with Alexia.

"Good afternoon, Mrs. Richardson," Pruitt said. "I'm glad you're present."

"Hello," Rena answered in a soft voice.

Pruitt continued. "I had a long meeting this morning with Joe Graham, the assistant solicitor assigned to the Quinton case. I laid out the information proving that my client could not have been involved in the death of Officer Dixon. Graham was skeptical, of course, and I suggested he call one of my alibi witnesses." Pruitt paused. "A police officer in Savannah."

"A police officer?" Alexia asked. "Quinton was hanging out with a policeman in Savannah?"

"Policewoman," Pruitt corrected. "And it wasn't voluntarily. She stopped him for failing to yield the right of way at an intersection. Quinton received a traffic warning, not a ticket, but the incident happened less than thirty minutes after Dixon's death. The officer confirmed everything to the solicitor, and I could see a distinct waning in prosecutorial zeal. The murder and theft charges should be gone by next week."

"Did you mention the videotape?" Rena asked nervously.

"Not directly. I referred to additional evidence not yet in my possession but didn't give any details. Frankly, I don't think it will be necessary."

Both Alexia and Rena sighed with relief at the same time.

"Did he ask you to explain the presence of Quinton's fingerprints on the door handle?" Alexia asked.

"Yes."

Alexia waited, but Pruitt didn't continue.

"What did you say?" she asked.

"Nothing that implicated your client."

"How about Rena's interview with Detective Devereaux?"

"After he realized his case against Quinton was going to crash and burn, Graham mentioned Rena's report of the theft."

"What do you think he's going to do?"

"I think there will be another round of questioning."

Rena groaned softly. Alexia glanced at the stack of Rena's files on the corner of her desk and had an idea.

"Would you be willing to represent Rena?" Alexia asked.

Rena opened her eyes wide and vigorously nodded her head.

Alexia continued, "Your knowledge of the videotape would then be protected by attorney-client privilege. I'm not a criminal-defense attorney, and Rena needs someone who can protect her as this situation unfolds."

"It's doubtful anything will be done," Pruitt responded. "Mrs. Richardson didn't accuse Quinton; she just falsely reported a stolen car. And as you know, criminal law is not my specialty either. I never get involved in a case unless charges have been filed or there is an imminent threat of prosecution."

"But you said the police are going to question Rena again."

"Maybe."

"What is she going to do about it? She can't lie and tell the same story."

There was another pause.

Alexia addressed another possible hurdle. "Money isn't a problem, is it Rena?" she asked.

"No," Rena said loudly.

"Sean, please hold on for a minute." Alexia pushed the mute button on the phone and spoke rapidly to Rena. "Can I ask him to help you deal with Giles Porter? I'll need to tell him about Baxter and what happened at the waterfall."

Rena nodded. "Yes. I like him."

"Are you sure?"

"Yes."

Alexia took the phone off mute and spoke. "And there is an unrelated investigation that involves a potential threat of prosecution."

"What is it?"

"Can we consider this phone call a consultation with a view toward possible representation?"

"Yes."

Alexia began by summarizing what had happened with Porter since she first met Rena at the hospital in Greenville. Pruitt asked Alexia a few questions and then quizzed Rena for almost an hour. Alexia could sense the Charleston lawyer's interest level rising.

"Ms. Lindale?" he asked.

"Call me Alexia."

"Okay. I'll be willing to represent Rena if you'll agree to remain as co-counsel. I assume you're going to handle the divorce, since that's your area of expertise, but it will be beneficial for me to keep you involved as a contact in Santee. We may also need to find an attorney in Mitchell County who can help."

Alexia glanced at the files stacked on the corner of her desk. Moving all of them, not part, out of her office had been her goal.

"Rena and I were discussing my total withdrawal from representation just before we called you," she said. "I believe she needs to put together a new legal team. Another divorce lawyer can help her and work with you as well as I can."

Pruitt's drawl took on a tinge of firmness. "My willingness to assume responsibility for the criminal issues is contingent on your continuing involvement. If I take on this aspect of the situation, it will leave you with what you know best, the domestic issues."

Alexia felt cornered.

"Please," Rena interjected. "I'm sorry I've been such a headache."

Alexia shook her head in resignation. "Well—" she began.

"It makes sense," Pruitt said.

Alexia hesitated a few moments then raised her hands in surrender. Perhaps getting rid of everything outside her legal comfort zone was the next best thing to total withdrawal.

"Okay," she said. "I'll do it."

23

Catch for us the foxes, the little foxes that ruin the vineyards.

SONG OF SONGS 2:15

Alexia hung up the phone. Rena, looking like a naive high-school girl, sat on her hands with a hopeful expression on her face.

"Thanks, Alexia," she said. "I know you're mad at me for not telling you the truth, but I was so scared that I made a mistake. I'm very sorry and appreciate you changing your mind about representing me."

"In a divorce case only. I'm not going to file any lawsuits against your father-in-law."

"Yes. I know I'll have to talk to Sean about all the other stuff."

Alexia stood up. "I'll send the extra copy of your records to him this afternoon. He should have it tomorrow."

"What should I do if Detective Porter comes back?"

"Call Sean."

Alexia opened a drawer in her desk and took out some papers, which she handed to Rena.

"This is an information packet I ask my clients to complete in divorce cases. I already have all your personal data, but put it on these sheets so it will be in the proper format. Of course, you can ignore the sections about children. As soon as I get this back from you, I can prepare the petition."

"Do I need to pay you any more money?"

Alexia thought a moment. "Not now, but send a retainer to Pruitt immediately. I have enough to get us through the first stages of the divorce. I'll be asking the court for interim payment of my fees from Baxter's assets."

"Both Ezra and Jeffrey have written me checks in the past week."

"Really? How much?"

"Ezra's was an odd amount—about thirty-two thousand. He put the word 'dividend' and the name of a company I didn't recognize on the bottom of the check. Jeffrey gave me twenty thousand."

"Okay. You realize their payments will stop when you file for divorce. They'll both be mad at you."

"Not Jeffrey."

Rena's comment aroused Alexia's old suspicions. "Why not?"

"We have an understanding about it, but even if he cuts me off, no amount of money is worth the suffering I've been through during the past few months." Rena put the information sheets under her arm. "I'll get busy on my homework."

After Rena left, Alexia sat staring at the far wall of the office. Gwen looked tentatively into the room.

"That was a marathon session," the secretary said. "What happened?"

Alexia gave her the sprinter's version. When she finished, Gwen nodded.

"You did the right thing. Rena is practically a kid. I have the sense she's had a hard time growing up and nobody ever stood beside her before."

"Yeah, she was raised by a stepfather near a little crossroads in the mountains outside Greenville. There's no telling what happened to her as a kid. I've been frustrated with her, but you may be right that she deserves a second chance. Whether good or bad, I'm in."

Gwen put some pleadings on Alexia's desk. At the top of the first page was *Rena Sue Richardson v. Baxter Calhoun Richardson*. It was a petition for divorce.

"When did you do this?" Alexia asked in surprise.

"Earlier today. It didn't take long, and I thought you'd need it to get started."

Alexia smiled. "So you were sure I wouldn't withdraw?"

"Not one hundred percent, but I've never seen you back down from a fight yet. This one was harder to predict because it's got more angles than usual. But with that lawyer from Charleston involved, you'll manage."

"I hope you're right."

Alexia drove to the house on King Street and parked in the narrow, concrete driveway. She walked slowly across the small yard. The front of the house was obscured from the street by a row of massive crape myrtles that had pushed beyond the ornamental stage and become small trees. She touched the smooth bark of a limb and gently bent a twig, feeling the hidden life that remained in the tree. The last of the small leaves from the crape myrtles lay in compacted piles on the ground beneath them. The first time Alexia visited the house, a few purple blossoms still clung to the tips of the branches. Now the trees were bare. Rachel had a plan to remove several plants and shape the others so they framed the house instead of hid it.

In the yard, sandy soil peeked through the spotty grass, but it would take only a bag of seed, some fertilizer, and an underground sprinkler system to turn the yard into a luxurious carpet. The soil around Santee never produced much cotton, but it grew great grass. The advent of the golfing communities allowed the soil to produce what it grew best. Alexia looked forward to kicking off her shoes at the end of a long day and taking a brief walk across the yard to enjoy the prickly feeling of grass beneath her toes.

Alexia hadn't put the key to her future office on her key ring. She rummaged around her purse for the loose key until she found it. Unlocking the front door, she went into the empty house. A slightly musty smell had taken over between occupants. She flicked on the lights in the dining room that would become her office. It wasn't hard to visualize her new desk in the center of the room with the art objects from her travels nestled in appropriate corners and attached to the generous wall space. The room was half again as large as her office at Leggitt & Freeman, and it would be nice to work in a less confining space. Although often specific in application, the law was innovative in theory, and it was easier to concoct new approaches to a problem in surroundings that didn't crowd out ideas.

She walked down the hall to the kitchen in the back of the house. The sink was old-fashioned but salvageable. The cabinets would need to be removed and replaced with storage space for office supplies. Taking her PDA from her purse, Alexia jotted down several ideas for the renovation. Even if her romantic involvement with Ted Morgan warranted caution, she still needed to give him direction concerning the renovation.

On the drive home, she didn't slow down when she reached the road leading to the Sandy Flats Church. She'd do well to take her relationship with Ted from personal to professional as quickly as possible. She'd cracked open the door of her heart to the minister, but she had time to ease it shut with minimal damage. She would dictate a memo to Gwen outlining some of her ideas for the renovation. Ted could read it, provide advice, and sign it.

———

Ted Morgan emerged from the crawl space beneath Marylou Hobart's house. The confined space could have been the movie set for a horror film on arachnids. In some places, the thick cobwebs hung from the floor joists all the way to the soil. Ted didn't suffer from any phobias about spiders, but he rubbed his head to remove the sticky strings that clung to him. Mrs. Hobart was standing outside, anxiously waiting for him.

"What did you find?" she asked.

"Some old termite tunnels, but no sign of current infestation. Do you remember when you had it treated?"

"Of course not, or I wouldn't have asked you to check it. Harriet Gibson up the road told me termites got into the wood under her back porch, and I couldn't sleep at night worrying that they might be chewing on my house."

"I can do a preventive treatment. Do you ever see any spiders in the house?"

"I got a splinter in my foot the other day, but it was my own fault. I shouldn't be walking around barefooted at my age. When I was a little girl, I never wore shoes and my feet were tough as rawhide leather, but the older I get, the more my skin turns to paper."

Mrs. Hobart's hearing deficiency sent normal conversations veering off in tangents. Sometimes Ted followed the tangents. Today, he tried to return to the initial topic. He spoke louder.

"I said spiders! Do you ever have spiders in the house?"

"Yes, that's another reason I shouldn't go barefooted. I stepped on one the other day in the kitchen. Good thing I had on my shoes. If I'd been barefooted, you'd probably be making my funeral arrangements. Did you get bitten while you were crawling around under there?"

"No, but there are a lot of cobwebs. It might be a good idea to spray under the house."

"Is that expensive?"

For sake of the old woman's dignity, Ted would occasionally charge Mrs. Hobart less than his supplies actually cost. Even then, she often complained at paying a price more consistent with 1950 than the present. Her reactions led Ted to a different strategy—let the older woman set her own price.

"I'll have to check and let you know. How much can you afford?"

Mrs. Hobart squinted in thought. "I get my check on the fifth. They used to mail it to the house, but now they can send it straight to my bank. It's a wonder they don't get it confused with all the other mail, but a nice girl at the bank told me it was better to do it that way. I agreed to try it for a couple of months, and so far they haven't missed a payment."

"The church does that too."

Mrs. Hobart opened her eyes wide. "I didn't know the government sent money to the church. I thought that was illegal. Not that I think it's wrong," she added quickly. "I know the Lord would bless this country if we quit trying to tell him that we don't need him. I know I do. I pray every morning and at night before I go to bed. I used to get on my knees, but recently I've started sitting on the bed when I pray because of my arthritis. I don't lie down because I'd go right to sleep, but I still close my eyes. Do you think that's alright?"

"Yes ma'am. What can you afford to pay to get rid of the spiders?"

"Oh, about thirty-five dollars, if it also includes the termites."

Ted nodded. "That's a good price. I can do it for that."

Mrs. Hobart smiled. "Do you want some tea?"

"Yes. That would be nice."

They walked to the back porch. A large sink stood in the corner of the screened area. In years past, the sink served farm workers who washed their hands before sitting down to a generous noontime meal included as part of their wages. Vegetables picked from the garden could be cleaned before bringing them inside. The property hadn't been a working farm in a generation, and Mrs. Hobart longingly reminisced about the big vegetable gardens of the past. As a result, Ted had set out a few tomato, squash, and okra plants that produced enough vegetables for Mrs. Hobart's personal use and extras she could proudly give to friends.

The old woman's tea was sweet, even by Southern standards. Ted always put a lot of ice in his glass and let it melt to cut the syrupy brew before drinking it. Extra lemon helped too.

"I'll get my own ice and cut up the lemon," he offered.

Ted knew his way around Mrs. Hobart's kitchen as well as the roof, toilet, windows, and now the crawl space. They sat down at a small kitchen table with the back door open to let in the cool afternoon air that drifted in from the porch.

"Are you cold?" Ted asked. "We can shut the door."

"No, you're probably hot from all your work. I'll be fine."

Mrs. Hobart took a sip of her tea. Ted shook his glass to hurry up the melting process.

"How is Alicia doing?" Mrs. Hobart asked.

"She's busy at work. She bought a house, and I'm going to fix it up for her."

"Where does she live now?"

"Another house near the marsh. This house will be her office. It's on King Street near the courthouse."

"She's a lawyer, isn't she?"

"Yes."

Mrs. Hobart sipped her tea. "They make a lot more money than preachers, except for the ones on TV. If everybody who watches the show sends twenty dollars, it could add up to a right smart sum of money. If you and Alicia get married, I hope you won't stop working on people's houses. I don't know what I'd do without you."

Ted laughed. "We haven't talked about getting married or what I would do if we did. I like her a lot, but I'm not sure if I'm involved in her life primarily to help her in her faith or if our relationship will lead to something serious."

Mrs. Hobart didn't respond. It was a long, complicated thought to communicate to the older woman, and Ted didn't expect a response. The ice in his tea had sufficiently melted so he could take a sip without risking the health of his teeth. He took a drink, thankful for a strong hint of lemon.

"You need to marry the right person," Mrs. Hobart said emphatically. "That's true for everybody, but you're a man of God, and I believe when you meet the woman who fits you, it will be clear as a morning after a rain."

Ted lowered his glass to the table. He leaned over and patted the older woman's wrinkled hand. "Thank you. You're right. And when you're sitting on the edge of your bed at night with your eyes closed, will you add that to your prayers?"

———

Exhausted after the encounter with Giles Porter and the pressure of Alexia's threatened withdrawal, Rena went home, collapsed on the sofa in the living room, and went to sleep. But she didn't rest. Every time she heard a car come up the driveway, she feared the detective had returned. Each time she looked, however, she discovered the nurses changing shifts. Suppertime had arrived by the time she awoke from a few fitful minutes of sleep. She went into the kitchen. Opening the refrigerator, she took out a peach yogurt. She'd lost over ten pounds since Baxter was hurt, and her appetite was fickle. Trying to get rid of Baxter appeared impossible, and now fleeing Santee the only viable option.

She flipped through the day's mail and picked up one of Baxter's wine magazines. The cover featured a man wearing a sweater and standing in a vineyard in California. Every wine magazine was identical—always a hillside of lush vines on the cover with the location rotating between California, France, Italy, or another European country. In the middle of the picture would be a man or woman with a relaxed expression and no cares in the world. The rain always fell in perfect increments on magazine vineyards. Rena tossed the magazine aside and sorted the rest of the mail. A few envelopes contained bills. Underneath, Rena uncovered the slip of paper on which Ezra had written his private phone number. Rena put it in a drawer. Picking up the phone, she called Jeffrey's cell phone. When it came to her desire for freedom, Rena could be stubborn. It was time to be blunt with her brother-in-law.

"What's going on?" he asked in a cheerful voice.

"This is a serious call."

Jeffrey's tone changed. "Is Baxter okay?"

"Yes, but I'm not. I can't go on living this way, and I've decided to file for divorce. Alexia Lindale is going to prepare the papers."

Jeffrey was silent for a few moments. "Do you realize this will have a negative effect on our plans?"

"No, I think it will help. Alexia can use the divorce proceeding to do what you wanted her to do in a suit against Ezra. She can ask questions and request information about business stuff that will put the same kind of pressure on your father as if I sued him directly. All you want him to do is back off from manipulating Baxter's interests so you can take more control, right?"

"So *we* can take more control," Jeffrey corrected.

"Forget the act," Rena responded. "You don't want me as a business partner any more than I want to be involved with you. If I can help you in your power play with your father, I'll do it, so long as you give me the money to finance my exit from Santee. I'll get something from Baxter in the divorce case, and then I'll be on my way."

"How will you manage Alexia Lindale?"

"What do you mean?"

"I don't want her prying into our affairs. If she thinks there is money to be found, she'll go after it. That's her reputation."

"I can tell her to stop whenever you want and say it's because I don't want a messy divorce. She's tired of the whole situation anyway. I was barely able to convince her to keep helping me at all."

"I don't like it. My plan is better."

Rena had tried the businesslike approach, but now she shifted tactics. Her voice wavered. "You don't realize what I'm going through. I'm going to do this no matter what."

"Don't test me, Rena."

Rena bit her lip. "If you're talking about the videotape, I've hired a lawyer in Charleston and told him all about it. He told me it wasn't a problem."

"Really? I'd think you'd be more concerned now that the theft and murder case against Quinton is going to be dismissed."

"How do you know that?" Rena asked in surprise.

"You're not the only person with a lawyer in Charleston."

"Did you talk to Sean Pruitt?"

"I don't know him, but I received word this afternoon that Quinton is off the hook, except for some charges related to a fight at a nightclub. If that's true, the police are going to be looking for someone else to prosecute, and I don't know a more likely suspect than you."

Rena shut her eyes as if the loss of sight would cut off her hearing too. "Stop it!" she exploded.

Jeffrey laughed. "Okay, okay. I'm kidding. You're much more help to me sitting at your kitchen counter than in a jail cell. I'll think about the divorce angle and let you know. You may be right. It might work just as well as a direct suit against my father, but I don't like being pressured into doing something."

Rena clicked off the phone and slammed it so hard against the counter that the back cover flew off and the battery slid across the floor. She stared out the window over the sink. She hated being trapped. She would find a way to deal with Jeffrey. She picked up the pieces of the phone and put it back together. As she was about to return it to its cradle, she had an idea.

Opening the drawer, she took out Ezra's number and dialed it. After five rings, she was about to hang up when a recording invited her to leave a message.

"This is Rena," she said in what she hoped was her respectful daughter-in-law voice. "Thanks for giving me this number. I've talked to Jeffrey and need to meet with you as soon as possible."

24

"For I know the plans I have for you," declares the LORD,
"plans to prosper you and not to harm you,
plans to give you hope and a future."
JEREMIAH 29:11

Wednesday afternoon, Alexia inwardly debated whether to attend the music-therapy session scheduled at midnight. Already feeling left out because she didn't have anything musical to contribute, she felt even greater apprehension over Ted's apparent interest in Sarah Locklear. She wavered between a pout and hurt feelings. Gwen buzzed her.

"Preacher-man Ted is on the phone."

"Put him into my voice mail."

Gwen continued. "We've already had a nice chat. He wanted to consult with me about your specific likes and dislikes and had no idea how much you crave watermelon. I suggested he order one from South America for a Christmas present."

"Liar."

"Are you sure you don't want to talk to him?"

Alexia sighed. Totally avoiding Ted was not a long-term solution.

"Alright," she said.

She waited for the call to come through.

"Just checking about tonight," Ted said cheerily. "Do you want to ride together? I could pick you up."

"Uh, I'm in the opposite direction. It would make more sense for me to pick you up."

"I know, but it will be late."

Ted didn't sound like a man wanting to distance himself from her.

"Okay," she said. "Do you remember the road that leads to my house?"

"Pelican Point Drive."

"That's right. Go to the end of the road and turn left on the driveway that runs along the marsh. I'll have a light on."

"I'll be there at eleven thirty."

Alexia paused. "Will Sarah Locklear be on duty tonight?"

"I haven't talked to her, but that's what I understand from the agency. I hope she's there, but even if she isn't, I still want to play. You and I can do it together."

Feeling ten times better about Ted Morgan, Alexia hung up and walked across the hall to Gwen's office.

"Got a date?" the secretary asked. "The watermelon story was bogus, but he still sounded like a man on a mission."

"We're getting together at eleven thirty tonight. He's coming to my house."

Gwen's jaw dropped open. "Now you're the liar."

Alexia shook her head. "It's the truth. You're welcome to hide in the downstairs bedroom and see if he shows up. He suggested it, and I agreed."

Gwen narrowed her eyes. "And then what?"

"We have plans. But you wouldn't understand. I'll let you know tomorrow how it goes."

Alexia returned to her office, closed the door, and counted to ten. Then she opened the door and looked across the hall. Gwen's chair was empty. Alexia chuckled. The secretary had probably scurried down the hall to find Rachel Downey.

———

Boris signaled Ted's arrival long before the doorbell rang. The dog, barking wildly, ran back and forth across the living room. Alexia flung open the door and saw the approaching headlights. She waved as Boris bolted past her. The lights stopped and began to back up. Alexia started down the front steps. Boris reached the vehicle and ran up to the driver-side door.

"Come on! This is the place!" she called out.

The lights continued to recede. Alexia reached the bottom of the steps as the vehicle backed into the sand and turned around. It wasn't Ted's truck. It was a blue car. Alexia ran back up the stairs.

"Boris! Come!" she yelled from the landing in front of her door.

The dog continued barking at the slow-moving car. The driver turned off the lights as he headed away, and Alexia couldn't see the license plate. A hundred yards down the road, the driver flipped on the lights and veered right onto Pelican Point Drive. Alexia slammed the front door shut and locked the dead bolt. She switched off the lights in the living room, went into the kitchen, and peered out the darkened window. A vehicle was approaching the house. She could see Boris's dark shape running down the road beside it. Closer it came; this time without slowing down. When it came under the spotlight on the corner of the house, she could see it clearly.

Ted's white truck.

Alexia closed her eyes for a few seconds and commanded her heart to slow down. Taking several deep breaths, she returned to the living room, unlocked the front door, and stepped onto the landing. Ted was standing beside his truck letting Boris smell the back of his hand. He looked up and smiled.

"I'm letting Boris make sure I'm friendly."

Alexia leaned against the railing at the top of the steps.

"Are you ready to go?" Ted asked.

"Uh, yes. I need to get my purse and put Boris in the house."

Boris obediently pattered up the steps and past her into the house. Alexia closed and locked the door. She left the lights on in the living room.

"Are you tired?" Ted asked when she reached the bottom of the steps.

Alexia shook her head. "No, let's go."

Ted opened the door for her. "You have a beautiful house."

Alexia didn't respond, but as soon as Ted was behind the wheel, she asked, "Did you see the blue car that passed you at the turn for Pelican Point Drive?"

"Yes."

"Did you see how many people were in it?"

"No, I didn't pay that much attention to it."

"When it approached the house I thought it was you, so I ran down the steps, waving," Alexia replied. "When the driver stopped and turned around, I realized that it wasn't your truck. He backed up and turned off his lights until he reached Pelican Point Drive."

"So you couldn't see the license plate?"

"Right."

"The vehicle you mentioned the other day was a van, wasn't it?"

"Yes, but there isn't any reason for someone to be on this road at midnight without headlights."

Ted turned onto Highway 17. "Unless they'd taken a wrong turn."

"Which happens," Alexia admitted. "But since the van forced me off the road . . ."

Ted drove toward Santee in silence for a few moments.

"Are you okay?" he asked.

"Still a bit shaky. I'm glad you arrived when you did. Boris makes a lot of noise, but he's not a protector."

They reached the edge of town and the deserted streets of Santee. They parked in front of the cottage next to the dark Richardson house. Alexia started to open the door of the truck.

"Wait," Ted said, touching her arm. "Let's pray. I don't want you to walk into the cottage feeling afraid."

"Okay, but I'm not sure what to pray."

"I'll do it." Ted kept his eyes open. "Father, I ask you to touch Alexia and take away all fear. Cleanse her soul from the effects of this attack upon her peace and security. Reassure her that you are her strong defense against every kind of enemy who would attack her. Restore and refresh her by the ministry of the Holy Spirit. In Jesus' name I pray, Amen."

As Ted prayed, Alexia let out a deep breath, and the inner tension relaxed.

"Thanks," she said. "It worked."

Ted grinned. "That's encouraging. It's supposed to work."

Inside the cottage, Baxter lay on his side with his face away from the door. Sarah Locklear peeked out from the kitchen at the sound of their entrance. Her dark hair was on her shoulders, and she was wearing light-blue scrubs. Ted set his keyboard on a chair beside Baxter's bed and greeted Sarah with a quick hug. Alexia glanced at the floor; her uneasiness returned.

"How is he?" Ted asked Sarah.

"Better. He's showing signs of improving mental ability—awareness of his environment, responding to commands, simple word phrases. When he tries to talk, it's jumbled, but at least he's making the effort.

He's complained of headaches, which is not a bad sign. The fact that he comprehends the presence of pain and where it's located is positive."

Curious, Alexia stepped closer to the bed. "Has he talked tonight?" she asked.

"When I came on duty he was alert. His eyes were open, and he turned his head to watch me cross the room. He asked for a sip of water, but he's been sleeping most of the time since."

Thinking about the visit from Giles Porter, Alexia probed further. "Has he been able to respond to questions about events in the past?"

"I don't know for sure, but I haven't seen it. He may have a surge in improvement and then lose ground. I didn't see anything in the notes indicating that he understands the seriousness of his condition. That will raise another category of issues."

"Depression?" Ted asked.

Sarah nodded. "And other things."

Ted connected the power cord to the keyboard. "Where is the nurse's aide?"

"She called in sick, and the agency couldn't find a replacement. I can handle the shift by myself." She looked at her watch. "My relief won't be here for about seven hours, so I'm not in a hurry, although you two may want to go to bed before the sun rises."

Ted turned on the keyboard. "I'm here for as long as it takes to do what we need to do."

"Me too," Alexia replied in a voice that even convinced herself.

Alexia retreated to a chair on the opposite side of the room where she had a clear view of Baxter's face. At the moment, he didn't looked troubled or in pain. Ted spoke.

"Healing and hope is the theme on my heart. Healing for now and hope for the future."

Sarah picked up a worn black Bible and turned the pages. She stopped and began to read.

"'For I know the plans I have for you,' declares the LORD, 'plans to prosper you and not to harm you, plans to give you hope and a future.'"

"Yes," Ted answered.

The minister began to play. Alexia had heard Ted play different types of music, but the sounds directed toward heaven on behalf of Baxter Richardson were unique. The keyboard might be cheap, but the intention rich. As she listened, Alexia could visualize the notes coming together in a purposeful pattern. After a few minutes, Sarah joined in with her vibrant alto voice.

"Lord, you have a plan," she sang. "For this man, Lord, you have a plan."

Over and over, the nurse repeated the words, calling forth a strategy born in the will of God.

It took time for Ted to build musical momentum that encompassed the breadth of hope. Back and forth, Ted and Sarah went until the sounds exploded in shouts of triumph from Sarah and powerful chords from Ted that summoned healing for Baxter's body, mind, and spirit. A stranger walking into the room at that moment might have stepped back in apprehension, but the sounds elicited intuitive agreement from Alexia.

She harbored mixed emotions toward Baxter. After all, the young man had tried to kill his wife, and his current physical status smacked of divine justice. Yet, somehow, as she listened to the music, Alexia couldn't rule out the possibility that God would reveal a purpose for Baxter down the road and around the bend. It was a staggering prospect. She ceased being an observer and began to long for a miracle. Chills ran over her. She watched Baxter's face. The music and singing had no apparent effect on him.

The nurse sang about prosperity, not in the financial sense, but a spiritual richness only God could provide. Ted added notes that piled up like stacks of heavenly coinage. They transitioned through the rest of the verse into the theme of protection. Several times Alexia closed her eyes. Each time she opened them, she looked at Baxter, who remained unaware. The music began to subside.

But not all at once. A few more roaring breakers washed over the room. Ted stayed in the upper reaches of the keyboard, musically standing on tiptoe to push the notes as close to heaven as possible. Sarah didn't sing; she stopped, raised her face to the ceiling, and lifted her hands in the air. Alexia suspected Ted and Sarah were in a place she'd never been, but the atmosphere in the room didn't tolerate jealousy. She sat as quietly as possible until the last note faded beyond the realm of hearing. Ted bowed his head for several seconds and then turned off the keyboard.

"That's it," he said.

Sarah lowered her hands and stepped closer to Baxter. She reached over and brushed his hair away from his forehead.

"He's hot," she said. "I'd better take his temperature."

She returned with a digital thermometer. Alexia stood on the opposite side of the bed. If Baxter was warm, he wasn't perspiring. He looked at peace. Sarah checked the reading.

"Ninety-eight point six." She looked across the bed at Alexia. "Touch his head."

Alexia rested her hand on Baxter's forehead.

"Wow, how can that be? He's on fire!"

Ted leaned forward and placed his hand on the spot Alexia had touched.

"It's a sign of anointing," he replied simply. "I don't think there's anything wrong with him. The presence of the Lord is so strong upon him that it's generating heat. The Bible says the Holy Spirit can be like fire."

"How long will it last?" Alexia asked.

"I don't know. But that's encouraging. Maybe the Lord decided to send a message that we are on the right track."

Sarah smiled. "Thank you, Lord."

———

Ted and Alexia left the cottage after 1:00 AM. Ted, in the world of his own thoughts, didn't speak. Alexia didn't either, until they turned onto Pelican Point Drive.

"That was probably my last chance to go to the cottage with you," she said.

"Why?" Ted asked in surprise.

"I shouldn't mention this until the papers are delivered to the clerk's office in the morning, but Rena is going to file for divorce. Once that happens and Baxter's father hires a lawyer, the ethical rules prohibit my contact with Baxter outside the presence of his attorney."

"But Baxter doesn't even know you're there."

"It doesn't matter. He might say or do something that she could use against his interests in court."

Ted frowned. "Why is she filing for divorce?"

"I can't tell you."

Ted's voice took on an edge. "I guess she didn't take seriously the vows at their wedding to stay married 'for better or for worse,' and 'in sickness and in health.'"

Alexia bristled. "She has legitimate reasons that have nothing to do with Baxter's condition. If I didn't think so, I wouldn't have agreed to represent her."

"Whatever he's done in the past, he's helpless now."

"True, but powerful family dynamics drive this situation. Rena needs to escape."

"That's what my wife thought too."

Alexia glanced at Ted's silhouette. "No, it's not the same. I can't tell you Baxter and Rena's history, but if I could, I don't think you'd condemn her."

"I'm not condemning her, but it's a decision that has no end. It affects the rest of life."

They reached Alexia's house. Ted turned off the engine. A full moon passing across the night sky cast light into the cab. Half of Alexia's face was in shadow, half in the light. Ted spoke.

"Can I ask you a question?"

"Yes."

"Do the things you know about Baxter and Rena affect your ability to pray for his healing?"

"It's been an issue," Alexia admitted. "But I've decided that if I want God to have mercy on me, I can't tell him not to have mercy on Baxter."

"Quid pro quo."

Alexia smiled. "Spoken like a lawyer. I'll never forget the feeling of overwhelming love I experienced when God touched me in your backyard. I wish everyone could have the same kind of encounter, no matter what they've done. If I thought otherwise, it would cheapen what happened to me."

"Okay," Ted replied.

"So I'm glad Baxter baked in heavenly heat while you played and Sarah sang. If that's the way God wants to touch him, I won't disagree. I don't understand it, but I guess that's not the most important thing."

"You know what?" Ted asked, his voice softening.

"Tell me."

"You're a remarkable woman."

Ted leaned forward and kissed her before Alexia realized what he was going to do. She received the kiss but didn't respond.

"Good night," she said.

"I'll stay here until you signal that everything is alright."

"Uh, thanks."

Alexia climbed the steps and unlocked the front door. The only living creatures in the house were two sleepy pets that belonged there. She stepped back to the door and waved.

This time, the correct person waved back.

25

Oh, what a tangled web we weave.
SIR WALTER SCOTT

Rena, sitting in a high-backed leather chair near the Palmetto Club's main dining room, waited nervously for Ezra to arrive. Half a bagel topped with cream cheese and a cup of coffee constituted a big breakfast for her, and the massive spread at the private club held no appeal. Ezra had designated the site for their meeting, and Rena didn't protest, even though it meant getting up at 6:30 AM to drive to the outskirts of Charleston.

It cost tens of thousands to join the club, and thousands a year to remain a member. Dues covered a certain amount of food, but Ezra Richardson's membership bought him something more valuable. Rena knew the large dining and smoking rooms were watering holes for the kind of big game Ezra hunted—businessmen and investors looking for opportunities to collaborate and earn even more money. Most cared less about spending money than about crafting a venture that netted an enviable profit.

A member of the wait staff dressed in white with a blue bow tie deftly balanced a large tray on his right hand and made his way to a private dining room. His feet made no noise on the thick carpeting. Rena looked again at her watch. Her father-in-law was fifteen minutes late. The possibility that he'd been called away on more important business crossed her mind. A hand touched her shoulder, and she jumped.

"Sorry I'm late," Ezra said. "I saw someone on the way in, and we had a brief chat in the bar. It's the best place for privacy at this time of the morning."

"That's okay," Rena replied. "This is a nice place to wait."

Ezra was wearing an open-collar shirt, slacks, and expensive black shoes.

Rena had taken time to make sure she looked as classy as possible. She'd swept her blonde hair away from her face and slipped on a stylish yet conservative dress that would meet with Ezra's approval. Wearing a nice dress to breakfast was not customary for the female inhabitants of the ramshackle five-room house in Nichol's Gap where Rena grew up.

"Have you had a cup of coffee?" Ezra asked.

"No, I waited for you."

Ezra raised his hand, and a waiter quickly approached.

"Good morning, Robert. Do you have a table for two by a window?"

"Yes, Mr. Richardson. Please follow me."

As they crossed the dining room, Rena felt multiple eyes tracking her progress. Annoyance flushed her cheeks. It wasn't unusual for heads to turn when she passed by, and the morning admiration from the club members differed little from the leers she received when walking across a nightclub dance floor.

She sat down. With a flourish, the waiter laid a cloth napkin in her lap.

"Coffee?" he asked.

"Black," Rena answered.

"Cream and half a sugar," Ezra said.

The waiter left. Her mouth suddenly dry, Rena took a sip of water.

"Don't be nervous," Ezra said. "We're getting off to a new start this morning."

The fact that Ezra sensed her tension made Rena even more uneasy.

"Uh, that's what I want too."

The waiter brought their coffee.

"What would you like this morning, Mr. Richardson?" he asked.

Ezra ordered an omelet with six specific ingredients. "And make sure they don't overcook it, Robert. I want it runny around the edges."

"Yes sir. Eddie is in the kitchen this morning."

"Good. Give him my regards."

Rena requested fruit. Left alone, Ezra took a sip of coffee and raised his eyebrows.

"You mentioned that you'd talked to Jeffrey. What did you discuss?"

Rena could be bold when given the opportunity to follow through with a plan. She launched immediately into her presentation.

"It was a follow-up to several conversations we had in Greenville while Baxter was in the hospital. He told me you were taking over Baxter's interest in several businesses and that if you followed through with your plans, Baxter and I would be ripped off. He asked me to help him gain greater control over the business interests of Richardson and Company. That way, both of us would come out ahead."

She saw Ezra's face harden. "How did he propose to do that?"

"He wanted me to file a lawsuit against you so that you would back off. He said that if my attorney mentioned certain companies in the legal papers and asked for information about them, you would get the message and let him do what he wanted."

"Which companies?"

"I don't remember. I have a list at the house."

"I'd like to see it."

"Okay, but no lawsuit has been filed, and I'm not going to do it."

Ezra eased back in his chair, and his shoulders relaxed.

"That's good. What changed your mind?"

"I don't believe Jeffrey told me the truth about you. I know you used the power of attorney to take money from our checking account, but you put it back."

"That's right, and I apologized."

Rena couldn't remember an apology but didn't argue. "And when you stopped by the house the other day and gave me your private number, I began to wonder who really wanted to do the right thing—you or Jeffrey."

Ezra didn't immediately respond. Rena felt her left cheek beginning to twitch and reached up to hide it.

"Have you decided?" Ezra asked.

"Yes. That's why I called you."

Ezra nodded. "Good decision. Did you see the dividend distribution I transferred to your bank account last week?"

"Yes, that also helped convince me."

The waiter brought their food, and conversation ceased until he left. Neither Rena nor Ezra took a bite.

"How much has Jeffrey been giving you?" Ezra asked.

"Twenty thousand whenever I ask."

"I'll do more, so long as we can keep the lines of communication open."
Ezra rubbed his temples. "I'm sorry you've been dragged into the middle of
this, Rena. It would be better if you didn't know anything at all. What else
did he tell you?"

"Nothing, but now I'm scared of Jeffrey."

"Why?"

"He's been threatening me if I don't do what he says. It has to do with
the man who stole my car and killed the sheriff's deputy in Charleston.
Jeffrey is going to tell the police that I had something to do with it."

Ezra didn't hide his shock. "That's insane."

"Jeffrey claims he has powerful friends who can influence the police
and prosecutors. I don't know. I'm just scared."

Rena brought her napkin to her face and covered her eyes but peeked
over the edge to gauge Ezra's reaction. He looked grim.

"Leave that to me," he said. "I'll take care of it."

"Are you sure?"

"Yes. Jeffrey's influence can't come close to mine. He's got a lot to
learn. Some of it may have to come the hard way."

"What should I do?"

"Nothing except trust me."

"That's all?"

"Yes."

"Thank you," Rena responded gratefully, lowering the napkin. She
took a bite of fruit. "This sure is good cantaloupe."

―――

The final draft of Rena's complaint for divorce sat on Alexia's desk with
the filing fee check on top. Gwen buzzed her.

"Rena is on the line."

"Good. I'll let her know that we're ready to go."

Fifteen minutes later, Alexia hung up the phone. She picked up the
divorce petition, walked across the hall to Gwen's desk, and dropped the
documents on the desk.

"Guess what Rena told me?"

Gwen looked at the top sheet of the petition. "After begging you not
to fire her, she hired another lawyer to represent her in the divorce?"

"Not even close. She wants me to hold off on the divorce until she gets some things worked out with her father-in-law."

"But she's not divorcing her father-in-law."

"Only his money. He's promised to bankroll her. Apparently she's started a bidding war for her help between Ezra and Jeffrey and wants to keep it going until she builds up a pot of cash. Then she'll cut ties with Baxter and skip town without feeling any immediate financial pressure while the divorce is pending."

"Why would Ezra and Jeffrey give her money? I heard Ezra didn't want Baxter to marry her in the first place, and Jeffrey is a self-centered jerk."

"Probably right on both counts, but Rena claims she knows details about Richardson and Company that both father and son want kept quiet."

Gwen's eyes grew big. "Hush money. Alexia, this is unreal."

"Oh, at least the money part is real. Ezra and Jeffrey have put tens of thousands into Rena's checking account in the past two weeks, and she tells me much more is coming in the near future. I can't say whether there is anything truly shady about Richardson and Company, although it wouldn't surprise me. At first, Rena's suspicions sounded off-the-wall, but now I'm not so sure."

"What are the Richardsons doing that they want kept secret?"

"Like I said, I don't know. The other day when we went to Charleston, Rena claimed they were up to something illegal, but they might just want to protect insider knowledge. Maybe they have a scoop about future road construction or a new commercial development that will affect the value of property they want to buy or sell. Ezra always had a new deal in the works. Secrecy can mean the difference between a huge profit and a loss."

Alexia decided not to mention Henry Quinton's comments about "bad people," which implied something more sinister than a crooked politician leaking information about roads.

Gwen pressed her lips tightly together before she spoke. "Where do you fit in?"

"I'm on the sidelines for now, which is fine with me. I'd rather let the dust settle. I'm tired of being Rena's yo-yo lawyer."

Gwen picked up the divorce petition and placed it on the other side of her computer. "I'll keep this nearby. When Rena jerks your string, it will be ready to go."

———

Alexia went to lunch alone at Katz Deli, a local place owned by a Jewish couple who moved to the coast from New York City. They planned to escape the pressures of life in Brooklyn and be close to multiple grandchildren; however, Arthur and Edith Katz brought their love of the great city south with them and decorated the restaurant with framed posters of the New York City skyline. The Statue of Liberty greeted patrons as they walked through the door. A panorama of Wall Street stretched along another wall with Central Park opposite it. A poster featuring the twin towers of the World Trade Center hung on the back wall. Edith had draped it in a sheer black cloth.

Alexia loved the Katz's Reuben sandwich with a fat pickle on the plate. Arthur greeted her when she walked through the door.

"Alexia! I hear you opened your own office. You should have moved to New York, where you could make some real money. A sharp female lawyer like you, representing super-rich women with apartments on Park Avenue and houses in Nantucket . . . oy! You could charge more than five hundred dollars an hour."

Alexia sat down at a table for two near the meat cooler. "If I billed that much what would a sandwich cost me?"

"Forty-seven fifty," the balding rotund man replied without hesitation. "And the pickle would be an extra five bucks. You know, there are places on Manhattan where it costs thirty dollars for a hamburger. One of my Reubens should be worth more than that."

"I won't argue with that," Alexia responded. "Where's Edith?"

Arthur came over to Alexia's table. "She's at home. Our third daughter and two of our grandchildren are coming for a visit this weekend. The house is a mess."

Arthur and Edith had more grandchildren than Alexia could keep straight without a chart. She doubted Edith Katz ever kept a messy house.

"And I bet she's cooking something special," Alexia said.

Arthur grinned. "The best blintzes you have ever put in your mouth."

"Please reconsider my request that you adopt me," Alexia pleaded. "I'll do the legal work for free."

Arthur patted her on the arm. "I'll save you a couple of blintzes if you promise to come in on Tuesday."

"It's a deal."

"How about today? Do you want the usual?"

Alexia nodded. "Yes."

While she waited, Alexia watched the two waitresses who worked the lunch crowd scurry back and forth with plates piled high with sandwiches and chips. She heard her cell phone beep the opening notes to Beethoven's Ninth Symphony.

"Hello," she said.

"Alexia, I hope I'm not disturbing your lunch."

Sean Pruitt's distinctive voice needed no identification.

"Not yet. It should be here in a few minutes."

"Things are heating up with Rena. The detective you mentioned from Mitchell County—"

"Giles Porter."

"Yes. He's been busy lobbying the local police to go after Rena. I received a call from Rick Bridges, the detective who was beaten up at the Beachcomber Club. He wants to interview Rena."

Arthur put a plate down in front of Alexia. She took a nibble from her pickle. It had the perfect crunch.

"You anticipated that would happen. Shouldn't you be contacting Rena?"

"Bridges wants to talk to you as well."

Alexia put down her pickle. "Me? Why?"

"It seems Porter claims you have illegally obstructed a criminal investigation."

"That's ridiculous!" Alexia said so loudly that the people sitting at nearby tables turned to look at her. She glanced around and continued in a low but intense voice. "I told him to leave Rena's property because he didn't have a search or arrest warrant, and I wouldn't let him interrogate Rena when we were at the hospital in Greenville. It's been several years since I took criminal procedure in law school, but I'm sure the Sixth Amendment preserves the right to have a lawyer present when a suspect is questioned."

"Of course, but there are limits on what a lawyer can do to protect a client. I'm not sure about the allegations, but I thought you would want to know as soon as possible."

Alexia stared straight ahead, racking her brain to recall anything that remotely crossed the line of improper activity on her part. Rena had deceived her about the theft of her car, but Alexia hadn't made any personal representations to the police about what happened.

"I'm clueless," she said. "Is there any way you can find out more details?"

"I can try. Do you want me to represent you?"

"Oh, yeah, I guess that's necessary."

"Don't worry about the fee at this point," Pruitt said before Alexia could ask him about it. "I'll just engage in a fact-finding mission. I have contacts at the police department who will give me information outside official channels."

Alexia had heard about similar arrangements nurtured by criminal-defense lawyers, some of which involved liquor, women, or drugs. She hesitated. One meeting with Pruitt wasn't enough to form a reliable opinion about his character.

"What kind of contacts?"

"Nothing shady. I have a friend who works for internal affairs, and a great aunt who has a clerical job."

"Who will you ask to help?"

"My aunt. She's the person who knows everything. I'll invite her over for tea. She loves visiting the house, and I'll let you know what I find out."

"What about Rena?"

"I'm calling her next. I'll fax you a representation letter this afternoon."

Alexia put the phone down on the table. Her sandwich smelled delicious, but her appetite had vanished. If she left the Reuben on her plate untouched, she would hurt Arthur's feelings. She motioned to one of the waitresses.

"Please box this to go."

26

No weapon formed against you shall prosper, and every tongue which rises against you in judgment you shall condemn. This is the heritage of the servants of the LORD.

ISAIAH 54:17 NKJV

Alexia took her sandwich directly to her office and shut the door. She stared at a blank legal pad on her desk, but there was nothing to write down, no plan of action. Without any idea what incriminating facts gripped the handle of the gun pointed in her direction, she couldn't formulate a defense. She mentally replayed the entire course of her representation of Rena, but no potentially unlawful incidents surfaced. Alexia could do nothing but wait for Sean Pruitt to drop a lump of sugar in his aunt's teacup and conduct a parlor-room interrogation.

She opened the Styrofoam container for her sandwich. It still smelled good, and she unwrapped the pickle covered in a thin sheet of white paper. On the paper, Arthur Katz had written, "Don't forget the blintzes!" The delicatessen owner's thoughtfulness made her suddenly teary. Nice people still lived in this world.

Her phone buzzed. She'd forgotten to push the do-not-disturb button.

"What is it?" Alexia asked.

"Ted Morgan is here to see you," the receptionist answered. "I wasn't sure if you were back from lunch."

Alexia didn't want to see anyone, not even Ted.

"Is he standing there in front of you so that he knows I'm here?"

"Uh, yes."

Alexia sighed. "Okay. I'll be right out."

The minister, wearing a pair of new white painter's overalls, waited in the reception area. He greeted her with a smile.

"I'm going over to the house this afternoon and need a key."

"It's in my office," Alexia replied flatly. "Come on back and I'll give it to you."

She led Ted down the hall and into her office. The smell of the sandwich filled the room.

"Sorry, I interrupted your lunch," Ted said. "Is that from Katz's Deli?"

"Yes, but I'm not very hungry. Would you like it?"

"No, thanks. Is something wrong?"

"It's not something I can talk about."

"Did someone else come near your house?" Ted asked with concern in his voice.

"No, everything is fine. It's a legal matter. Here's the key." Alexia held out the key and dropped it into Ted's hand. "What are you going to do at the house?" she asked.

"Prep work. Take off the old wallpaper in the living room, back bedroom, and dining room. If it doesn't rain this afternoon I'll also begin scraping paint from the exterior. It's especially bad on the north side of the house. And I need to repair a leaky section under the eaves and make sure the gutters are flush against the house."

Alexia wasn't paying attention. "You're the professional. When do I need to pay you?"

"Not before the end of next week. I have a charge account at the lumber yard, and I'll keep up with my time."

"I know about time records. Try to keep it as low as possible."

Ted gave Alexia a puzzled look. "You can save money if you help strip the walls. But you'll probably come out ahead billing your minutes on cases instead of breaking a fingernail scraping off wallpaper."

Alexia managed a weak smile. "I don't know about that."

Ted took a step backward from her desk. "Are you sure there isn't anything I can do to help you?"

The tears that had touched the edges of Alexia's eyes moments before returned before she could suppress them. Ted Morgan also appeared on the list of good, decent people who walked the earth. And he'd touched her life much more deeply than Mr. Katz. Alexia quickly rubbed her eyes, but couldn't hide her emotions. Ted's look of concern deepened. Alexia held up her hands in front of her.

"I really can't tell you—"

"I understand."

Alexia paused to sniffle before continuing, "But when you prayed for me while we were sitting in the truck last night, it helped. Could you do the same thing now without knowing what's going on?"

"Sure. The most important thing is not what I know, but that we ask the One who does."

"Then, please, do it."

Alexia leaned forward in her chair and wiped her eyes with a tissue. Ted sat across the desk. Alexia closed her eyes. Several seconds of silence passed before Ted spoke.

"Alexia, a verse just came to mind. I'm going to quote it as a prayer and statement of God's will for you." The minister spoke slowly and distinctly. "No weapon formed against you shall prosper, and every tongue which rises against you in judgment you shall condemn. This is the heritage of the servants of the Lord."

As Ted spoke, the words became like fire behind Alexia's eyelids. She bit her lip. Ted stopped. Alexia waited.

Her eyes still closed, she spoke, "Say it again."

Ted repeated the verse. Each word landed with impact upon her heart, and Alexia felt a confidence that the words were true, not just in a general sense, but specifically for her.

"One more time," she asked.

Ted complied. Alexia listened intently, wanting to linger in the presence of God as the pressures of the finite world shrank before the power of words from heaven. The spiritual atmosphere in the room cleared. Tears of gratitude, not sadness, touched the edges of her eyes.

The moment passed, but the strength it imparted remained. Alexia wiped her cheeks with the back of her hand and kept her eyes closed tightly for several more seconds before opening them. When she did, she saw through blurry vision Ted, his face sober, watching her.

"Thank you," she said through sniffles.

She sat quietly, letting the message soak in. In a few moments she spoke.

"Is this what you're doing for Baxter Richardson?" she asked.

Ted tilted his head to one side. "In a way. I'm trying to be specific in what I play so that it's relevant to his need, but the fact that my prayers are musical instead of spoken makes their effectiveness more difficult to gauge."

"But they're real," Alexia said with renewed strength. "I know it. Would you quote the verse one more time? I want to write it down."

Ted repeated the words, and Alexia wrote them on a blank legal pad. "Anything else?" he asked.

Alexia smiled. "Go strip some wallpaper?"

"I'll be there all afternoon if you want to come by and help."

After Ted left, Alexia didn't feel like working. She leaned back in her chair and read the words on the legal pad over and over until she memorized them. Her sandwich was cold now, but she didn't mind. She closed the box lid. Something more effective than food had reinvigorated her. There was a knock on her door, and Gwen peeked inside.

"That was a quick lunch," the secretary said. "You left a minute before me, and I didn't hear you come back."

"I picked up a sandwich to go at Katz's. When I returned, Ted Morgan was here. He's working at the King Street house this afternoon and needed the key."

Gwen looked closer at Alexia's face. "Have you been crying?"

Alexia nodded. "Yes. But Ted really helped me. He's like nobody else I've met in my life." She paused and spoke more rapidly. "Gwen, he's the kindest, most sensitive man I've ever met. Whether that equals the ultimate romance, I'm not certain. He has what I want and need, but I'm not sure I have anything to give to him." She sighed. "A one-sided relationship isn't going to work in the long run."

Gwen frowned and shook her head. "You're a special woman, and I bet he sees it. Don't sell yourself short."

"You're prejudiced."

"And I know the truth."

Alexia smiled slightly. "Thanks, but it's hard to figure out where he's coming from. I'm not sure he thinks of me as anything more than a project."

Gwen rolled her eyes. "You're making this too complicated. He's a guy; you're beautiful. He wouldn't be normal if he weren't attracted to you."

"I know he's a man, and he may leave his dirty socks on the floor, but he's one of the least self-centered people I've ever met."

"Has he kissed you?"

"Yes. The first time was inside the church on a Sunday morning after everybody left."

Gwen clapped her hands together. "Then you're practically married. Grab him and spend the rest of your life finding out what's underneath the surface. Good men are scarce. The Marines may find a few, but I've never been so lucky."

———

Rena hung up the phone. She had to be at Sean Pruitt's office at ten thirty in the morning.

The lawyer didn't seem worried, but anxiety would not leave Rena alone. She went into the kitchen and drank a glass of water. The liquor bottles in the cabinet in the corner had been beckoning her with promises of better sleep through the endless nights and anesthesia for the fear and worry that plagued her.

But Rena resisted. She'd suffered too much at the hands of her stepfather; four shots of cheap whiskey never failed to unleash irrational rage that sent all children scrambling for places to hide. Many nights she'd lain in bed pretending to be asleep as he stood over her cursing under his breath for what seemed like hours. On good nights, he would turn away and tromp down the hall to the room where her brothers slept. In a few seconds, she would hear the thumps of the blows raining down on them. Crying out was forbidden, but often her younger brother couldn't suppress his screams. On bad nights, the cruel fists would strike Rena. She would turn her face to the pillow and bite the pillowcase so that no noise escaped her lips to fuel his wrath. Even when drunk, Vernon Swafford took care not to strike the children in the face. Clothes hid their bruises when they went to school the following day. Not until he went to prison did the truth come out.

Rena didn't think about those nights of eternal darkness. She'd filed the horrible memories in a place reserved for nightmares that weren't true. The counseling she eventually received failed to straighten the place within her twisted and deformed by scars of the past. Baxter lying paralyzed in the cottage proved the potency of her stepfather's cruelty and her failure to break free from it.

The agony of looming failure drove Rena to the liquor cabinet. This would end. Now. No matter the cost. She would rid herself of this miserable life, of her miserable father and husband, of the whole miserable Richardson family. She picked up a small bottle of brandy and hurled it against the wall.

The phone rang. The caller ID revealed it was Jeffrey. Rena calmed herself before answering.

"What's going on?" Jeffrey asked.

"Not much. I need some more money."

"Why? I gave you twenty thousand a couple weeks ago."

"The police want to talk to me again about the car theft and the officer's death. I need fifty thousand as soon as possible. I've hired a lawyer in Charleston. He's very expensive."

"Fifty thousand for the lawyer? That's ridiculous. You haven't paid that much to Alexia Lindale for all she's done. Why can't she take care of it?"

"She's a divorce lawyer. Sean Pruitt is a criminal-defense attorney. He has to have all his money up front in case I'm charged and have to go to trial."

"I don't know—"

"Stop it!" Rena interrupted, her voice rising. "Fifty thousand is nothing to you! Do you realize what could happen to me?"

Sean Pruitt had asked for ten thousand dollars, but Rena believed she could pull off the deal over the phone. In person, she feared she would falter. She steadied herself mentally, watching the brandy slowly drip down the wall and pool around the shards of glass.

"We need to get together," Jeffrey responded.

"There's no time. I have to be in Charleston in the morning."

"I can come over now."

Rena bit her lip and looked out the window. "Will you bring the money?"

"Yes. I'll have a check with me."

"Okay, but I'll only be here for another thirty minutes."

"I'm on my way."

After she hung up, Rena calmly mopped the pungent liquid with a towel and swept up the broken pieces. When everything was as it had been, she took out a bottle of expensive whiskey and poured herself a drink. She looked at the clear, amber liquid for a few seconds before taking a sip. It burned her throat. She took another sip. It went down easier. A third followed. And she felt stronger. Her mind cleared, and she had an idea.

———

The receptionist brought a fax and laid it on the corner of Alexia's desk.

"This just came for you."

Alexia saw the cover sheet but didn't touch it. "Thanks."

When the young woman left, Alexia picked up the representation letter from Sean Pruitt and scanned it. It was standard language, nothing fancy. She put it on her desk beside the verse Ted had given her. Even up against the reality of what lay ahead, the words from the Bible didn't retreat. Alexia read both the letter and the verse and remained confident. She signed the representation letter and sent it back to Sean. After feeding it into the machine, she returned to her desk and spent the rest of the afternoon working on her cases. She hardly noticed the hours pass.

———

Rena changed clothes before Jeffrey arrived. She dressed up to bolster her claim that she had to attend a dinner party and couldn't talk very long. She finished a second glass of whiskey as he drove up the driveway. The liquor was already making her feel lightheaded, and she welcomed the sensation. She felt relaxed and beautiful. She flung open the door before Jeffrey rang the bell.

"Come in," she beckoned. "I'm off to the Nickersons's house in a few minutes."

"Nickersons? I don't know them."

"They're new. Just moved here. I met Betty at the tennis club. She's a fabulous player, and when she found out about Baxter, she invited me over for dinner to get me out of the house."

Jeffrey came into the foyer. "You look great," he said.

Rena smiled. "Thanks. Did you bring the check?"

"Let's sit down."

Jeffrey turned toward the living room. Rena didn't want him to get too comfortable.

"No, come into the kitchen," she said. "I need to do a little cleaning up before I leave."

Jeffrey followed her. She rinsed her glass under the faucet for several seconds and put it into the dishwasher. Moistening a dishcloth, she began rubbing the kitchen counter.

"Go ahead," she said.

Jeffrey sat on a stool beside the island.

"I'm willing to consider paying for your lawyer in Charleston, but there are other things that need to be done as well."

"I know." Rena sighed as if talking to an incorrigible child. "Putting pressure on your father. We've been over this. I'm going to do it as part of the divorce proceeding. You acted like a jerk when I mentioned it, but it makes more sense to do it indirectly than to attack your father head-on."

"There's no need to get upset—"

Rena threw the wet cloth down on the floor at Jeffrey's feet. It landed with a loud *splat*. "Listen! You either help me or leave! You're not the only person willing to give me money for information." Jeffrey seemed to jump off the stool in slow motion. Maybe it was the whiskey.

"What are you talking about?"

"Your father, you idiot! Don't you realize he suspects you're up to something?"

"What did you tell him?"

"I didn't tell him anything. He told me. I had breakfast with him at the Palmetto Club. Check it out with his favorite waiter. Robert, isn't it?"

Jeffrey didn't respond, and Rena could tell he knew she was telling the truth. She relaxed.

"He'll tell you we were there," she continued. "Ezra put eighty grand in my bank account last week as a dividend distribution to Baxter. He wants to put our past disagreements behind us and offered to give me a lot more money whenever I ask."

"But he doesn't have a videotape, does he?" Jeffrey shot back.

"I don't think that matters. Go ahead, give it to the police. Then who will help you?"

Jeffrey started to speak, hesitated, and then asked, "What did my father tell you?"

"He's suspicious, but he doesn't know what you're planning to do. He asked me to find out."

Jeffrey swore. Rena thrilled. This was the first sign of weakness she'd seen in her brother-in-law.

"But if I wanted to help him, I wouldn't be talking to you," she quickly added.

"What did you tell him?" Jeffrey repeated.

"That I'd find out what I could. He doesn't know about the divorce, so that will be a complete surprise to him. You won't be involved in the divorce, so you can't be blamed for anything that happens in it. Until Alexia Lindale files the papers, I'll let you tell me what you want your father to know."

Jeffrey sat back down on the stool. "Why are you doing this?"

"Because you will give me the money I need and don't care if I divorce Baxter."

"And I have the videotape."

Rena rolled her eyes. "Yeah, whatever you want to think."

Jeffrey slowly leaned over, picked up the washcloth, and tossed it back to her. "You're not fooling me, Rena," he said in a matter-of-fact tone of voice. "You can stop the act."

Rena stared at his face, but his expression didn't waver. Her thin veneer of confidence cracked. She had no backup plan. If Jeffrey cut her off, she wasn't sure Ezra would keep her on. She didn't trust herself to speak and grabbed hold of a thin thread of hope—a vision of herself far away from this place, perhaps in California, free of this inhumane cruelty. Jeffrey continued.

"You've always been a gold digger. That's the reason you married Baxter in the first place. He was too stupid to realize what you wanted and walked into the marriage blind." In a flash Rena tried to slap him, but Jeffrey grabbed her arm. California faded. "But I don't blame you. You're doing what everybody does—trying to find an angle to get ahead. I'll steer some money your way, but I'll be keeping closer tabs on you to make sure you don't double-cross me. Since Quinton's arrest, your guardian angels have been on vacation. I'm going to put them back to work, and they'll let me know what you have for breakfast, lunch, dinner, and every snack in between."

"How?"

"There's technology for everything." Jeffrey let go of Rena and took out a single check. "I'm going to write you a check for one hundred thousand. I doubt the lawyer in Charleston is charging you fifty, but I don't care. Tell him the videotape is in a place where no one can touch it. You should destroy the copy I gave you."

He placed the check on the counter and quickly filled it in. He handed it to Rena.

"This is what I want you to tell my father. Listen carefully, because I'm going to make sure you do everything exactly as I'm instructing you."

Rena nodded.

27

My life is like a stroll upon the beach,
as near the ocean's edge as I can go.
HENRY DAVID THOREAU

Wearing her black wet suit and old dock shoes, Alexia pulled the little boat away from its mooring underneath her house and began moving steadily backward. Hearing a noise, she glanced over her shoulder and saw a white vehicle turn onto the narrow road that led to her house. Anxiety hit her for a moment before she realized it was Ted Morgan's truck. She dropped the tongue of the trailer and waited. The minister pulled up to the house and got out. Boris left his post beside the boat and delivered a rambunctious greeting. The dog jumped up and added paw prints to the brown smudges dotting the front of Ted's formerly clean overalls. The minister tried to brush off the new spots as he walked toward Alexia, but the mud merely smeared.

"What are you doing?" he asked.

"Launching my boat. Boris and I are going for a swim. What are you doing?"

"I'm reporting to the construction-site supervisor about the renovation of the house on King Street."

Alexia hoped he could stay for a while. "If you want to talk to me, you'll have to go for a boat ride. I may not be in the water yet, but Boris won't forgive me if I turn back now."

"Can I help?"

"Yes, by not getting in my way until the boat is in the water. There's no way I can pull you and the boat."

Ted stepped forward and took hold of the tongue of the trailer. "I'll lend a hand."

"It's not necessary, and I don't want you to get your boots wet unless they double as flippers."

Ted looked down at his scuffed but dry work boots. "I'll be careful."

Together they pulled hard on the boat, and it shot forward toward the marsh, quickly gaining momentum. They reached the edge of the water so fast that Alexia almost fell down trying to halt the boat. The dark mud grabbed hold of Ted's shoes and wouldn't let go. He leaned against the boat and pulled them out, only to sink again.

"This is like sin," he called out. "Once you're in, it's hard to escape."

"And you should have followed the advice of your lawyer and avoided any problems."

Ted struggled back to solid ground. Alexia held the boat.

"We have a problem," Alexia continued. "I didn't get the boat turned around so that the stern faces the marsh. I can't get traction in this mud to push it backward far enough to maneuver it."

"Which means?"

"You'll have to take off your boots and let your toes revel in the mud."

Ted grimaced but didn't argue. Finding a dry spot covered with grass, he sat down and pulled off his boots and socks. Rolling up his pants, he waded out to Alexia.

"This water is cold. I don't usually go swimming this time of year."

"Don't worry, the piranhas are in hibernation. On the count of three, push on the tongue of the trailer."

Alexia counted, and together they backed the boat away from the marsh. Alexia stepped onto the sand and turned the boat around. Ted remained standing in the shallow water near a clump of reeds.

"You can come out now," Alexia commanded. "As soon as the boat is in the water, climb in the bow. Boris will show you how to do it."

She lifted up the tongue and let the boat slide into the water while she held on to the bow rope. Boris leapt into the boat and ran to the stern. Ted followed at a much slower pace.

"I forgot my boots," he said as soon as he was over the side.

Alexia hopped into the boat beside Ted. "You won't need them where we're going. They'll be here when you get back unless a family of crabs decides to turn them into a duplex."

Ted sat in the middle of the boat. Alexia stepped around him and started the motor. Letting it run a notch past idle, she turned the boat around and steered into one of the narrow canals that meandered back and forth across the marsh. Boris stood proudly in the bow. Ted turned around so that he faced Alexia.

"What happened with that situation you were worried about?" he asked over the sound of the motor. "Did you work it out?"

Alexia brushed a strand of hair blown by the early evening breeze from her face. "No business talk allowed on this voyage. Enjoy the ride."

Ted faced forward. Alexia watched his head as she navigated and turned to see what he saw. She never tired of the marsh. A breeze blew the reeds so they swayed like a field of wet wheat. A white egret glided over-head and descended in a semicircular descent to a shallow area beside a sand bar. The bird's thin legs blended in with the reeds. In a few seconds, its head shot down into the water and came up swallowing a slender fish. Boris barked wildly at the egret, but it didn't abandon its fishing spot until the boat came down the channel directly across from it. The heavy season for insects had passed, but a few hardy water striders skated across the inky surface. Alexia felt content, secure in a place worry could not mar.

Alexia made a sharp turn into the narrow stretch of open water between the marsh and the barrier island and revved the engine.

"Get ready to land!" she called out. "Follow Boris! He knows what to do."

Ted turned and nodded. As soon as the boat touched the sand, Boris bounded out and ran up a dune and over the top. Ted went after him and followed without looking back at Alexia, who was left to bring the boat out of the water and tie it off to a scrubby bush. Beach bag in hand, she climbed the dune. Reaching the top, she looked down. Boris was already chest-deep in the surf. Ted was standing in shallow water that washed over his feet and waving his arms at the dog. Alexia descended the dune and dropped her bag on the sand.

"What are you doing?" she yelled out to Ted.

Ted retreated from the water and joined her.

"I'm acting excited like Boris. I'm not going to wade out to my chest, but I can at least copy his enthusiasm."

Alexia laughed. "Good job."

She took her goggles from the beach bag and slipped them over her head. She glanced down at her watch.

"I'm going for a swim. The island is about a mile long, and sometimes I swim all the way to the south end. Today, I'll only stay in the water about twenty minutes. Boris paddles along beside me. We don't set any speed records, but we've always returned to dry ground."

"That's good to know. I'll explore on foot."

Alexia walked into the water and greeted Boris, who came close and shook himself. She rubbed his head and slipped the goggles over her eyes. Wading into the chilly water, she dove through a wave and began swimming.

After a few strokes, she turned her head toward the beach, but a swell blocked her view, and she couldn't see Ted. A stiff breeze made the water choppy. It wasn't perfect swimming weather, and it took a minute to synchronize her strokes with the water. All waves in a sequence are not alike; every seventh wave is slightly larger. Alexia timed her strokes to reach the crest of the largest wave and slide down the other side. The thrill didn't compare to surfing, but it gave Alexia a feeling of accomplishment. By cooperating with nature's peaceful beat, she could move forward faster than if she fought it. Boris swam with the consistency of a metronome.

When she finally had a clear view of the beach, Ted had disappeared.

She glanced at her watch. Twenty minutes had passed. Though she'd struck a good rhythm, she turned toward the beach. Boris paddled a few more feet, then followed. Alexia body surfed to the shore. Boris occasionally caught a wave by accident but didn't know how to utilize its power, and he struggled against the forward force of the water. What his arrival on the beach lacked in grace, he made up for in enthusiasm. Alexia reached the shallows and shook the water from her hair. Taking off the goggles, she looked up and down the beach.

"Where's Ted?" she asked Boris.

Alexia was Boris's universe. Even if the dog had understood the question, Ted was nothing more to him than a minor star in an obscure constellation. Boris simply wagged his tail. Looking up, Alexia saw the minister crest a dune farther down the beach. Alexia waved, and they walked toward one another.

"What did you find?" Alexia asked.

"Beauty everywhere. I understand why you like this place. It's like having your own island."

"Especially this time of year. A few people will come for the day in the summer, but the rest of the year, it's deserted."

They walked slowly toward the place where Alexia left her beach bag. Boris ran ahead. The air was cool against Alexia's wet skin, but she felt comfortable sharing her simple paradise with Ted. She would have been disappointed if he hadn't appreciated it. She walked between Ted and the ocean along the undulating line where departing waves left tiny flecks of foam on the sand.

"You are totally different from earlier today," Ted said.

"The verse you gave me has stayed with me all afternoon."

They walked farther. A family of sandpipers scurried across the wet sand in front of them.

"I have a question," Alexia said.

"What?"

Alexia hesitated. "Do you know what it is?"

Ted laughed. He looked up at the sky, which was beginning to darken at the eastern edge. "God, what is Alexia's question? And while you're at it, give me the answer."

They took a few more steps. The sandpipers rose into the air and glided farther down the beach.

"I have it!" Ted exclaimed. "Yes! The answer to your question is yes."

Alexia shook her head. "No, you have to tell me both the question and the answer."

Ted hesitated. "Uh . . . yes, I know how to swim, but not as well as you."

"That's okay, but the question has to do with me, not you."

She stopped and turned so that she faced him. The breeze blew a few strands of her dark hair alongside her face. Ted stood just beyond the reach of the waves. Alexia spoke.

"Do you want to spend time with me because I need your help, or are you interested in me as a person?"

"Both," Ted responded immediately.

"I mean, are you interested in me as a woman?"

Ted didn't immediately answer, and Alexia's heart sank toward the sand at her feet. Ted tilted his head to the side.

"Alexia, if I wasn't interested in you as a woman I wouldn't have kissed you. Romance is not a game to me. I've been divorced for almost twenty years, and the idea of another relationship is scary. I've dated some, but it's been years since I've let myself think seriously about a woman. I mean, I want to help you because I see God's hand on your life in a wonderful way, but I'm very attracted to you as a woman. I could list—"

Alexia reached up and touched his lips with her index finger. "Not now. That's enough. But I have another question."

Ted ran his fingers through his wiry hair. "Don't make me guess."

"I won't. It's about Sarah Locklear. Ever since you met her for supper I've wondered if she might be a better fit for you than I am. She's musically gifted, closer in age to you, and understands God a lot better than I do." Alexia paused. "And she's beautiful."

"Is that your way of telling me that I should back away from you?"

"No!" Alexia replied with more force than she intended.

"Then I'll make you a promise," Ted said. "If my thoughts about you change, I'll let you know."

"Okay."

"Will you do the same?"

Alexia nodded. "Yes."

"Anything else?"

Alexia grasped the straps of Ted's overalls and pulled him closer to her. "This seals the deal," she said.

Alexia initiated the kiss, but Ted prolonged it. When their lips parted, Ted looked down at her and smiled.

"There's nothing quite like a salty kiss while standing at the edge of the surf."

"Too salty?" she asked.

"No."

Alexia raised her head. "Try this. I'll try to make it salty and sweet."

28

O tiger's heart wrapped in a woman's hide!
HENRY VI, ACT 1, SCENE 4

Too nervous to read a magazine, Rena sat in the parlor waiting for Sean Pruitt. She'd already handed a check for ten thousand dollars to the attorney's bookkeeper. The receipt for the retainer lay in her hand, and she'd folded and unfolded it so many times it threatened to fall apart. She stood and paced and then sat down again and considered abandoning her appointment. This was a waste of time. Almost an hour passed before the dark-haired attorney came into the room and greeted her. He was wearing a blue suit, white shirt, and a yellow tie.

"Sorry I'm late. I was delayed in court for a hearing. While there, I saw Detective Bridges and told him you don't have anything else to say at this time."

"Won't that make him suspicious?"

"He's already suspicious, and we don't need to give him any additional reasons to focus the investigation on you."

"But I didn't do anything wrong. Why can't I repeat the same story I told earlier?"

"No, I can't let you do that. It's better to keep quiet."

Rena pouted. "What happens next?"

"Hopefully, nothing."

A knock sounded on the door of the parlor.

"Come in!" Pruitt called out.

The attractive receptionist opened the door and peeked around the corner.

"Detective Bridges is here to see you."

"What's he doing here?" Rena blurted. "You told him I wasn't going to talk to him!"

"I did. It may not be about you. He's also interested in the remaining charge against Henry Quinton. Bridges is the officer beaten up at the Beachcomber Club. I'll be right back."

Pruitt left Rena to continue folding and unfolding the receipt. Several long minutes passed. Waiting was one of her least favorite things to do. She stood up and walked about the room. With all the antiques, the parlor appeared frozen in time a hundred years earlier, except for a sleek, modern phone and recessed electrical lights. Rena picked up several knickknacks to inspect them more closely and wondered about the value of the oil paintings on the walls. She sat down, fidgeted, and got up to pace the room several more times. He should be paying her for her time rather than the other way around. Finally, Pruitt opened the door and slipped inside.

"What took so long?" she asked.

"I'd rather Bridges talk to me than you."

"Is he gone?"

"Yes."

"What did he ask?"

"About other matters, though he repeated his request to talk to you. I told him it wasn't necessary unless he had a specific question. He asked about the car, and I told him you sold it."

"Did that satisfy him?"

Pruitt shrugged. "I don't know."

"Is there anything else I should do?"

Pruitt looked at her with a level gaze. "Don't talk to anybody about this. No exceptions."

"Not even Alexia Lindale?"

"Correct."

———

Gwen buzzed Alexia.

"The receptionist says a police officer is here to see you. I sent the complaint in the Wallen matter to the sheriff's department yesterday. Do you have any other papers that need to be served?"

Alexia scanned her desk. "No, I'll go up front and find out what he wants."

Alexia entered the reception area expecting to find a uniformed deputy. Instead, a tall man in a suit waited for her. He extended his hand.

"Ms. Lindale?"

"Yes."

"I'm Detective Jefferson with the Santee Police Department. Is there a place where we can talk in private?"

"Uh, yes, in one of the conference rooms."

Alexia led him into the room where she'd watched the videotape with Rena. She closed the door.

"What can I do for you?" Alexia asked.

The detective held out a sheet of paper. "I have a subpoena for production of a videotape that may be in your possession."

Alexia took the sheet of paper, a grand-jury subpoena from Charleston County. The lines reserved for description of the items to be produced listed a "videotape depicting the activities of Rena Richardson" and gave the date of Officer Dixon's death. Alexia read the subpoena twice to give her time to formulate her response and then spoke in a quiet voice.

"Ms. Richardson is a client of mine, and I'll need to consult with her before responding."

"I know. I also have a subpoena for her; however, she wasn't present when I went by the Richardson home a few minutes ago."

Alexia stiffened. "As her attorney, I'll accept her subpoena as well."

The detective handed a second subpoena to Alexia. It was identical except for the change in name.

"And the tape?" the detective asked.

"I'll consult with Ms. Richardson and notify you."

The detective's eyes narrowed. "You're refusing to deliver the tape?"

"Yes, and I'm not admitting that it exists."

"You're an attorney, Ms. Lindale. I'm sure you realize the possible consequences of refusing to honor a grand-jury subpoena."

Alexia's eyes stayed fixed on the detective. He might be effective at striking fear in a guilty suspect, but she wouldn't yield to intimidation.

"That doesn't change my answer," she said.

The detective shrugged his shoulders and relaxed. "I'll indicate your response on my return to the court. I'm sure the solicitor will be in touch with you."

After the detective left, Alexia returned to her office, shut the door, and called Sean Pruitt. After holding briefly, he came on the line.

"I was going to phone you later," he began amiably. "I talked with my aunt last night. She's going to find out why Bridges is making noise about obstruction of justice and get back to me."

"We have another problem," Alexia replied grimly. "Five minutes ago I was served with a subpoena for Rena's videotape from the grand jury in Charleston. They also issued one to Rena."

"What did you do?"

"I told the officer I would have to consult with my client and sent him on his way."

"Have they served Rena?"

"No, she wasn't at home, so I accepted service on her behalf."

"Good. Did you try to call her?"

"No, you're first. What are you going to do?"

"Rena doesn't have the tape, so I can file an answer denying possession—"

Alexia cut him off. "How do you know she doesn't have another copy?"

"That would be stupid."

"Rena has been known to act contrary to her best interests," Alexia responded dryly.

Sean hesitated before responding. "If she doesn't have a copy, we can deny. Otherwise, I can claim her privilege against self-incrimination. As to you, we'll need to file a motion to quash the subpoena."

"Will that work?"

"Probably not, but it will buy time. Fax me the subpoenas so I can look them over."

"What about Rena? When are you going to tell her?"

"Nothing for now. I need to decide on a strategy. There's nothing she can do."

"Except become hysterical."

"Which isn't legal grounds to quash a subpoena."

"Okay. It's on the way."

Alexia prepared the cover sheet herself and sent the subpoenas to Sean's number. She then put the originals in the drawer with the tape and forced herself to work on another file. A few minutes later, Gwen buzzed her. Alexia pressed the button for the speaker phone.

"What is it?" she asked.

"Rena Richardson is here," Gwen said. "I don't see her on your calendar. Does she have an appointment?"

Alexia looked up at the ceiling in exasperation.

"No. Tell her I'm busy and find out what she wants."

Alexia tried to concentrate on the papers in front of her, but the words blurred. There was a knock on her door, and Gwen peeked inside.

"She doesn't need to see you. She's here to pick up a videotape that she left with you a few days ago."

Alexia's eyes narrowed, and she bit off her words. "Tell her to wait. I'll be there in a second."

Gwen raised her hands as she retreated. "Hey, don't kill the messenger."

When the door clicked shut, Alexia redialed the number for Sean Pruitt. Extricating herself from Rena was proving more difficult than Br'er Rabbit trying to escape the sticky embrace of the tar baby.

"I have the subpoena," Pruitt began as soon as he came on the line. "I pulled up a few cases after we talked. If I had the videotape in my office, it would be safe. As Rena's attorney for any criminal charges, I wouldn't have to give up the tape, because it's evidence of past crimes. You're her lawyer, too, but I haven't found out if your representation as a civil attorney in a noncriminal matter makes a difference. I may do some research in other jurisdictions—"

"That's academic," Alexia interrupted. "I have an immediate practical problem. Rena is standing in my reception area and wants to pick up the videotape."

"Oh," Pruitt said and then stopped. "What does she want to do with it?"

"I don't know. Burn it in the fireplace? Toss it in the ocean? Give it to you? I haven't talked to her, but I have a big problem giving it to her. You can file a motion to quash, but when I'm questioned about my possession of the tape, I'll have to admit that it was in my office when the detective served the subpoena. I don't think a judge will accept that I can't produce it because I subsequently gave it to my client. That might justify an obstruction of justice charge against me even if there's no basis for one now."

"Yes."

"And it also creates a conflict of interest between Rena and me in seeking advice from you. As Rena's lawyer, you want the tape to disappear or materialize in your desk drawer instead of mine. As my lawyer, you don't want me to do anything that will cause me to lose my license."

"I'm not going to let either of you do anything illegal or unethical. That's not the way I play the game."

"Okay. But what next?"

"Bring Rena into your office and put us on the speakerphone."

"What are you going to say?"

"I'm still working on it."

Alexia walked to the reception area. Rena was standing in the middle of the room.

"Where's the videotape?" she demanded in a low voice so the receptionist couldn't hear. "I need to pick it up."

"It's in a drawer in my desk."

Alexia led Rena back to her office. Gwen glanced up as they passed her door but kept typing.

"Have a seat," Alexia said. "I have Sean Pruitt on the phone."

"I just left his office. All I need is the videotape—"

"There's a problem with that," the Charleston lawyer interjected. "Alexia has been served with a subpoena to turn the tape over to the police. There is also one outstanding against you."

Rena stared at the phone and her face turned white. "How do they know about it?"

"I'm not sure."

Rena turned toward Alexia. "Did you give it to them?"

"No," Alexia replied. "Do you have another copy?"

"Of course not. That would be stupid."

Sean continued, "Listen, Rena. I'm going to file papers in court to try and block their attempt to make Alexia turn over the video. This all happened in the past few minutes, so there's nothing else to tell you except that I'm going to fight it as hard as we can."

"Give the tape to me," Rena replied. "Then Alexia won't have anything to turn over."

"That won't work for two reasons. First, Alexia will be subject to questioning and can't commit perjury if asked about the location of the tape at the time the detective served the subpoena. Second, Alexia accepted service on your behalf for an identical subpoena requiring you to turn over the tape. Right now, I can file a response that you don't have it. If you take the tape from Alexia, things get a lot more complicated."

Alexia watched Rena for signs of an outburst or meltdown. She simply looked stunned.

"I have money," she said slowly. "Maybe it's time for me to run."

"No!" both Alexia and Sean spoke at once.

"We can't ever advise you to do that," Pruitt continued. "But the situation is still uncertain. There is a lot that can be done legally to help you."

"Not if they get the tape!" Rena shot back. "Who is going to believe me when I tell the truth about what happened to the fat deputy? All the police want to do is find someone to blame!"

Sean kept his voice level. "They want a legitimate explanation of what happened. I beat the charges against Henry Quinton because he wasn't guilty. It's the same with you."

Rena put her head in her hands and didn't say anything. Alexia resisted the urge to wade into the conversation; Rena only needed to hear one voice of counsel. Sean spoke.

"My next step is to file the motion to quash and try to find out what the police already know about the tape."

Rena looked up at Alexia and spoke in a subdued voice. "If Jeffrey gave it to them, they wouldn't be trying to get the copy from you and me, would they?"

"Probably not."

"What was that?" Sean asked. "I couldn't hear you."

Rena repeated her question.

"Has anything happened to make you think he would contact the police?"

"I don't think so."

"Then it may be Quinton," Sean replied. "I'll make a quick trip to the jail and find out. In the meantime, the tape stays with Alexia."

The phone clicked off before Rena could protest or ask another question. She looked forlornly at Alexia.

"What am I going to do?" she asked.

"Let your lawyer take care of it. That's why you hired him."

Alexia looked down at the verse she'd written on her legal pad when Ted came to see her and considered reading it to Rena. The young woman needed it as much as Alexia did. Trying to decide on a way to broach the subject, the lawyer cleared her throat.

"Could I see the tape?" Rena asked before Alexia could speak.

"Why?"

Rena shrugged. "To face my tormentor."

Alexia leaned over and opened the desk drawer. She picked up the tape and held it up. "Let's hope it stays right there," she said.

Rena stood up. "I'm going home. Do you think I should call Jeffrey and ask him—"

"No," Alexia responded. "You heard Sean. Let him take care of it."

As soon as Rena left, Alexia sat at her desk for a few seconds and then buzzed Gwen.

"Please, come here."

"Is it safe?" the secretary asked when she appeared.

"What do you mean?"

"Are you going to start acting like Ralph Leggitt? You know, you set up your own firm, and the next thing I know you're asking me to fix your coffee and take your clothes to the cleaners."

Alexia smiled. "I wasn't that bad."

"No, but I want to weed out any of those tendencies before they get a chance to sprout."

"Let me tell you why I was on edge."

Gwen sat down and listened, interrupting with several questions about Jeffrey and Rena that revealed the same suspicions that had crossed Alexia's mind.

"There may have been something going on between them at one time," Alexia said, "but now it's a mess. I suspect Rena is stirring the pot without realizing what she's cooking. Until this business about the tape is settled, I want to open a safe-deposit box and keep it in a safe place."

"I'll call the bank. Who else will be a signatory?"

Alexia hesitated. "You, I guess. But under no circumstances are you to give Rena the tape unless you hear it from my lips."

———

Later that afternoon, Alexia met with a prospective client. Even in her temporary office, Alexia's practice continued to grow—proof that the key to an expanding law practice did not depend on fancy furniture. All the new clients who had contacted her since she left Leggitt & Freeman had been referred by other clients and therefore entered the door with a pre-existing level of trust in Alexia. When she finished the intake information for the latest client, Alexia placed the papers beside the computer monitor on Gwen's desk.

"Please open a new file for this woman and give it to me. Her husband has already filed for divorce, and the answer is due next week. I don't want to ask for an extension."

"Okay," Gwen said. "And Sean Pruitt called again. We talked for a minute or two. Is that Rhett Butler accent for real?"

"If it's not, he's a better actor than Clark Gable."

Gwen handed her the slip with the phone message on it. "You probably have his number memorized by now, but here it is. How old is lawyer Pruitt? It's hard to tell over the phone."

"Sorry," Alexia replied. "He's about my age."

Gwen sniffed. "You're going after an older man. Why can't I investigate a younger one?"

Alexia smiled. "Be my guest. He drives a silver Ferrari."

"I'm not sure what that looks like."

"It sits as close to the ground as a go-cart, and everybody stares at you when you pass by. Used ones go for over a hundred thousand."

Gwen's eyes widened. "My left knee is stiff in cold weather and makes it hard to get down low, but I could take a pain pill before going for a ride."

Alexia pointed to the paperwork. "Please open the file. Then you can go on the Internet and look at Ferraris. I can see you cruising along the Battery on a Saturday night."

Alexia went into her office and returned Sean's call.

"What else can happen today?" she asked.

"Just research. I don't think the motion to quash is going to fly unless we can assert that you're also representing Rena on potential criminal charges."

"I stepped between her and the detective from Mitchell County several times. Would that count?"

"Maybe. Neither of us has filed an appearance as counsel for her because no charges have been filed in any court, so there's no public record identifying her attorney. The slate is still blank, and we can fill it in with whomever we choose."

Alexia felt a twinge of conscience and sighed. "But the reason she hired you was to handle the criminal aspect of her problems. I specifically told her I wasn't a criminal-defense lawyer and wouldn't represent her in a criminal prosecution."

"You could change your mind."

"But would that relate back to before I received the subpoena?"

"That's unclear, but your role is bolstered by your previous interaction on Rena's behalf with the Mitchell County authorities. I recommend we include the attorney-client privilege in the motion, and let the judge sort it out."

"Would I need to sign the motion?"

"Yes."

Alexia hesitated. "As my attorney, what do you advise me to do?"

Sean chuckled. "Get a third opinion."

"I don't know anybody to call about this type of issue."

"Did anybody with your old firm leave the door open for future interaction?"

"Not really, and none of them is a criminal-defense lawyer. They'd be trying to remember a lecture from law school."

"Then I'll give it more thought and let you know. How much longer will you be at your office?"

Alexia looked at the clock. It was almost 5:00 PM. "About an hour. The receptionist goes home in a few minutes, so I'll give you my cell phone number."

29

Be thy intents wicked or charitable,
thou com'st in such a questionable shape that I will speak to thee.
HAMLET, ACT 1, SCENE 4

Rena couldn't sit still. The possibility that the videotape might soon be a lead story on the evening news pushed her beyond the limits of self-control. She paced across the kitchen floor. Several times she banged her fist on the wooden surface of the island. Finally, she stopped and leaned over the sink to splash cold water on her face. Patting her cheeks dry and feeling slightly calmer, she decided to go upstairs and sit in a bubble bath. She turned away from the sink.

Blocking her way to the dining room and the stairway beyond stood Baxter.

Rena studied him closely. Every detail of his appearance was more real than even a life-size wax statue. The slight crease on the left side of his jaw, the way his hair parted slightly higher than normal on his head, the position of his hands with his thumbs inside his fists as he stood motionless—all added to the sense of realism. Barefooted, he wore the pajamas Rena gave him the previous Christmas.

"This has nothing to do with you," Rena said casually.

Baxter blinked. And Rena felt fear. Always before, he'd been as lifeless as a mannequin.

Suddenly, Rena doubted everything that had happened during the past weeks and months. The hike along the wooded trail to Double Barrel Falls. The struggle at the edge of the cliff. Her husband lying motionless and presumed dead on the rocks as she crept forward to retrieve the keys to the SUV from his pocket. The maddening sound of the hospital ventilator that breathed for Baxter when the doctors did not know he could breathe on his own. The encounters with Giles Porter, the grotesquely scarred detective. Her entire world turned into a question mark.

She stepped back. Baxter, his expression not changing, stepped forward.

Rena suspected it might be possible to live in an unending world of delusion. But if all was false, then what was true? She stared hard at the figure, trying to bore a hole through him with her gaze. He remained impenetrable. Real in appearance, yet unnatural in conduct. If actually present in the room, he should speak—greet her, curse her. Not that she wanted him to do either. Communication from him would validate her insanity. By remaining silent, he remained an enigma. Rena decided to risk all.

"Say something," she demanded in a voice that trembled slightly.

Baxter's lips parted. She could see his teeth, including the crooked pair on the bottom row. She held her breath. His mouth opened wider. His tongue licked his lips. She could sense the words about to come forth. Rena shut her eyes to absorb the impact and waited. No sounds came. She opened her eyes.

She was alone.

She reached out and steadied herself against the island. Shaken by the persistence of Baxter's appearance, she crept forward to the place where he'd stood and looked down at the floor. She knelt and touched the place where his feet moved, checking for a hint of residual warmth. The floor was cool. She was still living in the real world. Baxter remained an interloper from another realm.

At nearly 5:30 PM, Gwen stuck her head into Alexia's office.

"I thought you'd already left," Alexia said.

"I had to open the file you gave me," Gwen paused, "and do some research on Ferraris. There are so many different models, and they only make a few thousand of each one. Which one does Sean Pruitt drive?"

"I have no idea. It was silver with a tiny horse on the trunk and the hood."

"They all have the horse, and they're all expensive."

"And I didn't tell you about his office. It's in a historic house owned by his family for generations. It's three stories tall, and he lives on the top floor. The parlor where we met was filled with antiques and fancy Oriental rugs. The car is parked in a garage at the rear of the property. We had to cross a courtyard with a massive fountain in the middle and incredible landscaping to get to it."

"You're making all this up."

Alexia shook her head. "No, it's all true. He's smart but a bit odd. I think his grandfather married a cousin."

"How close a cousin?"

"I made that part up," Alexia admitted.

Gwen nodded. "If he makes a trip to see you or Rena, let me know, and I'll put him under personal surveillance. I admit he's too young for me, but I have two nieces who deserve to marry a rich guy. They wouldn't need medication to ride in a fancy sports car or climb three flights of stairs with bags of groceries in their hands."

After Gwen left, Alexia logged onto the computer and began researching the subpoena issue herself. She found a relevant case and was scrolling down the screen reading the majority opinion by the court when her cell phone rang. She glanced at the caller ID.

"I'm still here," she said in answering. "I'm reading an interesting case by a divided court on the subpoena issue."

"With Judge Fain writing for the majority?" Sean Pruitt responded.

"Yeah."

"That's the one."

"According to this, we might win," Alexia said.

"Yep. I'll e-mail the motion to you tomorrow so you can sign it. Leave the brief in support of the motion to me, but I'll need you at the hearing. When will you be available?"

Alexia opened the screen for her calendar and gave him several dates.

"Is there any chance you could bring the motion to Charleston on Friday?" Pruitt asked.

"Hm, I'd rather send it back via overnight courier."

"Would it make a difference if I took you out to dinner at The Cypress?"

Alexia hesitated. Pruitt's antebellum eccentricities amused her, but she felt allegiance to her developing relationship with Ted, especially after their time on the beach.

"No thanks. I'm dating a man here in Santee," she replied simply.

"If you like, we can consider it a business meeting. I thought The Cypress would be nice."

Alexia loved the fish at The Cypress, a Bay Street restaurant. She hesitated. A business dinner was not a date.

"What time?" she asked.

"Seven at my office. We'll leave the motion here and go to the restaurant."

———

On her way home, Alexia detoured to the Sandy Flats Church. Several days had passed since she last slipped into the back of the sanctuary to listen to Ted play. His truck was parked at the old parsonage, but she went directly to the sanctuary. Pushing open the door, she met the music minister in the narthex.

"Hey," she said. "Am I too late for the concert?"

"I wasn't playing. I've been checking repairs I did earlier today to a couple of pews. After a hundred years or so, the backs begin to protest. If they break, we'd probably be sued."

"I'm not here looking for lawsuits. Piano music is my preference."

Ted rubbed his hands together. "What would you like to hear?"

"One of the *Études Tableau* would be nice."

"I can handle that."

Alexia followed Ted into the cool sanctuary, lit only by the moonlight filtering through the window.

"Do you want me to turn on the lights?" he asked.

"Not unless you need them."

Ted smiled. "I like it better in the dark. It makes the sense of hearing a tiny bit sharper."

He went around the altar rail to the piano. Alexia sat on the front pew closest to him and admired his strong profile. He focused on the piano, then began to play.

The melodies, countermelodies, and suspended harmonies woven by Rachmaninoff resulted in some of the most beautiful piano music ever written. As with many things Russian, the composition bore an element of sadness, but the sorrow was so beautifully adorned that it was transformed into an antidote for suffering. It melted the heart, and Alexia let the music penetrate her soul. When Ted finished, she held on to the lingering sound of the last note as long as possible.

"Wonderful," she said simply. "I hope someday my mother can hear you play. It would make her weep."

Ted ran his fingers through his hair and stood up.

"Can you do one more thing?" Alexia asked.

"What?"

"The verse that says no weapon formed against me shall prosper—could you play it?"

Ted looked past Alexia toward the rear of the sanctuary. A shaft of pale light from outside fell on his face, and Alexia could see a glint in his eyes.

"Yes, but it won't be lyrical. There are weapons on both sides of the fight."

Alexia relaxed against the pew, and Ted resumed his seat. He sat motionless for several seconds before striking the keys. Unlike other spontaneous compositions he'd played, the sounds were technically complex from the outset.

It didn't take Alexia long to visualize the picture painted by the notes. Ted began in the lower octaves, stoking the fires in which weapons of divine power are forged to combat the enemy's. It took time to purify the metal and prepare the molds. When the molten liquid was white-hot, he poured the notes into the place he prepared for them, let them cool, and then brought them forth with the sound of challenge.

Then the battle began.

His fingers flew over the keys. Alexia shivered. Back and forth the conflict raged. Alexia wondered if there was a key he didn't touch. Malevolent sounds in the lower octaves had the greater power in this war. A melody repeatedly tried to emerge in the upper registry, but the unrelenting onslaught from beneath kept swallowing it.

And then a clear note rang out, a tiny trumpet at the far end of the keyboard, coming from a place where few musicians bothered to look. At first, Alexia wondered if such an insignificant sound could survive. But it lived. And it grew in persistence. The lower notes railed against it, mocking, reviling, insulting, challenging, but each time the smoke cleared, the trumpet remained on the field of battle. Undaunted by overwhelming odds, it continued to sound a clear call, summoning its power from an unseen place linking heaven and earth. When it sounded, the opposing foe could only retreat. The attack weakened; the trumpet increased.

Until finally, nothing else remained.

Ted lifted his hand from the keyboard. They sat in silence. Alexia sensed that all future assaults against her were already vanquished. Total victory is already assured for those whose God fights for them. No weapon formed against them shall prosper.

"Thank you," she said.

Ted pointed up. "Thank Him."

They let the silence envelop them again as the influence of the music lingered. Respect for a higher authority sealed their lips and kept them quieter than a small child sleeping on its mother's lap. And then the presence lifted. Both of them realized it at the same moment. Ted stood and stretched. Alexia uncurled from the pew and leaned forward.

"What do you call this?" she asked.

"The music?"

"Yes."

"Besides playing the piano?"

Alexia nodded.

Ted shrugged. "I'm not sure. I imagine David had similar experiences when he wrote the psalms, only I'm interpreting scripture, not writing it. He probably composed most of his music spontaneously, sitting on a grassy hillside with his harp in his hands."

"A psalmist," Alexia replied thoughtfully. "It has a nice ring to it. Now I know what to give you for Christmas—five hundred business cards with 'Ted Morgan, Psalmist' engraved in gold ink. With a little piano underneath your name."

"That would take some explaining."

"The piano on the card could be a Steinway."

Ted patted the massive black instrument. "It won't fit."

They walked together from the sanctuary. The salt breeze had cleaned and cleared the evening air, and Alexia inhaled deeply. They stopped beside Alexia's car. Ted rested his hand on the roof.

"Sarah Locklear left a message on my answering machine this afternoon, and I called her back before I came to the sanctuary," he said. "She's going to be on duty Friday evening and mentioned that she could let the aide go to supper around seven thirty. That way, we can have uninterrupted time with Baxter for about an hour."

"Good."

"I guess you can't come because of the divorce."

"Well, actually it's on hold."

Ted brightened. "I'd love for you to come then. Do you want me to pick you up about seven o'clock?"

"Uh, no," Alexia answered with a hint of regret. "I can't make it. I have a meeting with another attorney in Charleston on Friday evening. We're working on a case together."

The euphoria Alexia felt while listening to Ted play didn't linger in the car as she drove home.

Except for an occasional headache, Rick Bridges had fully recovered from the injuries suffered at the Beachcomber Club. The bruises and bumps left first; the dizziness and ringing in his right ear lingered another week before disappearing.

The detective's file on Rena Richardson had grown thicker in the past few days, though it remained scanty. Several people in the Santee area had characterized her as a moody loner with expensive tastes that Baxter seemed eager to satisfy. Rena was apparently a good tennis player who formed no close friendships with other women. Beyond her interest in physical exercise, her life was as private as a locked diary.

Bridges incorporated Giles Porter's research about Rena's background into his records. Porter told him Rena's mother died when she was a little girl, and her stepfather, Vernon Swafford, was a habitual felon with multiple stints in South Carolina and Georgia prisons. Within the past few months, Swafford had been arrested in Macon on an aggravated-assault charge. Porter doubted Rena knew or cared about the latest charges. Violence had been part of Rena's life until she ran away from home as a teenager to live with an aunt in Spartanburg. From that point forward, she appeared to lead a more normal life.

Porter claimed Rena hadn't told the truth about Baxter's accident. Bridges politely listened to Porter's theories but kept his focus on the responsibility assigned to him. The Charleston detective was certain of one thing: given her rough background, Rena had greater potential to commit a crime than the vast majority of the residents of Santee.

30

Always be prepared to give an answer to everyone who asks you
to give the reason for the hope that you have.

1 PETER 3:15

Alexia finished reading Sean's well-argued motion and brief and put it on her desk. Unless the assistant solicitor assigned to the case was a former law clerk to the judge or cited an appellate court decision not discovered by Pruitt, the motion to quash had a reasonable chance of success.

Alexia walked to Gwen's desk. The secretary was reading a romance novel.

"Busted," Alexia said.

Gwen put down the book and scratched the side of her nose. "I transcribed everything you dictated this morning, and I've finished setting up the new case-tracking system, including entry of all the relevant data. You'll never miss a statute of limitations again."

"When did I miss one in the past?"

"As far as I know you haven't, but it's not the sort of mistake you want to experience." Gwen held up the book. "This is the story of a woman attorney who falls in love with a handsome young male lawyer on the opposite side of a case. She missed a filing deadline, and I'm about to find out if he's going to have mercy on her because he loves her or send her client down the tube to the tune of a half-million dollars."

"Ouch."

Gwen shrugged. "If she loses her law license, she can marry him and have a house full of fat babies."

"I doubt that's what will happen."

"Me too. But you'll be interested to know the guy drives a Lamborghini. He doesn't like Ferraris."

"I'm going to see the silver Ferrari owner this evening when I go to Charleston. I have to sign a motion he prepared in Rena's case."

"Thanks for letting me know." Gwen reached for her purse. Opening it, she took out two photographs and handed them to Alexia. "These are my nieces. Their names and birthdays are written on the back. Either one will be a good wife. Betty June is cuter, but Nancy Kate is smarter and would be a better housekeeper."

Alexia held the pictures up in front of her. "What would they say if they knew you wanted me to show these pictures to Sean Pruitt and tell him to take his pick?"

"They'd blush with embarrassment, but they're too young to appreciate what really counts in a man."

Alexia handed the pictures back to Gwen, who returned them to her purse.

"Actually, I'd rather they meet someone like Reverend Ted," Gwen said.

"He's going to be at the cottage tonight playing music for Baxter."

"How is Baxter doing?"

"He has moments of consciousness, but he's still not communicating much. Rena hasn't told me anything about him recently. I don't think she's spending much time with him."

"I'm not surprised. The divorce papers are ready at a moment's notice if the yo-yo flips in a different direction."

"It could happen," Alexia replied, "although Rena is more worried about the videotape right now than anything else."

Gwen answered a phone call. Putting her hand over the receiver, she mouthed, "It's Mrs. Claxton."

"Tell her I left a message for her husband's lawyer. He hasn't returned the call, but as soon as he does, I'll let her know."

Gwen complied and hung up the phone. "Will you return from Charleston in time to join Ted?"

"No. Sean Pruitt is taking me out to dinner after we review the legal paperwork."

Gwen leaned forward. "Alexia, what are you up to?"

"Nothing," Alexia insisted. "He invited me to go to The Cypress. I told him about Ted, and he said he'd consider it a business meeting."

"What kind of business?" Gwen sniffed. "Two cocktails and a man's idea of business is pretty broad."

"Yeah," Alexia admitted sheepishly.

"And what would Ted think?"

"He knows, kind of. I told him I had a meeting with a lawyer in Charleston."

"Oh, that's full disclosure."

Alexia sighed. "It also leaves Ted alone with the nurse who sings."

"Who?"

Alexia told Gwen about Sarah Locklear. She concluded by saying, "Ted reassures me that he's interested in me, not her."

"That doesn't surprise me, but some men can't handle even the hint of competition."

"Ted has no competition. I promise."

Gwen closed her book without marking the place. "This is better than what I'm reading. I expect a detailed report, dictated and ready for transcription, on Monday. Don't leave anything out."

———

Alexia wasn't sure how to dress. Too conservative wouldn't fit with the restaurant. Too dressy would send the wrong message. She settled on a black dress with silver jewelry that she hoped was in-between.

The sky grew darker as she drove to Charleston. She arrived fifteen minutes early and drove around the Broad Street area to pass time. After one loop past the Battery, she quit stalling and parked in front of Sean's office. Two flickering gas lamps lit the way to the front door. After business hours, the building resembled a residence more than an office. She climbed the steps and lifted the shiny brass lion's-head knocker on the front door. When no one came, she knocked again. At least a minute passed before the door opened.

"Sorry," Sean said. "I was in my office and thought you would come on in. It's not my habit to keep beautiful women waiting on my doorstep."

It was a corny comment, but the way Sean said it sounded sincere. Alexia entered the foyer and handed him a folder containing the motion and brief.

"This looks good," she said. "I didn't make any changes."

"Thanks. Come to my office, and we'll sign the original. I'll file it Monday morning and ask the court administrator to set a date consistent with your availability."

They walked past the reception area and down a short hall. Sean turned left into a room with long windows facing the street in front of the house. Alexia had never seen a more elegant office. In the middle of the room rested a partner's desk with a burgundy leather top trimmed in gold leaf. A credenza sat behind the desk with a small Tiffany-style lamp at each end. Sean's high-back chair, made of the same shade of leather as the desktop, faced three delicate chairs positioned around a low table with graceful legs. Two ancient yet lustrous carpets partially covered the wooden floor. Multiple paintings adorned the walls. Alexia touched the corner of the desk.

"It's beautiful," she said.

"It came from England more than 150 years ago. It's designed so two men could work on opposite sides."

"Doing what?"

Pruitt shrugged. "Trading cotton futures, most likely."

"And the lamps?"

"They're real."

Alexia laughed. "This isn't an office; it's a museum."

"I heard your office is unique as well."

Alexia visualized her current work environment with its cheap paneling that rippled along one wall.

"Not really."

"No? Gwen told me about your office at Leggitt & Freeman and the collection of artifacts from your travels."

"Oh, those are in storage while I renovate my new location. Right now, I'm renting space from a real-estate firm. It's plain." She chuckled. "What else did Gwen tell you?"

"Not much, except that she thinks you're the greatest lawyer on earth."

Alexia smiled. "She's a good friend. We've worked together for a long time."

"I wish I could say that of someone. I've had four secretaries in six years and two paralegals in the past nine months."

Alexia sat in one of the chairs beside the little table. Pruitt picked up some papers from his desk and joined her.

"Here's the motion and brief," he said, flipping it over to the signature page.

"Any changes from what you sent me?"

"No."

Alexia signed, and Pruitt scooped up the papers and put them on his desk.

"Could I have a copy of the signed pleadings?" Alexia asked.

"The copy machine is turned off and takes several minutes to warm up. I'll mail a set to you together with the notice for the hearing."

"Okay."

"Ready to go?"

"Yes."

They passed the parlor where Alexia and Rena had first met with Sean and went to the rear door leading to the courtyard.

As they descended the steps, Alexia asked, "Did Gwen ask about your car?"

"No, we just talked about you."

"What exactly was the 'not much' you found out?"

Sean opened the door leading to the garage. "Am I subject to cross-examination?"

"On matters relevant to me."

He pressed the button that raised the garage door.

"She told me you live alone in a house on the marsh and have two dogs."

"A dog and a cat."

"Okay. I don't have my notes with me. You like to swim in the ocean, even when it's so cold that no one but a woman with Russian ancestry would consider getting into the water."

"She told you about my mother?"

"Yes. A great story. I'd like to know more."

Sean opened the door for Alexia, who lowered herself into the car as gracefully as possible. As they drove to the restaurant, Sean asked Alexia for a fuller version of her mother's defection to the United States and their recent interaction with relatives near St. Petersburg.

"They're still struggling. It's a hard country."

"A hard country that produces great artistic talent. Gwen didn't have to tell me about your love for classical music. I assume you prefer the Russian composers?"

"Yes."

Sean launched into a discussion of music that left Alexia's head spinning. He didn't know as much as Alexia about the Russians but proved knowledgeable about the Germans and Austrians. They arrived at the restaurant both talking at once.

The Cypress was one of a row of Bay Street restaurants that attracted both tourists and local residents. The crowd outside signaled a long wait, but when the hostess saw Sean, she immediately escorted them to a table for two in a corner. Alexia ordered she-crab soup and crab-crusted wahoo. Sean chose a salad and lamb.

"No seafood?" Alexia asked after the waiter left.

"No tonight. I like to cook what I catch. The fresh fish from my own kitchen rivals anything prepared here."

"You're a fisherman and chef?"

"Yes, I have the same boat my father and I used when I was a boy."

"Do you go out together?"

"No, he died in a small plane crash in Tanzania when I was eighteen. He was on a photographic safari with some of his friends."

"Oh, I'm sorry."

Sean shrugged. "It made me grow up a little faster." He took a sip of water. "I promised you a business meal, and I always try to keep my promises. Can we talk business while we wait for the first course?"

"Sure."

"I know how the police found out about the video."

"Quinton?"

"Not directly. He denied everything at first, so I had to do some additional investigation through another contact I have at the jail."

"Who?"

"A man I represented in the past. He told me about a cellmate who overheard Quinton talking on the phone about the video. The cellmate reported the conversation to a guard, but instead of getting an extra dessert at mealtime, he ended up with a black eye and knot on his head for eavesdropping."

"Quinton beat him up?"

Sean shook his head. "That's not the way it works. Someone punched him on behalf of Quinton. There's a hierarchy in jail, and guys like Quinton quickly rise to the top. When I interviewed him the second time and mentioned the name of the man with the black eye, he told me the eavesdropper should have kept quiet."

"Why would Quinton care if the police get the video? It's further proof of his innocence."

"That's not the only thing he cares about. The fact that someone shot the video could lead to more questions about his activities. For obvious reasons, he's a private person."

"Which makes me nervous to think he may start snooping around my house soon. How long will he stay locked up?"

"The assault case could be around for a while, and he's facing extradition to Rhode Island on an old murder charge."

"Murder?"

Sean told her what he knew about the death of the Rhode Island police officer. "Quinton has already hired an attorney in Providence. I talked to the lawyer the other day, and the chief witness against Quinton has dropped out of sight. Without him, the Rhode Island attorney claims the State doesn't have a case."

The waiter brought the soup. Alexia tasted it.

"This is good," she said. "Different from mine, but tasty."

"You make crab soup?"

"Yes, but it's never the same. I throw a variety of things into the pot. Whatever is fresh gets included."

"Do you catch your own crabs?"

Alexia nodded. "I have two traps that I'll set out in the marsh near my house. The hard part is sorting out the keepers from the babies. When you lift them out of the trap they're all grabbing each other."

"I've had clients like that. Instead of cooperating, a group with common interests turn on one another."

"Why are you a plaintiff's lawyer who dabbles in criminal law?" Alexia asked. "It doesn't fit with your background."

Sean smiled. "You think I should be writing wills for rich people who knew my grandparents?"

"Yeah, that would fit."

"Why do you handle divorces? Doesn't it make you feel slimy? You could be shuffling corporate documents for more money and less hassle."

"Most of my clients are women who need a champion."

"And mine don't?" Sean speared a cherry tomato and put it in his mouth. "I never wanted to specialize in criminal defense. To make it work financially, I'd have to represent the people who hired Quinton."

The waiter brought their entrees. Alexia tasted the fish.

"If your fish is better than this, it would be worth another trip to Charleston," she said.

Sean smiled. "That could be arranged."

They ate in silence for a few moments.

"How is your personal-injury practice going?" Alexia asked.

Sean put down his fork. "Civil trials are more fun than criminal cases, and the pay is a lot better."

"Any big cases?"

"Yes. I hit a couple of home runs last year. A former university professor died following some neglect in a nursing home. The defense lawyer argued that my client was going to die anyway, and the jury didn't buy it. The other claim was a wrongful death case against a trucking company. They sent a driver out on the road knowing that the brakes on his truck needed to be serviced. The truck ran away from him on a hill and killed my client and a young woman with a husband and two children."

Alexia had never been able to consider taking a personal-injury case at Leggitt & Freeman. Her former firm, oriented exclusively toward business clients, tolerated her divorce practice but wouldn't allow her to expand into other areas.

"Occasionally, a former client calls me about a personal-injury matter," she said. "Would you be interested in a referral?"

"If it's a good case. Or we could work together on a claim."

Alexia nodded thoughtfully. "Do you come here often?" she asked.

"Not really. I have several favorite spots, and I like to check out new places that open." Sean took a sip of the Chablis he'd ordered. "But you struck me as a Cypress type of person."

Alexia felt warm and comfortable. Six months previously, she would have flashed her brightest smile to reward Sean for the compliment. Tonight, she gave a slight nod. Sean Pruitt was affable and charming, but Ted Morgan had introduced her to a new realm of romance that made other relationships seem like black-and-white TV. They finished the meal with coffee.

"Thanks for a very nice meal," she said.

Sean stared at her for a few seconds.

"You're welcome," he said. "I suggest we adjourn to my office for a few minutes and discuss the motion."

Alexia was quiet as the sports car rumbled through the peaceful streets. Traffic in the downtown area wasn't heavy this time of year, even on the weekend. Sean opened the door of his garage by remote control, pulled the car into its place, and turned off the engine. They crossed the courtyard. A security light caused the fountain to cast a long shadow that reached the brick and iron wall surrounding the enclosure. The muted sounds from the street didn't reach the area, and Alexia's shoes made a slight clicking sound as she walked across the slate pavers.

"Do you get lonely in your house on the marsh?" Sean asked as they climbed the steps to the rear entrance. "Even the best dog and cat can't be enough company."

Alexia stood beside him as he unlocked the door. "I'm around people all day and need space to be alone. The house is my refuge, but I have no desire to be a hermit."

Sean chuckled. "No plans to enter a convent?"

"No, my faith has been drawing me out into the world, not calling me into a cloister."

Alexia followed him into the house. He flicked on the lights and led the way back to his office. They sat in chairs around the small coffee table. The Tiffany lamp cast a colorful glow on the wall above them.

"Tell me about that," Sean said as he flicked on the second of the two lamps.

"About what?"

"Your faith."

Alexia could have talked for hours about music, but discussions about Jesus had been for Ted's ears only. She stalled.

"Why do you want to know?"

Sean sat down in the chair next to her. "Because I can tell that it's important to you, and I'm interested in finding out why. I'm not antagonistic, I promise, just curious. You're dating a music minister who is an accomplished pianist, and my guess is that he's encouraging this aspect of your life."

"Did I tell you about Ted, or is this information from Gwen?"

"You mentioned a boyfriend, but Gwen provided the details, including the fact that he was the pianist who filled in at the benefit concert."

"How did you get so much information from her?"

"It wasn't hard. You're one of her favorite topics of conversation, and of course, as your attorney, I assured her everything she told me would remain confidential."

Alexia smiled. "Okay. What do you want to know?"

"The truth, the whole truth, and nothing but the truth."

Beginning with her first encounters with Ted, his music, and the stained-glass windows of the Sandy Flats Church, she continued to her backyard epiphany, when the reality of God's love and the influence of her grandmother's prayers overwhelmed her. She didn't take any shortcuts. The poignant power of the moment returned in the telling, and she had to retrieve a tissue from her purse. She paused until she regained her composure.

"I've discovered there is a spiritual reality I never dreamed existed. Part of it is inside the church, but for me, most of it has showed up in other places."

"Is that what you meant by going out into the world?"

"Yes, and, as my grandmother told me, let my light shine."

"Give an example."

Alexia thought a moment. "Part of it relates to Baxter Richardson, Rena's husband."

Sean gave her a puzzled look, and Alexia tried to explain what Ted, Sarah, and she were doing around the paralyzed man's bed. The more she talked, the less confidence she had that she was making sense. Sean confirmed her feelings.

"I don't get it," he said when she finished. "Music can have a soothing effect. That's one reason I enjoy it myself. But using it to restore function to a damaged spinal cord is a fantasy."

"If you could be there and hear it, you'd understand," she said. "I'm not much more than an observer myself, but I know the presence of God is in the room."

"You don't sing?"

Alexia gave a wry smile. "That would send Baxter back into a coma. Ted asked me to pray, so I sit in a chair and ask God to touch Baxter in the same way Jesus touched the people he healed."

"Then the proof will be in the results."

Alexia looked at her watch. "It's late, and we haven't talked about the hearing on the motion to quash the subpoena."

Sean reached over to his desk and retrieved a manila folder. "It won't take long. Here is my research and the questions I will ask you."

Thirty minutes later, Alexia closed the folder. "So it's primarily a legal argument, isn't it?"

"Yes. I don't anticipate much in the way of cross-examination. The more questions the solicitor asks, the clearer it will be that you've been Rena's attorney in multiple matters long before the incident with Deputy Dixon."

"When do you think the hearing will be held?"

"I'm not sure, but I'll call you or Gwen as soon as I know."

Sean walked Alexia to the front door and down the steps to her car. "Tonight has been even more interesting than I anticipated," he said.

Alexia reached her car and faced him. The playful look that had been in his eyes at the restaurant was gone.

"I had a nice time," she said. "Thanks for listening."

Sean took her hand and kissed it. At the moment, it seemed the most natural, proper thing in the world. The lawyer still had a toe firmly planted in the nineteenth century.

"Good night," he said. "You've answered your grandmother's prayer tonight."

"How?"

Sean released her hand. "You've let your light shine on me."

31

Ted woke up early on Friday morning. Diffused light peeked around the edges of the shades in his bedroom. His usual routine involved a hearty breakfast as one of the first activities of the day. Ted's mother always fixed a big breakfast for his family, and he'd never abandoned the childhood routine. Thinking about what to prepare, he realized he wasn't hungry. He didn't feel sick, just uninterested in food.

He sat on the edge of his bed and offered a quick prayer for insight. No sooner was the request released from his lips than he realized the obvious implication—God didn't want him to eat and had taken away his appetite in order to help him obey.

Going into the living room, he reclined in his reading chair and opened his Bible. He read a few chapters, but nothing leaped off the page as a spiritual reason to fast. He mentally scrolled down the activities planned for the day. Nothing arrested his attention until he came to Baxter Richardson. The paralyzed young man had exhibited slight improvement after several sessions of musical intercession, and the music minister couldn't deny the sense of God's presence in the room while he played and Sarah Locklear sang. Even so, Ted wasn't satisfied. Something deep within him continued to chafe at the lack of dramatic improvement in Baxter's condition.

He flipped open his Bible again and read about a healing in the ministry of Jesus. Prayer and fasting had been required to heal a deaf-mute boy. Ted read the passage several times, entering into the scene in his mind's eye and praying for the same power to manifest on behalf of Baxter.

Throughout the day, Ted's thoughts returned with anticipation to the time planned that evening at the cottage. He'd hoped to play the piano for an hour in preparation for the evening, but fixing a plumbing problem took much longer than he'd hoped, and he barely had time to shower before going to the cottage.

Sarah opened the door and looked behind him.

"Where's Alexia?" she asked.

"She had a meeting with a lawyer in Charleston and couldn't make it. It's just us tonight."

Keyboard under his arm, Ted entered the small living room. Baxter lay on his back with his eyes closed. Ted plugged in the keyboard and placed it on a chair.

"Something is going to happen tonight," Sarah said. "I've felt it all day."

"Me too," Ted responded. He started to mention his fasting, but Jesus' recommendation to keep the practice secret stopped him. After a brief pause, he asked, "What has God put on your heart?"

She picked up her Bible from a tray near Baxter's bed and opened it to a slip of yellow paper that served as a bookmark.

"I've been thinking about two passages since our last session. The first is the story of Jesus healing a crippled man at the pool of Bethesda."

She read the verses while Ted listened. Sarah's vibrant voice made the words come alive—as if they were striving to leave the realm of print and step into the three-dimensional world.

"That's good," Ted acknowledged when she finished. "We have a stained-glass window at the church depicting the scene, and the miracle fits what we want to see happen for Baxter. What is the other passage?"

Sarah found another thin slip of paper. "This one is less clear," she said, "but it has been rolling around in my mind for days."

She began to read the story of the deaf-mute boy. Ted was stunned. When she finished, she touched the edge of the sheet covering Baxter and looked at Ted. Her dark eyes were filled with compassion.

"This is a difficult case," she said. "It would be easier to believe God could touch someone with less severe problems than Baxter's, but he's the one placed in our path. I believe we have to be persistent if we want to see a breakthrough."

Ted started to mention his early-morning study but stopped. Perhaps Sarah was being called to believe without human confirmation.

"I agree," he replied simply. "Let's get started."

Ted began with the account of the miracle at the pool of Bethesda. As he played, the notes came easily to his fingers, and with little effort he began to paint a musical picture of the scene at the pool—squalid conditions that would have been a breeding ground for despair, the sick and lame longing to enter the waters and be healed, each one desperately wanting to crawl through a window of hope so narrow that the most seriously ill had no chance to enter the waters when stirred by an angel.

Suddenly, upon the scene came a man who did not need Bethesda's waters in order to heal—the waters of life within him flowed freely with healing power. Jesus engaged the lame man in casual conversation, and with a simple statement shattered thirty-eight years of demoralizing routine. Standing at the foot of Baxter's bed, Sarah began to sing.

"Take up your mat and walk," she called out in a voice that was more command than lyric.

Ted increased the intensity of the music. Sarah stayed for many minutes on the same theme, slave to no clock. When she finally fell silent and Ted lifted his fingers from the keyboard, over two hours had passed. Yet Baxter was unaffected. They both stared at his motionless form.

"What next?" Ted asked.

Sarah's eyes took on a look of determination. "Do it again."

Ted didn't argue. Not eating was fasting; worshipping on behalf of another, a form of prayer. If they were right, Baxter needed both. He began again. The sound resembled what he'd already played, but he sensed the music expanding, going deeper or higher; he wasn't sure which. Soon Sarah joined in. Her rich alto voice filled the room. When they reached the place where Jesus revealed his authority, the atmosphere in the room seemed to pop with expectation. Ted closed his eyes for several minutes, while Sarah again issued the command to rise and walk. Suddenly, Sarah stopped singing. Ted opened his eyes. The nurse was at the end of the bed staring down at the sheet covering Baxter's feet.

"He moved his right foot," she said in a quiet voice. "Watch."

Ted stood up to get a better look. Nothing happened. He glanced at Baxter's face. The young man's eyes were closed; his breathing regular.

"Baxter," Sarah said in a steady voice. "Move your right foot."

Ted stared at the end of the bed. Nothing happened.

"Could it have been an involuntary—"

Sarah interrupted him.

"Baxter! Move your right foot!"

Unmistakably, the form beneath the sheet shifted. Ted looked at Baxter's face. His eyes were open.

"Do it again," Ted blurted out.

The foot moved.

"What about your left foot?" Sarah asked in a more normal tone of voice. "Can you move it?"

Baxter's foot did not respond. Sarah came to the side of the bed closer to Baxter's head.

"Do you understand what I'm saying?" she asked.

"Yes," Baxter croaked. "Thirsty."

Sarah took a cup of water from the tray table and held up his head for a sip. Baxter shut his eyes for a moment and then reopened them. Sarah pulled the top sheet away from his upper chest and torso. His thin arms lay pale against the bed.

"Move your right hand," Sarah said.

Baxter twitched his index and middle fingers. Ted was amazed.

"How is this possible?" he asked.

Sarah smiled. "I think this is what we asked God to do."

Baxter turned his eyes toward Ted. "Who?"

"I'm Ted Morgan, a music minister."

"And I'm Sarah, one of your nurses. Can you move your left hand?"

Baxter glanced down in the direction of his left hand. Nothing happened.

"What?" he asked with obvious puzzlement in his eyes. "Why?"

Sarah looked across the bed at Ted, and then in simple words, she explained to Baxter that he'd been in an accident, which left him in a coma and paralyzed. Partway through the explanation, he closed his eyes. Sarah gently touched his cheek.

"Are you awake? Can you hear me?"

The sandy-haired young man didn't respond.

"How much of that do you think he understood?" Ted asked.

"It often takes many repetitions. The head injury complicates things. He will have occasional lucid moments. When that happens we try to pour in the right information to help him understand. It's like pointing out handholds to someone climbing a rock face. The hope is that he'll eventually be able to reach the top."

"And the movement of his foot and hand," Ted said. "What do you think?"

Sarah laughed. "I think it's the preview to a miracle. Neurologically, it's staggering. Only the right side showed recovery, but it's incredibly significant. His chart doesn't indicate the spinal cord nerve was severed when he fell, but it's the first sign that a return of function is possible. We'll notify his doctor first thing in the morning."

Ted looked at his watch. It was almost 2:00 AM. Sarah saw him.

"You can go home and get some sleep," she said.

Ted shook his head. "No. There is someone we need to thank and praise."

———

Alexia thought about Ted and Sarah during the drive from Charleston to Santee. She'd not been with them at the cottage, but she ventured out on her own journey of faith by talking to Sean Pruitt. Even though it was late, she called Ted's number at the old parsonage. The phone rang several times before the answering machine came on. She left a message and tried his cell phone. It, too, routed her to an answering message. A report to and from the minister would have to wait for the following day.

Saturday morning, Alexia decided to go to the office for a few hours and catch up on paperwork. When she arrived, there was a message with a name and phone number in the seat of her chair: "Urgent—call ASAP." When she saw the name on the slip of paper, Alexia didn't need the phone number. She had memorized Rena's numbers weeks before, as every call from her client routinely fell in the urgent category. Alexia buzzed the receptionist. Saturday was a busy day for Rachel Downey, and she kept a full staff on duty.

"Did you leave the message on my chair?"

"Yes."

"Did the caller give any other information?"

"No, the woman didn't even want to leave her name at first. She sounded upset."

Alexia picked up the slip and called the number.

"Where have you been?" Rena asked anxiously. "I tried all your numbers, but you didn't answer."

"I forgot to turn on my cell phone when I left the house and just received your message at the office. What's going on?"

"Your minister friend spent the night at the cottage with the night-duty nurse, which could get her fired if I cared about that sort of thing. But anyway, when I saw him leave, I called over to find out what was going on, and the morning nurse told me that during the night Baxter moved his foot and hand."

"He moved his foot and hand?"

"It wasn't more than a twitch, but that's not the problem. They also talked to him, and I don't know what he said. We have to do something before he wakes up and starts causing trouble."

Alexia's head was spinning.

"He moved," she said softly, more to herself than to Rena.

"Are you listening to me? I'm afraid that he will try to blame me as a way to direct attention away from himself. I mean, if he talks to Detective Porter, there's no telling what he might say. And I know the detective will believe anything that accuses me of doing—"

"Hold on," Alexia interrupted, regaining her focus. "Let me get this straight. Did you go over to the cottage after you talked to the nurse?"

"No. We just talked on the phone."

"Did the nurse say that Baxter accused you of anything?"

"No, she didn't mention it, but I'm not sure what happened."

Alexia looked at the clock on the corner of her desk. Sarah Locklear's shift would have ended over an hour earlier.

Rena continued to speak rapidly. "She said Baxter wanted to see me, but I don't want to go over there by myself. I'm scared."

"I'll be right over and go with you," Alexia responded.

"Will you be there as my attorney?"

"Yes, I'm still representing you."

"Which means that no matter what Baxter says, you won't repeat it to anyone?"

Rena's paranoia constantly kept Alexia testing the limits of ethical guidelines. She wanted to see Baxter for herself but chose her words carefully since her visit could have legal implications for Rena.

"There might be exceptions, but Baxter doesn't pose a threat to you or anyone else."

"He would if he lied," Rena shot back.

"No, you don't understand. The only thing I would have to report would be the possibility of future criminal conduct. Any accusations he makes against you would be about past events and protected by the attorney-client privilege."

"Oh, I wasn't worried about the future. I'm getting out of here as soon as possible."

Alexia remembered Rena's threat to become a fugitive. "But not before we take care of the situation in Charleston. I met with Sean Pruitt last night. He's done a good job on the motion to suppress the subpoena for the videotape and will schedule a hearing as soon as possible. Once that is settled, you can go wherever you want."

"I don't want to talk about that right now. How soon can you get here?"

"Within five minutes. Stay in the house and watch for my car."

Before staring the engine, Alexia hit the memory button for the old parsonage. The answering machine responded. She left another message for Ted.

———

Rena opened the front door of the house and came outside as Alexia parked beside the cottage. Alexia stood beside her car and waited. Rena had not taken time to properly brush her hair. She wore workout clothes that didn't match.

"How do you want to handle this?" Alexia asked.

"You do the talking. Tell the nurse and the aide to leave the room, and I'll stand where Baxter can't see me."

"What do you want me to ask him?"

"I thought about that while waiting for you. Get him to admit that he tried to push me off the cliff."

Alexia's mouth dropped open in amazement. "How do I do that?"

"You're the lawyer. That's your job."

Rena started to walk toward the cottage, but Alexia didn't budge.

"Most people don't willingly admit to attempted murder," Alexia said. "We have no idea whether—"

"Come on," Rena interrupted. "You've got to go on the offensive and nail down his story before anyone else can try to manipulate him."

Alexia walked slowly behind her. "I thought you were concerned that he was going to accuse you."

"I am, but if you get him to tell the truth while he's weak, it will be hard for him to change his story later." Rena slipped her hand in the pocket of her pants and pulled out a digital voice recorder. "I brought this, and I'll be standing close enough to the head of the bed to pick up his voice."

They reached the front door of the cottage. Rena cracked it open, peeked inside, and motioned with her hand. A nurse that Alexia had never seen before came to the door. She was obviously excited.

"The night nurse called and told me Baxter was more alert," Rena said.

"Yes, but the most amazing thing is that he exhibited voluntary movement in his right hand and foot. We've left a message with the neurologist's answering service."

"Is he awake?" Rena persisted.

"No, he's sleeping."

"Have you talked to him?"

"No."

"Okay. I'd like to be alone with him."

The nurse nodded. "The aide and I will be in the kitchen."

"No," Rena responded. "I want total privacy. Go over to the main house. The front door is open, and the kitchen is to the left through the dining room. There's coffee in the pot on the counter."

Though Rena was agitated, Alexia could see clearly that she had a plan to carry out.

"If he has any distress—"

"I'll let you know, and you can be here in less than a minute."

Alexia watched the bewilderment in the nurse's eyes and could see her evaluating whether to refuse a direct order from her patient's wife.

"Alright," the nurse replied. "But please keep the visit short. This is outside our protocol."

"The only problem you'll have is if you tell me I can't have private time with my husband. I want to see for myself how he's doing."

The nurse's brow furrowed at the direct threat. She turned toward Alexia. "Who are you?"

"Alexia Lindale."

"A friend of mine," Rena added before Alexia could say anything else. "Please get the aide and leave. We're not going inside until you've left."

While they waited, Alexia said, "You didn't have to be so rough on her. She'd already agreed to leave."

"She needs to know that I'm the boss. I'm sick and tired of doctors and nurses telling me what I can and can't do. Ever since the first meetings with the doctors in Greenville, they've tried to run my life."

Alexia didn't answer. Rena's state of mind didn't accommodate diplomacy at any level. The nurse and aide came to the door. The aide glanced nervously at Rena, who ignored the look.

"Help yourselves to coffee," Rena said. "There is cream in the refrigerator and bagels on the counter if you want a snack. Cups are in the cabinet above the dishwasher."

As soon as the other women left, Rena turned to Alexia.

"Was that nice enough?"

"I don't think it's wise to make a big deal out of ordering them off the job."

Rena shrugged. "It won't show up in their notes because they don't want to get into trouble."

Rena pushed open the door and peeked inside.

"His eyes are closed," she whispered. "I'll sneak in quietly and go to the head of the bed. As soon as I'm there, you come in and wake him up."

"Do you want me to ask him to move his foot?"

"No," Rena hissed. "The nurse already told me it wasn't much."

Alexia started to argue, but Rena spun around and went into the cottage.

Alexia counted to ten and opened the door. Rena was standing directly behind Baxter's head and motioned for her to come inside. Alexia usually had more than thirty seconds to prepare for an important interview and didn't share Rena's expectations about the benefits of cross-examining Baxter. Most damaging admissions Alexia obtained in her cases came only after many hours of research and hard work. However, an opportunity to protect her client couldn't be ignored.

She approached the bed. Baxter lay on his side with his eyes closed. A foam wedge behind his back kept him stable. It was warm in the room, and his bare right arm rested outside the sheet. She sat in a chair near his head. As she did so, she thought about Ted. A few hours before, the music minister occupied the same spot for a different purpose. She leaned close to the sleeping man's face.

"Baxter," she said in a soft voice.

Rena shook her head from side to side. "Louder," she said in an intense whisper. "No one else is here."

Alexia took a deep breath, and spoke in a voice that could have filled a courtroom. "Baxter!"

The young man opened his eyes and looked directly at her with the gaze of a person waking from a nap. No confusion or disorientation marked his countenance. He opened his mouth to speak.

"Who are you?" he asked.

When he spoke, a thought shot into Alexia's mind. She spoke distinctly but without extra volume.

"I've been coming with the man who has been playing music for you."

Baxter licked his lips. "Good. Sing?"

"No, that's one of the nurses. I pray."

Alexia could see Rena gesturing but ignored her.

"I can't move my arms and legs," the young man said.

"Yes, you can," she said. "Try to move the fingers on your right hand."

She stared intently at the right hand inches from her face. The fingers moved. Alexia glanced up at Rena.

"Did you see that?" Alexia asked in excitement.

Rena pointed at the voice recorder.

"The doctor is coming to see you later," Alexia continued. "He'll tell you how you're doing."

Baxter closed his eyes. When he opened them, he asked, "Where is Ted?"

"Uh, he's gone home," she said. "He was here all night with you. Did you talk to him?"

Baxter licked his lips again. "Yes."

"Are you thirsty?"

He nodded slightly.

"Would you like some water?" she asked.

"Yes, please."

Baxter had been an inanimate object in Alexia's mind for so long that the simple request caused an involuntary wave of sympathy to well up within her. He had done a terrible thing to Rena, but Baxter was still a human being. On his tray was a slender wooden stick with a tiny orange sponge on the end. Alexia dipped the sponge in a cup of water, took it out, and rubbed it across the paralyzed man's lips. He took it into his mouth and sucked a few drops of fluid from it.

"Thanks," he said.

Rena leaned forward with her eyes blazing and mouthed the words, "Ask him!"

Alexia leaned closer.

"Baxter, do you remember what happened at the waterfall before you fell?"

He didn't answer but looked past her.

"Rena," he said and then stopped.

"Yes, she was there. What did you try to do?"

"Grab," he managed.

"Did you and Rena get in a fight?"

"Yes."

"Did you try to grab Rena?"

"Yes."

Alexia looked up at Rena, who nodded and held up the recorder with its red light glowing.

"Did you try to push her off the cliff?"

A puzzled look crossed the paralyzed man's face.

"Push, Rena," he responded. The tone sounded affirmative but was less clear when combined with his facial expression.

"Will you tell me why you tried to push Rena off the cliff?"

"No," he said a little bit stronger.

He looked at Alexia and slightly shook his head.

"Will you talk to me?" she asked.

Baxter closed his eyes and didn't open them. Alexia remained beside his head. Rena peeked over the top of the bed and then walked softly out the door. Alexia pushed back her chair and joined her outside.

"I think I got it," Rena said. "I'll rewind the tape so we can listen."

"Did you see his hand move?" Alexia asked.

"Yes. I read on the Internet that sometimes paralyzed people will have slight motion, but it doesn't mean they will return to normal. It scares me to think that Baxter might recover his strength and come after me. Let's listen to the tape."

Rena pressed the play button. Alexia's questions were distinct. Baxter's responses were fuzzy but audible.

"You nailed him down pretty good," Rena said. "I knew you could do it. I wasn't sure why you mentioned the music minister until I saw Baxter's reaction. That was smart. It got behind his defenses so he would tell the truth."

Alexia cringed at the characterization of her methods. "I wasn't trying to get behind his defenses, and I thought his answers were somewhat ambiguous. We'll need more than what he just said to build a case in court."

"What was ambiguous?" Rena asked sharply. "He admitted the fight and that he grabbed me and tried to push me from the cliff."

"All that could be explained away by claiming that he was still coming out of the coma and didn't understand what I was asking."

Rena held up the recorder. "Well, it's enough for me. He mentioned the music minister by name, which shows he is oriented to his current surroundings, and his answers to your questions made sense without any extra words."

Alexia tilted her head to the side. "Have you been doing a lot of studying about the characteristics of paralyzed coma victims?"

"Yes, and what's happening with Baxter fits the information I read."

"Maybe," Alexia replied. "But I'm going to check with Ted Morgan and find out what else took place last night."

32

The fixed sentinels almost receive
the secret whispers of each other's watch.
HENRY V, ACT 4, CHORUS 5

When Alexia returned to the office, Gwen was at her desk playing a card game on her computer. The secretary glanced up from the screen.

"What are you doing here on Saturday?" Alexia asked. "Besides playing solitaire."

"I stopped by to find out what happened," Gwen responded. "I want every detail."

Alexia leaned against the door frame. "I talked briefly with Baxter, but I'm not sure he understood me. But the most incredible thing was—"

"No," Gwen interrupted. "I meant with Sean Pruitt. I called your house and when you didn't answer, I checked here and found out you were working. The more I thought about lawyer Pruitt after our talk yesterday, the more fascinating he seems to me. I like Ted, but aristocratic-sounding Sean with lots of money, an expensive sports car, and a fancy house in Charleston deserves a serious look."

Alexia hesitated. Her thoughts were still on Baxter, but perhaps it was wise to avoid discussing his ability to move his fingers until the doctor had examined him.

"Sean and I had a nice evening," she answered simply.

"Details," Gwen demanded.

Alexia obligingly summarized the previous evening's conversation. She concluded by saying, "Maybe you shouldn't have given up so quickly on your novel. Any romance between Sean Pruitt and me won't generate enough suspense to make it to chapter two."

Gwen wrinkled her nose. "It's your life, but it seems to me that you and Sean have a lot in common."

"We'll be in court together as soon as he gets a date for the motion to suppress the subpoena."

Gwen closed the screen for the card game. "Give it room to grow. Have you talked to Ted about his time with Baxter?"

"No, but according to Rena, Ted spent all night at the cottage with Sarah Locklear."

"You're kidding."

"No, and I don't doubt that it's true. I didn't want to call Ted this morning because he's probably sleeping. He needs his rest."

Gwen's eyes narrowed. "That's nice of you," she grunted. "And you seem pretty nonchalant about the fact that he spent the night with another woman. Baxter Richardson is in no shape to chaperone."

"Oh, I know what they were doing."

"What would that be?"

"They were worshipping God and praying for Baxter."

"All night long?"

"Yep. What else would they do?"

Gwen threw her hands up in the air. "I give up. Bring me back into your story when it reaches a place that makes sense."

Alexia patted the older woman on the shoulder. "Real life is always more unpredictable than fiction."

———

In the downstairs storage room, Rena held the slip of paper in front of her nose as she turned the dial for the wall safe. The safe was hidden behind a shelf containing cans of furniture polish, insect spray, and bathroom cleaners. The shelf swung outward, revealing the square beige door of the safe. Baxter rented a large safe-deposit drawer at a local bank but installed the safe so Rena wouldn't have to run to the bank every time she wanted to wear expensive jewelry that couldn't be left unsecured in their bedroom.

The last tumbler clicked, and Rena opened the door. She pushed aside velvet-covered boxes containing diamond and sapphire earrings, a diamond pendant necklace Baxter purchased in Brussels, a unique antique bracelet once worn by an antebellum Southern belle, and a collection of rings worth more than some people in Santee made in a lifetime of hard labor. When it came time to leave, the jewelry would supplement the cash Rena gleaned from the Richardson family. No one could deny her claim of ownership to the contents of the safe, gifts freely and voluntarily given to her. Although she expressed delight when Baxter presented each bauble, they had no sentimental value to her, and Rena wouldn't hesitate to dispose of them when needed for the right price. This morning she secured a more precious possession—the digital recorder containing Alexia's questions and Baxter's answers. She set it beside the bracelet, closed the door of the safe, and returned the shelf to its place.

An hour later, the phone rang. Rena put down her second cup of coffee and glanced at the caller ID. Jeffrey.

"I'm sitting in my car in front of the house. Can I come in for a few minutes before I visit Baxter?"

Rena stepped to the front door and peeked out one of the sidelights. She could make out Jeffrey's figure in a black Mercedes coupe.

"Okay," she replied.

Her brother-in-law, dressed for the golf course, entered the foyer.

"It's going to be warmer this afternoon, and I have a golf date in Hilton Head," he said. "But I wanted to stop by, see you, and then talk to Baxter."

"Why are you going to see Baxter?"

"It's not to shake his hand, though I hear he can at least wiggle a finger."

"How do you know about that?"

Jeffrey's face was serious. "I warned you that I would know everything you said or did. That includes what goes on at the cottage."

"Did the nurse call you?"

"No," Jeffrey scoffed. "Do you remember when the heating and air-conditioning crew serviced the unit at the cottage last week?"

Rena vaguely remembered a work van with lettering on the side parked beside the small dwelling.

"Uh, yes."

"They did more than check the heat pump." Jeffrey took a step toward the living room. "Rena, you're living in a reality show without knowing it."

Rena's face paled. "You mean, there are cameras—" she stopped.

"Let's sit down and talk."

Numb with shock, Rena followed Jeffrey into the room. He sat in the large green leather chair Baxter always preferred. Rena sat at the end of a couch as far from her brother-in-law as possible. Jeffrey put his hands together in front of him and leaned forward.

"I'll get to the point. Did Baxter try to push you off the cliff at the waterfall?"

"Is that what you heard?"

"Just answer me. The video surveillance tape shows the parts of the conversation that the voice monitor picked up, but I need to hear it from you."

Rena swallowed hard and in a quiet voice said, "Yes, he did."

"Why?" Jeffrey demanded.

"Does it matter?" she asked, fighting back tears.

"You might as well tell me. I'll find out eventually."

Rena rubbed her eyes before responding. "Okay," she said with a sigh, "but you're not going to like it."

"That will be for me to say."

"It's not very complicated. Baxter was jealous. Not ordinary jealousy, but crazy jealousy. It started before we were married. I had to reassure him constantly that I stopped looking at other men when I met him. I thought everything would get better after the wedding made our commitment official. But it got worse. I suggested the trip to the mountains so we could be together away from everyone else and talk it out. On the hike, he accused me of seeing someone else. Of course it wasn't true, and he seemed to settle down, but when we reached the waterfall, he brought it up again. We got into a big argument. He grabbed me and pushed me. I fought back. He slipped and fell. That's it."

Rena put her head in her hands and waited.

Jeffrey considered this silently before speaking in a subdued voice. "Baxter was jealous about his girlfriend during senior year in high school, but I had no idea it had become such a big problem."

Jeffrey's admission of a prior similar tendency emboldened Rena. She raised her head but didn't look at her brother-in-law. Instead, she stared at the carpet in front of the sofa as she spoke.

"I thought Baxter and I could solve the problem ourselves. I mean, if I stayed with him, he would have to realize how much I loved him. My family taught me to show love, not just say it. That's why his attack came as such a total shock. We'd had arguments, but Baxter never threatened me physically. You know him. He's not an aggressive person."

Jeffrey nodded. "Why didn't you tell the police what happened?"

Rena shook her head. "Looking back, that's what I should have done, but I thought he was dead and I didn't want to embarrass your family. When I found out he was alive, I didn't know what to do."

"So you tried to terminate his life support."

Rena felt her face flush. She looked Jeffrey in the eye. "No! Keeping him alive paralyzed from the neck down and in a coma was the cruel thing to do. I forgave him enough to let him go. I'm the victim in this mess. Don't accuse me—"

Jeffrey held up his hand. "I'm sorry. It will take time for me to work through this."

"I haven't completely dealt with it, either," Rena said. "And when he started waking up, I became terrified that he would make up a story trying to blame me for what happened. That's why I asked Alexia Lindale to talk to him. I hoped that he would admit the truth before he had a chance to think through a lie. Did you hear his answers?"

"The audio was faint, but it was obvious from your lawyer's questions what was going on. Did you record the conversation?"

Not sure about the range of the camera, Rena was afraid to deny it. "Yes."

"Did it pick up Baxter's answers?"

Rena nodded.

"What did he say?"

Rena summarized Baxter's responses, emphasizing the incriminating implications. Jeffrey's face was hard and impassive. He pressed his lips together.

"Where is the tape?" he asked when she finished.

"Alexia Lindale has it."

"What are you going to do now?"

"Just what I told you. With the information on the tape, I don't think Baxter can hurt me with a false accusation. I want to divorce him and leave Santee. I need money, and I'll help you maneuver into a better position with your father if I can stay out of danger."

Jeffrey nodded. "It changes my perspective too. Even if Baxter wakes up and regains some use of his arms and legs, I don't want to be associated with him."

Rena pointed in the direction of the cottage.

"Does your father know about the surveillance camera?"

"Of course not."

"Do you know everything that goes on over there?"

Jeffrey shrugged. "Once a day, I receive a written report, but I don't spend hours watching Baxter lying on his back. Last night was bizarre. Lindale's music-minister friend brought in an electric keyboard and played for several hours while one of the nurses sang and read from the Bible."

"That's what they call music therapy. One of the doctors in Greenville recommended it."

"I thought it was nuts. Your visit this morning was much more interesting." Jeffrey paused. "I still don't know why you didn't tell me all this about Baxter when we met in Greenville. I could have taken the truth, even if my father couldn't."

Rena held firm. "Would it have made any difference?"

Jeffrey didn't immediately answer. "Not really," he admitted. "I guess nothing has changed except that I know why you want out. And I can't blame you."

Rena sat back against the soft cushion of the sofa in triumph. "As horrible as all this has been, it feels better to share it with someone besides my lawyer."

"Is she the only other person you've talked to?"

"Yes. No one else knows the truth."

———

Alexia worked through lunch, opting to eat an apple at her desk. She rarely spent a full Saturday at the office. Shortly after two o'clock, she clicked off her dictation unit and took a stack of files to Gwen's desk. The secretary would have more to do on Monday morning than increase her win/loss rating at solitaire. On her way out the back door, Alexia met Rachel Downey coming in.

"I passed by your new office a few minutes ago," the Realtor said. "There were a couple of trucks parked in front. What are they doing?"

"I'm not sure," Alexia responded in surprise. "I haven't talked to Ted today. I thought he would be sleeping."

Rachel waved a ring-encrusted finger at her. "You haven't been keeping him up too late, have you?"

"No," Alexia replied with a straight face. "He spent all last night with another woman, and I didn't want to disturb him by calling his house."

Rachel dropped her hand. "Quit it, Alexia. That's not funny."

"I'm not trying to be funny. It's the truth. Call Gwen. She knows the details."

Rachel opened her mouth but no words came out. Alexia grinned at the minor miracle of rendering the glib saleslady speechless.

"I've got to go," Alexia said. "I was going home, but I'd better stop by King Street and make sure Ted's okay. I wouldn't want him to work while he's exhausted."

She brushed past Rachel and headed out the door. The sky was cloudy, and a cool breeze that had brought a dusting of snow to the mountains near the North Carolina border caused her to shiver. The humidity in the coastal air made the temperature feel colder than it would in a dryer climate. She turned on the heater in her car as she drove the few blocks to King Street, but the engine didn't have time to warm the car before she arrived. Ted's white truck and another work truck were parked in the driveway.

Alexia pushed open the front door. Inside, she could hear a banging sound from the rear of the house. She passed through the foyer and dining room into what had been the kitchen. The old sink was gone, and the counters had been pulled away from the wall. Ted and another man were working on the row of slightly rusted white metal cabinets suspended over the space where the counters had been. Ted had a paint sprayer in his hand, and one of the cabinets now glistened with a shiny, deep cherry color. He looked up when Alexia entered the room and pulled a mask away from his nose and mouth. A faint dusting of red paint framed the area of his face protected by the mask. He spoke to the other man, who also turned in Alexia's direction.

"Jackie, this is Alexia Lindale, the owner."

The other worker was a very thin, white man who looked to be in his sixties. He nodded in Alexia's direction without taking off his mask.

"I don't want to interrupt your work," Alexia began. "I just stopped by for a second."

"No, it's fine. I can take a break. Jackie knows more about these cabinets than I do. He works in an automobile body shop and knows how to paint anything metal."

They walked into the dining room. Ted slid the mask over the top of his head. His fingers were tinged with red.

"Actually, this was the only day Jackie could work for me."

"But aren't you tired? Rena called me this morning and told me that you and Sarah were at the cottage all night."

Ted nodded. "Yes. It will hit me harder in a few hours."

Alexia decided not mention her visit. "What happened?"

Ted's brow furrowed and became more serious. "I'm still sorting it out myself. I'd rather talk about it when we have more time. Are you coming to church tomorrow?"

"Yes."

"Let's get together for lunch after the service."

"With or without Mary Lou Hobart?"

"Without. She'll understand, and I'll promise to take a fried-fish platter to her house for supper one evening next week."

Rena was restless the remainder of the day. Shortly after Jeffrey left, her confidence in the protection offered by Baxter's taped confession began to wane. She left the house for several hours and went shopping, but nothing caught her fancy. As she walked past a rack of expensive dresses at a chic shop on the outskirts of Charleston, she longed again for a permanent end to her husband's threat. Divorce could not eradicate the possibility that Baxter might someday incite Giles Porter or some other detective to track her down. The only sure solution would be to silence

Baxter, once and for all. Rena's attempt to figure how to introduce a fatal secondary infection had come up empty. The stronger Baxter became, the more likely his chances of survival.

She picked up a yellow chiffon dress and held it up in front of a mirror. It would have looked good on a brunette, but it made her blonde hair look washed out. She remembered a dark-haired classmate from college. The young woman, a fierce rival for a boyfriend, would have loved to include the dress in her clothes arsenal. Rena looked at the price tag. It cost more than six hundred dollars. If she'd had money in college, Rena would have bought the dress without blinking just to keep the other girl from discovering and wearing it. She returned the dress to the rack. Money was the key to power. It could keep things from happening, or it could make sure they did.

33

Obstinacy in a bad cause is but constancy in a good.
SIR THOMAS BROWNE

A lexia arrived a few minutes late at the Sandy Flats Church. A light rain had settled over the coast, and she shook out her umbrella on the steps outside the front door. She found a seat in the almost-full sanctuary a couple of rows from the rear.

Ted sat on the piano bench playing a portion of a Bach fugue originally written for the organ. Alexia doubted anyone would complain. She settled into the pew. During the sermon, her mind drifted, and she looked at the stained-glass windows that lined the walls of sanctuary. The cloudy day muted the colors. Each panel depicted a miracle performed by Jesus, and the scenes had served as illustrations during her first conversations with Ted about faith. In her favorite, the healing of the crippled man at the pool of Bethesda, the face of Jesus came alive when viewed from a specific spot on a sunny afternoon. Today, the Savior's gaze was trapped in the one-dimensional glass realm.

Alexia continued to daydream until she heard the minister finish the closing prayer, and Ted began playing a piece that bore the marks of an original composition. Alexia had listened to Ted enough to recognize his creative musical voice. She remained in the pew as the congregation quickly exited the sanctuary. Ted saw her and smiled in her direction as he finished with a flourish. She clapped as she walked down the aisle to the piano.

"Why the big crowd this morning?" she asked when she reached the low altar rail.

Ted closed the keyboard cover. "When the weather gets cooler and wetter, the sanctuary fills up. Where do you want to eat?"

"How about Cousin Bert's? There's nothing like a bowl of soup and cornbread on a day like today."

"Sure. I haven't been there for a couple of months."

They walked to the back of the sanctuary. Ted slipped off his robe and put it on a hanger in the foyer. The rain had increased, so no one hung around the parking lot to talk. Ted didn't have an umbrella, but he held Alexia's over her head as they walked to her car. She glanced sideways.

"You're getting soaked."

Ted didn't answer as he shielded her head while she unlocked the door of the car.

"Tell me about Friday night," Alexia said as she drove from the parking lot. She still wanted to hear Ted's account without any input about what she'd seen.

"It was wonderful and troubling," he said.

Alexia waited. She turned onto the road leading into the center of town. The rain began to fall harder. The windshield wipers for Alexia's car rapidly beat back and forth.

"I'm listening," she finally said.

"Which do you want first?" Ted asked. "The wonderful or the troubling?"

"Good news before bad news."

Ted summarized what took place. He'd reached the place where Sarah confirmed the scripture he'd read about prayer and fasting when they arrived at the restaurant.

"You're not fasting now, are you?" Alexia asked.

"Nope. God's will for my life today includes a big piece of cornbread."

The restaurant wasn't as crowded as usual, and they didn't have to wait for a table. Most of the patrons were churchgoers. A family sitting near the door greeted Ted by name as they passed by to a table in the rear.

They ordered their drinks and meals at one time. Both selected a bowl of seafood stew—a concoction not unlike Alexia's homemade gumbo, but with a greater concentration of garden vegetables. Cornbread came with the meal. Ted added a vegetable plate of collard greens, mashed potatoes, and okra with tomatoes. After the waitress left, Ted described the initial musical session.

"It was similar to what we've done in the past, but not having to conform to a schedule made a big difference. We went on for much longer than usual."

He related how Baxter moved his right foot and fingers in response to Sarah's command. "That's the good news," he said.

Their food arrived, and Ted prayed. But he didn't limit the blessing to thanks for stew, cornbread, and collard greens seasoned with vinegar. He extended the request toward Baxter Richardson.

Alexia ate a bite of cornbread. "Is that all the good news?"

"No, we took a break for coffee and then had a time of praise and thanksgiving. I've never heard anyone sing like Sarah Locklear. Her voice is clear, and I don't mean technically. There is spiritual power in her singing that touched me as much or more than it did Baxter."

Alexia tried to suppress the familiar twinge of jealousy. It was impossible not to compare herself unfavorably to the nurse.

"That's wonderful," she managed, inwardly kicking herself for being childish.

Ted continued. "As far as I could tell, Baxter slept through the worship time, but when we stopped about five o'clock in the morning, he woke up. I was sitting beside the bed, and he looked up at me. He didn't have that glazed-over, disoriented look on his face.

"Did he talk to you?"

"Yes," Ted chased down a bite of collard greens with his fork. "And that was the troubling part. Sarah went into the kitchen. He asked me to lean close and spoke in a whisper."

Ted stopped and looked over Alexia's shoulder. She turned around as two men at an adjacent table got up to leave. There was no one else within earshot. Ted lowered his voice.

"What did Rena tell you caused Baxter to fall from the cliff?"

"I can't tell you because it's protected by the attorney-client privilege."

"Why?"

Her first response had been a legal reflex. The second question made her stop and think. She took a sip of tea.

"Rena told me information with an expectation that I'd keep it confidential. She hired me to protect her interests and needs to be able to confide in me without fear."

Ted's face remained serious. "Does she always tell you the truth?"

Alexia winced. "I can't answer that without violating my ethical rules."

Ted looked down and stirred his tea with a short, stainless-steel spoon. "Then perhaps I shouldn't tell you what Baxter said to me."

Alexia wanted the information. "Why? Was it troubling?"

Ted shook his head. "You're not going to cross-examine me."

Alexia flushed slightly. Ted was being unreasonably obstinate.

"You don't have any confidentiality rules to restrict you. I'd tell you what happened at the waterfall if I could. Did Baxter accuse Rena of something?"

Ted took a sip of tea. "Isn't there legal protection for conversations with a minister?"

"Yes, but the person has to know that you're a minister, and it must be in a counseling situation. Does Baxter know that you are a minister?"

"Yes."

"But that alone doesn't mean he was seeking counsel."

"What is the difference between counsel and help?"

Alexia bit her lip. "Ted, I need to know what's going on. We can talk in circles or you can tell me what Baxter told you."

Ted shook his head. "I don't think it would be right to discuss my conversation with Baxter unless Rena agrees to let you talk openly with me."

"You mean unless she waives the attorney-client privilege?"

"Yes."

Expanding the circle of those with sensitive information exponentially increased the risks of uncontrolled disclosure. Alexia hesitated before responding.

"I could discuss it with her, but I doubt—" Alexia paused as an idea came to her. "Remember when I asked you to consider counseling Rena?"

"Yes."

"I never mentioned it to her. But that might be a way to solve this.

She could talk with you as a ministerial counselor with the understanding that what she tells you will remain private."

"Does she want counseling?"

"I'll see if she's open to the possibility. I can tell her how much you've helped me."

"Would you be there too?"

"Of course."

"Where would we meet?"

"The church would be my choice."

Ted nodded. "Okay. I'm willing to help her. That might be the best thing to do."

———

Dr. Simon Leoni didn't come to Santee until Monday morning. After conducting a neurological examination of Baxter, he walked out of the cottage with Ezra. They stood facing each other on the sidewalk.

"Movement to his extremities is definitely returning," the doctor said. "The scans taken in Greenville after the accident showed significant displacement of the spinal cord, but it wasn't severed; however, this degree of improvement isn't common. I would have given him less than a 25 percent chance of regaining even the limited motion we saw today."

"What about his left side?"

"I elicited a trace response in his left arm. His leg is still at zero. Given what I found today, he may possibly regain some level of functioning in both his arms and hands. The legs are more difficult to predict. If you'd asked me a week ago if he would ever walk again, I would have told you no. Now, I'm not so certain. I'll schedule another MRI to see if there has been any decrease in displacement of the spinal cord."

The two men parted. Ezra walked over to the house and rang the doorbell. No one answered. He rang it again. In a few moments, Rena cracked open the door and motioned for him to come inside. She quickly shut the door behind him. She was barefooted and wearing a quilted housecoat.

"I didn't feel well this morning," she said, blowing her nose on a tissue. "The nurse called when the doctor arrived, but I didn't want to expose Baxter to whatever I have."

Ezra relayed the information he'd received from Dr. Leoni.

"Did you talk to Baxter?" Rena asked.

"He was groggy. He knew I came to visit but didn't want to keep his eyes open. How is he responding to you?"

"Oh, we've had some sweet times together, but he's still very confused. One minute, his thinking is clear; the next, he's talking nonsense."

Ezra glanced past Rena toward the kitchen. "Do you have any coffee?" he asked.

"Sure. Come into the kitchen, and I'll pour you a cup."

Ezra liked Rena's coffee. She set the cup on the island in the middle of the kitchen. Ezra took a drink before he spoke.

"What's the latest from Jeffrey? I've been out of town for several days and just returned last night."

Rena put an index finger to her lips. Taking a slip of paper from a pad near the phone, she wrote on it and passed it to her father-in-law. *He's listening.*

"Oh, he's fine, I guess," she answered in a casual voice.

Ezra gave her a startled look and then wrote on the pad. *Jeffrey?*

Rena nodded.

Ezra continued to write. *When can we meet?*

"That's good," he said. "I haven't talked to him since I returned."

Rena slid the note back. *I'll be followed.*

"I've got to go," Ezra continued. "Thanks for the coffee."

He scribbled beneath Rena's words. *Tomorrow, my office—3:00pm—$$*

Rena nodded. "I'll take something so I feel better."

———

Gwen cornered Alexia around ten thirty the following morning. Coming into the lawyer's office, she closed the door.

"I've told the receptionist to hold your calls for five minutes," she said. When Alexia started to protest, she continued. "Except for Sean Pruitt. I know you're waiting on notification of the hearing in Charleston. Let's have it."

Alexia pushed her chair away from her desk. "Okay. I talked to Ted, and it's just what I suspected. He and the nurse spent the night praying for Baxter, who is regaining use of his right arm and leg. Their time at the cottage was like being in church."

"Which is where you first kissed the minister, if I recall my facts correctly," Gwen retorted.

Alexia smiled. "Guilty, but the whole deal with Baxter is different from anything I've been involved in. For Ted, it's completely unselfish."

"And for you?"

"I'm like a kindergartener who barely knows the alphabet. Until I met Ted, I never considered that God might do miracles. The stories in the Bible were no more real to me than fairy tales."

Gwen was thoughtful. "Did you actually see him move his hands and legs?"

"On the right side. I started to tell you on Saturday, but you were focused like a laser beam on Sean Pruitt."

Alexia told Gwen about her visit to the cottage, leaving out the recorded conversation. Scoring points on cross-examination with a worthy opponent was rewarding, but the lawyer couldn't escape a twinge of guilt at taking advantage of a barely conscious man. Gwen stood when Alexia finished.

"What does Rena want to do?"

"She wants out more than ever. I wouldn't be surprised if she gave me the go-ahead to file the complaint for divorce within the next few days."

After Gwen left, Alexia phoned Rena at the house. Rena answered and curtly told Alexia that she would call back at a more convenient time. In a few seconds, a return call was routed to Alexia's office.

"What's going on?" Alexia asked.

"It's Jeffrey."

Rena proceeded to tell Alexia about the electronic eavesdropping.

"Surveillance!" Alexia exclaimed. "He has no right to do that. It's not his house!"

"You tell him," Rena replied. "Right now I'm standing on my deck in a cold wind talking to you since I don't know whether he's bugged my house or not."

Alexia's mental wheels were turning. "Maybe Sean can find out from Quinton."

"But he's been in jail for weeks."

"And according to Sean still maintains his contacts on the outside."

"Go ahead and ask him then, but in the meantime we'd better communicate on cell phones."

"Which can also be tapped. What else did he tell you?"

When Rena finished, Alexia asked, "Did Jeffrey claim that the equipment at the cottage picked up my conversation with Baxter?"

"I don't think so. That's why he asked me about the tape."

"What else?"

Alexia could hear Rena sigh. "I told him what really happened at the waterfall. He could hear your questions and that made it impossible to avoid the issue. He asked me point-blank whether Baxter tried to push me off the cliff, and I told him everything—our argument about the Richardson companies, what I'd tried to do to handle the problem on my own, and how crazy Baxter acted."

"How did he take the news?"

"He was shocked, but now he understands why I want to divorce Baxter. I think he's more willing to help me now."

"Did you tell him about the subpoena demanding a copy of the videotape?"

"No, it didn't come up. The whole thing with Baxter blew him away. We didn't talk about anything else."

"Did he say anything about what happened with Ted Morgan and the nurse the night before?"

"He thought it was a waste of time."

"Did he mention any conversations Ted Morgan had with Baxter?"

"No, weren't you going to talk to Ted about it?"

"I had lunch with him yesterday, but he wouldn't tell me. He wants to hear your side of what happened at the waterfall before letting me know what Baxter said to him. I can't do that without your permission, and it's risky anyway. But I think I know how we can address it."

"How?"

"You can go to him for counseling."

"I don't need counseling from a music minister!"

Alexia explained her strategy to Rena, who remained skeptical.

"It's the only way to find out what he knows and at the same time keep your comments to him confidential," Alexia insisted. "You won't have to meet with him again or establish an ongoing counseling relationship."

As soon as she spoke the words, Alexia felt a bit dirty. At the heart of her idea was a nugget of deception.

"Okay," Rena replied. "Set it up, and I'll go so long as you'll be with me."

34

And after all, what is a lie? 'Tis but the truth in masquerade.

LORD BYRON

Sean Pruitt called Alexia. The hearing on the motion to quash the sub-poena was set for Wednesday afternoon at 3:00 PM.

"Should I bring the tape in case the motion is denied?" she asked. "It's in a safe-deposit box at the bank, and I'll need to get it out before I leave Santee."

"Bring it. If we win, I'd still prefer to have the tape in my possession. If we lose, it will save you a trip to deliver it to the solicitor's office."

"Should Rena come?"

"I've already filed a response that she doesn't have a copy of the video, so it's not essential that she be there. No warrant for her arrest will be issued until the tape is reviewed."

"Okay."

Pruitt paused. "Is something else going on with Rena?"

"What do you mean?"

"I can hear it in your voice. Something is troubling you. Has the detective from Mitchell County returned?"

"I don't think so. If he tried to see Baxter, Rena would have let me know. But *I* had a chance to talk to Baxter."

Alexia explained what happened at the cottage.

"I agree. His statement's not definitive," Pruitt said when she finished. "But it helps, and together with Rena's testimony could create a credible argument for self-defense."

"Rena is convinced it's airtight."

"She bounces around a lot, doesn't she?"

"Gwen and I call her 'the yo-yo client.' The only problem is that I'm the yo-yo she's constantly yanking on."

"I'll try to ease some of the yanking for you. Has the divorce been filed?"

"No, but it will be as soon as we tell her that she can leave Santee and not look back."

"Wednesday will determine the next step."

"Oh, there's one other thing," Alexia added. She told him about her conversation with Ted Morgan.

"I'm not sure it's a good idea for Rena talk to anyone. Who knows what she will say?"

"I'll be there with her."

"Will that make any difference?" Sean asked. "It didn't deter her in Charleston. Perhaps you can tell the minister what Rena told you, and she can simply nod her head that your account of the facts is correct. Keep her from opening her mouth."

"Which I should have done when we first met with you."

"Probably."

"Okay."

———

Rena didn't try to hide the fact that she was driving to Richardson and Company headquarters. Even before Baxter's injury, she avoided the building, unknown territory inhabited by people she didn't know and couldn't trust. She'd been to Ezra's office only one other time. She parked in the parking place marked, "Reserved for Baxter Richardson."

Expertly landscaped grounds, as carefully manicured as the golf courses developed by the firm, surrounded the two-story stone and brick structure. A small stream flowed across the ground in front of the building, and the path to the entrance crossed a narrow bridge. The original golf-equipment-manufacturing facilities were farther down the road. Gold lettering on the wall above the door proclaimed, "Richardson and Company."

Rena entered the spacious lobby. A young woman with an unfamiliar face sat in the middle of a circular reception desk made of dark wood. She looked up when Rena entered.

"May I help you?" she asked.

"I'm Rena Richardson. I'm here to see my father-in-law."

The woman's eyes grew big. "Of course, Ms. Richardson. Shall I let him know you're here, or do you want to go directly to his office?"

"I'll go myself. Is Jeffrey here?"

"No. He's out of town today."

The second floor could be reached by either a winding staircase or an elevator. Rena walked up the staircase. Jeffrey and Baxter had offices at one end of the floor. Ezra's suite occupied the opposite end. In between were many smaller offices of the middle-management personnel who kept the wheels of the business well-oiled and turning out a profit. As she passed several closed doors, Rena wondered how many of the employees knew the real source of the company's recent prosperity.

Thick, dark-green carpeting covered the hallway. The first time Rena visited the office, she took off her shoes and let her toes enjoy the luxuriance, so different from the crude floor covering in her bedroom in Nichol's Gap.

A set of wooden double doors led to Ezra's area. Rena pushed open one door and peeked inside. Ezra's secretary, an attractive woman in her midthirties, looked up from her desk and waved Rena inside.

"Come in," she said. "Mr. Richardson is expecting you."

Two walls constructed of glass panels boasted beautiful views. Her father-in-law's massive desk sat in the center of the room, and a comfortable seating area filled the left. Ezra was nowhere in sight. Rena stood awkwardly in the middle of the room and waited. In a moment, one of several doors in the opposite wall opened, and Ezra motioned for her to join him. She joined him in a small, windowless room with a table surrounded by four chairs and dark paneling. There was a small TV in a corner as well as a computer terminal and a telephone. Ezra closed the door and turned a lock.

"Have a seat," Ezra said. "This is a safe room. We can talk freely here."

Rena glanced around. If she'd suffered in the least from claustrophobia, the room would have been intolerable.

"How are you feeling?" Ezra asked.

It took Rena a second to remember her fake cold.

"Uh, much better. I took some vitamin C." She sat down in a small leather chair. "Does Jeffrey know about this room?"

"Of course. We meet here all the time."

"And Baxter?" she added without thinking.

"I think he's been here," Ezra responded vaguely. "But we need to get down to business. What is going on with Jeffrey?"

Rena was ready with her speech. "He's talking with some of the people who buy golf balls made in the Caribbean for ten thousand dollars a dozen."

"He told you about that?"

"Yes, and he's hired people to watch me ever since Baxter's accident. He says they're protecting me, but I think they're spies. The man who shot the videotape on the day my car was stolen is one of them."

"What's his name?"

"I'm not sure, but he works with a man named Henry Quinton, who is in jail in Charleston."

Ezra made a note on a pad in front of him. "Who are some of the other people helping Jeffrey?"

Rena shook her head. "I don't know. He gave me a list of companies that my lawyer should mention in any lawsuit filed against you, but there weren't any names on it."

"Where is the list?"

"At my lawyer's office."

"Lindale?"

"Yes."

Ezra tapped the pad with his pen. "Get it back. And I'd very much like to know the names of Jeffrey's friends. Find out the next time you talk to him."

Rena looked at the floor. "That may not be possible. Jeffrey only tells me what he wants me to know so he can manipulate me."

"Tell him Lindale needs to verify the information you've given her. I only need one or two names to unravel this web."

Rena looked up, entreating him with her eyes. "Would you be willing to send people to watch out for me? If Jeffrey knew that I'm talking to you, there is no telling what he might do to me."

"That might tip my hand to Jeffrey. I'd rather he not know what I'm doing."

Rena ignored his obvious lack of concern for her safety. "You could set it up to look like they're working for me. I'll even pay them, so long as you give me the money."

Ezra put his fingers together in front of his face. "That's an interesting approach. They could monitor the surveillance activity and provide data that might allow us to identify Jeffrey's contacts."

Ezra paused, and Rena waited.

"Very well," he said, sitting up straight in his chair. "I'll do it. But I still want you to send me the list of companies and try to find out who is helping Jeffrey. What you're telling me fits with a rumor I heard on a trip to the Caribbean a few weeks ago."

"Will the people working for you contact me?" Rena asked.

"Yes, and you'll pay them. I never get directly involved with things at that level."

Ezra's comment mirrored what Jeffrey had told Rena and slightly unnerved her—father and son, the same.

"Someone will get in touch with you very soon. You'll know that he's working for me because he will bring a work-order for a security system you want to have installed due to break-ins in the neighborhood."

Ezra picked up an envelope, which was beside the television, and handed it to Rena.

She opened it and found a cashier's check for $250,000 inside. The remitter was a company whose name was unfamiliar to her.

"What is this company?" she asked.

Ezra smiled. "One set up especially for you."

"How much should I pay the guard?"

"He'll tell you. The first thing he'll do is provide a secure way for you to communicate with me." Ezra walked to the door and flipped the dead bolt. "Try to find out who is helping Jeffrey. The information will be very valuable to me and you."

"Will you be visiting Baxter soon?"

"Yes," Ezra replied, his voice lighter. "Isn't it wonderful that he's improving? When he is able to function again, I know that the three of us will have a much better relationship."

Rena smiled. When she did, she knew it made her eyes sparkle.

———

Rena's cold was bogus. The respiratory infection that entered Baxter's room on the right index finger of the nurse's aide was not. It was alive and thriving, ready to leap onto a new host. The young aide wiped her little girl's nose with a tissue before kissing the child good-bye at a day-care center. She intended to wash her hands as soon as she began her shift, but the nurse on duty needed help as soon as she walked through the door.

"We need to turn him more frequently," the nurse said. "I noticed a small sore on the left side of his lower back. That can lead to big trouble. Hold his head steady while I turn his body."

While shifting the patient, the aide's finger touched the corner of Baxter's mouth. A few seconds later, Baxter licked his lips, and the germs entered his mouth, where they found a warm, moist place to multiply. Within minutes they had migrated to his lungs. Twenty-four hours later, his temperature began to rise. It wasn't the exotic infection Rena had hoped for, but it was enough to send Baxter in the same direction—off the cliff.

And this time, Rena had nothing to do with it.

———

Alexia and Rena got out of their cars at the Sandy Flats Church.

"I saw you looking in your rearview mirror a lot," Alexia said. "Do you think we're being followed?"

"Always," Rena shrugged.

"Going to a church is probably not a suspicious activity on anybody's list."

They walked up the front steps. When they reached the top, Rena stopped.

"I haven't been inside a church in a long time," she said. "Baxter and I were married at his father's place on the river."

As an associate at Leggitt & Freeman, Alexia had known about the wedding but didn't receive an invitation. After the event, Ralph Leggitt placed a photograph on his credenza of himself with Ezra standing beside a flower-bedecked gazebo.

"Until I met Ted, I didn't attend church either," Alexia replied.

"My aunt used to take me, but it wasn't a happy place for me. The kids in the Sunday-school class never talked to me because I didn't wear the right kind of clothes."

Alexia glanced at Rena's outfit. Her shoes probably cost more than a prom dress for a local high-school student.

"You wouldn't have to be ashamed now," Alexia said.

"It doesn't matter. Every church is the same. All of them are filled with hypocrites."

Rena joined Alexia in the narthex. Piano music drifted from the sanctuary. Alexia looked at Rena and put her finger to her lips.

"Let's listen for a minute," she whispered.

It was Bloch's *Visions and Prophecies*. Written in the 1930s, it contained five short movements. Ted was playing the adagio.

"I can hear," Rena responded impatiently. "And I don't have time to waste."

The adagio was followed by a very fast poco agitato that lasted less than two minutes. Alexia wanted to hear the rapid section. "It will be over soon."

Rena plopped down in a small chair in the narthex and pouted. Her conduct made it hard for Alexia to enjoy the music. Ted stumbled a few times in the closing section.

"He needs to practice that part," Alexia said quietly.

The notes fell silent. Rena stood up. "Let's see him before he starts something else," she said.

When they stepped into the sanctuary, Alexia called out. "Hello! We're here!"

Sitting on the piano bench, Ted looked up. "Come to the front. I'll get a chair."

Alexia and Rena walked down the aisle and sat on the front pew facing the piano. Ted lifted a chair across the altar rail and positioned it so he could face them. Alexia introduced him to Rena and watched as Ted, his face serious, shook her client's hand.

"Thanks for letting me play for your husband," he said.

"Whatever you want to do is fine with me," Rena responded with a flip of her hand. "I'm not a classical music fan like Alexia, so none of it makes sense to me."

"I don't perform music written by a composer when I'm with Baxter."

"I'm unfamiliar with all of it," Rena responded and then quickly added, "and I'm not interested in a classical-music lecture."

"Of course, and that's not why we're here. Alexia wanted to ask me questions about a conversation I had with Baxter recently at the cottage."

"Yes, I know all that."

"But first, I wanted to hear from you what happened at the waterfall."

Rena looked at Alexia.

"Ted, can you reassure Rena that our conversation is confidential?"

"That depends on whether this is a counseling session, doesn't it?"

"Yes," Alexia replied slowly.

Ted turned toward Rena. "Do you want me to help you?"

Alexia winced. She'd hoped Ted would disclose his conversation with Baxter without trying to establish a bona fide counseling link with Rena.

"I need all the help I can get," Rena responded emphatically. "I've had a rough time my whole life, and it didn't stop when I married Baxter. It all started with my stepfather."

Alexia glanced at Rena in surprise. The only unfailing characteristic Rena Richardson possessed was the inability to keep her mouth shut. For the next forty-five minutes, she poured out a tale of woe that would have awakened sympathy in the most hard-hearted person. She didn't cry, but the subdued way in which she related hardships, beginning with her earliest memories, didn't diminish their impact. Ted interrupted a couple of times with questions but otherwise gave Rena free rein. Alexia sat on the edge of the pew, constantly ready to pull the plug, but didn't intervene until her client reached the events at the waterfall.

"It would be more efficient if I told you what happened, Ted," Alexia interjected. "It's hard for Rena to talk about it. It was an accident, but not an unfortunate slip and fall on slick rocks. Baxter tried to push Rena over the edge of the cliff. They fought, and he fell. Is that right, Rena?"

Rena nodded.

Ted turned toward Alexia. "Why won't you let Rena tell me about it?"
Alexia felt her face flush. "It's so painful."

Ted gave her a skeptical look. "More painful than what she's already told me? It would be hard to rank the horrible things that have happened to her. They're all bad." He looked at Rena. "Would you add anything to what Alexia said about the waterfall?"

Rena shook her head. "I've talked too much already, but you have the kindest brown eyes I've ever seen. I felt that I could tell you anything, and you wouldn't condemn me."

Alexia didn't want Rena to become more bizarre. "We need to move on. Rena has another appointment." She turned to Ted. "What can you tell us about your conversation with Baxter?"

"He agrees that there was a fight at the waterfall, so I don't think there is any difference on that point." The music minister leaned forward. "But Baxter claims Rena tried to kill him." Rena's face grew pale, and her eyes opened wide.

"What did he say?" Alexia asked. "Be as specific as possible."

"Baxter spoke in a whisper and told me it was Rena's fault that he fell. I asked him how, and he told me there was a fight at a waterfall, and she pushed him over the edge of the cliff."

"That's not what he told Alexia!" Rena blurted out. "And we have it on tape! There was a fight alright, but he was the one who tried to push me over the edge!"

"What else did he say?" Alexia asked, trying to remain calm.

"Nothing. I realize he's coming out of a coma and might say things that don't make sense or be correct, and I obviously wasn't at the waterfall and don't know what happened. That's why I wanted to find out what Rena had to say. I'd hoped there wasn't a fight at all and we could chalk the whole thing up to delusion. But after hearing her . . ." he stopped.

Alexia seized the opening. "Ted, you've heard about Rena's past. Trouble has stalked her since she was a little girl. This is another chapter in the same story."

"I'm not saying that I believe Baxter, but you can understand why I'm concerned."

"Of course, and what happened to Baxter is a tragedy. But it would be a worse tragedy for Rena to come under suspicion for something that he did to her."

Ted looked toward Rena. "Tell me exactly what happened."

Rena glanced at Alexia, who decided to scuttle Sean's advice.

"Go ahead," Alexia said.

Rena repeated the story she'd told Alexia. Ted didn't take his eyes off her. Several times, Rena glanced sideways at the lawyer for encouragement. Once, Alexia reached across and lightly patted her on the shoulder.

When she finished, Ted ran his hand through his hair. "I needed to hear what happened from your lips. Baxter is so completely helpless that I never considered what he might be like as a man and husband."

"I've told you everything," Rena said, leaning back against the pew. "You can ask me anything, and I'll tell you the truth."

"No, I've heard enough." He looked at Alexia. "What else?"

"The more I learn, the more I believe Rena that the Richardsons are involved in something illegal and they want it kept secret."

"So you believe her?"

"Yes, I do. And you?"

Ted got up and walked to the piano. He hit a few notes and then spoke to Alexia. "Yes. I'll keep everything we've discussed confidential."

"When are you going to see Baxter?" Alexia asked.

Ted glanced down at the floor and shook his head. "I'm not sure that I will."

35

Giles Porter finished the slow process of transcribing his conversation with Baxter Richardson. He relied on his memory, not a tape recorder, to recall what was said. His verbatim recollection wouldn't be admissible in court, but it was more than adequate for investigative purposes. He pushed the print button and waited patiently for the three pages to inch out of the ancient printer connected to his computer. He slipped the sheets in a folder and glanced at his calendar. It would take a full day to return to Double Barrel Falls and half a day to talk to the trauma-unit doctor at the Mitchell County Hospital.

When Rena arrived home, a white van with "East Shore Co." neatly painted on its side was parked in front of her house. She couldn't see through the van's tinted windows whether anyone was sitting in it. She entered the house by a side door. Less than a minute later, the doorbell chimed. Going into the foyer, she could see a skinny young man standing on the front landing. He adjusted the white cap on his head. She opened the door.

"What do you want?" she asked.

The young man shifted from one foot to the other. "I'm sorry to bother you. I'm here to install a security system for Mrs. Baxter Richardson."

Rena looked again at the tall young man, who stared back at her with brown eyes that revealed nothing. Rena noticed the blemishes on his cheeks. He held a tool kit in his left hand. A patch on his shirt identified him as "Rudy."

"Can I please see the work order?" she asked.

"Yes ma'am." He handed her a folded sheet of paper, which Rena took and examined. It was blank. "There have been a lot of break-ins in the neighborhood. You can't be too careful these days."

Rudy had definitely been sent by Ezra. But the package didn't fit her expectations.

"Is this an inconvenient time?" the young man asked.

"No," Rena said. "Come inside."

The young man stepped into the foyer. As soon as Rena closed the door, he dropped to his knees and opened the tool kit. It didn't contain a single pair of pliers. Instead, it was filled with electronic gadgetry. He flipped two switches on a box that looked like a walkie-talkie before he spoke.

"This will jam any attempts to eavesdrop within a ten foot radius,"

Rena peered over his shoulder. He took out a cell phone and handed it to her.

"Use this phone after you turn on the unit."

"How do I turn it on?"

The man showed her what to do. "It's very simple."

"What about video surveillance?"

"I'm going to check the house. I won't disturb anything, but I'll let you know what is safe and what is not secure."

"What should I do?"

The young man smiled with a glint in his eyes that caused Rena to reevaluate his apparent innocence.

"Do whatever you would do if a worker came in to tinker with your house."

Rena retreated to the kitchen. She could hear the man moving through the house, moving furniture in one of the bedrooms upstairs, walking down the hallway. Anxiety overtook her. What if he was planting bugs, not finding them? She quickly climbed the stairs. He was in her bedroom looking up at the light in the middle of the room. He spoke when she entered the room.

"I know security in this room is important, Ms. Richardson. We can install sensors on all the windows as well as under the carpet on the stairs leading to the second floor."

Rena stared at him for a second and then abruptly turned around and returned to the kitchen. She poured a drink of whiskey and fidgeted for thirty minutes before he reappeared. Taking a small handheld device from his pocket, he walked around the room, moving his hand from side to side. After two thorough sweeps, he slipped the device back into this pocket.

"You keep a nice, clean house, but you could use an exterminator in a couple of rooms. There's a mic in your bedroom, and a mic with camera in the living room."

"Can we talk in here without using the jamming device?" Rena whispered.

"Yes. They're not very sophisticated devices. I expect they're more for harassment than for gathering information."

That fit with Jeffrey's style. Rena relaxed.

The man continued. "Carry on as normal, but if you have something confidential to say, avoid those two rooms and turn on the jamming device as an extra precaution."

Rena nodded. "Thanks. What do I owe you?"

"Five thousand."

Rena's mouth dropped open. "You weren't even here for an hour."

"But I knew what to do with the time."

Rena started to protest but remembered Ezra's instructions. She took her checkbook from her purse and set it on the counter.

"Make the check payable to East Shore Company," he said.

"Not to Rudy?"

"East Shore Company," he replied. "I don't know anyone named Rudy."

Rena took out a pen and began to write. "If I knew your real name, I could write a check to you too."

The man took out the jamming device and turned it on. "Why would you want to do that?"

Rena tore out the check and handed it to him. "If I could hire you to do something for me, I would write you a much bigger check than this one."

"How much bigger?"

"A lot. And if you told me your name I would give it directly to you."

"What did you have in mind?"

By Wednesday morning, Baxter started coughing. The nurse on duty took his temperature and noted the increase in his chart. By noon, his breathing became raspy and she called Dr. List Cabot, the local internist who monitored Baxter's general health status.

"Have you been able to talk to him about his symptoms?" the doctor asked when she took the call.

"No, he's been lethargic and nonresponsive."

"Any mucus?"

"Yes. It's rust-colored."

"I'll be there shortly."

In a few minutes, the doctor arrived. She was a small woman in her late thirties with black hair and narrow glasses. She placed a stethoscope against Baxter's chest, listened, and then tapped his chest. The nurse stood beside her.

"Does he have pneumonia?" the nurse asked when the doctor took the stethoscope from her ears.

"His chest crackles when he breathes, but I hope it's only a very bad cold. His body is already so weak that he'll have a tough time fighting a severe respiratory infection."

The doctor took Baxter's hand in hers. His fingernails had taken on a dark tinge.

"Do you see that? His body isn't processing enough oxygen. I'm going to order a chest X-ray and ask the radiology group to send a portable unit this afternoon. Call me as soon as they finish."

———

Alexia spent a couple of hours Wednesday morning reviewing a detailed memo she'd received from Sean Pruitt about her testimony at the afternoon hearing. The Charleston lawyer's research impressed her. He had spent a lot of time outlining the issues, identifying the relevant documents from Rena's files, and listing the questions he intended to ask Alexia, as well as possible attacks she could expect on cross-examination. Gwen made copies of the documents needed and labeled them for easy identification. An hour before she left, Alexia loaded everything into the larger of her two briefcases.

She'd not heard from Rena in a couple of days, and the silence had been a welcome relief. Being a witness was going to be a different experience for

Alexia, and Rena's presence would have compounded the pressure. Gwen buzzed her.

"Rena is on the phone."

Alexia hesitated. "Okay, I'll take it."

"Is the hearing in Charleston this afternoon?" Rena asked.

"Yes, I'm leaving in less than an hour."

"What's going to happen?"

Alexia gave her a synopsis of the issues and Sean's strategy.

"So we're going to win, right?"

"If the judge agrees," Alexia replied. "Nobody can guarantee results in this type of proceeding. The judge can do what he likes and make us try to overturn his ruling on appeal. But even then, there is dispute in the case law about the timing of appellate review for denial of a motion to quash."

"Huh?"

"Don't worry about it now. I've got to get ready to go."

"Will I have to say anything?" Rena asked.

"You're going?" Alexia asked in surprise.

"Of course I'm going. It's really about me, not you. But I don't want to have to testify. That almost killed me at the hearing about terminating Baxter's life support."

Alexia flashed back to Rena on the witness stand in Greenville. It was true. She had been a horrible witness.

"There is no plan to call you as a witness, but I can't afford to be late to Sean's office. I have to walk out the door in thirty minutes."

Rena paused, and Alexia hoped the need for imminent departure would deter Rena from joining her.

"I'll be at your office in five minutes. I'm already dressed. We'll ride together."

Alexia hung up the phone and sighed. Five minutes passed without any sign of Rena, then fifteen. After twenty-five minutes, Alexia walked out to Gwen's desk.

"Any word from Rena? We're supposed to leave in a few minutes."

Gwen shook her head. "Go on. If she shows up, I'll give her directions to the courthouse."

"Maybe she won't come."

"Do you want to go alone?" the secretary asked.

Alexia nodded. "Yes."

"Then you've officially left the office."

Alexia picked up her heavy briefcase and walked out the back door. She almost ran into Rena coming around the corner of the building. She was wearing a dark, navy dress suitable for court.

"Sorry I'm late," she said. "I parked along the side of the building so I wouldn't take up any spaces in front."

"That was considerate," Alexia said with a hint of sarcasm. "Let's go. I want to make sure we arrive early at Sean's office in case he has any last-minute instructions for me."

"I'm looking forward to seeing him," Rena said. "Don't you think he's good-looking?"

"You're still married," Alexia said flatly.

"You're not."

"My mind is on what I need to do today."

Alexia shook her head and got in her car. As soon as they pulled into traffic, Rena started asking questions about Sean Pruitt. Alexia provided monosyllabic answers, but Rena was so persistent that she even dragged out information about their dinner at The Cypress.

"Jeffrey likes Magnolias," Rena said. "Did you know the same people own both restaurants?"

Alexia grunted in reply. As the miles fell away, Rena refused to let the conversation lag.

"Tell me about Ted Morgan," she said. "I haven't been able to get his eyes out of my mind. It's like he looks into your soul, only not in a bad way. I mean, I've got nothing to hide except my pain, and when he listened to me talk, I sensed everything would be alright. Even though he didn't say much, I felt his sympathy for me."

"He has an ability to communicate to the heart," Alexia admitted.

"Has he done that with you?"

Alexia hesitated for a few seconds and consciously pushed aside the resentment she felt toward her client.

"He's been a door opener."

"What do you mean?"

"He's opened my eyes to the reality of faith in God."

For the first time since she'd joined Alexia that afternoon, Rena didn't say anything.

After a moment, Alexia continued, "Do you want to hear about it?"

"Sure."

Alexia couldn't tell if Rena's response was sincere and glanced sideways. By all appearances, she was giving Alexia her full attention. So, for the second time in the past few days, Alexia recounted the sequence of events that led to her encounter with God in Ted's backyard. Rena listened without interrupting. When Alexia finished, Rena turned her head and stared out the window. Several miles passed. Alexia's curiosity broke the silence.

"What do you think about my story?" she asked.

Rena continued staring out the window. "It's different from anything I've ever heard."

They rode in silence until they reached the outskirts of Charleston. Rena spoke again.

"Do you think I should divorce Baxter?"

Clients had directed this very question at Alexia many, many times. Women knew ending a marriage wasn't the lawyer's decision but couldn't resist the urge to ask. Alexia had a stock answer, which always rolled off her tongue with ease—divorce was a choice each woman had a right to make. She would then proceed to explain her role to legally analyze the practical ramifications of all options and zealously pursue the one chosen by her client. In Rena's case, Baxter's conduct made the option to stay married less supportable. Alexia opened her mouth, but her usual speech didn't emerge from her lips.

"No," she said. Then she quickly tried to correct herself. "I mean, the petition is ready when you are. It's up to you. It's your choice."

Rena didn't answer.

———

They navigated the downtown streets of Charleston to Sean Pruitt's office. As they walked up the steps to the front door, Rena saw Alexia leaning sideways to counter the weight of her briefcase.

"What is in there?" she asked.

"Some of what I've done for you. I left the rest in Santee."

The receptionist asked them to wait in the parlor. The room exuded the comfortable atmosphere of a place where people once enjoyed un-hurried conversations as they whiled away long, lazy afternoons. But the environment failed to help Alexia relax. She felt tension rising at the core of her being. She always felt a hint of nervousness before the first blow in a hearing or trial, but today's anticipation touched a different set of nerves. Her responsibility as a witness was about to take her into unknown territory. Rena sat down and began to flip through a magazine.

After a few minutes, Sean Pruitt came into the room. He was dressed in court clothes—dark-gray suit, white shirt, yellow tie. Rena was right. If good looks alone could persuade a judge or jury, Sean's appearance would guarantee a high win-loss record. He showed no surprise at Rena's presence.

"Ready?" he asked.

Alexia nodded. "Yes, I've reviewed the questions, and my secretary has organized and indexed the documents you requested."

"Good. We'll hit the important parts of your testimony on the drive to the courthouse. It won't be complicated."

"Will you ask me any questions?" Rena asked.

"Maybe."

"What?" Alexia said.

"I don't want to testify!" Rena added. "Ask Alexia, I'm a terrible wit-ness."

"I didn't know you would be here," Sean responded nonchalantly, "but it may help corroborate Alexia's testimony if I ask you a few ques-tions about the formation of your attorney-client relationship. I'll test the waters and determine what we need to do."

Rena started to argue, but Alexia spoke up. "Don't panic. Maybe you should review her testimony on the way to the courthouse instead of mine. I have my script memorized."

The women followed Sean across the courtyard to the garage. The silver sports car had been replaced by a more mundane BMW similar to Alexia's.

"Where is your car?" Alexia asked in surprise.

"In the shop for repairs. This is a loaner."

Alexia sat in the backseat so Sean could focus on Rena. He led her through a series of questions that she handled with ease.

"That wasn't too bad," she said when he finished, "but what will the prosecutor ask me?"

"He's called an assistant solicitor in South Carolina," Sean replied. "Alexia, why don't you pick a few areas for cross-examination from the information I sent you."

Alexia took the memo from her briefcase and quickly mentioned a few areas. Rena interrupted her.

"I know all that stuff too."

"Yes," Alexia replied. "So there's no need to panic."

———

Sean found a parking space near the front door and went inside. One of the security guards joked with him as he walked through the metal detector.

"Put your gold coins in the tray, Mr. Pruitt," he said.

Sean pulled his pockets inside out to show they were empty.

After they passed through and walked down the hallway, Alexia asked, "What was that all about?"

"I represented his brother in a lawsuit against a local business. It was an odd case. After we won, the defendant paid the judgment in Krugerrands. He kept them in a plastic bag in a well on his property to protect them from foreign invaders."

"Foreign invaders?"

"Yes, an unusual defendant makes an odd case."

They took the steps to the second-floor courtroom. Several lawyers were milling around and chatting in the hallway. Sean opened the door for Alexia and Rena. Inside, on a bench in front of the bar, sat five manacled and cuffed criminal defendants wearing orange jumpsuits. Sean looked at his watch as they sat down on a bench behind the bar.

"I hope you don't have to be back to Santee for anything today," he said. "There's a lot of business to be disposed of before any motions are heard."

A short young attorney with brown hair and wearing a blue sport coat entered the courtroom through a door behind the bench. Sean nudged Alexia.

"That's Joe Graham, the assistant solicitor."

The government attorney was followed by the judge, a stocky, black-robed man with bushy gray eyebrows, salt-and-pepper hair, and dark eyes.

"All rise," the bailiff proclaimed. "This court is now in session, the Honorable Michael Moreau presiding."

Judge Moreau sat down behind the bench and scanned the court-room. Alexia sensed his eyes stop for a second when he reached them before continuing down the row of prisoners seated to their left. The judge picked up some papers and cleared his throat.

"The Court calls In re Grand-Jury Subpoena, Motion to Quash Subpoena."

Having settled in for a long wait, Alexia was startled. Sean was imme-diately on his feet.

"Ready for the motion, Your Honor," he announced.

Graham stood behind the table used by the State's attorneys and spoke in a deeper voice than Alexia expected from such a short man.

"Your Honor, as you can see, we have several prisoners in the court-room. With your permission, I'd like to handle those matters before taking up the motion."

The judge looked down at the bench. "Why aren't these on my after-noon calendar?"

"They were added after lunch. I thought an amended calendar was delivered to your chambers."

"It wasn't," the judge replied with obvious irritation.

"Do you want me—"

"Get on with it," the judge interrupted.

Three of the men entered not-guilty pleas, but two pled guilty. It was a tough day to plead guilty in front of Judge Moreau. In both cases the solic-itor's office had reached agreements with the defense lawyers; however, the judge kept everyone guessing whether he would accept the State's proposal.

"Is he always like this?" Alexia asked.

"No, but he's the most moody judge we have. One day he's accom-modating; the next he's a bear."

Alexia had no doubt which judicial temperament had come out of his den and ambled into the courtroom today. When the last defendant had slunk from the courtroom, Graham picked up the only file remaining in the rack before him.

"We're ready to hear the motion to quash, Your Honor."

Sean turned to Rena and whispered, "Wait here."

Alexia followed Sean past the bar to the other counsel table. The judge picked up a thin stack of papers and straightened them.

"I've reviewed the subpoena and your motion, Mr. Pruitt," he said. "Proceed with your proof."

"Your Honor, I call Alexia Lindale to the stand."

"Let the witness come around and be heard," the judge boomed.

Alexia walked up to the witness stand and faced the judge while he administered the oath. She lowered her hand and sat down in the witness chair.

36

The people are turbulent and changing;
they seldom judge or determine right.
ALEXANDER HAMILTON

Sean didn't immediately launch into questions about Alexia's representation of Rena, but methodically established her educational and professional qualifications. Remembering the advice she had given many clients, Alexia shifted in her seat so she could look up at the judge as she responded.

"And I've been in private practice in Santee since passing the bar exam," she said.

"What is the primary nature of your current practice?" Sean asked.

"Domestic relations."

"How about representing clients in criminal proceedings?"

"During the first three years of my practice I handled both misdemeanor and criminal cases, mostly for indigent defendants."

"Did any of these cases go to trial?"

"A few, but of course I prepared to try more cases than I actually tried."

"Who presided?" Judge Moreau interjected.

"Judge McNeill served as our General Sessions Court Judge at the time," Alexia replied.

"Were you with a law firm?" the judge continued.

"I was an associate at Leggitt & Freeman in Santee."

The judge leaned forward. "Ralph Leggitt's firm?"

"Yes, Your Honor. He and Ken Pinchot were my supervising partners."

The judge paused for a second. "But now you're on your own, is that correct?"

"Yes sir."

"Were you a partner at Leggitt & Freeman?"

"No."

Alexia had moved on with her legal career, but her failure to become the first female partner at Leggitt & Freeman still left a bitter taste in her mouth. The judge grunted and looked down at his papers. Sean resumed questioning.

"Were you still working at Leggitt & Freeman when you began representing Mrs. Rena Richardson?" he asked.

"Yes, the Richardson family has been a client of Leggitt & Freeman for many years. Mr. Leggitt sent me to Greenville after Ms. Richardson's husband was critically injured. There were questions about a durable power of attorney and health-care power of attorney signed by Baxter Richardson that affected decisions about his medical care."

"Who is Baxter Richardson?"

"Rena Richardson's husband."

"During this time in Greenville, what contact did you have with Rena Richardson?"

"I saw her at the hospital and helped mediate several sessions involving Rena Richardson, the physicians treating Baxter, and Ezra Richardson, Rena's father-in-law."

"Please describe for the judge the formation of the attorney-client relationship between yourself and Rena Richardson."

"At first, it was my goal to assist the entire Richardson family. However,—"

Movement over Sean's shoulder caught Alexia's eye. The back door opened, and a short man with a familiar disfiguring scar entered the courtroom. Detective Giles Porter walked up the aisle and took a seat on the bench behind Rena, who continued to look forward, unaware of his presence. Sean followed Alexia's gaze and quickly glanced over his shoulder. Alexia shifted in the chair before continuing.

"It became obvious that a conflict of interest existed between Ms. Richardson and her father-in-law regarding control of medical and property issues. Ms. Richardson had a clear, reasonable expectation that an attorney-client relationship existed between us—"

"Objection, Your Honor," Graham said, rising to his feet. "Ms.

Richardson's internal thought processes are outside the scope of this witness's knowledge."

"Sustained," the judge replied before Sean could respond.

Alexia glanced again at Porter, who sat impassively behind Rena. He was wearing the same brown suit he'd worn when he appeared at the hearing to terminate Baxter's life support.

"What discussions establishing the attorney-client relationship did you have with Mrs. Richardson?" Sean asked.

"First, she shared information with me that she considered confidential—"

"Objection, hearsay," Graham interrupted.

The judge looked at Sean. "Is Ms. Richardson going to testify?"

"She's here in the courtroom and available if necessary."

Alexia saw fear flash across Rena's face.

"You may present your proof however you like, Mr. Pruitt," the judge responded, "but I'm going to sustain the hearsay objection."

Sean didn't immediately retreat. "Your Honor, the attorney-client relationship is a bilateral agreement. It would not be hearsay for Ms. Lindale to explain the basis upon which her side of the contract of representation was formed."

"That's not what I hear you asking," the judge replied. "Mr. Graham is correct. You're asking her to read Ms. Richardson's mind."

"May I rephrase the question?" Sean asked.

The judge looked down his nose at Alexia. "Did Ms. Richardson sign a contract of representation at the time you're referring to?"

"No sir. That took place later in Santee."

Sean continued, "But it's not essential that the contract be formalized in a written document so long as confidential information is shared for the purpose of obtaining legal advice."

"Maybe not, but I'm going to need more than supposition if you expect me to seriously consider your motion." The judge waved his hand. "Move on to something relevant."

Sean stepped back to the table and picked up a stack of papers. After they were marked by the court reporter, he furnished a copy to the solicitor and handed the originals to Alexia.

"Could you please identify those documents?"

"These are my billing records. The oldest ones are from Leggitt & Freeman and explicitly state that Rena Richardson is the client. After I left the firm, all bills were sent to Ms. Richardson from my office. Over half of the charges in this stack represent work performed weeks before Officer Dixon's death. I've represented her on other matters, primarily related to her husband's condition."

"Did she seek your legal advice and counsel after Officer Dixon's death?"

"Yes. She asked me to be with her when Detective Devereaux from the Charleston County Sheriff's Office interviewed her in Santee about the circumstances related to her car."

"Please identify the bill for your services on that date."

Alexia turned to the sheet and marked the entry with a yellow highlighter.

"This is it," she said. "It states, 'Conference with client and Detective Devereaux at client's residence. 1.5 hours.'"

"How else do your records support the existence of an attorney-client relationship between yourself and Mrs. Richardson as to any inquiry into Officer Dixon's death?"

"I made phone calls to the Charleston County Sheriff's Office and wrote a follow-up letter to Detective Devereaux in which I identified myself as Ms. Richardson's attorney."

Sean returned to the table and picked up the phone records. He handed a copy to Graham. "First, the phone records. Please identify pertinent sections for the judge."

Alexia walked the Court through tedious but irrefutable evidence, grateful that many a legal case has been won or lost based on a telephone bill. Interested only in documenting information to justify charges, the phone company keeps records with consistent impartiality. After the bills were admitted into evidence, Sean handed Alexia a copy of the letter she'd sent to the Charleston County Sheriff's Office.

"Please identify this document."

"This is a letter I sent to Detective Byron Devereaux confirming information about our meeting with Ms. Richardson. As you can tell from the first line, I identified myself as Rena Richardson's attorney. The letter goes on to state—"

"I can read the letter," the judge interrupted. "It's admitted into evidence as a business record. Hand it up to me."

Sean took the letter from Alexia and passed it to the judge before continuing.

"At what point did you begin furnishing legal advice to Mrs. Richardson about the circumstances associated with Officer Dixon's death?" Sean asked.

"On the same day it occurred."

"When did you stop giving her legal advice about this matter?"

"I haven't. Even after she retained you, I have continued to provide representation."

"Do you have a written contract of representation with Mrs. Richardson?"

"Yes, and a letter that sets the amount of retainer required. My standard practice is to bill against a retainer."

Alexia hoped to make it through this sticky point unscathed. The attorney-fee agreement Rena signed was general, not specific, and it didn't mention representation in any criminal case prior to the date Alexia received the videotape. Sean handed Alexia a copy of the agreement.

"Is this the agreement?"

"Yes."

"What services did you provide to Mrs. Richardson after she signed this agreement?"

Alexia counted off the items with her fingers. "I assisted her in decisions affecting her husband's medical care, discussed legal issues related to her father-in-law, answered questions posed to her by a detective from Mitchell County, advised her about personal domestic matters, and counseled her regarding the situation we're here about today."

Alexia looked at Giles Porter as she spoke. Rena still hadn't noticed her nemesis.

"How did you come to possess the videotape described in the subpoena?"

"Ms. Richardson gave it to me because she had questions about its legal significance. I viewed the tape with her and kept it for further evaluation."

"What was your understanding of the reason for Mrs. Richardson's decision to entrust the videotape to you?"

"She did so only after I assured her that I would keep it confidential."

"Why did you refuse to deliver the videotape to the officer who served the subpoena?"

"Because my client gave it to me based on the fact that I am one of her lawyers. I could not obey the subpoena without violating my client's Sixth Amendment right to counsel and the South Carolina ethical rule protecting privileged information shared by a client with an attorney."

"I'll be the one to decide if that's the case," Judge Moreau said.

"Yes sir," Alexia replied.

Alexia knew that Sean had intended his question, not the judge's comment, to be the final direct testimony offered by her. He stood still for a second. Alexia knew he was trying to decide if another question was necessary to end on a strong note.

"That's all from this witness," he said.

The judge looked toward Assistant Solicitor Graham.

"You may ask, Mr. Graham."

Younger than Alexia, Joe Graham had shaggy brown hair, uncharacteristic for a prosecutor, and wore wrinkled slacks. Top law-school graduates did not generally seek assistant-solicitor positions, known for low compensation and miniscule raises. It was a great job, however, for a young lawyer who wanted to gain trial experience as rapidly as possible. After a few years in the trenches, most assistant solicitors migrated to firms where their courtroom skills commanded a much higher salary. Others who harbored political ambitions that could be advanced by the publicity available to a prosecutor remained in the solicitor's office. Joe Graham didn't look like judicial material.

"Ms. Lindale, does your client own a red convertible?"

"She did. I believe it was recently sold."

"Did she still own it on the date of Officer Dixon's death?"

"Yes."

"Did she ever notify the Santee police department that the red convertible had been stolen?"

"That's my understanding."

"Was the vehicle, in fact, stolen?"

"Any conversation I had with her about the status of the car was related to my legal representation of her."

Sean was on his feet. "And protected by the attorney-client privilege, Your Honor. We object to this line of questioning."

The judge scowled at Sean. Alexia sat completely still. Graham had started with questions she'd not expected until later in his cross-examination.

"I'm going to sustain the objection at this time, but I may allow you to bring it back up, Mr. Graham."

Graham didn't appear upset by the judge's ruling, and Alexia breathed a sigh of relief. He picked up the attorney-fee agreement signed by Rena and handed it to Alexia.

"Please point out the specific language in this agreement that states you are representing Ms. Richardson in a criminal investigation in Charleston County."

"That is covered by the words 'general representation,' which includes any legal matters, civil or criminal."

"Are you telling Judge Moreau that based on this agreement you would be willing to represent Ms. Richardson in any conceivable type of case?"

"Unless something came up outside my area of expertise."

"Antitrust, patent infringement, estate planning? Are these covered?"

"Not specifically, but I could have at least pointed her in the right direction for any type of legal work."

The assistant solicitor held up the fee agreement in his hand. "Is the language contained in this agreement identical to contracts signed by clients who specifically retained you in the past to represent them in criminal cases?"

"No," Alexia admitted.

"How is it different?"

"Well, usually, the agreement identified the nature of the charges and the fee for my representation. In this case, representation began before Officer Dixon's death, and my advice and counsel flowed out of my ongoing legal assistance to her."

"But the agreement is completely silent about legal representation for criminal charges in the past, present, and future, isn't it?"

"Except for the general-representation language."

Alexia realized she shared with Graham an unwillingness to leave an issue until scoring a point by attacking it in slightly different ways. The next questions did not surprise her.

"And you referred Ms. Richardson to Mr. Pruitt to represent her in any criminal investigation, didn't you?"

"But I remained cocounsel."

Graham's voice grew louder. "As a subterfuge, because you never legitimately undertook representation of Ms. Richardson in this matter but merely wanted to manufacture a way to block a grand-jury investigation into a police officer's death."

Alexia didn't answer. It wasn't a question.

"Isn't that what's really going on today, Ms. Lindale?" Graham persisted.

"Objection, argumentative," Sean said.

"Overruled."

"No," Alexia said. "Ms. Richardson is my client, and she has repeatedly shared information with me as her attorney in confidence for the purpose of obtaining legal advice."

"So, am I correct in stating that your discussions with Ms. Richardson about the contents of the videotape fall within the attorney-client privilege?"

Alexia hesitated. She didn't want to agree with anything the prosecutor said but couldn't see a way to deny the statement.

"Yes, that's partially correct."

"What part is incorrect?"

Immediately, Alexia wished she'd simply agreed. She'd fallen for the old trick of refusing to admit the obvious as a way to discredit a witness.

"I can agree with your statement."

"Without reservation?"

"Yes."

Graham looked down at the legal pad in his hand.

"Does the videotape contain confidential communications between yourself and Ms. Richardson?"

"What do you mean?"

"Are you talking with Ms. Richardson on the tape?"

"No."

"Then shouldn't the discussions about the videotape be protected from grand-jury investigation rather than the videotape itself?"

Alexia glanced at Sean, who stood up when she caught his eye.

"Objection, Your Honor. You will be the one to decide that issue."

"Overruled. I'd like to know what Ms. Lindale thinks, since she's the one asserting the privilege."

Sean sat down. Alexia was on her own.

"No, because the videotape was entrusted to me by my client as part of a confidential communication, just as occurs with a document or other type of record."

"Has Ms. Richardson discussed the videotape with anyone else besides yourself and Mr. Pruitt?"

Alexia felt her stomach sink.

"Not in my presence," she answered.

"What about outside your presence? Has she mentioned discussing it with another attorney?"

"Only Mr. Pruitt."

"Then who else is in the circle of information?"

"She told me as part of a confidential communication."

Judge Moreau's voice boomed from the bench before Graham could say anything else.

"Answer the question! If your client has discussed this matter with another person, it may waive her right to assert the attorney-client privilege now."

Alexia was aware of the rule. She glanced at Sean, who wore his attorney game face in an effort to appear impervious to bad news. Alexia looked up at Judge Moreau.

"With her brother-in-law, Your Honor."

"And what is his name?" Graham asked.

"Jeffrey Richardson."

"Does he live in the Santee area?"

"Yes."

"Where does he work?"

"With his father at Richardson and Company."

A sharp cry caused everyone in the courtroom to suddenly look toward the seating area. Rena was running from the courtroom. Alexia watched her retreating form. Giles Porter shrugged and rubbed the side of his face with a stubby finger.

"What's the basis for this commotion?" the judge asked sharply.

Alexia was about to answer when she saw Sean stand up.

"Mrs. Richardson had to leave the courtroom. I'm not sure why and apologize for the interruption."

"Do you want to proceed without her?" the judge asked.

Sean looked at Alexia, who nodded. Rena could not exist in the same confined space with the Mitchell County detective.

"Yes sir."

"Very well. You may ask, Mr. Graham," the judge said.

"Has your client discussed the contents of the videotape with anyone else besides her lawyers and brother-in-law?"

"Not to my knowledge."

Graham flipped over another sheet of his legal pad.

"Ms. Lindale, isn't it also true that documentation indicating the occurrence of future fraud or criminal activity is not protected by the attorney-client privilege?"

Alexia would not be trapped again by failing to admit the truth.

"Yes, but the tape does not contain information of future fraud or criminal activity."

"That's your opinion, but how can the grand jury make a determination without seeing the tape?"

Sean stood up. "Judge, I object to this line of questioning. It would be the Court's prerogative to review the tape in private in order to make that decision."

"Which is where this hearing is going regardless of any further testimony," the judge replied.

Graham stepped away from the witness stand. "That's all I have, Your Honor."

Alexia returned to her seat at the counsel table.

The judge looked at Sean. "Do you have any other witnesses?"

Sean answered without consulting Alexia. "No sir. We will not be calling Mrs. Richardson to the stand."

"Where is the videotape?" the judge asked.

"Ms. Lindale has it in her briefcase."

"Hand it up," the judge ordered.

Alexia opened her briefcase and gave the tape to Sean, who stepped forward and gave it to the judge.

"How long is the tape?" the judge asked.

"Less than five minutes."

"I'll review it in my chambers and then listen to any closing arguments." The judge banged his gavel. "The court will be in recess for fifteen minutes."

37

'm going to find Rena," Alexia said to Sean when she returned to the table. "The man with the scar on his head is the detective from Mitchell County."

"Go ahead. I need to stay here."

Alexia walked down the aisle. As she passed Giles Porter, their eyes met. He looked at her without emotion. Outside the courtroom, Alexia quickly scanned the hallway. No Rena. She went to the ladies' restroom and found her client standing at a sink with water dripping from her chin, a paper towel in her hand.

"He was there," Rena said.

"I know. He came into the courtroom while I was testifying. It made it hard for me to remain focused."

Rena faced her with an incredulous expression. "You saw him?"

"Of course. He sat down behind you."

"No, no. He was in the jury box on the first row, third seat from the end. He had the most awful expression on his face, and when he laughed out loud, it was so cruel—" Rena stopped.

"Who?"

"Baxter."

Startled, Alexia remembered that Rena briefly saw an apparition of her husband in the courtroom in Greenville. Rena stared straight ahead as she continued.

"But it was different from any of the other times—he was so real, and

I couldn't make him go away. I shut my eyes. I tried making a noise. I looked away at other people. I dug a fingernail into my arm until it bled. But nothing made a difference. And then the sound of his voice." Rena closed her eyes and her face contorted. "The laugh. It was beyond description. I had to get out."

"Rena, I had no idea. You told me in Greenville, but—"

"You don't want to know." Rena leaned over and splashed her face with more water. She patted it dry with a towel. "But you saw him too?"

"No," Alexia answered. "I thought you were talking about Giles Porter. He was sitting behind you."

Rena rested her forehead against the mirror. She closed her eyes.

"What is he doing here?"

"I don't know. It's an open hearing, so he can come and listen. I haven't tried to talk to him."

Rena stood up straight. "I'm going crazy. Baxter didn't kill me at the cliff, but he's going to kill me from his hospital bed."

Alexia routinely counseled distraught women, but Rena fell into a different category. Alexia racked her mind for a plan.

"Don't go back to the courtroom," she said after a few moments. "We'll find a chair in a hallway where you can wait for me."

"What's going to happen? I thought I might have to testify."

"No, it's not a good strategy, and you're in no shape to face cross-examination. Right now the judge is doing an in camera review of the videotape."

"He has a camera?"

"No, it's a legal term for a judge looking at evidence in his office without anyone else present. He's going to watch the tape before making a decision."

Rena spun, her eyes wild with fear.

"That's no good! We've lost! They're going to charge me with murder!"

Alexia tried to remain calm. "It's not unusual for a judge to review potential evidence in private. I should have mentioned it to you earlier. Trust me. Just because the judge sees the tape does not mean anyone else will know about it. It's part of the process."

Rena banged her fist against the sink. When she did, Alexia could see the place where she'd gouged her left forearm. A bruise was spreading around the cut.

"You can't stay in here," Alexia said. "Let's go find a place for you to sit."

Rena wadded up the paper towel and threw it in a trash can. "What's the use? I'm going to be treated like garbage."

Alexia found a police officer and asked about a place where Rena could sit.

"There's a snack room on the lower level," the officer replied.

They rode the elevator. Neither spoke. They stepped out and found the snack room.

"Do you have money for the machines?" Alexia asked.

Rena nodded.

"Stay here until I come back to get you. It won't be long."

Rena found a small table with one chair beside it and sat down.

"Are you going to be okay?" Alexia asked.

Rena waved her off. "Go, do your lawyer thing."

Reluctantly, Alexia returned to the elevator. She couldn't dismiss a nagging thought that Rena wouldn't be in the snack room when she returned.

Alexia rejoined Sean and checked her watch. Judge Moreau had not returned and Giles Porter was gone.

"Did you find her?" Sean asked.

"Yes. She's upset, and I took her downstairs to the snack room."

Sean didn't probe. He flipped through the pages of an appellate-court decision he'd marked in several places with a yellow highlighter. Alexia left him alone. She glanced over at Joe Graham, who was intently studying some papers on the table in front of him.

Judge Moreau reentered the courtroom.

"All rise!" the bailiff commanded.

The judge resumed his place on the bench. Nothing in his face revealed his thoughts about the video.

"Proceed for the movant," he said. "I'll give you no more than five minutes."

Sean stood but stayed behind the table.

"Your Honor, the U.S. Supreme Court has described the attorney-client privilege as 'the oldest of the privileges for confidential communications known to the common law.' In *United States v. Zolin,* the Court explained that its purpose was 'to encourage full and frank communication between attorneys and their clients and thereby promote broader public interests in the observance of law and administration of justice.' This purpose requires that clients be free to 'make full disclosure to their attorneys' of past wrong-doings in order that the client may obtain 'the aid of persons having knowledge of the law and skilled in its practice.'

"The attorney-client privilege is not without costs, since it has the effect of withholding relevant information from investigative and fact-finding bodies; however, unless the information sought relates to a future crime or fraud, the sanctity of the privilege must be protected."

Sean stepped from behind the table. "In this case, the evidence un-equivocally shows that Mrs. Richardson shared information, including the videotape, with Ms. Lindale as part of a confidential communication in which she was seeking legal advice and counsel. Our own Supreme Court emphasized this point in *State v. Owens* and held that once the attorney-client relationship is established, privileged communications must be protected from coerced disclosure. Having seen the videotape, you are able to make a judgment that it does not fit within the future crime or fraud exceptions to the general rule prohibiting disclosure. To allow the grand jury to obtain the videotape under the facts of this case would violate a principle that has been part of our jurisprudence for hundreds of years."

Sean picked up copies of the exhibits from the corner of the table. "You have our documentary evidence; you've received the testimony of Ms. Lindale; you are familiar with the guidelines given by our appellate courts. Our brief cites other judicial precedent, which time will not allow me to emphasize. Your full consideration of all arguments is requested, and on behalf of Mrs. Richardson, I respectfully urge you to grant the motion to quash the subpoena."

Sean sat down, and Graham stood up.

"Judge Moreau, opposing counsel would make this case more complicated than it is. We're not here to overturn principles established by the U.S. Supreme Court, and Ms. Lindale certainly has the right to file the motion to quash as a means to resolve her ethical dilemma. However, the motion must be denied because the State is not asking Ms Lindale to force her client to incriminate herself."

Graham held up a copy of the subpoena. "We're here to protect the ability of a grand jury to uncover relevant information necessary for the administration of justice. Attached to this subpoena is an affidavit from Detective Rick Bridges establishing probable cause to support the grand jury's request for the videotape. This document alone justifies issuance of the subpoena. A grand jury can force a potential defendant to provide a DNA sample. How much more a videotape?"

Graham placed the subpoena on the table. "According to the testimony of Ms. Lindale, the videotape does not depict privileged communication between lawyer and client. If the court grants the motion, it means that an individual can deliver nonprivileged documents or data into the hands of a lawyer and thus place it outside the reach of a bona fide legal investigation. This is not the intent of the appellate courts in any of the cases cited by Mr. Pruitt. General summaries of the attorney-client privilege are not applicable to the facts of this case. Ms. Lindale should not be able to deny the grand jury access to the video, and the solicitor urges the court to deny the motion."

Alexia heard the back door of the courtroom close. She glanced over her shoulder and saw Giles Porter take a seat on the back row. Judge Moreau cleared his throat. Alexia suspected the judge would take the case under advisement and issue a ruling in a couple of days. All the attorneys remained seated.

"Come forward, Ms. Lindale," the judge said.

Puzzled, Alexia approached the bench. The judge handed the videotape to her.

"Ms. Lindale, deliver the videotape to the solicitor instanter. Mr. Graham, prepare a suitable order denying the motion."

Sean was on his feet. "Your Honor, we request a delay pending a decision whether to appeal."

"Denied. Anything further?"

"No sir."

Alexia walked over to Graham and handed him the tape. She saw no hint of a smirk on the solicitor's face. He took it from her and put it in an expandable file on the table. Judge Moreau and the assistant solicitor left the courtroom. Alexia nudged Sean and pointed to the rear of the courtroom. Porter walked up the aisle toward them.

"We're not finished," she said.

When Porter reached the bar, he put his hand inside his coat pocket and took out an envelope. Alexia and Sean faced him across the low railing.

"Good afternoon, Ms. Lindale," he said. "Mr. Pruitt, isn't it?"

"Yes," Sean replied.

Porter spoke. "I'm here to arrest your client on a charge of assault and battery with intent to kill Baxter Calhoun Richardson." He glanced at Sean. "I believe that's Code section 16-3-620, counselor. Here's the warrant."

Porter handed the envelope to Sean, who opened it and removed a sheet of paper. Alexia stood to the side so she could read it over his shoulder. The hammer had finally fallen. Rena faced a multiple-front war with battles to be fought in the mountains as well as the coast.

"I need to serve your client with the warrant," Porter said. "Where is she?"

"Downstairs in the snack room," Alexia answered.

Porter turned and began walking to the door.

"Wait. We're coming with you," Alexia said.

The detective stopped while Sean threw the remaining papers from the hearing into his briefcase. The two lawyers and the detective left the courtroom together. They rode the elevator to the bottom floor of the building in silence.

As the elevator doors opened, Alexia asked, "Will you let me tell her? I won't take her anywhere private; just let me break the news to her and let her know what to expect. She's emotionally fragile, and I'm not sure how she'll react to this news."

"Alright." Porter nodded.

"Do you want me there too?" Sean asked.

"No."

They walked to the snack room. Alexia went inside while Sean and Porter waited in the hallway. Three teenagers with spiked hair dyed blue, red, and purple were eating candy bars and drinking soft drinks at a table in the middle of the room. An older man sat near the drink machine reading a newspaper. The table where Alexia left her client was vacant.

Rena was gone.

Alexia scanned the small room in disbelief, though intuition had warned her Rena might run away. She stood still long enough to collect her thoughts and then returned to the hallway. Sean and Porter were talking.

"I'll check the ladies' restroom," she said casually.

Porter watched her closely as she passed by. The restroom around a corner at the end of a hallway was empty. Alexia leaned against the sink and flipped open her cell phone. Service was poor in the basement of the building, but she scrolled down to Rena's number and hit the send button. The phone rang until Rena's answering message responded.

Alexia kept her voice calm. "Call me when you get this message. I'll have my phone on."

She returned to the hallway but stopped beside a water fountain. She couldn't face Porter without a plan in place. Again taking her phone from her purse, she called Ted. He answered on the second ring. Alexia spoke rapidly.

"I'm at the courthouse in Charleston and don't have long to talk. A detective from Mitchell County is here to arrest Rena for trying to kill Baxter. She left before finding out about the Mitchell County warrant. I have no idea where she's gone, but I suspect she'll go to her house to pick up some things and then try to leave town."

"Why would she do that if she doesn't know what's going on?"

"She's been talking about running away for weeks. She's under pressure from every direction. Psychologically, she's very fragile."

"What do you want me to do?"

"Go over to her house. She didn't have a car here so she would have to take a taxi."

"A taxi from Charleston to Santee?"

"Yes. A hundred dollars for a cab ride is not a problem for Rena."

"What do I do if she shows up?"

"Stall her. If the detective thinks she's fleeing, she'll have a much harder time obtaining bond. Don't mention my call. I'll tell her what's going on when I get there."

"What proof does the detective have that Rena did anything wrong?"

"None that I know of. But he did have a warrant."

"What are you going to do?"

"Get to Santee as fast as I can."

Alexia shut the phone and rounded the corner. Porter peered over Sean's shoulder in her direction, and she knew from the look in the detective's eyes that telling him what had happened would be a formality.

"She's not here," Alexia said. "Once she knew that she wasn't going to testify, she probably went back to Santee."

"Did you try to contact her?" Porter asked.

"Yes. I left her a voice message on her cell phone."

"Did you mention the warrant?"

Porter had no right to pry into Alexia's communication with her client, but she decided not to antagonize him and risk precipitating a manhunt for Rena.

"No. I suggest we go to her house in Santee. You can serve the warrant there."

Porter rubbed his hand across the top of his head. "I'll contact the Santee police and ask them to keep an eye on the house until I can get there. I don't want to have to chase your client across the country."

"Will you wait until I arrive to arrest her?" Alexia persisted. "I have to pick up my car at Mr. Pruitt's office."

"As long as I don't encounter any problems, I'll give you a few minutes leeway."

Alexia and Sean walked quickly out of the courthouse together. When they were beyond earshot, Sean asked, "Where is she?"

"I have no idea, but she was hallucinating in the courtroom before she ran out. She saw Baxter sitting in the jury box."

"That's bad."

While they drove to Sean's office, Alexia told him the gist of her conversation with Rena in the bathroom.

The Charleston lawyer considered the information before replying.

"Ever since the day I quizzed Rena over the phone, I've not been satisfied with her answers about the incident at the waterfall. Have you considered the possibility that Porter is right? If Rena flips in and out of reality, her actions may be unpredictable."

"It's crossed my mind," Alexia admitted. "But if that's the case—" she stopped.

"You'd have to admit that you've been wrong." Sean turned onto the street in front of his office and pulled in behind her car. "I don't know the truth, but regardless of the facts, Rena needs legal representation."

"Do you want to follow me to Santee?" Alexia asked. "Rena will need both of us."

Sean shook his head. "No. I have something more important to do."

"What?" Alexia asked in surprise.

"Arrange for Rena's bond. I have a law-school buddy who practices in a county adjacent to Mitchell County. I'm going to see if he can contact a local magistrate and clear the way for a bond before Porter drags Rena to the mountains. I don't want to go there myself until we have a preliminary hearing."

"What can I do to help?" Alexia asked.

"The most difficult part. Convince Porter to let Rena turn herself in at the police station in Santee. The time it takes for them to process her will give me time to see what I can do. I'll call you. As soon as Rena turns herself in, she will be subject to bond."

"And if Porter won't cooperate?"

"Rena is going to have a long ride to Mitchell County in the back of a patrol car. Do you really think that's what Porter wants?"

Alexia couldn't guess the detective's motivations. He might take perverse delight in hauling Rena two hundred miles so he could hear the door slam at an archaic jail.

"I'll try," Alexia said doubtfully.

"That's all you can do."

"And if she isn't at home?"

Sean put the car in gear. "Then we're representing a fugitive."

38

But now I am cabined, cribbed, confined,
bound in, to saucy doubts and fears.
MACBETH, ACT 3, SCENE 4

Ted arrived at the Richardson house behind an ambulance, which parked beside the cottage. Two EMTs hurried in. Ted ran up the steps to the main house and rang the doorbell. No one answered, and he peered through the sidelight into the dark foyer. He decided to try the cottage. A nurse's aide who had been on duty one evening with Sarah came out the door carrying a thick folder.

"What's wrong with Baxter?" Ted asked.

"He has pneumonia. Both lungs. They're taking him to the hospital to start him on oxygen and monitor his vitals more closely. The internist has already begun a high dose of antibiotics."

Ted could see into the cottage. Baxter lay on his back with an IV pole beside him.

"Which hospital?"

"Santee. There's no point taking him farther away. They can do everything locally that could be tried in Charleston." The aide shook her head. "It's a shame. He was starting to turn the corner."

"How bad is it?"

"Very bad. He doesn't have much pulmonary function left, and he's losing the little he has. They'll do more tests at the hospital."

"Is his wife here?"

"No. The doctor called her. She's on her way back from Charleston."

"Oh, I see."

So Rena's return to Santee was linked to concern for her husband, not fear for herself.

"And his father?"

"I'm not sure if he's been notified yet. But the family will eventually be contacted so they can come to the hospital."

"It's that serious?"

The aide nodded.

Ted looked again through the door of the cottage. He wasn't sure what to think. The aide spoke.

"I was on duty with Sarah Locklear one day when you played and she sang, and I read in the chart that you've been back recently. It's beautiful what you've done for him. I've never heard anything like it. I've pecked away on the piano since I was a kid, but you have a special gift. If I'm ever seriously ill, I hope you will play for me."

An EMT came out of the cottage and opened the back door of the ambulance. Now, no one seemed in a hurry. They acted like mortuary workers picking up a corpse. Ted and the aide stepped aside as they wheeled Baxter past. The young man's face was ashen; his eyes closed. Ted had seen a similar pasty appearance before—on people at the edge of death.

A sudden wave of emotion swept over Ted, and his eyes stung with tears. He cared, and not just about the investment of his musical gift or the hours spent at the cottage. He'd invested his whole heart and soul in seeing Baxter Richardson healed. But it had been in vain. The EMTs lifted the gurney into the ambulance. Ted rubbed his eyes with the back of his hand. The aide saw him.

"I know. It's sad. We've done everything we can to care for him, but in the end it's not in our hands." She pointed up. "It's in his."

The ambulance rolled down the driveway. No lights flashed or siren screamed. Ted left the aide and went into the empty cottage. The state-of-the-art hospital bed was empty, the room itself hopeless. Ted's emotions shriveled in the stale atmosphere. Baxter had left behind the aroma of death. There was no hope here. There was no hope where Baxter was going. There was no hope for Baxter Richardson on the other side of his last breath.

Ted returned to his truck. He sat behind the steering wheel, leaned his head against the back glass, and closed his eyes. He couldn't argue with the justice of Baxter's fate. Rena's husband deserved whatever happened to him. But the signs of restoration—waking up from the coma, the slight movement in hand and foot—bore the marks of divine intervention. In some ways it would be easier to face total failure than grapple with modest success cruelly snatched away.

Ted sighed. Why would the Lord touch Baxter and then withdraw? God is good, but his ways are not our ways. The rain falls on the just and the unjust. Ted would probably never grasp the complex enigma of healing either.

The sound of a car entering the driveway interrupted his thoughts. A black limousine parked in front of the cottage, and the driver opened the rear door. Rena stepped out. The nurse on duty came out to see her. The two women talked briefly, and then Rena put her hands over her face. Ted waited, not wanting to intrude. The nurse returned to the cottage, and the limo left. Rena walked slowly toward the house. Ted got out and stood in the driveway. Rena came up to him.

"I'm sorry," he said.

Rena's eyes were red, but she wasn't crying. "I don't know how much more I can take. I'm so confused."

Ted considered putting his arm around her shoulders but decided the gesture was outside the propriety of his current role.

Rena moved closer to the truck. "It helped the other day to talk to you and know that you believed me. Before we filed the petition to terminate Baxter's life support, I had to forgive him for what he did to me at the waterfall. Alexia and I talked about it, and she made sure I wasn't motivated by anything except what I believed Baxter would want me to do. But when you talked to him and he accused me of deliberately pushing him, every negative thought and fear has flared back up. Now it's hard to let go of the hate. How could he be so evil?"

Ted just listened.

"Part of me wants him to die and get out of my life. Another part wants to divorce him and run away. A third part wants him to wake up and ask for my forgiveness."

Ted paused for a second before speaking. "If he did wake up and ask your forgiveness, would you give it to him?"

Rena looked into Ted's eyes. "I don't know."

"I don't know if I could either. But it's important for you to forgive him even if he dies and never has the chance to ask for forgiveness. No one in your position could do this in her own strength. It takes the power of God's grace to forgive when there's no reason to do so. But that is what God did for us. The Bible says that while we were still sinners, Christ died for us. We didn't deserve it, but he did it anyway."

Rena nodded.

Ted continued. "Have you ever asked God to forgive you for your sins?"

"Sure, a bunch of times."

Rena's glib response threw Ted off guard.

"Uh, well, that's what you can do for Baxter. Forgive him a bunch of times."

"It's easier to think about now that he's so sick. When he was waking up and threatening me, I wanted to lash out at him." Rena looked past Ted's shoulder. "I'm thinking about divorcing Baxter, but I know it's probably not the right thing to do. Do you think I should stay with him?"

Even though his own divorce was initiated by his wife, Ted always felt vulnerable when someone brought up the topic of divorce and asked his opinion.

"I guess it depends on whether he would be a threat to harm you in the future."

"Only with his mouth. His body is broken. Alexia says it's my choice whether to stay married or file for divorce."

"Maybe we can talk about that later when Alexia is with us."

"I'd like that." She turned her full gaze into the minister's eyes. "Talking to you has a way of calming me down."

"I'm glad."

"Did you come today to play for Baxter?" she asked. "I enjoyed listening to you at the church."

"No," Ted answered. He wasn't adept at subterfuge. "Alexia phoned from Charleston and asked me to check on you. She was worried when you left the courthouse without letting her know where you were going."

"Oh, I should have told her, but she was in a hearing, and I didn't want to interrupt. Did she tell you what happened?"

"No, but she was concerned that you might have gotten scared and run away."

"Of course not. I don't have any reason to flee." Rena straightened her shoulders. "I have to face the future, no matter what it brings."

A Santee police car pulled to the end of the driveway and slowed down. Ted leaned his head to see where it stopped. Rena turned around.

"What do they want?" she asked with irritation.

"Do you want me to find out?"

"Yes."

"I'll go ask. Wait here."

Ted walked down the long driveway. He glanced back once at Rena, who had moved toward the front door of the house. She glanced at Ted before going inside. Ted approached the policeman, an older man with iron-gray hair cut in a flattop, and introduced himself.

"Is there a problem?" Ted asked.

"Not at the moment."

Ted waited for further explanation but none came.

"Are you coming up to the house?" he asked.

"No more questions, Reverend. You're free to come and go, but you might want to leave."

The officer raised the window of the car. Ted, certain the officer's presence had something to do with the warrant Alexia had mentioned, slowly retraced his steps toward the house. He had no role to play in the legal process and considered taking the officer's advice to leave. But he'd promised to stay with Rena until Alexia arrived. He walked up the steps and rang the doorbell. Rena opened the door a crack and peeked out.

"The officer wouldn't tell me why he's here."

Rena put her index finger to her lips. "Don't talk here," she whispered. "Come into the kitchen."

Ted followed her into the house.

"There is a bug and camera in the living room," Rena said in a soft voice as soon as they were in the kitchen. "Jeffrey had it installed."

"Why would he do that?"

"Because he's as bad or worse than Baxter."

Ted's face revealed his skepticism.

"You don't believe me, do you?" she asked. "I guess Alexia hasn't told you anything about what they're trying to do to me."

"We don't talk about her clients."

Rena stepped closer to him. "I could tell you things about the Richardson family that—"

Rena's cell phone chirped from the counter beside the sink. She picked it up and answered.

"Yes, I'm at home. Baxter has pneumonia, and they've taken him to the hospital. That's why I left the courthouse. The doctor called me while I was waiting for you in the snack bar. What happened in court?"

As Rena listened, Ted saw her eyes widen.

"What do you mean, that's not all?" she asked, her voice rising rapidly in volume.

There was another, longer pause. Rena's lips began to quiver.

"He's coming here! No!"

Another pause. "Is he going to arrest me? I'd rather die!"

Rena bit her lip and stared straight ahead.

"Uh, there is a police officer at the end of the driveway right now. Ted tried to talk to him, but he wouldn't tell him anything. How soon will you be here?"

Rena listened for a few more seconds and then clicked off the phone.

"Do you know what's going on?" she asked frantically, running her fingers through her hair.

"Some of it."

"Why didn't you tell me?" Rena's voice accused.

Ted stepped back. "Alexia asked me to let her tell you. She's your lawyer and can tell you a lot more than I could. She also asked me to make sure you were okay until she arrived."

"Okay?" Rena practically screamed. "What is okay about this? I'm going to die!"

Ted responded in a soft voice. "You've got to believe that the truth will come out. Remember what you told me a few minutes ago."

Rena gave him a blank stare.

"That you would face your future, no matter what it brings."

Rena turned away and looked out the window over the sink. "He's here!" she cried out, pounding the metal sink with both hands. "Standing beside the police car!"

Rena moved away from the window and sat down at the kitchen table. She put her head in her hands and began to moan. Ted looked out the window and saw a short, slightly chubby, bald man in a brown suit talking to the police officer.

"No, no, no!" she said over and over.

Ted didn't move to comfort her. Words wouldn't penetrate this situation. He began to pray silently. Looking outside, he saw Alexia's car roll to a stop behind his truck. The lawyer got out and waited for the man in the brown suit to join her. They talked in the driveway and then walked together toward the front door. The doorbell chimed.

"Do you want me to answer the door?" Ted asked Rena.

"No, no, no," she continued to moan. She dropped her head to the table with a low thud.

Ted left her and went into the foyer. He glanced over his shoulder into the living room, wondering about the location of the video camera. He opened the door and faced Alexia and the man in the brown suit.

"Where is she?" Alexia asked.

"In the kitchen. She's very upset."

Alexia turned to the man in the brown suit. "I'll get her."

Alexia left Ted with Giles Porter. They introduced themselves, but it seemed unnatural to Ted—shaking hands and exchanging names while Rena writhed in the throes of a psychological meltdown. They waited in silence. Several minutes passed. Ted continued to pray. Porter stepped back onto the front stoop and stared across the yard. Alexia returned with Rena, eyes barely open, leaning on Alexia's arm.

"We're ready to go," Alexia said.

Porter stepped forward and put the warrant in Rena's right hand. She didn't grasp the paper, and it fell to the floor. Porter didn't pick it up.

"Ms. Richardson, this is a warrant for your arrest charging you with felony assault and battery with intent to kill Baxter Calhoun Richardson. Come with me."

39

A sound of cornered-animal fear and hate.
ONE FLEW OVER THE CUCKOO'S NEST

Ezra Richardson slowly replaced the phone receiver in its cradle. He buzzed his secretary.

"Is Jeffrey in his office?"

"I'm not sure, Mr. Richardson. I'll check and let you know."

Ezra turned in his chair and looked out the window at the sunny afternoon. A pair of workers in white uniforms left the manufacturing facility and walked across the parking lot. He could see smiles on their faces. One of the men laughed. A knock sounded on his door.

"Come in!"

His secretary stuck her head inside. "He's coming up the stairs. Do you want to see him?"

"Yes. Send him in immediately."

Ezra stared unseeing across the room. Neither the fine paintings on the wall nor the imported marble bust on a stand drew his eye. The healthy balance sheet on his desk gave him no satisfaction. The door opened without a knock, and Jeffrey strode in, straight from the golf course. He took off his golf visor and tossed it on a leather chair.

"What is it?" he asked.

"Sit down."

Jeffrey plopped down across from the desk.

"They're taking Baxter to the Santee hospital and want us to come. He has pneumonia. I just got off the phone with his internist. It's very serious."

"Pneumonia is treatable," Jeffrey scoffed. "It's like a bad case of the flu."

"According to his doctor, it's the most life-threatening problem he's faced since the fall."

Jeffrey's expression sobered. "Okay. I'll clean up and meet you at the hospital." He stood to go.

"Sit down," Ezra replied with an authority that caused Jeffrey to immediately lower himself into his seat. "I had another phone call that we need to discuss here, not at the hospital."

The older man fixed his gaze on his son until Jeffrey gave a nervous laugh.

"So, what was it about?" Jeffrey asked.

"We've both been fools," Ezra replied grimly. "Especially you."

"What do you mean?"

"Nicholas Valese lost his job."

"Really?" Jeffrey cleared his throat. "I talked to him a couple of days ago."

"And his boss also lost his job. Apparently neither of them will ever work again."

Jeffrey paled. "They're dead?"

"And your link with them is out in the open."

Jeffrey looked around the room.

Ezra spoke in a softer voice. "Jeffrey, I'm your father. If I didn't want to save your hide, would I be talking to you?"

Jeffrey's shoulders slumped. Ezra continued.

"Baxter is on the brink of death, and even if he lives, what kind of life will he have? My hope for the future is in you, not him. I have control of this company, not because of the number of shares I own, but because of the people on my side. Don't try to buck the status quo. If you're patient, you'll get everything you want. Otherwise, I can't protect you."

Jeffrey swallowed.

"Are you listening to me?"

"Yes."

"And Rena has been playing us against one another like schoolboys. Do you know about the criminal investigation against her in Charleston?"

"I knew it might happen. It has to do with a—"

Ezra interrupted with an edge in his voice. "Surveillance videotape.

She told me all about your petty blackmail. An hour ago, a judge in Charleston ordered her lawyer to turn over the tape to a grand jury. We have to distance ourselves from her and cut off all support and contact."

"Yes, sir."

Ezra paused for effect. "She told me about your plan to file suit against some of our shell companies."

Jeffrey's anger flared. "That little traitor!"

Ezra's fist came down hard on the desk. "No! You're the one to blame! She's a mountain hick in a pretty shell who wouldn't know how to find her way across a street unless someone pointed her in the right direction. But she's passed along information to her lawyer. That's who I'm worried about. What information did you give Lindale?"

"Just a list of names. Nothing else."

"Which ones?"

"There were ten."

Jeffrey counted off the companies on his fingers. When he reached MetBack, Ezra exploded. "You idiot! Why did you list them?"

"They buy a few golf balls. What's so special about it?"

"It's the board of directors! Two men in that group are now under constant watch by the authorities. They stay on the board because their cover is already blown, and there's no use in resigning. The business itself is defunct. We haven't done any business with them for six months."

"So what's the problem?"

Ezra held up the balance sheet, which crumpled in his hand. "The first five months of the year we shifted a total of twenty-five million dollars on four occasions for MetBack and earned a two-million-dollar commission. I handled it myself while you were out partying!"

Jeffrey seemed to shrivel in the chair.

"How did you even know about them?" Ezra demanded. "We've never discussed it."

"Valese told me."

Ezra sighed. "His mouth was his downfall. We'll have to watch the situation with the lawyer. Rena is supposed to give me her copy of the list."

"And the lawyer?"

"Send a cleaning crew to Lindale's office to purge her records. Make sure they check her computer files too. Keep it neat, everything returned to its proper place."

"What if either of them keeps a copy?"

"Rena wouldn't know what to do with it if she did. Your job is to make sure the lawyer doesn't have that option."

"Yes sir."

Ezra relaxed slightly and leaned back in his chair. "Do you know whether she actually had anything to do with the deputy's death?"

Jeffrey shook his head. "It was a freak accident. He stopped her for speeding and when she opened the car door, he fell backward and broke his neck. She panicked, drove away, and lied to the police."

Ezra shrugged. "It really doesn't matter. I have friends in Charleston who will keep her busy. Her ability to cause us trouble is about to end."

Jeffrey bit his lip. "Maybe not. Did she tell you what really happened at the waterfall?"

———

Giles Porter allowed Rena to ride to the Santee jail with Alexia, who phoned Sean as soon as they were in the car. She set the phone in a holder and set it on speaker mode.

"She's with me," Alexia told the Charleston lawyer. "Porter is going to let her turn herself in."

"Good job. My friend Skip Ayers is waiting at the magistrate's office in Mitchell County. As soon as the magistrate knows that Rena is in custody, the magistrate will set a bond. With any luck, Rena won't have to spend the night in jail."

Rena, staring out the window, made no response.

"Whom do I call?" Alexia asked.

"Call Skip. Does Rena have immediate access to money for the bond?"

"Yes, so long as we know the amount before five o'clock. We called the bank before we left her house."

"If you have any problems, call me."

Alexia clicked off the phone. She wanted to say something reassuring to Rena, but her client had descended into a noncommunicative state.

The jail, a small but modern facility, had only three cells in the women's area. From an objective standpoint, however, the Santee jail provided better accommodations than some of the cheap motels on the outskirts of Myrtle Beach.

Alexia parked beside Porter's vehicle and accompanied Rena to the waiting area, a sparse, pristine room. Porter was speaking to a female deputy who sat behind a glass enclosure. The deputy eyed Rena with curiosity. A male officer, all business, came in from the back.

"Ms. Richardson, come with me."

Her head down, Rena followed the officer through a heavy metal door that clanged shut behind them. The fight had left Rena. Alexia turned to Porter.

"Will you let the Mitchell County magistrate know that she's voluntarily come in for processing? We have an attorney standing by to file a request for bond."

"Yes."

The detective stepped over to the female deputy.

"Where can I make a telephone call?"

"You'll have to use one back here."

Porter left Alexia alone. She phoned Skip Ayers and relayed the information to him.

"The magistrate is ready for me," Ayers said in a voice that revealed the same Lowcountry roots as Sean Pruitt. "I'll call you back as soon as I have an answer."

Alexia put her phone in her purse. She wished she could find out how Rena was doing. The two women's lives had become so intertwined that Alexia, now unable to provide immediate help, felt a measure of separation anxiety. Porter didn't return to the waiting area, and Alexia began to suspect the detective was lurking around the booking section, waiting for Rena to blurt out something incriminating. She inwardly kicked herself for forgetting to remind Rena not to provide any information other than her name, age, and address. Alexia's phone played the opening notes of Beethoven's Ninth Symphony.

"The magistrate gave us a bond," Ayers said with a hint of excitement in his voice.

"How much?"

"Two-hundred-fifty thousand, but only twenty-five thousand in cash will secure her release so long as she signs for the full obligation."

Alexia nodded her head. "We can handle that."

"And he's agreed to set a preliminary hearing next Friday afternoon. That was the earliest date Sean could come. Are you at the jail?"

"Yes."

"Get the fax number and I'll send the order granting bond. The magistrate is going to let me use his fax machine. He's been very cooperative."

Alexia got the information from the deputy and repeated the number to the attorney.

"Got it," Ayers responded. "Will you be coming to the preliminary hearing?"

"Probably."

"I'll try to make it myself. I've heard Sean is very smooth."

When they hung up, Alexia waited a couple of minutes and asked the deputy to check the fax machine. The woman officer left her desk and returned with a sheet of paper in her hand.

"It's here."

"I need to see my client so we can make arrangements with the bank." Alexia held up a blank check on Rena's account. "I need her to sign this check so I can get the money to post her bond."

"I have to stay here to answer the phones," the deputy replied. "They'll let me know when they've finished booking her."

Alexia glanced at her watch. The bank would close in less than thirty minutes. Without the money, Rena would spend a night in jail. Alexia paced. It was unethical for an attorney to post bond; otherwise, Alexia would take care of it herself. She tried to think of someone who could come to her rescue. She called Gwen.

"How did it go?" the secretary asked.

Alexia realized Gwen meant the hearing in Charleston, which seemed days rather than hours ago.

"Well, a lot has happened that I can't go into right now. Is Rachel Downey in the building?"

"Yes, I saw her a few minutes ago."

"Please get her on the phone for me."

The phone went silent, and Alexia waited. The Realtor's familiar voice spoke.

"Hello, Alexia. How are things with the house renovation?"

Alexia didn't have time for the usual banter.

"Great. Ted is a real craftsman. You'll have to see what they've done with the old kitchen."

"Let's grab a bite to eat the first of next week and go by the house."

"Yes," Alexia replied. "Rachel, I need a check for twenty-five thousand payable to the State of South Carolina—"

At that moment the door opened, and the deputy who had taken Rena to the rear of the building spoke.

"You may come back, Ms. Lindale."

"Never mind," Alexia said to Rachel. "We'll do lunch."

"Did you say twenty-five thousand?" Alexia shut the phone.

Alexia followed the deputy through the metal door and down a short hallway. Another heavy, metal door opened into the correctional area. Wire mesh surrounded the small booking area, and Alexia did not see Giles Porter. An obviously inebriated man in scruffy clothes sat in a metal chair in the hallway. He leaned his head against the mesh and moaned softly. When he saw Alexia, he spoke in a plaintive voice.

"Don't let them beat me!" he begged.

He turned sideways and showed Alexia a nasty cut above his left ear.

The deputy with Alexia grunted. "He got that trying to walk through a sliding-glass door at his ex-wife's house."

"That's a lie!" the man bellowed. "I was in cell number five, and you hit me with a blackjack!"

The deputy opened the door to an interview room. Rena didn't glance up when Alexia entered.

"We have a bond," Alexia said in a chipper voice. "It only requires a twenty-five thousand dollar cash payment against a guaranteed amount of two-hundred-fifty thousand. Fill out a check, and then I'll go to the bank so we can get you out of here."

Alexia sat down and put the check on the small, metal table in front of Rena. Her client stared downward without making a move to pick it up.

"We don't have much time before the bank closes." Alexia said patiently. "Fill out the check."

Rena didn't budge.

"Rena!" Alexia said sharply. "Look at me!"

Rena's head stayed bowed for a moment, and then slowly raised. The look in Rena's eyes caused Alexia to recoil. It was a mixture of malevolence and despair—a look of death inhabited by hate.

"I don't care what happens to me," Rena said in a voice that sounded more husky than usual. "I'm going away to another place where you can't go."

"Don't talk nonsense," Alexia responded in a businesslike tone. "We're getting you out of here today. A preliminary hearing has been set in Mitchell County at the end of next week. It will be an opportunity for Sean to find out what Porter claims to have in the way of evidence against you. Everything is being handled quickly and efficiently."

Rena dropped her head. Alexia stared at her for several seconds, uncertain what to do. She could handle frantic Rena; withdrawn Rena was someone new. Alexia took out her pen and filled in the check. She slid it back in front of Rena with the pen beside it.

"Sign the check. I'll leave for a few minutes and then come back to get you."

Rena didn't respond.

Alexia leaned back in her chair and considered her options. Perhaps she should leave Rena at the jail. It might be the safest place for her. It would be necessary to inform the officers on duty to place her on suicide watch. As she mulled over the possibility, Rena reached forward with a trembling hand and picked up the pen. Instead of signing the check, she raised it up in the air.

"What are you doing?" Alexia asked in alarm.

"I'm signing the check!" Rena screamed in a voice that reverberated in the tiny enclosed space.

With a violent flourish, she scribbled her name across the bottom of the check and threw the pen across the room.

"Get me out of here!" she screamed again.

Alexia picked up the check and retrieved the pen. When she looked back at Rena, the young woman's blonde head was again bowed, her gaze shielded, her chest heaving. On her way out of the jail, Alexia stopped at the booking area.

"Please keep an eye on my client. She's very upset."

———

Alexia rushed to the bank. The assistant vice president on duty gave Alexia a cashier's check and locked the door of the bank behind her. Back at the jail, it took a tedious hour to process the paperwork as communication flowed between Santee and Mitchell County. Alexia asked about Porter and learned he'd left as soon as he talked with the Mitchell County magistrate. After the last fax was sent, Alexia waited anxiously for Rena. When the metal door opened and her client appeared, Alexia breathed a sigh of relief. Life had returned to Rena's eyes.

"Thanks," her client said gratefully. "That was rough."

"I know. Let's get you home."

On the ride to the house, Alexia explained the next steps in the process. Rena responded appropriately.

"I'll phone Sean after I drop you off," Alexia said. "I'm sure he'll want to increase the retainer, but he's worth every penny."

"I understand."

"What are you going to do tonight?" Alexia asked with a touch of apprehension. "Do you need to spend the night with a friend?"

"No. After I rest for a few minutes, I'm going to the hospital and see Baxter. Ted and I talked about the whole divorce issue this afternoon, and I need to see Baxter even if he doesn't know that I'm there."

Alexia put no faith in the logic of her client's decision-making process but didn't really want to discuss it. Rena continued. "Would it look bad in the criminal case in Mitchell County if I got a divorce?"

Alexia mulled over the question before answering. "It could go either way. If you file for divorce, you could explain it as a response to Baxter's actions at the cliff. Any juror would agree no woman should remain married to someone who wants to kill her. On the other hand, it could also send a message that you're a selfish person who tried to kill Baxter for his money and now wants to abandon him, taking a pile of cash on your way out the door."

Rena humphed in response.

———

Alexia didn't bother stopping by the office, but left a message on Sean's voice mail and went straight home. No client in her career had ever drained Alexia's emotional tank to the same extent as Rena.

It was dark and way past supper time. Boris heard her car coming, ran to greet her, and proudly accompanied her to the house. Alexia trudged up the steps. Misha met her in a sulky mood. To placate the feline, Alexia scratched her neck and shared a few bits of tuna from the salad she threw together for a quick meal.

Afterward, Alexia went upstairs and turned on her computer. She put a Rachmaninoff CD in her player and peacefully searched the Internet for vacation spots with white sandy beaches and gentle surf. St. John in the Caribbean looked nice, and she checked the price of flights. Before turning off the computer, she decided to do a quick cleanup of unused files. She quickly deleted several items. The folder containing information about the Richardson companies popped onto the screen. The likelihood that Rena would want to pursue a claim against her father-in-law appeared remote. Cooperation had proven more profitable than confrontation. Alexia considered pressing the delete button when the phone rang. Turning away from the keyboard, she answered the phone.

"How are you?" Ted asked.

"Tired. It's been an unbelievably stressful day."

"Can you talk for a few minutes?"

"Sure. You're not a person who wears me out."

"How is Rena?"

"She's on the brink of a nervous breakdown."

"What's going to happen?"

Ted had become so entwined in the loop of information that Alexia felt comfortable expressing her general opinion. She explained the most likely legal scenario.

"We're just beginning what will probably be a very long war. The next big step will be the preliminary hearing in Mitchell County. It's the best opportunity for a defense lawyer to find out what the prosecution has in its file."

"Did Rena tell you about Baxter?"

"Not much. I know they took him to the hospital with pneumonia."

"It's very serious."

"Life-threatening?"

"Yes, according to the nurse's aide."

"Rena is going to see him tonight, in part because of her conversation with you."

"Really? I wasn't sure I made any sense."

"It's hard to know with Rena. She's difficult to read." Alexia paused. "Ted, are you sure you believe Rena's story about what happened at the waterfall?"

"Yes. I think she's telling the truth."

"Sean Pruitt isn't so sure."

"Has he sat down and listened to her?"

"We had a long conference call a couple of weeks ago, but Rena was sitting in my office, and Sean was in Charleston."

"It's not the same. I watched her face when I met with her in the sanctuary. I don't think she is lying."

"That helps me." Alexia yawned. "Thanks for calling. I'm about to drop."

"Good night. I want to give you a private concert soon to energize you. How about Saturday night? You pick the music."

They set a time. As Alexia clicked off the phone, she smiled. At least there was one person in Santee who didn't always think of himself first. Her screen saver projected an underwater ocean scene with brightly colored fish.

Alexia turned off her computer.

40

That bide the pelting of this pitiless storm.

KING LEAR, ACT 3, SCENE 4

Ezra, Jeffrey, and Rena stood in silence around Baxter's bed. The patient lay motionless, a rich mixture of oxygen flowing through his nostrils and a high dose of antibiotics dripping into his veins. Ezra cleared his throat, but it did nothing to dispel the tension in the room.

"I'd better be going," he said. "I left instructions for the doctor to call me in the morning with an update."

Jeffrey glanced toward his father, who frowned and cut his gaze toward Rena.

"I'm going to stay a few more minutes," Jeffrey responded.

Rena stepped toward the door.

"Will you hang around?" Jeffrey quickly asked her.

Rena hesitated. Ezra held up his hand.

"No need to walk out with me," he said. "We can talk later."

Rena stopped. As soon as Ezra left, Jeffrey stepped closer to her.

"Do you still have the list of companies I gave you?" he asked in a low voice.

"Uh, it's somewhere. I'm not sure. Why?"

"Find it and give it back to me. I've decided to take a different approach in dealing with my father."

"Fine. I don't need it. I've decided not to file for divorce."

"Really?" Jeffrey asked in surprise. "Why not?"

Rena pointed at the bed. "Look at him. He may not live another week. I'd rather wait and see what happens."

"But he tried to—" Jeffrey stopped.

Rena turned toward her brother-in-law.

"And he's still trying to destroy me," she said without emotion.

"What do you mean?"

Rena looked first at Baxter and then faced Jeffrey. She spoke in a level voice.

"When Baxter started getting better, he talked with a detective from Mitchell County and convinced him to file charges against me. I've had to hire a lawyer to take care of it."

"Wait," Jeffrey said. "Are you saying Baxter took out a warrant for you?"

"Not him, but he persuaded a redneck detective to do it for him. I'm going to have to tell the truth, no matter what it does to your family."

Jeffrey inwardly swore. If a Richardson and Company shareholder had attempted to kill his wife, the news would appear in all the newspapers, in boardroom gossip, and in negotiations with competitors. It would be very bad for business—not fatal, but crippling. How many opportunities would Richardson and Company lose?

"Maybe not," he said. "My father could intervene. He knows a lot of powerful people."

"In Mitchell County?"

"I don't know, but don't say anything yet."

"There's not much time," Rena said. "I have a preliminary hearing at the end of next week."

———

The following afternoon, Alexia went for a swim. The waves pounded the beach underneath an overcast and stormy sky. The choppy water made her hesitate before venturing in, but only for a moment. In New England such wind would have held the promise of a coming nor'easter, sweeping down from the north Atlantic to buffet the rocky coast. Boris sniffed the air and barked wildly.

"You're as rambunctious as the waves, aren't you?" she yelled at the dog as they waded through the shallow water.

Boris answered, but his bark was overwhelmed by a larger wave that crashed against his legs, causing him to stagger.

Alexia, too, was feeling untamed. Even after getting a good night's sleep, she felt restless. She needed a physical release from the inner spring wound too tightly by events of the previous week. She didn't need a weather report to inform her that it was not a good day for swimming, but without any sign of an imminent storm, she decided to risk a quick dip in the water. Fighting the waves would at least be a different type of struggle than contending with the enemies swirling around Rena Richardson.

She plunged headfirst through a breaker and came up on the other side. The water was rocking and sloshing all around her. She swam farther from the beach. Several times, she lifted her arm from the water and plunged it into air as she fell into a trough. At other times, she couldn't get her arm clear of the waves, as the water followed her arm and forced her higher and higher. Boris swam beside her gamely, but she couldn't keep him in view. In fact, she suddenly realized she couldn't see the shore either. Forcing herself up, she tried to regain her bearings.

All she saw, in every direction, was water.

A wave sloshed across her face and filled her mouth. Some of the salty water found its way down her throat, and she choked and gagged. At that moment Boris slid down in the same trough. She caught hold of his ruff in an effort to steady herself. He turned his head slightly, and she saw fear in his eyes.

"Oh no," she said.

She let go of his fur and flipped onto her back. Alexia floated easily, but it was impossible to turn herself into a wooden stick capable of bobbing on top of the waves. She had to move and kick in order to keep from being swept under. She took off her goggles and stared at the sky in an effort to determine the location of the sun. But the clouds were thick, and it was too late in the day to fathom a guess.

And then the rain came.

It fell hard and coarse, cold rain mixed with tiny pellets of ice. The miniature hail popped the water all around them. Alexia caught a wave to the top of the water and again tried to find land, but even from the crest, visibility extended only a few feet in any direction. Boris slid down next to her. He continued paddling, and she realized his efforts were focused on staying close to her. If they died, it would be together. Alexia passed beyond hope in her ability to save herself.

Before a swell could separate her from the dog, she yelled into his ear, "Beach! Go to the beach!"

It wasn't a command they'd practiced. The Labrador knew the individual words; whether he could make sense of them in the context of the moment remained to be seen. Alexia repeated the command.

"Go to the beach!"

Boris kept swimming without any apparent sense of direction. Alexia focused all her energy on staying beside him. Every few seconds she would repeat the command. The rain continued to fall in sharp sheets. The hail stopped, but the visibility didn't improve. It was impossible to tell if they were moving in a specific direction or swimming in circles. Waves began to look familiar. Alexia knew that her mind was playing tricks on her. She fought to stave off the disorientation.

"Go to the beach!"

Boris looked sideways at her. Fatigue had replaced the fear in his eyes. If an indomitable swimmer like the black dog was tired, Alexia knew the adrenaline fueling her own limbs would soon run out. They rode up a particularly large swell, came down, and then rose again. The second swell crested and curled forward. It swept them forward for several seconds and dropped them in water that came up to Alexia's waist. She tried to stand but fell forward when another wave crashed into her. Her fingers scraped sand beneath the water, and she came up with a few grains clasped in her hands. A fistful of diamonds wouldn't have been more precious.

Boris continued swimming until his feet were on solid ground. He turned around as Alexia stumbled forward. She reached solid ground and collapsed. The rain abated as quickly as it had started. Alexia raised her head. Boris was running down the beach, barking the story of his adventure into the wind. Alexia sat up, looked out to sea, and wondered where she'd been. Boris returned and licked the side of her face. Alexia grabbed his head.

"Good boy," she said.

The sound of her voice brought tears. She held on to Boris's neck with her right hand and wiped her eyes with her left hand.

"Good boy," she repeated. "You know the beach better than I do."

She sat still for several more minutes. Boris lay beside her, panting.

The sky grew dark again, and she got up. Whether on land or water, she didn't want to be caught in another storm. She turned toward home.

———

Several hours later, the thick blanket of clouds had broken up. Alexia stood on her deck as the sun sank beneath the horizon, and the sunset reflected a deep red against the bottom of the remaining clouds. Alexia looked up with gratitude. Her whole body ached, not because she'd had to swim so long, but because every muscle willing to respond had been tense and taut as she struggled to survive in the water. A unique sunset was a treat on any evening, but tonight she especially appreciated the fact that she could stand on solid ground and gaze at the painted sky.

The red had given way to dark gray by the time her car's tires crunched across the church parking lot and stopped. A few puddles, the only sign of the afternoon's heavy rain, stood on the brick sidewalk leading from the sanctuary to the church office. The sandy soil had an enormous capacity to soak up moisture. Alexia turned off the lights of the car and quietly entered the church.

No matter how often she stepped into the narthex, Alexia never lost the sense of wonder at encountering the sounds floating from the piano in the sanctuary. Music sustained her soul, and each encounter with Ted's gift was a fine meal to be appreciated in its own right. Tonight's first dish was Mozart, the irrepressible genius who from boyhood to an untimely death astounded a continent.

He was playing one of the DuPort's Variations, a reflective theme that matched Alexia's poststorm mood. Alexia listened until the end before entering the darkened sanctuary. The outline of Ted's form was visible on the piano bench.

"It was perfect!" she called out.

Ted turned toward her, and even though Alexia couldn't see his face across the length of the sanctuary, she knew the expression he wore. The moment struck a new awareness in her. The minister's countenance had become part of the picture gallery of her heart. She walked down the aisle and sat in her familiar place on a front pew.

"What do you want to hear?" Ted asked.

"Mozart."

"But he's not Russian."

"I can pretend you're playing in an ornate drawing room in St. Petersburg."

"Okay. I have another from the same group. It's fast, not in a minor key."

Ted touched the keyboard and launched into an exhilarating display. Alexia closed her eyes, again glad that she was alive. The last note faded away, and she felt refreshed.

"Thank you," she said simply.

Ted kept his fingers on the keyboard. "What else?" he asked.

Alexia stood and came over to the altar. "Let me see your hands," she said.

The minister turned sideways on the piano bench and tentatively held his hands in front of him. Alexia reached out across the altar rail and held them. They were rough and strong—the outward appearance camouflaging the talent within. Without letting go, Alexia knelt down on the narrow cushion that lay in front of the railing. Ted started to pull away, but she held on firmly. Lowering her lips, she gently kissed each finger and then released him. Ted sat up straight; Alexia remained on her knees and looked up at him.

"Why did you do that?" he asked softly.

"Because you deserve it. If a woman could wash Jesus's feet with her tears and dry them with her hair, I can bless your fingers with a kiss."

"I consider myself blessed."

Alexia stood up. "No more performances tonight. I'm hungry. Where can I take you for dinner?"

"Across the parking lot. I have something at my house."

They walked together to the old parsonage. The smell of good food greeted them as soon as they entered the house.

"What's cooking?" Alexia asked.

"Lasagna."

"You made lasagna?"

"If taking it out of the box and putting it in the oven counts. I thought we could make a salad together."

As they passed the fireplace, Alexia patted the mantel. "And have a fire with dessert?"

"Uh, I don't have any dessert except ice cream."

"Oh, that's perfect. Ice cream to cool my tongue and fire to warm my bones."

They went into the kitchen. Alexia, still experiencing the euphoria of being alive, enjoyed every domestic nuance. She washed the lettuce while he cut up the tomatoes. She sliced the cucumbers while he grated some cheese. When everything was ready, they sat at the little table in the kitchen, and he lit a red holiday candle.

"Where's the lemonade?" Alexia asked.

"I didn't think about it," Ted said apologetically.

"I'm teasing. It's not the season or the type of meal. Water with a twist of lime is better."

When Ted prayed, Alexia kept her eyes open and watched him. The minister's hair was very curly. She guessed that if he didn't brush it regularly and keep it closely trimmed, it would quickly become bushy.

After a few bites, Alexia said, "This is some of the best lasagna I've ever eaten. Are you sure you're not Italian?"

"Stop it," Ted responded.

Alexia reached across and patted his hand. "The key to great lasagna is the care with which the cook puts it in the oven."

They ate in silence for a few moments. The only sound in the room was the click of their forks against the plates. Alexia wiped the edge of her mouth with a napkin.

"I'm glad to be alive," she said.

Ted was chewing a mouthful of salad, "Me too," he mumbled.

"No, I really mean it. I had a scare in the water this afternoon."

Alexia told Ted about her experience without revealing how close to death she'd come.

"Animals are amazing," he said after she related the help she received from Boris. "He's a good dog."

"That's what I told him."

"I'd like to go back to the island with you," Ted said. "I enjoyed my salty kiss."

"Those are rarer than an unbroken sand dollar," Alexia replied with a smile. "You have to be in the right place at the right time."

They finished eating and washed the dishes by hand at the sink.

"I'll wipe up," Alexia said. "Go start the fire."

Her mind wandering, Alexia started at the sound of a sudden knock at the kitchen window. She jumped back from the sink and then realized it was Ted, who'd gone outside to retrieve some wood.

"That was juvenile," she sniffed when he reappeared.

"You have to be careful about the graveyard. Strange noises come from there on nights after a big storm."

Alexia swatted at him with a dish towel.

When she walked into the living room, she found a small fire beginning to intensify in the fireplace. A wallpaper-sample book lay on the reading table beside Ted's chair.

"Is that for my office?" she asked.

"Yes. I thought we could look at it together."

They sat beside one another on a couch that faced the fireplace and flipped through the pages. Ted made notes on a pad.

"You really need to see the paint colors to make a decision," he said. "Did you go by the store and get some color cards?"

"Yes, they're at the office."

Alexia nestled against the armrest at the end of the couch and watched the tiny dancing flames.

"Would you like a cup of coffee?" Ted asked.

"That would be wonderful."

Ted went into the kitchen, and Alexia glanced at the picture of Ted's daughter on the mantel. She wondered if the talented young woman would like her.

"No coffee!" Ted yelled out.

"That's okay!"

Ted stuck his head in from the kitchen. "No, it's not. I want a cup and need some for the morning. Stay here. I'll be right back."

"No, I'll ride with you."

Outside, the wet weather had given way to a chilly cold front.

"Brr," Alexia said.

"Wait, I'll get you a coat."

Ted grabbed a coat from the closet in the foyer and handed it to her. It had flecks of white paint on one sleeve and several colors on the other.

"It's clean," Ted reassured her.

The coat swallowed Alexia's arms and hands. Ted opened the door of his truck for her. They drove into town and stopped at a convenience store not far from Rachel Downey's office.

When he returned with the coffee, Alexia said, "Let's swing by my office and get the paint cards."

The detour took only a couple minutes. When they arrived, Ted started to park in front of the building.

"Go around back. I don't have a key for the front door."

The rear parking lot was dark.

"I'll run in," Alexia said. "Keep the truck warm."

Alexia fumbled at the lock before finding the keyhole and turning it. The light switch for the overhead was at the other end of the hallway, so she entered in the dark. Her office was immediately to the left. She heard the door behind her open and spun around.

Ted.

"You've got to quit scaring me."

"I don't remember the color of the wood stain on your office furniture," he said. "We'll need to take that into consideration when we think about paint color."

Alexia opened the door to her office and flipped on the light. Before her eyes could adjust to the sudden brightness, the lights went out and someone shoved her across the room. She stumbled but didn't fall.

Alexia screamed.

When she did, a hand grabbed her hair, and another hand wearing a thin latex glove clamped over her mouth and nose. She could see a dark shape across the room. Ted came running through the door.

"Alexia!" he yelled.

The figure grabbed the minister. Alexia, desperate for air, struggled and opened her mouth enough to bite the hand suffocating her.

The man holding her yelped and jerked back her head. Forced to look up, she could see him raise a dark object in his right hand. He brought it down directly toward Alexia's face. Just before it struck her, something knocked it away. Alexia heard a low crunch and crashed to the floor. She lay there dazed.

"Let's go!" an unfamiliar male voice cried out.

A few quick steps, and the assailants were gone. Alexia heard moaning on the floor beside her. She felt her face, and her hand came away wet with blood.

"Ted!" she said.

"Yeah," he responded before crying out in anguish.

Alexia staggered to her feet and turned on the light switch. When her eyes adjusted, she saw Ted sitting on the floor holding his left hand. His face contorted in agony, he looked up at her.

"Alexia! Your face!"

Alexia touched her nose again. "It's just a bloody nose. I'm calling 911."

Alexia went over to her desk and dialed the emergency number. Ted, continuing to wince, stood up.

"My hand is broken," he said. "I can't move my fingers."

Alexia looked down at his left hand. A gash creased the back, and his fingers bent at an unnatural angle.

"Don't try to move anything. Someone will be here soon."

41

You may break, you may shatter the vase, if you will, but the scent of the roses will hang round it still.

THOMAS MOORE

Alexia, wringing her hands, sat in the surgical unit's waiting room at Medical University Hospital in Charleston. The long wait stretched into the predawn hours. The emergency room doctor in Santee had evaluated Ted's hand and immediately sent him via ambulance to Charleston for surgery. Alexia picked up a magazine, but the words were irrelevant and the pictures inane. The abstract world of print couldn't touch the reality of her anxiety and concern.

Finally, a short, older doctor with a surgical mask hanging from his neck came into the waiting area. He lifted his bushy gray eyebrows and scanned the room.

"Mrs. Morgan?" he called out.

Alexia tentatively raised her hand. "I'm with Ted Morgan."

The doctor approached her.

"Let's go to a consultation room," he said.

Two small rooms stood off the larger waiting room. They entered the nearest one.

"I'm Dr. Hayes," the surgeon said. "Have a seat."

"How is he?" Alexia asked.

"He's in the recovery area and should be in a regular room within an hour. He had a comminuted fracture of several bones in his left hand. That means multiple bones in his hand were shattered. The chart indicates he was the victim of an assault. Is that correct?"

"Yes. There was a break-in at my office, and we surprised the burglars.

He blocked a metal object aimed for my face. I think it was one of those big flashlights. All I suffered was a bloody nose."

"You're fortunate. If the damage to his hand is any indication of the force involved, you could have been seriously hurt or worse if the blow had fallen directly on you."

"But what about him? He's a music minister and very talented pianist."

Dr. Hayes gave Alexia a serious look.

"I put his hand back together the best I could. In addition to broken bones, he has nerve and tendon damage caused by jagged pieces of displaced bone. I repaired and reattached the damaged tendons, but the nerve damage may be permanent. Pins and screws in his hand will greatly limit his ability to perform rapid finger movements or stretch out his hand. He will be able to do activities requiring gross manual dexterity, but I can't make any promises about whether he'll use it to play the piano."

Alexia couldn't believe what she was hearing.

"You don't understand," she said. "He's not just an ordinary pianist who plays a few hymns on Sunday mornings. He has concert talent. A few weeks ago he filled in at a benefit concert at the Francis Marion."

Dr. Hayes eyebrows shot up. "Really? My wife was there and told me what happened."

Alexia continued to shake her head in disbelief.

"Is there a chance he will regain full use of his hand?" she persisted.

Dr. Hayes shook his head. "No. I can't restore what is totally gone, only give back as much as possible. I'm deeply sorry this happened."

Alexia blinked back tears. "Thanks," she managed.

"The attendant will be able to tell you his room number within the hour. I'll be by to check him tomorrow afternoon."

The doctor left, but Alexia didn't move. Running through her mind were snippets of musical passages from the times she'd eavesdropped in the narthex of the Sandy Flats Church. Rachmaninoff, Beethoven, Debussy, Chopin, Weber. The possibility that the glorious sounds would be forever silenced placed her in even greater shock.

"This can't be," she spoke aloud to the empty room. "Not to Ted."

She stared unseeing across the room at a bare wall. In a few seconds, scenes from the sanctuary floated before her mind's eye—Ted on the piano bench in front of the altar rail, his head bowed, his hands giving voice to his talent as they moved up and down the keyboard. Images at the church were joined by scenes from the cottage, where the music minister poured out his gift unselfishly for a young man he didn't even know. Alexia closed her eyes, but the pictures continued.

"Stop it!" she called out.

The images stopped. But as soon as they did, she regretted her command.

"No," she said, burying her face in her hands.

She kept her eyes closed without considering the passage of time. When she raised her head, she looked at her watch. Perhaps Ted had been taken to a room. She walked over to the attendant and asked him to check on Ted's status. The young man made a phone call and then gave her the room number.

Alexia took the elevator to the proper floor. Before going down the hall, she stopped at a restroom to check her appearance. She was a mess: her eyes bloodshot, her face puffy, her nose beginning to turn purple on the right side, her hair stringy. All she could do was run a brush through her hair. She left the restroom and walked down the hall to Ted's room. The door was cracked open. She slowly pushed it open. The first bed in the room was empty.

Ted lay on his back with his eyes closed, his right hand limp on top of the sheet with an IV drip attached to it, and his left hand out of sight under the covers. Alexia walked slowly over to the bed.

"Ted," she spoke softly. "It's Alexia."

Ted's eyes opened slightly at the sound of her voice, but he didn't speak. Alexia started to speak again but didn't. He needed to rest. The things she wanted to say to him would have to wait until he was able to understand. He fell asleep, and she quietly left the room.

———

Jeffrey Richardson shifted in his seat in Ezra's office.

"What happened?" the older man asked.

"Lindale and Morgan surprised the cleaning crew, but they got away without a problem. It's an old building without any type of security system. Morgan is in the hospital in Charleston with a broken hand. Lindale wasn't hurt."

"And the information?"

"They got the hard copy of the list from her file and checked her computer for any records. It was clean. Unless she made some phone calls, there's no indication that she'd begun any research. The crew was almost finished when she came into the office. If she'd been a minute later they would have been gone."

"What about the police investigation?"

"Word on the street says it was a routine break-in, probably people looking for money to buy drugs."

"Was any money stolen?"

"Yes, they took a petty-cash drawer from the secretary's office as a diversion."

Ezra leaned back in his chair. "Okay. That's one less thing to worry about."

"What have you done about Rena?" Jeffrey asked.

"Nothing directly. The solicitor in Mitchell County is a man named Vince Kinston. He's been in office a long time, and I'm told his enforcement of the law is more flexible than most. A subtle word at the right time will probably keep everything quiet. As soon as that happens, we need to eliminate the risk."

"What do you mean?"

"We must make sure Rena doesn't create any problems in the future. We can't let her dictate to us; we have to dictate to her."

"How?"

Ezra pressed his lips tightly together before he spoke. "We need a permanent solution."

Jeffrey shook his head. "Don't ask me to do anything like that."

"I won't. All you'll do is place a phone call to the right person at the right time."

———

Late Sunday afternoon, Alexia returned to the hospital. Word of Ted's injury had swept through the congregation of the Sandy Flats Church, and a steady stream of visitors flowed through his hospital room all afternoon. She passed a man and woman with familiar faces as she walked down the hall. They gave her a close look as well. Alexia wasn't sure if they recognized her or simply couldn't ignore the large purple splotch spreading out from her nose to her cheek. She knocked softly on the door of Ted's room. A familiar voice answered.

"Come in!"

She pushed open the door and found Ted alert and sitting up in bed. Several arrangements of flowers brightened the windowsill. His left hand was hidden under the sheet.

"Hey," she said tentatively. "How are you?"

"Glad that I don't have to do anything except lie here. How is your nose?"

"Just bruised, thanks to you."

Ted's right hand was still connected to an IV, but he raised it slightly and gestured toward the flowers. "Why would people send flowers to a guy?"

Alexia smiled. "Because they care about you. What would you rather have?"

"For you to sit beside me."

Alexia pulled a chair close and sat down. She could see the outline of Ted's left hand underneath the sheet.

"That's better," Ted said.

"How is your hand?"

"It hurts. I'm on pain medication but nothing that knocks me out. I wanted to be able to talk intelligently to the people who came by."

"And enjoy your flowers."

"Which look much better with your face in the foreground."

Alexia glanced again at his left hand. "Have you talked to the doctor?"

"Yes, he came by after lunch. He said that he'd talked to my wife last night."

Alexia flashed a sheepish grin. "I didn't correct him because I wanted to find out about your condition."

"You're forgiven. He spent quite a bit of time explaining the damage and what he'd done to correct it. Did he discuss the prognosis with you?"

Alexia nodded. "Yes."

Suddenly, tears pooled in the corner of her eyes. She bit her lip.

"And he told me that if you hadn't reached out your hand—" she stopped, her voice choking. The tears in her eyes overflowed.

Ted pulled his left hand from beneath the sheet. It was swathed in bandages with only the tips of his fingers visible. Raising it to her face, he gently touched her cheeks, capturing her tears in the clean white gauze.

He spoke softly. "There's no need to cry."

Alexia looked down. "The thought that you won't be able to play again . . . I feel so responsible."

"No," Ted answered in a strong voice. "I would do it again." He held up the bandaged hand. "I would rather have this than see you badly hurt. You are so beautiful."

Alexia broke. She buried her face in the sheets and sobbed. After a few seconds, Ted put his left hand on her head. Neither spoke. Finally, Alexia lifted her face. Her eyes were red and swollen.

Ted spoke. "Maybe I'm still in shock, but I feel the grace of God to cope with this."

"I don't understand."

"Neither do I, but for now I'm at peace. That's more than I could hope for, and I want you to have faith that everything will be alright too."

Alexia looked at the bandaged hand, and her lip trembled. "I'll try."

"Let me rest my hand on yours."

Alexia put her right hand on the edge of the bed. Ted carefully laid his left hand on top of hers. They sat together quietly. No visitors disturbed them.

———

The police left Alexia a voice mail at her home number informing her about the money missing from Gwen's petty-cash drawer. Early Monday morning, Alexia returned to the office. Gwen was waiting for her. When the secretary saw Alexia's face, she wiped away a quick tear and gave her a hug.

"Rachel called me yesterday. I tried to reach you in the afternoon, but you weren't home."

"I was at the hospital with Ted."

"How is he taking it?"

"Like a saint."

Alexia told Gwen what had happened. Both women ended up with tissues in their hands.

"I don't know what to think," Alexia said when she finished. "It's beyond me."

"I know what I think," Gwen said.

Alexia raised her eyebrows. "What?"

"That you should get him down the aisle of that old church where you've been hanging out as soon as his finger is well enough to be fitted with a gold ring."

Alexia smiled through teary eyes. "That's up to him."

Gwen smiled back. "That's never been true for any man. A woman's influence is the key to a man's decision."

The two women walked into Alexia's office. It looked exactly as it had the previous Friday.

"Is anything missing?" Gwen asked.

"I haven't found anything out of place except the few dollars in your drawer."

"So what did the thieves want?"

Alexia shook her head. "I don't know. I just don't know."

Alexia spent much of her morning fielding phone calls from sympathetic acquaintances who had learned about the break-in. Near lunchtime, Gwen buzzed her.

"Rena is on the phone."

"Did you talk to her?"

"Yes, for a minute. She didn't know about the break-in."

Alexia picked up the phone.

"Your secretary told me what happened," Rena began. "That's horrible. Are you okay?"

"I have a bruised nose, but otherwise, I'm fine. Ted is the one with serious injuries."

Rena listened without interrupting as Alexia told her the details.

When Alexia finished, Rena asked, "Do you know what they were after?"

"The police think they were looking for money. They took a small amount of cash from Gwen's drawer."

"That's not what I believe," Rena responded.

"What do you think?" Alexia asked in surprise.

"That it's not a coincidence. Like the person who tried to run you off the road near your house. It's all connected to the Richardson family."

Alexia could count on Rena to come up with a conspiracy theory that put herself at the epicenter. She considered ignoring the comment but couldn't resist a further question. At least her client no longer seemed on the verge of a mental breakdown.

"Why do you say that? What do I have that they would want?"

"The list of companies Jeffrey gave me," Rena answered. "Jeffrey called me a couple of days ago and asked me to give him my copy. Didn't he fax you a copy too?"

"No, you did. Jeffrey and I talked about the list but never discussed any specifics. He was going to contact me with more information but never did."

"Do you still have the list?"

"Let me check."

Alexia put the call on hold and went to her filing cabinet. Rena's files took up almost half a drawer, but she knew exactly where she'd deposited the sheet. Taking out the folder, Alexia quickly flipped through it without finding the list of companies. Slowing down, she checked again. It was gone. She returned to the phone.

"It's not where I put it," she said.

"See, I told you."

Alexia started to mention that she still had the information on her computer at home, but stopped. She couldn't trust Rena to keep anything confidential.

"Why would he go to that much trouble?" she asked.

"Because the Richardsons are crooks. I've been telling you that for months."

"Did you give Jeffrey your list?"

"Yes, but I'm not stupid. I kept a copy."

Alexia's mind was spinning. Why would the Richardsons go to so much trouble to hide the names of corporations whose existence was a public record?

Rena continued. "If you research those companies, you'll find something illegal."

"But why would I do that? I don't work for the police. Have you changed your mind about suing Ezra or filing for a divorce?"

"No, but if I'm going to be falsely accused of trying to hurt Baxter, I want everyone to know the truth about his family. They're behind the charges filed against me."

"No, Giles Porter took out the warrant."

"They're manipulating him then. Ezra has powerful friends across the state. He's always taking a big-shot politician out to play golf."

If Rena's previous accusation had proven groundless, Alexia would have ignored her second claim. As it was, she made a note on her legal pad.

"I'll talk to Sean about it. I need to call him about the preliminary hearing anyway."

"Do you want me to send you another copy?"

Alexia thought about Ted's hand and the danger the other list had caused. "No. I'll let you know if I want it. How is Baxter?"

Rena sighed. "Weaker and weaker. I don't like to go to the hospital and run into his family though, so I've been calling the nurses' station to find out what's going on."

42

*For God so loved the world, that he gave his only begotten
Son, that whosoever believeth in him should not perish,
but have everlasting life.*
JOHN 3:16 KJV

A lexia pushed the speakerphone button and continued talking to Sean
Pruitt. The Charleston lawyer's shock and genuine concern about the
weekend events made Alexia realize he cared about her as a person, not
just a professional colleague. Alexia shifted their discussion to prepara-
tions for the preliminary hearing in Rena's case.

"It will be your chance to dissect Giles Porter," Alexia said.

"Yes, and according to Skip, the magistrate assigned to the case is
right friendly to defense lawyers."

"When are you going to Mitchell County?"

"I'll fly up early Thursday morning so I can talk to potential witnesses. I may even hike to the waterfall. Will you be able to bring Rena
on Friday morning?"

"Yes. Is anything happening with the grand jury in Charleston?"

"Not yet. They don't meet until next Monday. They'll probably watch
the videotape, but they'll need additional evidence to support an indictment against Rena for anything other than lying to the police."

———

Alexia had trouble concentrating on her work. Toward the middle of the
afternoon, Gwen buzzed her.

"Ted is on the phone."

Glad for the interruption, Alexia picked it up. "How are you?"

"Sitting in my living room. Dr. Hayes released me late this morning
and told me to come back next Monday. A member of the church drove
me home."

"Were you ready to leave the hospital?"

"I could have stayed, but my health-insurance company thought otherwise."

"What about the bandages on your hand?"

"My family doctor can change the dressings, but for now I have a private-duty nurse who is going to take care of me."

"Who?"

"Sarah Locklear. She left the house a few minutes ago."

"Oh, how did she find out what happened?"

Alexia's concern for Ted overshadowed any vestige of jealousy.

"One of the aides heard about it and phoned her. Sarah and I talked quite a bit about Baxter."

"Has she gone to the hospital to see him?"

"Yes, and she says his prognosis is poor. He never started moving enough to build up his muscles, and his body is slowly shutting down. But Sarah thinks we should continue music therapy as long as he's breathing."

"But how can you—" she stopped. There was no use stating the obvious.

"Of course, I can only play with one hand. But Sarah convinced me that even if I can't play normally, we should do what we're supposed to do."

"I thought you didn't want to go back after finding out what Baxter tried to do to Rena."

"I didn't. But after talking to Sarah, I realize that's not the issue."

"You didn't tell her, did you?" Alexia asked in alarm.

"No, I'm not that heavily medicated, but her perspective convinced me I was off-base. What I learned distracted me from what I'm supposed to do."

Alexia leaned back in her chair. "Okay, I guess. When are you going to the hospital?"

"Tomorrow night if I feel up to it. Do you still have a copy of the music-therapy prescription?"

"Let me check."

Alexia returned to the drawer and found the authorization from the neurosurgeon.

"Yes. It's here," she said.

"Good. Sarah says that Baxter has a private room, but it would be good to have the prescription in case anyone questions what we're doing."

"I'll bring it. What time will you be there?"

"I'll call and let you know."

Alexia slowly hung up the phone. She didn't have a tidy descriptive category in which she could place Ted Morgan.

———

Rena argued with Sean Pruitt before dropping her demand that he expose the Richardsons' corruption during her preliminary hearing. Her ears perked up, however, when the lawyer mentioned traveling to Mitchell County a day early and going to the waterfall.

"I'd like to go with you." she said into the phone.

"Why?"

"I can help you understand what happened, and it will get me away from this place."

"I can't be with you the whole time. I need to get ready for the hearing."

"I want you to do your job, but it's my freedom at stake."

Silence crossed the phone line.

"Okay."

Rena gave the lawyer directions to her house. After she ended the call, she glanced out the window. She had not seen any sign of Jeffrey's men for several days. She opened the drawer in the kitchen and found the phone number for Rudy.

"Do you have everything ready?" she asked.

"I'm waiting on the people in California to do their part. I'll be ready next week."

"That's not soon enough. I'm going to be in Mitchell County on Thursday and Friday."

"Why?"

"That's not important, but it gets me out of town. That's when you need to do it."

"How can I contact you?"

"I'll call you."

"Yeah, that will work better."

"I thought so too."

"I'll call California as soon as we hang up."

Rena set the phone on the kitchen counter and walked into the foyer. Looking into the living room, she saw the back of a man's head. He was sitting in a leather chair and facing in the opposite direction.

Rena screamed.

The head stayed completely still, and Rena knew it was Baxter. She stepped slowly into the living room, aware of the surveillance camera, yet unable to resist the need to confront this ghost. She crept toward the chair, terrified that the figure might turn and face her with a lurid expression. She stopped a couple of feet behind the chair. The head seemed to move slightly, and she clasped her hand over her mouth to stifle another scream. But the head didn't turn completely. Baxter ignoring her was worse than some of their face-to-face confrontations.

She lowered her hand from her mouth and reached toward the chair. Her hand trembled as she touched the back of the chair and felt the rich texture of the upholstery. It was solid, not imaginary. Her fingers inched forward to the back of the head. She cut her eyes to the ceiling where she knew the camera was recording her movements. She didn't care. Let the camera capture what her imagination could see. She looked back at the chair.

It was empty.

———

Alexia fixed a bowl of soup and ate supper at the little table in her kitchen. Looking out the windows to the dusky horizon, she could see the lights of an ocean freighter sailing toward Charleston. Working as a deckhand would be a straightforward life with well-defined parameters in a finite world. Routine would be the order of the day, a predictable life that went about its business under the panoramic night sky without the diffusion of city lights. The ship passed out of sight. Darkness had fallen by the time she finished her soup. It was time to go to the hospital.

———

Ted's hand throbbed in a steady four-four rhythm. He turned the steering wheel of his truck with his right hand and pulled into a parking place at the Santee hospital. He'd avoided taking a pain pill because he wanted to be alert for his session with Baxter. Now he wondered if he'd made a mistake. He saw Alexia walk through the front door of the hospital. Somewhat awkwardly, he managed to pick up his keyboard and prop the instrument against the side of his truck while he locked the door. Alexia and Sarah waited in the hospital lobby. As they walked together to the elevator, Alexia fingered a copy of the prescription for music therapy.

Baxter's room was on the second floor. They stopped outside the door while Sarah retrieved his chart from the nurses' station and read it. She filled them in.

"He has a common form of bacterial pneumonia. The irony is that his lungs are filling with mucus because the body is trying to isolate and destroy the infection. He's slowly drowning in the substance intended to heal him."

"Is it better or worse than when you came by the other day?" Ted asked.

Sarah ran her fingers down a list of numbers. "Leukocytosis with a left shift, decreased CO_2. He's slightly worse, and they have him on a CPAP machine to assist his breathing. Pneumonia with a bedridden patient is always serious." She closed the chart and returned it to the nurses' station. "But none of that determines what we're going to do."

Baxter's room reminded Alexia of the ICU unit in Greenville. Tubes and monitors filled every space—a constant reminder of the fragility of life and the efforts needed to sustain it. Baxter, a mask over his mouth and nose, lay motionless in the bed. Ted walked up to him.

"Hello, Baxter. It's Ted Morgan."

There was no response.

"I'm going to play, and Sarah Locklear is going to sing." Ted glanced at Alexia, who shook her head.

"Don't mention me," she whispered. "I'll sit near the door."

Ted placed the keyboard on a chair and plugged it in. He looked at Sarah and spoke.

"Now that we're here, I'm not sure I have the faith to play for a healing. I don't feel very good myself, and there's no telling how exhausted Baxter must be. He's been fighting for a long time."

Sarah came forward and stood beside the bed. Ted waited for her to disagree and encourage him to believe. She put her hand on Baxter's head and closed her eyes.

"You're right," she said after a few moments. "He's dying, and I don't want to ask for healing. My heart cry is that he be made ready for heaven, not held to earth. This life is about to end. He needs life everlasting."

Peace immediately replaced the unsettledness in Ted's spirit.

"Yes, but can he hear and respond?" he asked.

Sarah gave a little smile. "That's where the faith comes in. We have to believe that the power of the Gospel can penetrate the fog of illness."

A nurse opened the door of the room. Sarah went over and spoke to her. The nurse left.

"We have thirty minutes," Sarah said. "She'll make sure we're not disturbed. They know how sick he is, and they extend more latitude when someone is near the end." She again touched the top of Baxter's head. "I've seen seriously ill patients respond to the Lord within minutes of death. As long as there is breath, there is hope."

Ted pressed his keyboard's power button.

"With only one hand I can't play anything fancy."

Sarah looked directly at him. "Don't play with your fingers, play with your heart."

Alexia watched. With his hand wrapped in a thick bandage, Ted looked like a patient himself. The sight of his left hand useless in his lap caused Alexia's sadness to return. She quickly dabbed at her left eye to wipe away a tear.

Ted touched the keys.

The sound was tentative, searching, unsure. It wasn't the music of Ted Morgan, whose gift Alexia had come to both esteem and take for granted. She cringed. It was hard to listen to his crippled effort and more difficult to watch.

Sarah continued to stand silently near Baxter's head. Ted's right hand moved over the keys as he searched for a sound in harmony with the moment. Always before, Alexia had listened in amazement and marveled at the divine presence that acknowledged the music. Tonight, nothing happened. No transformation overtook the room. No hint of divine life filled the music. Alexia shut her eyes and began to pray. Ted stopped, and they all sat in silence. Time passed. He touched the keys again.

And in a few moments, a melody came.

It was simple, yet profound, unlike anything Alexia had ever heard.

It wasn't borrowed from a classical composer and recycled for contemporary use. The fresh combination of notes flowed across the room with both message and emotion. Alexia didn't try to stay the tears that streamed down her cheeks.

Sarah, her hand still resting on Baxter's head, began to sing.

Theme rather than rhyme linked her words. They took Alexia back to the evening in Ted's backyard when the love of God invaded her own soul. Jesus Christ came to earth to save her. He also came for Baxter Richardson. With all her heart, in spite of all his faults, Alexia longed for Baxter to know the same divine acceptance she'd experienced. No matter the past, the eternal future belonged to the God who lived outside time. In that future, enemies could embrace as friends; those separated by hate could enter into glorious unity.

As if prompted by Alexia's thoughts, Sarah began to sing a song of forgiveness. Forgiveness for Baxter through the blood of Jesus. Forgiveness for others, because the genuine fruit of the Gospel makes heavenly reconciliation possible. The young man's opportunity for ultimate freedom opened before him. His body might be wrapped in the chains of death, but Alexia sensed the moment of liberation for his spirit.

Ted responded with as much emotion in his one hand as Alexia ever heard him display with two. The sounds confirmed the power of forgiveness and transformation. Baxter stirred. His head moved under Sarah's touch. He wasn't struggling; he was agreeing. Sarah stroked his sandy-colored hair.

"Seal it," she said.

And the minister transitioned to a new sequence of notes that spoke an emphatic "Amen." Alexia listened and understood that she had taken part in an event she would never forget. Ted slowly reeled in the music and lifted his hand from the keyboard. The room was the same, the people in it forever different.

"That's it," he said. "It is finished."

43

Alexia drove home with a sense of peaceful euphoria. She didn't pay any attention to the familiar twists and turns in the roads to her house. Her mind stayed in Baxter's hospital room and the hoped-for entrance from life into death into life everlasting. She turned onto Pelican Point Drive and onto the narrow driveway toward her house. The headlights for her car cast glimmers across the black water at the edge of the marsh. It was high tide on a moonless night.

Another vehicle's headlights suddenly flashed directly in her eyes. She swerved to the right as a car passed by her and accelerated toward Pelican Point Drive. Her heart pounding, she could see the vehicle turn right in the direction of Highway 17. Alexia eased back onto the driveway and pulled close to her house. She saw no other cars. Her headlights illuminated tire tracks left in the sand by the vehicle that had passed her. She pulled under her house and turned off the engine. Getting out, she heard the rustle of wind moving through the marsh grass. Alexia tentatively climbed the steps to the front door and stopped.

The front door stood open.

Her first impulse was to rush into the house. Immediately on its heels came the urge to dash down the steps and escape. She stood still, straining to hear a sound or sense movement.

All was silent.

No sound of an intruder. No bark from Boris. No sign of Misha.

At the thought of her pets, Alexia overcame her fear. She stepped forward and flipped on a light just inside the front door. She quickly scanned the living room. Nothing had been disturbed since she left for the hospital. She walked slowly into the house and crossed the living room into the kitchen. It, too, was untouched. She glanced at the soup bowl and spoon she'd placed on the counter. Every nerve alert, she walked down the hallway past one of the two downstairs bedrooms.

A noise came from the room. Alexia turned to flee but when the noise came again she recognized the sound of scratching. She turned on the light and went into the bedroom. Opening the closet door, she was almost knocked over by Boris, who bolted past her through the house and out the front door. Alexia returned to the front stoop and could hear Boris, invisible in the night, thrashing through the underbrush beside the house.

Going back inside, she picked up the cordless phone in the kitchen and called the police to report the break-in.

"We'll have a car on the way," the dispatcher replied. "Was anything taken?"

"The downstairs looks fine. I haven't been upstairs."

"You can check or wait for the officer."

"I'll go up. My dog wouldn't have left the house if an intruder was still here."

Still holding the phone, she walked upstairs and turned on the light in her bedroom. Misha walked around the corner of the bed. Everything appeared normal until Alexia's eyes reached her computer. It was demolished, the screen broken, the processing unit ripped open and parts scattered on the floor. A few papers were strewn about underneath the small computer table.

"Wait," she said. "My computer has been destroyed."

———

Sean Pruitt turned the steering wheel of the rented SUV sharply to the left. The gravel road shrank to one lane, making it almost impossible to avoid a head-on collision with a vehicle coming from the opposite direction.

"You should honk the horn as you enter the curve," Rena said. "It's dangerous up here. Baxter hadn't driven on narrow roads in the mountains, and I had to tell him what to do so we wouldn't get hurt."

"I'll keep that in mind. How much farther is it to the trailhead?"

"Not far. We're almost there."

Rena checked her cell phone. "I'm out of range. I called the hospital while you were renting the SUV but couldn't get a nurse. I'm not very impressed with the hospital in Santee."

"Couldn't they move him to Charleston?"

"They say it wouldn't make any difference."

Several minutes and two hairpin turns later, Rena said, "That's it to the left."

Sean cut the wheel, and they came through a narrow gap in the trees into an empty clearing large enough for five or six cars.

"Nobody comes this time of year," Rena said. "The leaves are gone, and we'll have the trail to ourselves."

Although close to noon, the chilly mountain air prompted each of them to put on a coat and gloves. Sean donned a baseball cap, and Rena wrapped a scarf around her neck. The trail went directly up a small knoll from the parking lot. When they reached the top, Rena turned around and looked down at the car.

"That's the exact place where Baxter and I parked," she said. "Do you have the keys?"

Sean patted his pocket. "Right here."

"Same pocket as Baxter."

"Why do you remember that?"

"I had to get them out of his pocket after he fell. I'll never forget how he looked. I thought he was dead, but his eyes were open."

The trail ran along the top of a ridge. They set out at a steady pace. With no leaves on the trees it was possible to see into the gullies on either side of the trail. The autumn's crop of leaves occasionally rustled along the ground as a breeze brushed against the side of the hill.

"I've been coming here ever since I was a little girl," Rena said. "I wanted Baxter to see it."

"Did you argue after you started walking?"

Rena shook her head. "Not until we reached the waterfall. I think we even held hands for a while."

After several minutes, they veered left from the top of the ridge and began a descent, occasionally broken by a short climb up.

"It's easier walking in than climbing out," Rena said. She stopped and picked up a dead limb. "We each found a walking stick. They were better than this one, but about the same size."

They continued on. Rena broke the tiny twigs from her stick as they walked along until it was smooth. They stopped for a drink of water.

"Didn't you tell me Baxter brought some wine?" Sean asked.

"Yes. He carried a small backpack."

"What else was in it?"

"Bread and cheese."

"No cups?"

"Oh yeah. He brought real glasses and a large white napkin we used for a tablecloth."

"Anything else?"

Rena replaced the cap on her water bottle. "Yes, he had a pocketknife with a corkscrew in it. That's it."

"Did he have a gun?"

Rena laughed. "Baxter? No way. Now, my stepfather always had a pistol in his pocket when we came here, but Baxter doesn't even own a gun."

"Okay. Lead the way."

They ascended a long, gradual climb before plunging downward in a succession of switchbacks. Eventually, Rena led Sean to the base of a stairway cut in the side of the hill.

"I can hear the waterfall."

"It's not far now."

The stairs rose to a flat rocky area covered with scrubby trees and bushes. They walked across two small streams no more than a few inches deep. The sound of the waterfall increased. The path disappeared in a bank of scattered rocks. Ducking under some low limbs, they came into an open area beside a bold stream. The waterway came in from the opposite direction and cut sharply to the left. In the middle of the stream, a large boulder split the water in two before both courses plummeted over the edge into the gorge below. In the distance, the hills marched westward toward the higher Appalachians.

"Nice view," Sean said.

"I used to think so," Rena answered flatly.

"I'm sorry."

Rena pointed her walking stick at a flat rock near the edge of the water. "That's where we ate. Baxter spread the napkin there and cut up the bread and cheese."

"And the wine?"

"I drank a little bit; he finished the bottle."

"So you were here for quite a while?"

"Yes. That's why we took the hike."

"Did you see anyone else on the trail or here at the waterfall?"

"No, it was just like today, only the leaves were just beginning to turn. We had the place to ourselves."

Sean sat on the flat rock. Rena walked past him and stood close to the edge of the cliff.

"Come here," she said.

Sean stood up and came toward her. He stopped a foot behind her.

"This is close enough for me," he said. "I'm not crazy about heights."

"I want to show you the rock where he landed."

Sean stepped back. "Maybe in a minute. Tell me again what happened."

Rena continued to stare out over the cliff. "I already did. Why do you want to hear it again?"

"That's why we're here, isn't it? So I can get a clear picture of what happened?"

Rena turned around. At its zenith, the sun shone down on her golden head. But her eyes, not her hair, caught Sean's attention.

"Don't you believe me?" she asked.

He looked away. "Just tell me. You were sipping wine and eating a snack. How did the argument start?"

Rena stepped away from the edge. "Everything was fine until he finished the bottle of wine. Baxter drank too much, and when he did, it changed his personality. I'm sure the records at the hospital show that he had more than his share of alcohol in his blood. He started asking me a bunch of questions about his brother, Jeffrey, and accused me of spending time with him when Baxter wasn't at home. It was crazy."

"Why would he think that about you and Jeffrey?"

Rena shook her head. "I don't know. I don't even like Jeffrey, and I'm not that kind of person anyway. Jeffrey is always flirting with women, but

I never responded. I told Baxter that he was being silly, but he wouldn't stop. He stood up and started pacing."

"Where were you standing?"

Rena looked around. "Uh, at first I was sitting beside the flat rock, but I got up and moved near where I am now."

Sean started walking back and forth. "Like this?"

"Yes."

"Did you lose your temper?"

"No. I mean, I guess I raised my voice to try to make him believe me, but it didn't do any good. I had the walking stick in my hand, and I told him that if he didn't stop I would knock some sense into his head."

"You threatened him with the stick?"

Rena stopped and tilted her head to one side. She spoke more slowly. "No, that didn't happen. I'm wrong. I thought about doing it but didn't."

Sean came closer to her. "Where was the walking stick after the fight?"

"I don't remember. I think I left the stick here after Baxter fell."

"How did the fight get physical?"

Rena looked over Sean's shoulder. "He came at me, grabbed my arms, and shook me."

"Where did that happen?"

Rena stepped back toward the edge. "I'd been backing up because he was so upset." She reached out and took hold of Sean's arms. "I held on to him like this. He pushed me backward, but I spun him around."

With surprising strength, Rena pulled Sean forward and with a swift move knocked him off balance and turned him so that his back was to the edge of the cliff.

"Stop it!" the lawyer cried out.

Rena didn't release her grip. Sean pulled to the side toward the stream. When he did, he stumbled and pitched backward. If Rena hadn't held on to him, he would have slipped over the edge. Instead, he went to his knees. Rena released him, and he quickly crawled away from the cliff.

Crouching on the ground, he cried out, "What got into you? I could have been killed!"

Rena stepped away from the edge and spoke in a level voice. "Don't be mad at me. You wanted to know what happened. The difference on the day of the accident was that Baxter pushed me, and when I turned the tables on him he went over the edge."

"But it was wrong to do that to me."

Rena stared directly at Sean. "Did you feel the fear? That's what I felt. I thought I was going to die."

Sean didn't answer. He stood and brushed off his pants.

"Let's go," he said.

"Do you have any other questions?"

"Not here."

———

From the outside, the Mitchell County Courthouse looked very similar to the First Baptist Church on the adjacent block. The church had a steeple housing a bell; the courthouse had a tower featuring a large clock face with Roman numerals. Both buildings were constructed of reddish brick with a few darker flecks in them. When air conditioning came to the mountains, the courthouse received the benefit of cool air two years before the people on the church pews could enjoy a long sermon on a hot August day.

A common assignment for third-graders in Mitchell County was to draw a picture of the courthouse clock tower and identify each Roman numeral. Julius Caesar would have been proud of Mrs. Kinnamon's current class. All twenty-three students correctly identified the numbers, and most successfully completed a few simple math problems that gave them heightened appreciation for the genius of Arabic numbers.

On Friday, Sean and Rena walked into the Mitchell County Courthouse a half hour before the preliminary hearing was scheduled. Skip Ayers had told Sean that preliminary hearings were rarely held in the main courtroom. Magistrates, lower-level judges who didn't wear robes, were shuffled into any available space where a few people could squeeze around a table. Today, however, the courthouse schedule must have been light; the hearing had been assigned to the spacious room where the grand jury met for its deliberations.

The room lacked a judicial bench for the magistrate, but a long table stretched across the front of the room with two smaller tables facing it. The lawyer put his briefcase on one of the two small tables but left it closed.

Rena, wearing a stylish burnt-orange wool skirt with a decorative sweater, thought she looked more like a graduate student going to a college football game at Clemson than a woman facing a felony criminal investigation. Maybe the innocent look would work in her favor today.

"Did you phone Alexia this morning?" she asked.

Sean paused for a split second before answering. "No, my cell phone is dead, and I left the charger at home. She said she would be here, so I expect her any minute. What about Baxter?"

Rena hadn't called the hospital, but it wouldn't sound right to admit it. She just shrugged. "He's about the same. They're fighting the pneumonia with antibiotics. There's nothing I could do if I was there." She indicated the room with a sweeping gesture. "And all this makes it hard to care what happens to him."

A heavyset man wearing suspenders under his suit jacket entered the room. He breathed heavily as he walked.

"Good morning," he said with a somewhat leering grin directed toward Rena, "I'm Vince Kinston, the solicitor."

Sean introduced himself. "I have several witnesses under subpoena."

"I know. We'll just have to see who shows up."

"If any witness doesn't honor a subpoena, I'll need the chance to reconvene the hearing and—"

Kinston waved his hand. "Don't worry, Mr. Pruitt. I've looked over the file. Unless the sheriff's department shows me a lot more than currently indicated, there's no way I'll present this case to the grand jury." The solicitor again directed his gaze toward Rena. "We'll have you out of here before supper time, honey."

Kinston shuffled out of the room. Sean peeked out the door.

"I guess he's going back to his office."

"Did you hear what he said?" Rena began excitedly. "He's not going to charge me with anything."

"Don't count on anything," Sean cautioned.

"He called me honey," Rena shot back.

"Which makes him look incompetent but doesn't mean he won't seek an indictment. A lot of these rural solicitors go deer hunting with enough men in the jury pool to get a conviction on questionable evidence."

Rena pouted. "You can be negative, but I'm feeling a lot better."

"Just sit tight, and remember not to say anything. This is our chance to find out what they have in the investigative file." Sean took out a blank legal pad and placed it in front of her. "If you want to tell me something during the hearing, write it down."

"Don't you think it would help if I told the judge what happened?"

"No!"

Rena stepped away and walked to a window behind the magistrate's seat. As she looked down on the sidewalk one story below, she saw a familiar figure approaching. The confidence that she'd felt moments before evaporated at the sight of Detective Giles Porter. She hurriedly returned to Sean's side.

"The detective is here!"

Sean was sitting at the table with his briefcase open. "Of course he is. I subpoenaed him. As the officer in charge of the investigation, he is the primary witness I want to question."

"We know what he thinks," Rena replied.

"But we want to know why he thinks it. Don't expect me to become antagonistic with him today. I want to find out as much as possible, not drive him into a corner. That type of cross-examination is what happens at trial."

"He's been awful from the beginning."

"Did you see Alexia?"

"No."

A slightly balding, middle-aged man wearing a wrinkled, gray suit entered the room.

"I'm Magistrate Simpson," he said. "We'll be ready to go as soon as Detective Porter arrives. This is the only case on my calendar for this afternoon."

Sean shook Simpson's hand. "I subpoenaed another officer, as well as the EMT workers who found Mr. Richardson."

The magistrate gave him a doubtful look. "Our local EMTs are too busy to come to preliminary hearings."

"Then I hope you'll allow us to continue the hearing at a later date."

The magistrate gave a noncommittal shrug. "We'll get started in a few minutes. I'll give you a chance to pose your questions to anyone who shows up."

Rena turned to Sean. "I need to go to the restroom."

"Okay. You have a few minutes."

Rena went into the hallway and walked to the top of the stairs. She looked down the stairwell. It was empty. The door to a room across from her was labeled "Law Library." She went inside. Bookshelves reached the ceiling. A single table sat in the middle of the empty room. Rena took out her cell phone and punched in a number.

"Where are you?" she asked.

"Outside the courthouse. I'm in a green pickup truck."

"Is everything ready?"

"Yes. What are you doing in there?"

"It's a court thing and should be over in an hour or so. It may not be a big deal after all."

"I don't like this spot."

Rena remembered noticing a convenience store when she looked out the window.

"Do you see the convenience store across the street from the courthouse?"

"Yes."

"Move there. We'll do it either today or tomorrow."

"You're staying another night?"

"Yes, but I'm sending my lawyer back to Charleston."

"Okay."

Rena clicked off the phone and returned to the grand-jury room. The court reporter hired by Sean arrived and set up at the end of the magistrate's table. Giles Porter had yet to appear.

"Where is the detective?" Rena asked in a low voice. "I saw him come into the courthouse."

"Probably huddled up with the solicitor." Sean checked his watch. "They'll come in at the last minute."

Rena sat beside Sean and fidgeted. Everyone in the room had something to do but her. Sean made notes on a legal pad. The magistrate looked at some papers. The court reporter was reading a book. Rena's stomach began to twist in a knot. She got up and walked again to the window. Alexia had still not arrived. The green truck, however, was in its new location. She breathed a sigh of relief. Escape from everything that haunted her was as easy as a walk across the street.

She glanced down at the sidewalk again and saw a man in a wheelchair at the bottom of the handicapped access ramp. When he turned his head, she recognized him.

It was Baxter.

Rena wanted to scream in frustration. She made a slight choking noise that caused the magistrate to turn in his chair and look at her. She raised her hand to her mouth and coughed.

"Excuse me," she managed.

She looked out the window again. This time he was gone, the sidewalk empty.

Turning away from the window, she confronted the flesh-and-blood nemesis who wouldn't disappear. Detective Giles Porter entered the room, followed by Solicitor Kinston. The detective's eyes met hers and grabbed her before she could look away. In that split second, all Rena's fears returned with a vengeance. The solicitor closed the door and sat at the other small table.

"Come forward and be sworn in, Detective Porter," the magistrate said. "We're ready to get started."

44

Do you solemnly swear that the testimony you are about to give in the matter before this court
will be the truth, the whole truth, and nothing but the truth, so help you God?

JUDICIAL OATH

R ena sat beside Sean. "Where's Alexia?" she whispered.

Sean seemed not to hear her. "Remember," he said. "Write what you want to tell me. Don't whisper."

Rena rolled her eyes and laid a pen across the top of the pad.

Sean began by asking Porter questions about the detective's training and experience. Rena glanced sideways at Solicitor Kinston, who took out a small pocketknife and began to pare his nails. Sean turned over the top page of his legal pad.

"Detective Porter, how did you become aware of the incident involving Baxter Richardson?"

"I was in a patrol car and received a call from a Mitchell County 911 operator that Ms. Richardson had phoned in an accidental fatality involving her husband."

"Did you initiate phone contact with Rena Richardson?"

"No."

"What did you do in response to the 911 call?"

"The operator was concerned about Ms. Richardson's physical condition, so I immediately proceeded to the forest service road in an effort to locate her. An ambulance was also dispatched, but I arrived on the scene first."

"Were you alone in the patrol car?"

"No, a deputy was driving."

Sean checked his notes. "Would that be Officer Dortch?"

"Yes. I requested that a rescue helicopter go to Double Barrel Falls to determine if Baxter Richardson was still alive."

"Why did you request a helicopter when the incident was reported as a fatality?"

"To save Mr. Richardson's life if it was possible to do so. Ms. Richardson told the 911 operator that her husband had no pulse, but if she was wrong, I wanted to attempt a rescue. In fact, the helicopter flew over shortly after I made initial contact with your client."

Rena remembered the sound of the helicopter. If not for the aerial rescue, Baxter would have died at the bottom of the cliff, and she could have gone on with life. She clenched her teeth.

"What is the first thing she told you?"

"She asked me not to stay with her but to go up the road because her husband had fallen from a cliff. When I informed her about the helicopter, she told me that her husband was dead and didn't have a pulse. When I asked if she was sure, she stated that she'd unsuccessfully tried to revive him, but his body was cold and lifeless."

The detective had yet to open the folder on the table in front of him.

"Do you have notes of your conversation with my client?" Sean asked.

"No, but I have a very good memory. While she was being checked at the Mitchell Regional ER, she gave me her phone number, address, and social-security number." The detective looked directly at Rena as he repeated the information.

Rena wrote her social-security number on the pad and underlined it.

"Show-off," she muttered.

"What else did she tell you about her husband's condition?"

"Nothing, but she raised my suspicions. One moment she wanted us to leave and check on him, and the next she told me any rescue attempt would be futile."

"So that made her a criminal suspect?"

Porter shook his head. "Not at that time—just a distraught woman who couldn't provide a coherent account of a traumatic event."

In response to further questions, the detective related the trip with

Rena to the main highway, where an ambulance met them and transported her to Mitchell Regional Hospital.

"Did you talk to her during the drive on the forest service road?"

"No, she was lying in the backseat. She claimed she was nauseated."

"Did she get sick?"

"Yes," the detective admitted.

"Did you accompany her in the ambulance?"

"No. Officer Dortch and I followed in the patrol car. Once she checked in at the hospital, I talked briefly with her in one of the treatment rooms."

"Tell me everything that was said."

The detective focused on Rena as he talked. She looked down to avoid his eyes but couldn't escape his voice.

"She told me that she'd gone to the area since she was a little girl and wanted her husband to see it. They drank a bottle of wine, ate a snack, and when it was time to leave, her husband got too close to the edge of the cliff and fell. She was a few feet away but couldn't do anything to help him. When I asked whether she remembered anything else, she mentioned looking over the edge and seeing that he was dead."

"Was she aware that he was alive at the time you talked in the ER?"

"No. We'd not yet heard from the helicopter crew."

"Did you ask any other questions?"

"Yes. She had several scratches on her face and a scrape on her left arm. I asked how they occurred and she told me that after her husband fell, she hiked down the trail to the bottom of the falls to check on him. She also mentioned giving him CPR."

"What else did you do at the hospital?"

"I requested that a sample of your client's blood be retained."

"Why?"

"For DNA. She'd told different stories about what happened, and I thought we might be dealing with a homicide. If so, some evidence might require DNA testing."

Rena's stomach twisted.

"How many times did you question her at the hospital?"

"Just once. I came back and gave her my card."

"When did you next have contact with her?"

"Outside the hospital, while waiting for the helicopter to arrive with her husband's body. I learned that he was alive and informed her."

"How did she respond to the news?"

"She was shocked."

"Was there further discussion at that time?"

"I told her the helicopter was taking Mr. Richardson directly to the trauma unit at Greenville Memorial. That's all."

"Did you go to Greenville?"

"Yes. I arrived before Ms. Richardson."

"Did you use blue lights and siren?"

"No."

"What did you do at the hospital?"

"I told the trauma physician the incident involved a potential criminal investigation and requested an opportunity to view the patient."

"Did that take place?"

"Yes."

"What did you find?"

Solicitor Kinston shifted in his chair. "Please pick up the pace, Mr. Pruitt. This is a probable-cause hearing, not a trial on the merits."

Before Sean could respond, Magistrate Simpson spoke. "I'm going to allow it, Mr. Kinston, especially since it seems none of the other witnesses subpoenaed are going to be here."

Kinston shrugged. "Very well."

Porter looked at Sean. "Could you repeat the question?"

"I thought that would be unnecessary given your prodigious memory."

The detective ran his fingers across the scar on the top of his head. "A nurse took me back into the area where they were treating Mr. Richardson. He had an obvious head injury, as well as a broken right leg. I asked the doctor to check his fingernails for traces of skin. I suspected a link between Mr. Richardson and the scratches on your client's face and left arm."

"Was that done?"

"They were trying to save the man's life, but one of the physicians left instructions for a nurse to trim Mr. Richardson's fingernails without cleaning them and provide the clippings to me."

While Porter talked, Rena wrote on her paper—*that happened when Baxter attacked me.* She slid it over to Sean, who glanced down but didn't stop questioning the detective.

"Did you receive any fingernail clippings at a later date?"

"Yes."

"Did you see the nurse trim them?"

"No."

"Tell me about the chain of custody."

Porter shifted in his chair. "They went from a nurse and then to me."

"Did other people have access?"

"Possibly."

"Do you have their names?"

"No, that's still being determined."

"Have DNA tests been conducted?"

"Yes, by Dr. Ari Schlicter, a forensic pathologist with the state crime lab in Columbia."

While Sean made a note of the name on his pad, Rena felt the room starting to shrink. The wall on the opposite side of the room began to bend. She shut her eyes and bowed her head.

"What were the results of the tests?" Sean asked.

"Skin under the fingernails matched your client's DNA."

"Did they determine how long the skin had been there?"

"You'd have to ask Dr. Schlicter that question."

"Were there any other DNA tests?"

"Yes, involving a stick that I found at the waterfall when I conducted an on-site investigation. We found traces of Mr. Richardson's skin embedded in the wood on one end."

Behind Rena's closed eyelids, she witnessed a graphic replay of the hiking stick scraping Baxter's neck as he staggered toward the edge of the cliff.

"Baxter Richardson confirmed my theory regarding what took place when I interviewed him in Santee on—"

At mention of the interview, Rena opened her eyes in shock and saw the door to the room swing slowly forward.

Baxter entered.

Wearing a long-sleeve green shirt that a golfing buddy had given him as a birthday present, he passed by in a wheelchair pushed by a middle-aged woman. His hair was parted on the correct side, but he needed a haircut. Even in profile his face had a thin, pinched look, and Rena could tell that he'd lost a lot of weight, especially in his chest. Baggy khaki pants draped his spindly legs, and he sat slightly hunched, a wraith suspended between death and life. An annoying nuisance.

There was a loud buzzing in Rena's head, and she shut her eyes and covered her ears with her hands. She knew Sean must be continuing to question Porter, but she couldn't capture the words as they traveled through the air. Wanting to avoid Baxter, she turned her head toward Sean and opened her eyes.

The lawyer was leaning over and talking to Alexia, who had taken a seat beside him. That explained the opening of the door; however, Rena could still see Baxter out of the corner of her eye. The wheelchair had stopped near the detective, and she could sense her husband silently accusing her. She considered glaring back at him until he disappeared but didn't want the magistrate to think she was looking at him. Instead, she tapped Sean's arm. The best antidote for combating Baxter would be to ignore him. The lawyer finished talking to Alexia and stood to his feet without acknowledging Rena.

"Could we have a brief recess?" Sean asked.

"Yes," the magistrate replied.

Relieved, Rena sighed. A break would give her time to wrestle her mind back to reality. The hearing had been harder to handle than she imagined. Instead of going to the restroom, she might bolt across the street to her new life and new identity. A change in geography could produce a change in mind. Close proximity to Baxter and those associated with him prevented her from breaking free of his grip. She looked at the magistrate, who appeared focused on the part of the room where she imagined Baxter sat immobile. Steeling her resolve, Rena forced herself to look too. Baxter turned his head toward her.

"Rena," he said.

Rena's mouth went dry. Never before had he uttered a sound. She needed to get out of the room.

"Why?" he asked.

Rena started to answer and then caught herself. She couldn't start talking into the air. Sean had left his seat and was talking with the solicitor. Rena leaned and turned toward Alexia.

"He's here," she whispered.

"Yes, I know," the lawyer responded. "He's real."

Without fully comprehending, Rena glanced back at Baxter. He shook his head sadly, the gesture of a flesh-and-blood human being.

"No!" Rena cried out, pointing her finger at her husband. "You are not here!"

Rising to her feet so violently that she knocked over her chair, Rena came around the table and charged the figure in the wheelchair.

"No!" Alexia yelled.

But Rena wasn't hearing anything. The nurse pulled the wheelchair away but couldn't keep Rena from crashing into Baxter's legs and knocking him backward. Insanity burning in her eyes, Rena reached toward his face, and her nails scratched her husband's cheeks as her hands sought his neck. Porter bolted out of his chair, dragged her away from Baxter, and threw her to the floor. Rena thrashed and howled like a wild animal caught in a trap. Porter pinned her arms behind her, but not before she kicked him, causing him to grunt in pain.

"Get a bailiff with handcuffs!" Porter called out.

Alexia came around the table to try to calm her client, but the look in Rena's eyes stopped her from speaking. Rena was gone. No one capable of listening to the voice of reason remained.

Porter dragged Rena, still screaming and struggling, away from the wheelchair. A bailiff finally arrived, and Porter snapped the metal restraints on Rena's wrists. She was undeterred and continued to scream as the two men half-dragged, half-carried her from the hearing room. The sound of her cries echoed in the hallway but grew fainter as she was taken farther away. Alexia collapsed in the chair beside Sean. Sarah Locklear checked Baxter, who moaned in a soft voice.

After several moments of shocked silence, the magistrate spoke to Sean. "Do you want to go forward with the hearing?"

Sean leaned over to Alexia and whispered, "What do you think?"

"You need to hear from him," Alexia said simply.

Sean looked at Baxter, who had stopped moaning. Sarah nodded at Sean. "Mr. Richardson, are you able to answer a few questions?"

"Yes," Baxter replied slowly. "That's why I'm here."

The magistrate handed a Bible to Sarah, who put it under Baxter's left hand.

"Can you raise your right hand while I administer an oath?" the magistrate asked.

Slowly, with trembling motion, the young man raised his right arm until his hand was beside his claw-streaked face.

Magistrate Simpson spoke. "Do you solemnly swear . . ."

45

If music be the food of love, play on.
TWELFTH NIGHT, ACT 1, SCENE 1

Sitting in her new office on King Street, Alexia hung up the phone. The Santee police department was closing the case on the break-ins at her office and home.

"Ms. Lindale, we've investigated your theory about a connection to Richardson and Company and cannot substantiate it," the detective said. "There are no other leads."

Alexia didn't argue. It would take a bigger net than the one cast by the local police department to catch the bad fish in the Richardson pond. She walked out to Gwen's desk and told her the news.

"Humph," the secretary snorted. "Just like my first husband. Always taking the easy way out."

"You're right." Alexia laid a file and dictation tape on Gwen's desk. "I'm leaving early to stop by the church."

A smile lit the secretary's face. "To see a man who won't give up."

Spring comes early to the Lowcountry, and daffodils, hyacinths, and for-sythia announce the change of season months before they dare venture forth in colder northern climes. But Alexia's favorite heralds of warmer weather were azaleas. Before turning into the parking lot, she slowed to admire the azalea bushes on the north side of the church property. They were at their peak, with white blossoms so thick that in a couple of weeks the ground beneath would look like a March snowfall.

Alexia parked in front of the sanctuary. She walked up the steps, opened the door, and quietly stepped into the narthex. The wooden floor creaked unexpectedly, and she flinched, but no voice called out. She sat in a little chair that rested against the wall of the sanctuary and listened to the music. It was Ravel's *Piano Concerto for the Left Hand*, written by the composer for a friend with an injured right hand. Of course, Ted played it with his right hand.

When she first heard Ted play after the attack, Alexia almost always lost the battle against tears. She felt as crushed as the bones in Ted's left hand. Though his injuries had healed adequately given the severity of trauma, he couldn't extend his fingers more than five notes, and his former ability to fly across the keys unhindered by gravity was now an impossibility. Dr. Hayes characterized Ted's piano playing as physical rehabilitation—it served the purpose of strengthening Ted's hand and fingers but would never again fill a room with music brought to life.

When he finished the piece, Alexia entered the sanctuary and walked down the aisle.

"I thought I heard you come in," Ted said.

"Why didn't you say anything?"

"Because you like to eavesdrop."

Alexia didn't argue. She sat in her favorite spot in the front pew.

"That was well done," she said. "How is the other hand?"

"I drove a few nails with it today. Did you know that I'm ambidextrous with a hammer?"

"Are you bragging?"

"Yes." Ted flexed his left hand. "Mary Lou Hobart gave me a special cream to rub on it. She makes it herself and says it works wonders for her arthritis."

"Does it help?"

"I'm not sure, but the smell would probably keep any mosquitoes from landing on me."

Alexia smiled. She turned her head and glanced toward the stained-glass window of Jesus healing the crippled man at the pool of Bethesda. The late afternoon sunlight illuminated the paralyzed man's face.

"I saw Baxter yesterday," she said. "He's put away the walker and started using a cane. He said he'd be here Sunday morning and would like to have lunch with us."

"Sure."

"A reporter for the religion section of the Charleston paper is considering an article about the healing, and Baxter wants to ask you more about your perspective so he can be accurate in what he says. I'm sure the reporter will want to talk to you too."

Ted laughed. "All I can do is tell the truth."

"Which will be more than enough to keep my interest through three or four columns of newsprint."

"I was helped almost as much as Baxter."

Baxter Richardson's healing had created a breakthrough for the music minister's faith. Still weak from surgery and hampered by the use of only one hand, he saw God's power bridge the gap between heaven and earth and learned that divine grace, not highly developed musical technique, brought undeniable results. God, plus the obedient faith of a one-handed pianist, proved more powerful than any infirmity.

The morning after Ted played and Sarah sang the message of salvation, Baxter awoke, not to a dull reality, but with a clarity of mind that shocked those assigned to care for him. His lungs began to clear, and he asked a nurse to call Ted, who came with wide-eyed wonder to see a miracle as startling as those depicted in the church windows. By Thursday night, Dr. Leoni authorized the trip to Mitchell County. Sarah Locklear was the obvious choice to accompany him in a specially equipped van.

"Has there been any change in Rena's status?" Ted asked.

"She's still recovering from her suicide attempt. There isn't anything for me to do, and I haven't talked to Sean in several weeks. Until she's mentally capable of assisting in her defense, there can't be a trial."

"Any visitors allowed?"

"No. Why?"

"Oh, I'd like to play for her sometime."

Alexia's eyes opened wide. "You're kidding."

"I talked to Sarah about it the other day. We thought that you, as her lawyer, could get us in to see her." Ted looked soberly across the altar rail. "Rena's no more hopeless than Baxter the first time we saw him."

Alexia nodded. "Okay, I'll check into it, but you'd better not mention it as a future project to the religion reporter."

"I'll take that as the advice of my attorney."

Alexia stood and stretched. "Yes. Always do what your attorney says. I'd better be going if I want to have time for a swim."

Ted remained seated. "One more question, counselor. Do you remember what I played the first time we met?"

Alexia thought for a moment. "Uh, I'm not sure. Tchaikovsky?"

"No, something more common that I can do as well today as I could then. Would you like to hear it?"

"Yes."

"Close your eyes," Ted said. "And imagine yourself standing at the back of the sanctuary the first time you came to see me."

Alexia obeyed. "Okay."

"Are you there?" Ted asked.

"Yes."

With a flourishing introduction Ted played the wedding march. Startled, Alexia recalled the moment. Ted thought she was a bride wanting to plan the music for her wedding. In fact, she arrived as an aggressive attorney seeking information from him as a possible witness in a divorce case.

When he finished, she said, "Yes, that's right. You play it as well as ever."

"Keep your eyes closed," Ted instructed.

Alexia complied. She sensed him come close. "The next time I play it," he said, "I'd like you to be standing at the back of the sanctuary with your eyes wide open, wearing a white wedding gown with this diamond ring on your finger."

She felt Ted press a tiny velvet box into the palm of her hand.

Alexia opened her eyes.

READING GROUP GUIDE

1. If you've read both *Life Support* and *Life Everlasting*, have your opinions of any of the characters changed from one novel to the next? If so, what events changed your opinion?

2. Who should fear Baxter's waking? Why?

3. What is Jeffrey's perception of Rena? Does Ezra have the same perception?

4. Why does Baxter keep appearing to Rena?

5. Why does Alexia like to live alone on the marsh? What are the advantages and disadvantages of living away from everyone as Alexia does?

6. How is Sarah a better relational match for Ted than Alexia? How is Alexia better?

7. What do you think about Sean? What motivates him?

8. What is your favorite food described in the book?

9. Describe ways in which Rena demonstrates her survival instinct. Do her instincts help or hurt her?

10. What is your favorite quote from the beginning of the chapters? What makes that particular one stand out in your mind?

11. Why is Ted resistant to performing in public?

12. What does Giles Porter contribute to the story?

13. In what ways is Alexia growing spiritually throughout the novel?

14. What do you think about the injury to Ted's hand? How does it impact the story? How does it affect Ted personally?

15. If you were going to write "the rest of the story," what would happen next?

ACKNOWLEDGMENTS

Many who helped in the writing of *Life Support* also assisted with *Life Everlasting*. My wife Kathy provided vital encouragement and practical suggestions. Ami McConnell ably supervised all editorial efforts. John G. Elliott (johnelliott-music.com) again opened the vast vaults of his musical knowledge.

However, just as fresh characters walk across the pages of *Life Everlasting*, support came from new sources. My daughter Anna named the book and inspired me to produce a novel worthy of the title, and editor Erin Healy offered insightful suggestions and superb technical assistance.

And to those who prayed. Be blessed.

THE LIST

Inherit the wind.

PROVERBS 11:29, KJV

The secretary whom Renny shared with two other associates in the banking law section of the firm buzzed the speakerphone on Renny's desk. "Attorney Jefferson McClintock from Charleston calling on line one. Says it's personal."

"I'll take it."

Renny shut the door of the windowless office he had occupied since graduating from law school three months earlier. If he continued working sixty hours a week, he had a fifty-fifty chance of a comfortable six-figure salary and an office with a view of the city in approximately twelve years. But for now he was at the bottom of the legal food chain. Of the 104 lawyers employed by Jackson, Robinson, and Temples in Charlotte, Raleigh, Winston-Salem, and Washington, D.C., his name, Josiah Fletchall Jacobson, was next to last on the firm's letterhead.

Renny picked up the phone. "Hello, Mr. McClintock."

"How are you, Renny?"

"I'm OK. Busy learning the ins and outs of Truth in Lending and Regulation Z."

"Bank work, eh?"

"Yes sir. I have to review all the forms used by the lending institutions we represent to make sure they contain the exact wording required by the regulations and print everything in the appropriate size type."

"Sounds picky."

"It is, but if I make a mistake, the banks can get hit with class-action lawsuits involving thousands of consumers who have a cause of action, even if they didn't suffer any financial harm."

"Our government regulators at work." The Charleston lawyer coughed and cleared his throat. "Well, move the law books to the side for a minute, and let's talk about your father's estate. With the help of two associates, I've almost completed the documents needed to probate your father's will, but there are several matters that need your attention."

Two associates. Renny knew how the system worked. Multi-lawyer involvement was McClintock's way to triple his money: charge for each junior lawyer's time and throw in another fee at time and a half for the senior partner to proofread a stack of papers.

"Any problems?" Renny asked.

"We need to meet and discuss some things," McClintock answered vaguely. "When can you come to Charleston? Tomorrow is Friday. Why not leave early and see me around two?"

Renny had worked until ten o'clock two nights earlier in the week and had billed enough hours for the week to sneak away by late morning on Friday. Besides, he wasn't going to let anything delay moving forward on the estate. "Could we make it three?"

"Let me see." McClintock paused. "Yes. I can move my three o'clock appointment up an hour."

"Do I need to bring anything?"

"No," replied McClintock, "we'll have the paperwork ready. See you then."

"With your bill on top," Renny remarked as he heard the click of the other lawyer hanging up the phone.

Renny let his mind wander as he looked around his office. Even though it wasn't much larger than a walk-in closet, Renny didn't complain. Landing a job at a big law firm in a major city was the ultimate prize for the masses of eager students passing through the law school meat grinder. Each one entered the legal education process hoping they would come out with *Law Review* on their résumés and filet mignon status in the difficult job market. Most ended up as hamburger, relieved to find any job at all.

Renny had an advantage. Although not on *Law Review* or in the top 10 percent of his class, he had something even better: connections. For once, really the first time he could remember, his father had come to his aid. Dwight Temples, one of the senior partners in the firm, had attended college with Renny's father at The Citadel in Charleston. Over the years they maintained a casual friendship centered around an annual deep-sea fishing expedition off the coast of North Carolina. When Renny mentioned an interest in working for the firm's Charlotte office, H. L. Jacobson called Dwight Temples, and the interview with the hiring partner at Jackson, Robinson, and Temples became a formality. Renny was offered a position on the spot.

Today was not the first call Renny had received from Jefferson McClintock, his family's lawyer in Charleston. Six weeks before, McClintock telephoned Renny with the news of H. L.'s sudden death on a golf course in Charleston. No warning. No cholesterol problem. No hypertension. No previous chest pains. The elder Jacobson was playing a round of golf with two longtime friends, Chaz Bentley, his stockbroker, and Alexia Souther, a College of Charleston alumnus and restaurant owner.

At the funeral home, Bentley, a jovial fellow and everyday golfer who probably received more stock market advice from Renny's father than he gave to him, had pumped Renny's hand and shook his head in disbelief. "I don't understand it. He was fine. No complaints of pain or dizziness. We were having a great round at the old Isle of Palms course. You should have seen the shot he hit from the championship tee on the seventh hole. You remember, it's the hole with the double water hazards. His tee shot must have gone 225 yards, straight down the fairway. He birdied the hole. Can you believe it? Birdied the last hole he ever played!" The stockbroker made it sound like nirvana to make a birdie then die on the golf course. "We were teeing off on number eight. Alexia had taken a mulligan on his first shot and hooked his second try into a fairway bunker. I hit a solid drive just a little left of center." Renny could tell Bentley was enjoying Souther's duff and his own good shot all over again. "Then your father leaned over to tee up his ball and, he, uh…never got his ball on the tee," he finished lamely.

Because of the circumstances of his death, the coroner had required an autopsy. The pathologist's report concluded death by coronary failure. H. L.'s family doctor, James Watson, had explained to Renny, "Your father's heart exploded. He never knew what happened. Death was instantaneous. The pathologist called me from the hospital after he examined the body and reviewed his findings with me. Given your father's good health, we were both puzzled at the severe damage to the heart muscle. We know how he died, but not why it happened as it did."

Renny grieved, but he and his father had not had a close relationship. H. L. was a harsh, critical parent whose favor eluded his son like the proverbial carrot on a stick. Renny tried to please, but the elder Jacobson often changed the rules, and Renny discovered a new way to fail instead. After his mother's death, Renny only visited his father a couple of times a year.

Since there was no one else with whom to share the considerable assets his father had inherited and then increased through savvy investments, Renny looked forward to the trip to Charleston. Once the estate was settled, he would become what some people called "independently wealthy." It had a nice ring to it, and Renny indulged in fantasies of future expenditures.

H. L. was not a generous parent; he paid for Renny's education but never provided the extras he could have easily afforded. After landing the job at Jackson, Robinson, and Temples, Renny sold his old car for three thousand dollars and bought a new charcoal gray Porsche Boxster convertible. The payment and insurance on the new car devoured almost half of Renny's monthly paycheck, but the sporty vehicle was a sign to himself and, subconsciously, to his father, that he had started up the ladder of success. Now he would be able to pay off the car, buy a house, perhaps even quit work and duplicate his father's exploits in the commercial real estate market. His stay at the bottom of the law firm letterhead might be very short indeed.

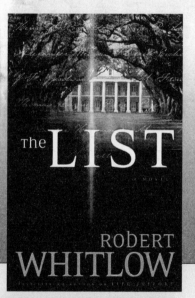

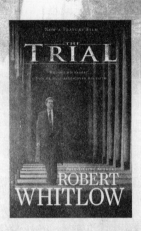
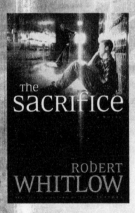

A poignant tale of innocence and courage in the tradition of *Huckleberry Finn* and *To Kill a Mockingbird.* Experience *Jimmy,* a story that will leave you forever changed.

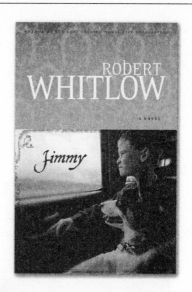

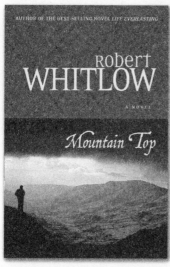

Can he trust his client's dreams and visions—even if they threaten to destroy his future?

The Tides of Truth series

A TIDES OF TRUTH | ROBERT WHITLOW

GREATER LOVE

A TIDES OF TRUTH | ROBERT WHITLOW

DEEPER WATER

"Whitlow's deep faith and legal skills shine."
TERRI BLACKSTOCK, bestselling author of *Last Light*

A TIDES OF TRUTH | ROBERT WHITLOW

HIGHER HOPE

"Writes in the tradition of John Grisham, combining compelling legal and ethical plotlines . . . but Whitlow has explicit spiritual themes." — *WORLD Magazine*